SHIFTING SANDS RESORT OMNIBUS

OMNIBUS

VOLUME 2

ELVA BIRCH
ZOE CHANT

For Rachel, who started this whole thing to begin with.

SHIFTING SANDS RESORT

Sun, surf, shifters, and secrets!

Escape to a shifters-only resort on a hot tropical island full of secrets and sizzling romance.

Shifting Sands Resort is a complete paranormal romance series with self-standing novels that interconnect in an intriguing mystery.

This omnibus edition is in the author's preferred reading order and includes:

Tropical Lynx's Lover (book 4)
Tropical Dragon Diver (book 5)
Treasure Sense (short story)
Tropical Panther's Penance (book 6)
A Christmoose Story (novella)
Dance Lesson (short story)
The Betting Pool (short story)

CONTENTS

TROPICAL LYNX'S LOVER

CHAPTER 1

Travis James stumbled into the empty staff house, dropping his toolbox just inside the door, where he also took off his sodden shoes and shrugged the work gloves off his hands to flop onto the floor like small dead things.

His lynx stirred at the idea of small dead things, twitching metaphorical ears in interest, then expressing disdain. *Living things are more fun to chase,* Lynx told him.

That eliminates us as "fun," Travis told him in return.

He felt like a zombie, limbs numb with exhaustion. Only shifter strength kept him stumbling forward at this point, and only hunger made him stagger into the kitchen instead of immediately finding his bed.

The harvest gold fridge revealed a treasure trove of food: cold cuts, fruit, deviled eggs, cold grilled fish, and even a few legs of crab standing guard over the bottom shelf, all of it leftover from the resort buffet. A cling-wrapped slice of cake said "Breck's. Eat at your own risk." Someone had left a sticky note on it in different handwriting: "I licked it."

"Don't eat Breck's cake," a voice behind him startled him, and only Travis' shifter-quick reflexes kept him from banging his head into the refrigerator door.

Bastian was standing at the door to the kitchen, and it took Travis a moment to realize that he looked strange because he was wearing something other than his bright-colored lifeguard uniform. The resort polo shirt was unexpected over the dragon shifter's chest, and the khaki pants made Travis realize he'd never seen Bastian out of shorts.

"At this point, spit doesn't scare me," Travis told him with a tired grin.

"You look like hell," Bastian told him frankly.

"Feel like it, too," Travis said briefly. "Been a long couple of weeks."

That was an understatement.

It had been an insane, demanding several weeks, as Shifting Sands Resort hosted the World Mr. Shifter male pageant.

Booked to capacity, as Travis suspected it had never been, the resort had performed well for a facility built in the eighties. Even though Scarlet had modernized most of it over the past several years following its long period of abandonment, it had required a flurry of last minute upgrades and Travis had spent the weeks leading up to the event putting cottages back into service, checking and monitoring the aging septic system, and upgrading the wiring and water heaters in anticipation of the influx of guests.

Considering how many people had descended on the resort, it had all gone very smoothly, Travis thought.

But that didn't mean it hadn't been a lot of very long days, running from task to task. The air conditioner in the hotel was down as much as it was up, and there wasn't a day that there wasn't some minor plumbing emergency. The laundry load had been higher than anyone had anticipated, and though Breck was able to help with some of the mechanical work, and most of the staff knew how to respond to blown fuses, Travis had been required to do any of the finesse work on the wiring, and troubleshoot the inevitable problems you had with generators run at full capacity for so long. Only he could do work that required welding or pipe replacement.

"You should get some sleep," Bastian advised.

"Oh, I plan to," Travis said. "Scarlet told me that if I showed my face before noon, she'd fire me. I'm pretty sure she wasn't kidding." The red-haired owner of the resort was not one to be trifled with.

"You'll miss a helluva party," Bastian laughed. "And I've got to get down to it now. Tex isn't back, so I've got to run the beach bar."

"Better you than me," Travis told him.

"You going to need any help?" Bastian asked, concerned.

Travis realized that he'd been staring blankly, standing with the fridge open and the cold air swirling over his feet. He shook his head. "Nah, I got it. Just going to have some food and then sleep until noon, as commanded."

"You do that," Bastian agreed, and he disappeared from the doorway. The front door slammed, and Travis could hear footsteps crunching away in the gravel through the open windows.

Travis left the cake alone, and went for a pile of meat. A slice of bread from the sealed loaf bin on the counter folded around it to complete the sandwich; he didn't bother with condiments or a plate. By the time he made it back to his bedroom, it was gone, all the crumbs inhaled, and he felt full enough to sleep.

He shucked off the filthy staff polo shirt, making his shoulders ache in new ways, and unbuttoned his heavy canvas pants.

The bed had been made up, though Travis was sure he had left it in disarray after too few hours of sleep far too many hours before. He was touched. The staff was usually self-sufficient about their own housekeeping, so one of his co-workers must have done it for him as a personal favor. The sheets even smelled clean, and Travis sighed. There was no way he was going to put his filthy body in those linens.

Not bothering with a bathrobe, Travis slipped his briefs off to join the grime-stiff pants and walked naked back out into the hall to the shared bathroom.

The marble and tile room that greeted him was more like a Greek steamhouse than a mere staff bathroom, even at an upscale resort like Shifting Sands Resort. It had not only a shower and separate tub, but also a steam room and a completely private water closet. The vanity had three separate sinks below an expanse of framed mirror.

Travis caught a glimpse of himself and grimaced.

He looked like a zombie as well as feeling like one. Fast-healing bruises from crawling under the cottages fixing plumbing problems showed purple through his golden skin along one flank. There was a scratch along one arm from a stray wire while fixing the circuitry for the ailing air conditioner in the hotel. The circles beneath his eyes were distinctly unflattering, and his short dark hair was stiff and wild with sweat and grease.

He turned away, and pulled the shower control to full heat and full strength, standing in the stream even before the heat from the tank had reached the shower. The rest of the staff would be away for hours; the World Mr. Shifter event was in its final, glorious throes, and the wrap-up party on the beach would keep the rest of the staff busy until morning. Travis didn't have to worry about saving any of the precious hot water for anyone else.

The water was running scalding hot now, and Travis lay his brow against the steamy tile and let it beat the stiffness out of his tired muscles.

There was a tremendous amount of satisfaction from the work. He took pride in keeping Shifting Sands running smoothly, and the staff was more like family than simply co-workers. The perks of the job included a beautiful place to live, all of the gourmet food he could eat, and most of the time, the workload was minimal. Scarlet listened to his advice when it came to remodeling and buying new equipment, and was fair and clear in her expectations.

It wasn't the work that was leaving Travis feeling hollow. He loved Shifting Sands, from the persnickety power grid to the steep, sprawling gravel paths. The resort was home, in a bone-deep way that even his Native village in Alaska had never been, and he was proud of how beautiful and functional it was, and how much it had improved in the past few years.

Maybe it was just exhaustion, making him feel like like something was missing.

Travis leaned against the shower control to turn it off, and stood there a weary moment, dripping.

The empty house felt unexpectedly lonely.

It took a ridiculous amount of time to reach for a towel and give himself a cursory pat-down. Scarlet didn't skimp on towels, so the thick, fluffy terrycloth absorbed most of the water even with half-hearted application. Travis barely got it back onto his towel hook before staggering back to his bedroom.

Even the fireworks couldn't keep him awake after that.

CHAPTER 2

*J*ennavivianna Smith wasn't floating.

For the first time in a very long time, she wasn't floating.

She wasn't all-Jenny, yet, but she wasn't as not-Jenny as she had been, and she kept her eyes screwed shut for a while after she was actually awake, trying to process what had happened.

"You're not sleeping anymore!"

At first, Jenny thought that it was her own thoughts. Her own, weirdly divided thoughts. The otter inside her that wasn't her, but was, all at once.

"You can't fool me," the voice said firmly, and Jenny remembered.

She remembered Gizelle, the slight, salt-and-pepper-haired woman who had talked her back into human form, and remembered seeing Fred again and feeling the sting of his betrayal, and Laura, oh, Laura! Her twin was there in her head again, that unspoken connection they'd always had was back and as strong and comforting as it had always been, even when they were at odds, or miles apart.

She opened her eyes. She was in a little square of neat lawn near a white gravel path, tall, flowering jungle brush on all sides. She could hear the ocean, and smell its sharp, salty tang, but she couldn't see anything through the dense foliage.

Gizelle was kneeling above her, hair wild around her face, big eyes earnest. "Come on, then, you've had a good sleep."

Jenny opened her mouth to protest that the sleep had been restless, and full of floating dreams, but it came out as half-trill and half-purr, and she snapped otter jaws together again.

"It takes a little while, that's all. Come and walk on two legs with me. See your sister!"

Jenny balked. The last time she had changed from otter to human, it had burned. She remembered the feeling of her bones cracking and resetting, the muscles stretching impossibly, the tendons snapping into new places.

"Don't be afraid," Gizelle said coaxingly.

"Don't baby me," Jenny wanted to tell her, but couldn't, through otter teeth. Nothing frustrated her more than being patronized.

Don't act like a baby, then, her otter told her. Its voice in her head was not scornful, exactly, but teasing, prodding.

Jenny felt more stung than she knew she ought to. *I'm not being a baby.*

Of course you aren't, her otter mocked. *You're a 'grown-up' coward.*

With an otter sigh of frustration, Jenny stretched.

At first, it was simply a stretch of otter limbs, then Jenny focused furiously, remembering human arms and human legs, and she reached and wrenched herself back into her own form.

Gizelle clapped her hands in delight as Jenny lay on the ground, naked and panting. "Good job!" she said enthusiastically.

"Don't baby me," Jenny was finally able to say, breathlessly.

Then don't-

Shut up. Jenny was dismayed to see that her fingers were still slightly webbed, and tipped with sharp claws. She ran her tongue over teeth that were too sharp and grimaced.

Gizelle took no notice of Jenny's crabbiness, simply offering her hands to stand up.

Let's go run around on those human legs you love so much, her otter suggested. *Maybe go swimming at the beach.*

I'm a little naked, Jenny reminded her, accepting Gizelle's offered hands and climbing to her feet.

I know, her otter purred back at her, full of mischief. Images of admiring men accompanied the rejoinder. Jenny felt her skin heat, hating herself for how the idea stirred in her loins.

"How do you do this?" Jenny demanded of Gizelle, standing unsteadily.

"I know, it's weird there's only two of them," Gizelle said comfortingly.

"Only two?" Jenny asked. Were there shifters with more than one extra voice?

"You just have to shift your weight between each one, and not think about it too much to keep your balance."

When Jenny looked blankly at her, Gizelle scampered away and ran in a circle. "Like this!" she called merrily.

"You meant *legs,*" Jenny realized. "Only two *legs.*"

Returning, Gizelle said, "Of course I meant *legs.* What else would I mean?"

"I thought you meant voices," Jenny said, feeling foolish.

"There are *always* more than two voices," Gizelle said solemnly, eyes big in her face.

Jenny had just started feeling like things made sense, and then suddenly she didn't again. She could feel her otter's amusement, and shunted it away. "There's more?" she said unhappily. She could barely stand otter's demanding voice, should she expect more of them?

"Voices that whisper. Voices in the sky with no sun. Feathered voices. Voices that-"

"Gizelle," said a new voice, gently chiding.

Jenny turned, half-crouching, and nearly let her otter take control of her skin again instinctively. *No!* she thought fiercely, fighting to stay in human skin.

The red-haired woman from the night before stood at the

opening in the hedge by the white path. She was neatly dressed, and Jenny was relieved to see that she was holding clothing in her hand.

It was her own dress, Jenny realized, and more memories flooded back. Laura, her twin, had come to the resort pretending to be Jenny, and of course she would have packed Jenny's clothing for the trip.

Naked would be more fun, her otter pouted at her.

Jenny ignored the voice.

"I'm Scarlet," the woman said, handing her the dress and looking politely aside while Jenny struggled to put it on. "I run Shifting Sands."

Jenny, still trying to work out how to get her head through the neckhole and feeling stumped by the armholes, was keenly aware of Gizelle staring at her.

"Gizelle," Scarlet said kindly.

"She's really bad at that," Gizelle said frankly.

"I need you to help Graham in the upper gardens, please." Scarlet's tone made it sound less like a request and more like a royal command.

Triumphant at last over the openings in the dress, Jenny pulled it fiercely down over her generous curves.

"Bye!" said Gizelle merrily, and she skipped off across the lawn and out the way Scarlet had come. Her footsteps were quiet on the gravel, and Jenny realized she was barefoot.

"I apologize for Gizelle," Scarlet said, sounding not the slightest bit apologetic. "She has taken great interest in you."

"She's not neurotypical, is she," Jenny observed. It felt ironic to say so, since she felt so much less than normal herself.

Normal is boring, her otter told her.

"We released Gizelle from a madman's prison less than a year ago and it took her a long time to shift from her gazelle form," Scarlet explained. "She remembers nothing about her life in his zoo. We have no idea how old she is, or where she came from before then. She may even have been born there." She gave Jenny an intense, appraising look. "How much do *you* remember?"

Jenny gazed back at Scarlet without seeing her. "I remember

driving. It was Laura's car, I was just going to get her a few things from the supermarket. There was an explosion — I lost control of the car, and it went off a curve. I remember going through the guardrail…"

She shuddered, remembering the scream of metal and the drop into the shattering ocean below, hitting her head, waves and water and sinking…

Comfort came from an unexpected source.

I caught you. I was there for you.

Jenny pushed back. She didn't want to be grateful to the interloper in her head.

"I shifted," she said woodenly. "I've never shifted before. I didn't know I could. I don't think I could, before."

Scarlet listened, but offered no comment.

Jenny worked her mouth, trying to find words for what came next. She had been more otter than herself, eating, swimming, floating in sleep. She was drawn south, swimming earnestly, day after day, through currents that became gradually warmer.

"I found Laura after her boat exploded. I didn't really think about things, only knew that I had to help her, and where I could find that help."

"Shifting Sands was always meant to be a safe haven for shifters," Scarlet said, nodding.

Jenny felt her eyebrows scrunch together. "Shifting… Sands. I worked on the contract for this place." Life before this seemed impossibly distant and long ago. "I was — I am — a lawyer."

"What else do you remember?" Scarlet asked gently.

"I remember Fred," Jenny said firmly. "He betrayed us. He was the one who sabotaged Laura's car, and her boat. And… our parents. He killed our parents, so long ago." Somehow, it stung as much now as it had when Jenny had first uncovered the treachery, weeks ago.

"He's in custody," Scarlet promised fiercely. "He will never be able to hurt you again."

Jenny tried to take comfort in the idea, and nodded.

Somewhere, far away, there was a beep of a car horn and

shouting voices, and Scarlet frowned. "Let me take you to the dining hall. You've missed lunch, but there's a buffet available and you must be hungry after your long ordeal."

On cue, Jenny's stomach rumbled, and she and her otter finally agreed on something.

"I'm famished," she admitted. Then she added, "Just please, tell me I don't have to eat raw fish or urchins for a long, long time."

She didn't think she would ever enjoy a sushi bar again.

CHAPTER 3

*T*ravis rolled out bed when he woke up, habit driving him
to get dressed before he registered that it was already
midday, and that he actually felt well-rested.

He got dressed and wandered to the kitchen to appease Lynx's
cries for food, and found a quarter of a pie dish full of shrimp kale
quiche with his name on it. The cake had a new note on it: "Dragon
germs don't scare me."

Through the open windows of the house, he could hear distant
sounds of the resort below, the ocean and the pool waterfalls making
a pleasant backdrop to the hum of activity. It was quieter than the
day before. Travis imagined the last guests, nursing hangovers,
hauling their luggage to turn in their keys and file into the van that
would take them to the little airfield on the far side of the island.
The resort staff would spend the day cleaning up at a leisurely pace,
putting everything back in order for the next, much smaller, wave of
guests.

Quiche inhaled, Travis went to find his tools. He knew there
would be work for him today, but he also knew that the insane pressure of the last few weeks was lifted, and his steps felt light and
eager for the first time in a long time. His work gloves and boots had

been dried, shaken out, and hung up. Travis gave a crooked smile for the thoughtfulness of his housemates.

His feet automatically took him to the largest building on the resort, the building that held the dining hall, kitchen, and conference room on the top level, the bar and mechanical rooms on the next level down, overlooking the pool below. The staff bulletin board in the conference room was where the calendar was posted, and where they left notes for each other about problems that needed fixed.

The calendar was marked "Travis: DAY OFF" and "Breck: Return the keys to rooms 7 and 12." The dry-erase board had a note: "Fix washer four." In new handwriting someone had added, "And dryer three."

Knowing he didn't have to handle it perversely made Travis want to.

There was singing coming from the kitchen, a tragic opera song in Chef's booming bass voice. Travis smiled to remember that Magnolia would be returning any day. The resort would feel normal again.

But normal still didn't feel… complete.

"Travis! What are you doing up so early?" How Breck, the head waiter, managed to look so fresh and energetic after what Travis knew could only have been a few hours of sleep was a mystery.

"It's after noon," Travis said skeptically.

"You still look like you need a week of sleep," the leopard shifter said critically.

"Thanks!"

"You're off the books today," Breck reminded him, frowning at the toolbox. "There are only about four guests left, so don't sweat anything."

"There will be more coming, though," Travis reminded him.

Breck was looking at the calendar and checking the notes. "Not until tomorrow, and next week will be cake compared to the last few." He gave Travis a suspicious look. "Speaking of…"

"I didn't touch your cake."

Breck gave him a theatrically skeptical look, then took off

towards the kitchen, opening the door with a surprisingly good harmony to Chef's song.

Travis shook his head and walked past the kitchen door as it swung shut, heading for the back staff stairs down to the laundry and mechanical room.

The relative stillness of the pool deck and the bar was welcome; it was strange, after the past few days, not to have to elbow through throngs of guests to get anywhere. Tex was behind the bar, and his new mate sat before him on a bar stool.

Our *mate*, Lynx said, unexpectedly in his head, and Travis had to freeze at the intensity of it.

That's Tex's mate, Travis assured him, shaken. Yes, she was a gorgeous woman, and Tex was lucky to have her, with that velvety dark skin and those beautiful curves, but that he would even give her a second glance felt like betrayal.

No, Lynx growled. *She's ours.*

All Travis could do was stare.

CHAPTER 4

*J*enny followed Scarlet up the winding white path to a pool deck that she vaguely remembered from the previous night. It looked quite different in daylight, brilliantly gleaming in the tropical sun. It was bigger than it had looked in the faint light of pre-dawn, and was edged with palm trees. What had only been the sound of splashing water proved to be twin waterfalls, flanking a grand staircase that came down into the pool from the upper deck.

Jenny was grateful for the dress Scarlet had brought her, but found herself keenly aware that she was wearing no underthings beneath it as Scarlet led her between scattered sun chairs. She was glad to see very few people, most of them looking hungover and dragging luggage.

"I suspect that Gizelle was not the best person to wake up to in a new place," Scarlet explained. "But she may be uniquely suited to helping you with your new shifting abilities, and she seems to want to. I apologize for not being able to stay longer and help you get situated, but I had a great deal of paperwork to do in the wake of your arrival."

It wasn't quite an accusation.

"I'm sorry, I don't know when I will be able to pay you for our stay," Jenny said hesitantly. "The money is going to be tied up in legal battles for a while." The life insurance money that had been denied to Jenny and Laura when her parents had been murdered would be difficult to access while the justice system unraveled the depths of Fred's activity. Jenny's head hurt, thinking about the layers of bureaucracy they were going to have to go through to put the whole sordid affair to rest. She usually loved a messy challenge to unravel; that was part of the reason she had dived into a career in law. But right now, the idea of facing anything more complicated than a sandwich felt overwhelming. She wasn't even sure if she'd be able to access her own slim accounts; her laptop had been destroyed and she couldn't remember any of the details or login credentials.

Scarlet looked as if she had been deeply offended. "You are our guest," she said in icy tones. "I will put you in touch with some legal council I have connections with once you feel up to it." Her skeptical tone made Jenny suspect Scarlet rather doubted her ability whether she felt 'up to it' or not.

The red-haired woman led her up a wide flight of stairs up to a deck that overlooked the pool and a collection of chairs and tables outside of an open bar. Tinny country music in Spanish was playing on a radio and Jenny's chest squeezed at the familiar sight of her wolf shifter sister, sitting in front of the bar.

"Jenny!" Laura leaped up from the barstool and tackled Jenny in a fierce hug.

Jenny was not sure if she should weep on Laura's shoulder or flee, suddenly feeling terribly unsteady. She clung to Laura much longer than she normally would have, and awkwardly hid her webbed hands behind her when they finally ended the embrace.

"Jenny," Laura said nervously. "I want you to meet Tex. Or, er, meet him again."

Tex was leaning over the bar, and Jenny immediately remembered his bear smell, and the beat up cowboy hat he was wearing from the night before. "I'm sorry about the hat," she said hesitantly.

There was something else familiar about him, and she couldn't put her finger on it until Tex's handsome face split into a grin and he put fingers automatically to the rim of the hat in question. "You don't have anything to apologize for, ma'am," he drawled, and he extended his hand to shake.

Jenny stared. "You're the bartender! From Texas!" It had been at least five years ago that they'd met; he'd been an absolute gentleman, and she'd been an embarrassment.

Tex smiled at her. "I am indeed the bartender from Texas."

Jenny winced to hear how stupid it sounded. His name was Tex, and he was standing behind the bar. "The other bar, I mean the bar *in* Texas." She realized Tex still had his hand out, but it had been offered too long now, and she didn't want to put her webbed fingers in his.

Laura sidled up beside her as Tex casually took his hand back, and Jenny could feel the energy and excitement that beamed from her. "Jenny, Tex is my mate."

Jenny looked from one of them to the other, marveling at the way they gazed at each other. She had never seen Laura look so content.

She started to smile, genuinely glad that her twin had found happiness, then remembered her pointed teeth and stopped. "Congratulations," she said, strained.

Scarlet had been waiting through the introductions impatiently, and finally said, so politely that it was verging on cold, "Please excuse me, I have a great deal to do." And she tapped off with a distinctive click from her low-heeled shoes over the tile.

"I've got the number from her for a guy back in America who works for a government shifter agency," Laura said, patting the barstool next to her. "He can expedite having Fred turned over to US custody, and help with getting the insurance money sorted. He may even be able to get things in motion regarding getting the cartel behind bars, I'll have to talk to him about that."

Jenny sat numbly on the stool and stared at her sister. Where had this capable, confident woman come from? How the tables had turned! Now, *she* felt like the screw-up sister, hardly able to make sense of simple words, and not even able to shift fully into her human form. She curled her webbed fingers into balls and winced when the claws scratched her palms.

I'm hungry, her otter insisted. Something smelled heavenly.

"There was food?" she said faintly. She didn't want otter to drag her out into the ocean after fresh fish for lack of options.

Laura and Tex both jumped. "Of course!" Laura said. "There's a buffet just upstairs, you sit here and I'll bring you a plate."

"I could get it," Tex offered, but Laura brushed him off.

"I know what she likes!"

They exchanged a swift kiss so intense that it made Jenny look away in embarrassment, and then Laura was slipping away through the backdoor of the bar, presumably to stairs that would take her up to the deck above them where the heavenly smells were coming from.

Tex put a bowl of mixed nuts in front of her, and poured a tall glass of pale juice. "You should get something in your stomach," he advised kindly.

Jenny tried to keep her hands low, positioning the glass between her fingers and Tex as best as she could. He seemed to sense her hesitation, and turned away to do obvious busywork at the far end of the bar. "I'm glad to see you up and about," he said without pressure. "Your sister is so happy to have you back again."

The drink proved to be lemonade, sweet and tangy, but not too strong. Jenny sipped it down eagerly and emptied the bowl of nuts without thinking about it.

Easing her hunger didn't bring the clarity of thought that Jenny had hoped for, but it did ease the overbearing intensity of her otter's presence a little.

She turned in her chair and looked out over the deck. Sunlight danced over the rippled surface of the pool, and dappled through the shade from the palm trees. The place had this strange sense of promise to it that Jenny had never felt before.

I'm hungry, her otter told her, and it wasn't the kind of hunger that a bowl of nuts was going to touch.

There was a man standing at one of the doors marked 'Staff Only' and Jenny tried not to stare. He was all lean strength, the staff polo shirt doing nothing to mask the muscles of his shoulders and arms. She thought he was Asian at first, with short, dark hair and golden skin, then he turned away from her abruptly, and the planes of his cheeks as the sun hit them made her think 'Native.'

He was gorgeous, like a sculpture, or a model, and Jenny was keenly reminded that she was still not wearing underwear. She squirmed on her stool, unable to look away as he yanked the door open and disappeared inside.

*I'm **hungry***, her otter repeated ferociously, and Jenny shuddered and cringed at the intensity and immediacy of it. If the otter had her way, they'd be scurrying over the white tile to catch the man, and her otter had very specific ideas of what they'd be doing with him once they caught him, regardless of where they were or who else was there.

She was still fighting down the carnal wave of need and animal lust when Laura returned with a platter full of Jenny's favorite food: glistening cubes of fresh fruit and cottage cheese, and a heaping green salad with slices of eggs and avocado, scattered with squares of real bacon and feta cheese and drizzled with a vinaigrette. A roll so fresh it was still warm topped off the plate.

Jenny was achingly glad there wasn't a hint of fish or seafood on the plate, and with a whimper, she fell upon it, channeling all of her energy to eating.

CHAPTER 5

*T*ravis shut the door to the laundry room without flipping on the light switch and leaned against it in the dark, breathing as heavily as if he'd just run a marathon.

Lynx, in his head, was suggesting other courses of action. Filthy, detailed suggestions that made Travis keenly aware of how long it had been since any hand but his own had been in contact with certain parts.

That's Tex's mate, he insisted desperately. *She's gorgeous, but she's not ours.* He had to wonder why Lynx hadn't had this reaction the first few times they'd met, but why-ever that was, he wasn't going to betray his code of conduct and so much as sniff in her direction if she belonged to someone else.

Travis turned on the light switch and winced in the harsh light. He had to adjust himself to kneel at the service port for the washer in question. Several of the other washers were churning along in their duties, and the piles of dirty laundry were epic, even though housekeeping was probably still stripping down beds as guests checked out.

She has a service port we could use, Lynx said slyly.

You are a dirty, dirty tomcat who ought to be fixed, Travis replied. *Tex's mate, remember.* **Tex's mate!**

He replaced the worn-out motor bearing that he knew was the cause of the washer's problem, gritting his teeth and ignoring Lynx's continued insistence that they fling the door to the mechanical room open and chase their mate down, fighting off Tex or anyone else who tried to stand in their way.

The dryer fuse was next to replace, as Lynx continued to demand that they pursue her, now, now, now, and Travis tried to shut out his persistent voice. Travis even moved laundry from the washer to the dryer when one of them stopped, and loaded up the two empty machines with new laundry from the piles.

He might have hidden in the mechanical room until night, but Lydia, the black swan shifter who ran the spa, opened the door and wheeled in a cart of laundry.

"Don't you have the day off?" she asked, in her rich Spanish accent.

"I slept in," Travis protested. "Aren't you supposed to be at the spa?"

"Everyone's gone, thank the stars," Lydia said, scooping towels and sheets and massage table covers out of the basket to add to the piles. "But we're down at least two housekeepers as well, so I'm helping out where I can."

Some of the staff had only been temporary, hired for the duration of the World Mr. Shifter event that had just ended. Travis hadn't expected to lose them so quickly, but Scarlet was nothing if not efficient.

"Did they take the extra staff back to shore in the boat, then?" he asked. "It's on my list to tune up the second engine."

Lydia stared at him. "You haven't heard! Oh, it was awful — the boat blew up with Tex and Laura in it! They barely made it back with their lives!"

Travis blinked stupidly at her. "I didn't hear about any of that," he said. His gut clenched at the idea of his mate — Tex's mate! He reminded himself — in danger. Also, "They sunk my boat? What about the whale watching tour?"

Lydia laughed, a musical sound. "You slept through quite a story..." she started.

Then the door opened again, this time with Bastian pushing another cart of laundry.

"One of the casters on this thing is off," the dragon shifter said, wiggling the cart to demonstrate. "Aren't you supposed to have the day off, Travis?"

"Aren't you supposed to be on the beach?" Travis countered crossly.

The lifeguard shrugged. "No one is there. One of the girls needed a hand with the laundry."

"I'll fix that," Travis said with a sigh. He kept a basket of extra casters in the back of the laundry room.

"Have you seen Tex this morning?" Bastian asked, with what Travis thought was exaggerated innocence.

Did staring at his mate from across the pool deck count? "Not really," Travis decided to answer, fishing through the basket for the correct caster.

"Had to pull him back to shore on the last sorry piece of your boat," Bastian said. "Guess his mate's friend-of-the-family wasn't such a great friend after all. The Civil Guard has already been here this morning to get him."

Travis stared. If the Civil Guard was involved, there must have been quite a sordid story. "Is that who was trying to kill Miss Smith?" He had to rein in Lynx's out of proportion desire for revenge.

"And her sister!" Lydia exclaimed.

"Though it turns out it was the French housemaid who poisoned her latte," Bastian added, shoveling laundry into the washer until Lydia clucked at him to stop and unpacked the over-stuffed drum.

Feeling very left out, Travis popped the new caster onto the bottom of the cart. "It sounds a pretty far-fetched story."

"Are you coming up to the staff room for dinner?" Lydia asked. "We can catch you up on it."

Travis bit back the question of whether Tex and his mate would be there. It didn't matter; she wasn't his mate.

Is too, Lynx insisted like a child, complete with stomping his big feet.

"I'm not really caught up on my sleep," Travis fibbed. "I'm just going to grab a quiet dinner out of the staff fridge and go to bed early."

He didn't really expect to sleep, given the grip Lynx had on his nerves, but remembering the contents of the fridge made him realize how hungry he was.

He followed Lydia and Bastian carefully out of the laundry, and was relieved to see that the bar was deserted. The sun was already setting, sinking down into the ocean horizon, and Travis was happy to slink away along the path to the staff house by the cliffs.

Breck's cake even sounded pretty good.

Lynx helpfully provided the picture of feeding it, bite by fluffy bite, to his mate. White frosting contrasted against her dark rose lips, and her tongue...

I'm going to give you a cold bath, you filthy tomcat, Travis threatened in return. *That is Tex's mate. Not ours.*

But Lynx's delicious image lingered, despite Travis' best attempts to squelch it.

CHAPTER 6

*J*enny stared at the computer screen. It was black, and for a long, confused moment, she had no idea how to go about turning it on.

Before she could confess to the unexpected gap in her knowledge, Scarlet grew impatient and reached over to press the space bar and bring the screen back from sleep.

"I very much appreciated your work with the World Mr. Shifter contract," the red-haired owner said. "Beehag's lawyer is making noises about trying to sell the property out from underneath us again, and I want a better understanding about our lease terms to fight him with."

"Of course," Jenny said faintly.

Scarlet opened the document in question with quick efficient motions on the touchpad while Jenny was still trying to remember what a touchpad was.

After a moment of stillness while Jenny fought down panic, Scarlet added, "I am, of course, happy to pay you your company rates for your time."

Jenny looked blankly at her, then realized that she wasn't going to be able to bluff her way through competence with this. "I'm sorry," she said shrilly. "I... I... can't read it."

The words on the screen might as well have been in a foreign language; Jenny could make no sense of any of it. The letters simply refused to order themselves into any kind of recognizable patterns.

It was a terrifying, helpless feeling, and Jenny was deeply ashamed to admit it.

Scarlet frowned at her, and Jenny told herself it wasn't probably wasn't meant to be a judgmental frown.

"Curious," the resort owner said blandly, giving a little shrug of dismissal. "We can try at another time when you feel up to it."

Jenny got to her feet, trying not to wring her webbed fingers nervously. "I'm so sorry," she said meekly.

Scarlet's expression softened. "I'm sure it will pass," she said kindly. "Your sister is at the bar if you'd like to go see her."

Jenny nodded, and let her feet lead her out of Scarlet's resort-top office and down the white gravel path to the bar. It had just stopped raining, and the sunlight was burning the raindrops off of all the jungle foliage; it smelled clean and delicious.

Laura had a swift hug for her in greeting when Jenny arrived at the bar.

"I'm about to go make up a few of the cottages with fresh laundry," her twin said. "We may or may not be millionaires, but sitting on my ass doesn't suit me, and who knows when we'll actually see any of that."

"Can I help you with it?" Jenny asked.

Laura looked skeptical, but covered it quickly with a smile. "Sure!" she said. "It will go faster with a second set of hands."

Unfortunately, it didn't. Jenny's claws snagged on the sheets and she was hopelessly clumsy about everything Laura tried to have her help with. Finally, she kept herself to merely sweeping, careful to keep the bristles on the floor so she didn't endanger any of the artwork or vases.

Laura took the time to catch her up. "I talked to Scarlet's contact in a government agency that deals with shifter affairs. His name was Tony, and he was able to get things expedited with getting the charges brought against Fred for killing our parents and with-holding our life insurance settlement. I even talked to him about bringing charges against one of the big players in the cartel, Black-smith — they were already trying to build a case and planning a sting, I guess, and they think my testimony will be enough to make things stick. He said the best thing to do was lie low here until it comes to trial. You'd have a better idea of how that will work than I do."

"I'm — I *was* — a civil lawyer, not a criminal lawyer," Jenny told her, marveling at how competent and self-sufficient Laura had become as she swirled through making beds. "And how did you get mixed up in the mob, anyway?"

"Cartel," Laura corrected. "You know me — I have terrible taste in men and worse judgement when it comes to work. Remember that MLM I lost my savings on?" She tucked a sheet in and pulled it smooth. Clearly, she had done this before, many times; she moved through the housekeeping tasks confidently. "I didn't ask questions I should have until it was too late. Blacksmith paid well in cash and didn't make me fill out a W2."

"As if those weren't warning signs," Jenny scoffed. She immedi-ately felt terrible and judgmental. This was why they always argued as children.

But Laura only chuckled with self-deprecating humor. "It's true," she agreed. "I was an idiot."

"What — what did you do for him?" Jenny wasn't sure she wanted to know.

"Sometimes I carried messages, sometimes I did odd errands. I went to the bank twice a week with a fake ID they gave me and made withdrawals for them. Sometimes they'd have me go to the store and make very exacting purchases. I delivered packages that probably had questionable things in them once or twice."

Jenny sucked her breath in. "Could you get in trouble?"

"Tony doesn't think so. A slap on the wrist at most. Maybe a fine, certainly no jail time. Testifying against Blacksmith could get me off the hook entirely."

Jenny swept her pile out the big double doors onto the deck and off into the tiny lawn below. "You've got everything figured out," she said, as they put the cleaning supplies back and shut the cottage behind them. There was no reason to lock empty buildings here.

Laura took her hand reassuringly, and though Jenny thought she startled at the feeling of the webbing between her fingers, she didn't let go. "You will, too," she said confidently. "I'll help you."

Jenny had to chuckle at how backwards everything seemed to be.

And if she didn't laugh, she'd probably cry.

CHAPTER 7

"*A*ren't you supposed to start looking better as you catch up on sleep?" Bastian asked frankly when Travis stumbled down mid-morning.

Travis muttered wordlessly, not wanting to explain that he'd gotten very little in the way of sleep because he couldn't seem to keep from lusting over someone else's mate.

"You do look awful," Breck agreed with Bastian critically.

"Don't you guys have jobs to do?" Travis asked crossly.

"Already done with the breakfast crowd," Breck shrugged.

"I put out the swim-at-your-own-risk sign," Bastian said. "It was raining, earlier. No one was in the water when I left, and I got bored. There's a big storm headed for us, probably hit us in the next few days. I've even heard a bunch of guests have canceled."

Travis went to the fridge with an unappreciative scowl for the waiter and the lifeguard.

"A hurricane?" Breck asked.

"I heard it could be," Bastian said. "They aren't supposed to get as far south as Costa Rica, but it's a category four right now and will still be pretty strong when it hits."

"You guys seen Tex?" Travis had to ask, retreating from the cool sanctuary of the fridge with an egg pastry of some sort and a pile of crispy bacon.

"He's staying with Laura over in cottage six," Bastian explained.

"Mates," Breck said with a shudder. "The horror."

Our mate is close by, Lynx reminded him, as if he hadn't spent the night trying to forget.

Travis made himself eat the suddenly tasteless food, sitting on one of the tall kitchen stools. The house the staff had taken over had a formal dining room, but it had already been converted into a weight and exercise room, sparsely filled with the leftover resort equipment and some rusty hand weights.

Bastian and Breck argued good-naturedly about the boat they wanted to buy to replace the boat that had somehow been sunk the day before — Travis still didn't know the story that went with that, but suspected it was quite a tale.

"What do you think?" Breck asked him abruptly.

Travis shrugged. "I have no opinion one way or the other," seemed like the safest answer, since he hadn't been listening at all.

"That's cheating," Bastian scoffed.

"What are you, Switzerland?" Breck rolled his eyes. "You know you want an inboard this time to run the whale watching tours."

But Travis couldn't focus on the conversation, no matter how invested he was in the outcome. He washed his plate and tossed his napkin.

"What's gotten into you?" Bastian asked, with genuine concern. "Are you okay?"

"I gotta talk to Tex," Travis told him, agonized, and left him more puzzled than ever in his wake.

Tex was sitting on the bar with his guitar, playing something uncharacteristically happy. His mate —

Our mate! purred Lynx.

His *mate!* Travis corrected in despair.

— sat a few chairs away, a glass of ice water covered with condensing droplets in front of her.

She looked up at his approach, and Travis could see both confusion and longing in her dark eyes.

Travis made the mistake of letting his feet stop, and was still trying to screw together the courage to walk forward again when someone brushed by him.

"Sorry, Travis," she said merrily, and Travis had to stare.

She was a perfect double, dressed in a red sundress compared to her mirror image's blue. She sat between Tex and the other version, and Travis couldn't believe that he had ever confused them. Tex's mate was gorgeous, but his mate —

Our mate! sang Lynx.

— was utterly perfect.

Relief made his knees feel like water. Travis wasn't crazy, it was the world that was crazy. There were two of them, twins, and he was sure he would never have a problem distinguishing them again.

"You alright, man?" Tex asked in concern, stilling his fingers on the strings of the guitar.

Travis could move again, and he strode forward with new confidence. "Never better," he declared. "Though you ladies had me doubting my sanity until now."

Tex's Miss Smith exchanged an amused look with him. "You didn't know there were two of us?" she asked teasingly.

"I thought I was going to have to skin my own Lynx for insisting that Tex's mate was our own," Travis admitted frankly. "I couldn't imagine a situation more impossible."

"Your mate?! Oh, Jenny, how perfect!" Laura's squeak was nothing but delighted, and Tex grinned congratulations at him.

Jenny only looked alarmed, not at all delighted, but Travis was still buoyed by the revelation that there were two of them.

He closed the distance between them and held out his hands. "My mate," he repeated firmly, almost giddy with relief and joy. "May I kiss you?"

CHAPTER 8

*Y*es, her otter insisted. *This is what we want. This is everything!*
The rest of Jenny was in a white-hot panic.

If she let this man kiss her, she would be lost forever to her otter, anything of her human self washed away in the passionate wave of the lust that threatened to consume her. She'd never have any kind of self-control again.

"No!" Jenny said firmly, standing up and pushing her chair back. Instead of sliding, it toppled over backwards with a crash. She was keenly aware of the stares of Tex, her sister, and most of all, of Travis.

He was perfect, she thought achingly. Gorgeous as a model, with golden skin in slanting planes, and shoulders that could carry the world.

He stood before her, hands outstretched, his look of delight and desire fading to confusion and puzzled rejection.

"Jenny," Laura said hesitantly. "What's wrong?"

"What's wrong?" Jenny repeated shrilly. "What's wrong is that I have webbed fingers and sharp teeth, and I can't eat anything without wanting to dunk it in salt water first." She heard her voice climb an octave. "What's wrong is that I've spent nearly two weeks in someone else's skin. What's wrong is that I can't even read any more, let alone make sense of words. I don't remember how to turn on a computer." She turned to Travis. "What's wrong is that you want to kiss me, and I don't even know you."

We know him, her otter insisted.

"I don't know you," she snarled, and she wasn't sure if she was replying to her otter, or to Travis, who was gazing at her as if she were hanging stars instead of having a ridiculous breakdown.

Rather than continue to stand there looking like an idiot as she ran out of words, Jenny turned away, and staggered out of the bar, knocking another chair over as she fled through the tables and out the back entrance.

Half-running, blinded by tears, she ran soundly into something soft but unyielding, just outside the bar entrance.

"Gracious, darling! We're on island time, nothing can be worth a rush like that."

The woman she'd barreled into was as tall as Jenny, and perhaps three times as wide, rolls of flesh bared at the shoulders and again at the knees, and otherwise swathed in swirls of magenta silk. Loose auburn hair hung to her waist. Despite her soft look, she didn't budge an inch at Jenny's collision, and if she hadn't put an iron hand at Jenny's wrist, the fleeing woman would have bounced off and fallen backwards. Instead, Jenny was steadied on her feet, and her shoulders were brushed off like an errant child.

"Oh, sugar, you've been crying," the woman said compassionately, and even if Jenny hadn't been crying already, that kindness would have undone her.

As she bawled anew, the woman drew her to a bench in the shade. It creaked alarmingly as they settled on it, and the woman pulled a piece of fabric from an orange beach bag to let Jenny wipe her face.

"Oh," sniffed Jenny as her claws snagged on the fabric. "This is silk... I shouldn't..." She tried to offer it back, tear-stained as it was.

"It will launder," the woman said dismissively, continuing to pat Jenny's shoulder in comfort. "Or it won't, no matter. What does matter is that you look like you've lost your best friend, and here we are at a beautiful resort where you ought to be enjoying the good food and good views." She put a hand at Jenny's chin and tipped it up to look into her eyes.

Were they human eyes this time? Or were they her otter's dark eyes with no whites?

Whatever the woman found there, Jenny forced herself to look steadily back. She had the most arresting violet-blue eyes.

"I'm Magnolia," the woman said, smiling and releasing her chin. "And that's a little better now, isn't it. Sometimes a good cry is just what you need to put things back into perspective."

"I'm Jenny, and I'm sorry to bother you," Jenny said, wiping away the last tears from her face. "I'm just... a little new to being a shifter." It seemed like the simplest explanation.

"Ah," Magnolia nodded. "That doesn't happen often, but I imagine it's quite an upset. Particularly if you think you have your life all figured out in a particular way."

Jenny stared. Was that why she was having so much trouble? She had been so sure about the path of her life. She was going to be the best lawyer, the best... sister.

Now, here she was, unsure of everything, right down to the shape of her body and the direction of her heart. Her sister was *better* than her, at *everything*, and Jenny was unexpectedly the one falling apart.

"Believe me, darling," Magnolia was saying, "I grew up on a very different island than this, and thought my life would play out in a very different way. But I chose differently, and haven't looked back, and you'll figure out the best path for yourself, too."

Without revulsion, Magnolia picked up one of Jenny's misshapen hands. "You may not be used to all the new features, but don't forget for a moment that you are the beautiful sum all your parts."

Jenny wished she had a fraction of the confidence the big woman exuded. "Thank you," she said genuinely. She couldn't consider the claws or the webbing beautiful, but she tried to remember that becoming an otter *had* saved her life.

"Oh honey," the big woman said cheerfully, "You are as

welcome as the dawn! Now, it's been two weeks since I had one of Tex's margarita's, and that is two weeks too many." She heaved to her feet, tucking the silk Jenny had cried on back into her big orange beach bag.

"Jenny! Oh, Magnolia, you're back!"

Jenny turned at Gizelle's cheerful call.

"Gizelle, honey!" Magnolia opened her arms, and Gizelle darted in and gave her a swift hug. "You're getting brave, darling," Magnolia told her proudly.

"There were so many people," Gizelle told her frankly. "It was noisy and smelly while you were gone. But I didn't break anything and I only shifted…" she counted silently on her fingers until she ran out.

"That's excellent," Magnolia told her before she could finish. From anyone else it might have sounded patronizing, but Jenny felt like it was genuine and gracious. "And you've met Jenny."

"She's a *twin*," Gizelle said, as if Jenny wasn't standing right there. "I'm *helping* her. She *needs* it."

"That's lovely of you, sugar," Magnolia said with an amused sideways look at Jenny.

Jenny wasn't sure if she should feel insulted or not, but decided she mostly felt touched by Gizelle's attention and Magnolia's kindness.

Gizelle took Jenny's hand, not appearing to notice Jenny's reluctance to give it to her. She didn't flinch at the claws or webbing. "I want to practice shifting with you before dinner," she said commandingly. "I'm *good* at it."

"You enjoy that," Magnolia said with a wave over her shoulder. "I'm off to the pool deck for the rest of the afternoon! I've missed the sunshine!"

Jenny let Gizelle lead her in the opposite direction. Perhaps shifting would take her mind off of the memory of Travis' heartbroken face while she decided what she was going to do about him.

It's not what we're going to do about him, her otter told her slyly. *It's what we're going to do **with** him.*

CHAPTER 9

$\mathcal{I}$n the wake of Jenny's stormy exit, Travis bent down slowly and picked up the chair she had toppled over. He put it carefully back in place on its feet, keenly aware of the presence of Tex and Laura, and the absence of his mate.

"Well," Tex said, full of false cheer, "that didn't go quite the way I expected it to."

"I'm sorry," Laura said, more sincerely. "She's going through a lot right now, of course."

"Of course," Travis agreed numbly. Lynx was pacing miserably in his head.

There was a moment of awkward silence, broken by the arrival of Graham, the lion shifter in charge of the grounds. It was odd that his entrance was the loudest thing in the room; he was as quiet as always.

Graham cleared his throat, looking from one uncomfortable person to another. "Storm hitting in a few days. Scarlet's got me shuttering the cottages that aren't being used," he said gruffly. "Said Travis might have some thoughts on electrical things that need extra protection."

"I'll come with you," Travis said, glad for the distraction. He picked up his toolbox and went for the stairs down. "Start at the bottom and work up?"

Graham gave one last suspicious look at Tex and Laura, then shrugged and answered by following Travis, his machete over a shoulder.

Graham was exactly the company Travis would have chosen for this task; he kept conversation to exactly what was necessary and no more.

The cottages were not built for strong winds; such weather rarely came to the island. Graham and Travis moved all the outdoor furniture and decoration into each cottage and made sure every door and window was latched securely, moving anything fragile back from windows that might get blown out.

Travis turned off the meters at each cottage, so no power would be running through them, and had Graham help him pull down a few solar panels in more precarious positions. He checked outdoor lights for stability, and screwed a few fixtures in more tightly.

Graham scanned the greenery as well, and judiciously took down branches overhanging the cottages that looked like they were a breakage risk.

Travis thought he muttered as he made every cut, and as they left the last cottage, asked curiously, "How'd you end up here, Graham?"

Graham had been the only other employee at Shifting Sands when Travis had started, though it hadn't been long before Bastian and Breck had been hired. A series of cooks had been fired in short succession before Chef arrived with Magnolia. Getting her to stay on as a long-term resident had been a coup for the kitchen, because Chef wouldn't have stayed without her, and he had proved to be a genius at food preparation, earning his nickname within a week.

Graham was quiet for so long that Travis had stopped expecting an answer. Then the gardener finally shrugged and volunteered, "Got a letter from Scarlet. Seemed like a better option than any of my others." He didn't elaborate about those previous options, but Travis wondered, as he had several times before, if there was a slight British accent to his words; he didn't sound *entirely* American.

"You?"

Graham's query was a surprise. He rarely pursued conversation, if he could be coaxed into it at all.

"Grew up in a Native village in the middle of nowhere, Alaska," Travis said briefly. "Went to the city to get my certifications, but cities don't really suit me. I saw an employment ad in an underground shifter magazine I subscribed to and it sounded like a nice change of pace. I sent a resume, and got a letter back inviting me out. It was supposed to be temporary, but Scarlet never ran out of work, and I honestly can't imagine living somewhere else now."

Could he? Jenny must have had a life established in California, maybe she was planning to return to it.

We would follow her, Lynx assured him, even though they both shuddered at the idea of a crowded Californian city.

Graham grunted, slicing down an overhanging branch efficiently and hauling it back out of the way into the hedge. Travis knew that their brief moment of conversation had ended. He finished the last power disconnect, and double-checked the latch on the door.

Whatever the storm brought the next evening, Travis was fairly certain that the resort was ready for it.

Whatever his mate brought, he'd be ready for that, as well.

CHAPTER 10

*J*enny wondered if Gizelle had forgotten about her. The tiny woman had demonstrated a shift into her gazelle form, then wandered away to nibble on the grass without a backwards glance. Currently, she was grazing earnestly across the little lawn where they had been meeting every day, ostensibly for Jenny to practice shifting.

Most days, Gizelle had Jenny shift several times, repeating her advice about thinking *as* the form she was aiming for, not *about* the form she was aiming for. Jenny's shifts had grown less painful, but she still dreaded them, and she was still never fully human.

This time, her fingers had no webbing, but the short, no-nonsense claws at the ends pressed little divets into her palms when she clenched her fists.

Jenny sighed and lay back in the prickly grass, looking up into sky. It was blue and clear, and the sun beat down with even more strength than the Californian sun. There wasn't the slightest hint of a breeze, and the early afternoon was sweltering. Jenny fanned the bottom of her sundress to cool her sweaty legs. Maybe she should bring a lawn chair out with her next time; the grass prickled distractingly at her skin, making her think of her otter's coarse fur.

She wondered if lynx fur was softer, and suspected it was. Laura had told her everything she knew about Travis, without Jenny asking. Her sister was clearly more excited about her mate than Jenny was, and seemed puzzled that Jenny was still trying to avoid him.

It wasn't that she didn't want him; she couldn't sleep at night without imagining him beside her. She fantasized about touching his golden-brown skin, running fingers through his short, thick hair, had to try to keep her mind from wandering to still dirtier topics.

Abruptly, there was a big deer-like face right above her, blocking the sunlight. Spiraled horns curving dangerously back from between her bell-like ears.

Gizelle snuffled at her, then shifted like mercury into her human form, crouching beside Jenny. "Are you napping?" She was so close that her long, wild hair tickled Jenny, and she didn't move back much when Jenny sat upright. She had an odd sense of personal space, Jenny had found, sometimes so close that it was uncomfortable, sometimes keeping so much space between them that conversation was awkward.

"No, I'm not napping," Jenny assured her, though she'd been comfortable enough that she might have.

"Oh good! Let's practice!"

Gizelle jumped to her feet in one fluid move, while Jenny stood up more carefully.

"Go!" Gizelle commanded, startling Jenny.

She shifted obediently, braced for the discomfort, and a few moments later was shaking off the last of the pain and scampering on four small feet in grass that suddenly seemed very tall.

A fleet-footed gazelle danced easily with her, leaping high into the air, then stomped an imperious foot and was standing as a human.

Jenny drew a deep breath into her capable otter lungs and tried to keep Gizelle's advice in mind. She thought about what it was like to be a human, how much taller she was, focusing on fingers without webbing or claws. She remembered what it was like to type on a computer keyboard, how long and nimble her hands could be. She ignored her otter, who scoffed and protested that otter fingers were just as clever.

Then she was panting with the effort and looking in triumph at her fingers.

They were her fingers again, free from each other and with her old familiar short fingernails.

"I did it," Jenny gasped, feeling exhausted with the effort. "I did it!"

Gizelle was looking at her curiously. "I... suppose," she said reluctantly.

"I feel like I ran a marathon," Jenny confessed, feeling a little deflated by Gizelle's lack of enthusiasm.

"It shouldn't be that hard," Gizelle said. "Can't you feel the power around you to shift with?"

"Power?"

Gizelle put on what Jenny was recognizing as her teacher face. "It takes energy to shift, of course. But it shouldn't have to come from your own reserves. There is power all around you to draw on, just reach out and use it whenever you need. You should only have to focus."

Was that a feature of all places, Jenny wondered, or just this particular strange island?

Gizelle continued, her expression growing distant and her voice taking on a sing-song tone. "There are wells of power that make the sunless sky, and they can make prison walls or set you free with the right key. Drink it down and you can taste the future and touch the chains that hold the world together..."

Jenny watched her with concern. "Gizelle?" She asked tentatively, hoping to distract her from the trance she was in.

Gizelle ignored her. "Voices of power. Spells set in violence and chaos. Prisons. Things that shouldn't be disturbed..."

Sometimes Gizelle seemed normal enough that it was easy to forget that she had spent many of her formative years imprisoned and forced to remain in her animal form. And then there were these fugue states, when she ceased to make sense. It was hypnotic, sometimes more than just figuratively. Jenny reached up to pinch her neck and keep from falling into the spell with her.

The side of her face exploded in sensation, and Jenny flinched away in alarm and surprise, yelping out loud.

"What?" Gizelle asked, puzzled, but back in reality with her.

Jenny reached a cautious hand up towards her face. "I felt... something."

Stiff, flexible fibers met her fingertips, and the barest brush sent a battery of sensory input to her face.

"Whiskers?!" Jenny shrieked. "I have whiskers!"

These weren't a grandmother's mustache-like whiskers, they were inches-long, and bristled out from her face like quivering array of antennae.

Gizelle shrugged dismissively. "They look lovely," she promised, but Jenny could picture what she looked like quite clearly and knew better.

In her head, her otter was holding her sides and rolling with laughter.

Jenny gritted her teeth. "Let's practice some more," she ground out, even though she was still tired from the last shift.

Gizelle shrugged, obviously mystified by her discomfort. "We can do it some more," she agreed.

"Until I'm me," Jenny declared. "*Just* me."

Good luck with that, her otter teased.

CHAPTER 11

"Want something stronger in your orange juice?" Tex offered. He was hauling trash bags in one hand and a milk crate stuffed with gathered glass bottles in the other.

The bar was empty and Travis was alone. Only two guests were in sight, both of them on the pool deck below.

Magnolia was lounging on one of the chairs by the pool, soaking up the last rays of the late afternoon sun, a margarita in hand.

The other guest was a thickly built man with short-cropped dark hair who looked uncomfortable lounging in his deck chair. He wore mirrored sunglasses and was reading a paperback novel. A bottle of water was gathering condensation on the table next to him.

Travis considered the drink Tex was offering, but finally shook his head. He had a feeling that if he started drinking, he wasn't going to want to stop. His heart hurt for his bewildered mate, and Lynx was yowling and pacing inside of him.

He settled for saying, "Nah."

Tex shrugged. "Suit yourself!" He returned to cleaning and emptying bins.

Travis couldn't get Jenny's face out of his head, and the lost, frightened look made him ball his hands into fists and want to fight something. But there was nothing to fight, and she didn't want his help. She had successfully evaded him for several days now.

There was nothing critical left to fix. The resort was as ready for the storm coming as he could make it. Everything was running perfectly smoothly. Even the heaps of laundry had finally been finished, and the big machines were still again.

When he looked up and saw Scarlet walking up from the pool deck, it seemed like perfect timing.

"What do you need?" he asked too eagerly. "What's next on the renovation schedule?"

Scarlet frowned at him. "You've done a lot of work these last few weeks, you do deserve some time off."

Travis frowned back, trying to figure out how to explain that he needed something to keep his hands busy while his newly-a-shifter mate decided what to do with him. Scarlet wouldn't appreciate an emotional confession or a rambling story about mistaken identity, and she wasn't the sort of person who invited intimacy.

Finally, he stuck with the simplest answer. "I don't really want any time off."

Scarlet gave him an appraising look and went to the bar. She came back to his table with one of the resort brochures. "We're going to have to get these updated with cottage numbers on the ones we put back into service," she said thoughtfully, spreading it out between them. "And we'll take the whale watching note off until we can get another boat."

Travis leaned over the colorful map. "Cottage five could use an upgrade to the bathroom and new windows."

Scarlet made a discouraging noise. "As busy as we were last week, we are not rolling in money. We have a boat that the insurance doesn't want to replace, we lost an entire shipment of groceries, and the air conditioner in the hotel was supposed to be a priority." She didn't have to add that several of the months before that had been in the red as the resort hosted dozens of refugees from a lunatic's shifter zoo on the other side of the island.

"What about the deck at cottage twelve?" Travis suggested, tapping it on the map. "It's got enough rotten decking to be a hazard as it is now, and we've got a bunch of treated lumber leftover from our last deck job. It should be enough to redo it."

Scarlet nodded. "That's an excellent plan."

"There's enough spare tile left to retile the bathroom in cottage five, even if we don't put in new fixtures," Travis suggested, knowing that the deck would only be a morning's worth of work.

"Let's do that, too," Scarlet agreed. "Be aware that there is a storm due to hit the island tomorrow evening. We almost never get hurricanes this far south, but it's still a category three and doesn't appear to be slowing down like usual. We should shutter up the cottages that aren't in use, and we should be prepared to stage repairs afterwards."

Travis nodded. "Already done. Bastian told me about the storm this morning, so I made sure all the cottages not occupied got shuttered and we've got some spare roof tile if we need it afterwards."

Scarlet looked pleased, with a slight, approving smile and a nod. "Excellent. We won't have many guests to worry about—"

She continued to say something else, but Travis could make no sense out of her words, because Lynx clenched claws into his heart just then, and he looked up to find Jenny watching them.

She was standing in the back of the bar, arms folded across her bountiful breasts. The royal blue sundress swished around her knees and left her perfect shoulders bare. She was still tucked up, like she was trying to hold herself in, but Travis thought her gaze was steadier, more sure. The sun was beginning its evening plunge into the sea, and the color of the light made her glow

He was warring with himself, trying to decide if it was better to give her space or give in to Lynx's desire to pounce now, while she was within reach.

Scarlet's sigh of disgust as she rose made Travis look around at her in embarrassment.

"There's no rush on any of those improvements," she told him with a single raised eyebrow, and then she clicked away in her short heels towards the back entrance, giving Jenny a brief nod of greeting as they passed.

Then his mate was strolling towards him, and Travis felt his breath stop at the beauty of her grace.

CHAPTER 12

*J*enny told herself she wasn't going to the bar to find Travis, she was going to find Laura, but she somehow wasn't surprised or disappointed to find her mate instead of her sister.

He was sitting with Scarlet in the setting sun, looking at a brochure spread out between them. The sunset colors made the owner's hair look like it was aflame, but Jenny was captured by Travis, looking seriously over the map. His face was drawn into concentration, and while she watched, he dragged a hand through his short, tousled hair. The play of golden light over his muscles made Jenny draw in a breath and fold her arms tighter across her chest.

Then he looked up, and the way his face lit up hit Jenny in the gut.

Whether she was ready or not, whether she deserved him or not, they were destined for each other. This was the man she was perfectly made for.

And it terrified her.

She made herself unclench her fists, glad at least that she and Gizelle had practiced shifting until she could be human without webbed fingers. The claws were still there, and the pointed teeth, and one of the practice shifts she'd had stiff whiskers protruding from her cheeks. But she knew that Travis wouldn't care about that, and it was oddly comforting to know.

Scarlet rose then, and passed Jenny with a cool nod of greeting, leaving them alone on the deck above the pool.

Jenny made her feet move, and her otter was wriggling in delight as they closed the distance to their mate.

He stood as she approached, and Jenny had to tip her head back to look up into his face.

"I wondered if you'd like to... take a walk."

It wasn't what her otter wanted to suggest, but it was a step Jenny was willing to make.

Travis gazed down at her with adoration that made Jenny squirm uncomfortably, then he cleared his throat and said politely, "That would be lovely."

He pivoted and offered Jenny his arm, which she took, shivering at the touch of his flesh under her fingers.

"Have you seen the gardens?" He asked with a gruff tone that made Jenny suspect that he was as affected by the touch of her skin as she was.

Jenny shook her head, not trusting her own voice.

Travis swallowed. "Would you like to?"

Jenny nodded wordlessly, and he led her out the back entrance of the bar to a gravel path that she had never taken.

Paths she hadn't taken was a theme that seemed to apply to a lot of her life lately.

The evening was a tapestry of purple and magenta, sparkled with stars. The garden was well enough away from the brightly-lit main areas of the resort that it was dark enough to see the features of the moonless sky, framed in the jungle trees that edged the garden.

Jenny marveled at her otter's night vision. If she weren't so busy resenting the otter's constant voice and unwelcome features, there were parts to being a shifter that she could grow to like.

She paused at a vine of white flowers that were climbing riotously up a trellis and reached for one of the blooms.

"Don't pick them," Travis warned.

Jenny froze. "Poisonous?" she asked.

Travis' laugh was her new favorite sound, and her otter practically did backflips of joy over it. "No, Graham is just really, really protective of his gardens. I wouldn't let him hurt you, but I'm not entirely convinced I would win in a fistfight."

Jenny glanced over at him, letting her eyes linger over the muscles under his polo shirt. She couldn't imagine that anyone would be able to beat him in a fistfight. He was not only broad-shouldered and strong, but he moved with a grace and efficiency of motion that made Jenny suspect he was underestimating his own proficiency.

Either way, she didn't want to be the cause of any more trouble at the resort than she already had been. She left the flower unmolested.

There was a bench tucked into one corner under a violet-flowered shrub, and they sat together. It was a small enough bench that Travis' thigh was against Jenny's, and she was keenly aware of how badly she wanted to have less clothing between them even than her thin skirt and his mid-weight khakis.

"I never meant to cause you discomfort," Travis said, awkwardly clearing his throat.

Jenny put an automatic hand on his thigh. "It wasn't you," she said, realizing how trite it sounded. "It was all me. I was... I am... in a really weird place. I don't want you to think I'm not... ah... interested."

"I'll be patient," Travis told her sincerely. "I'll make Lynx be patient."

"No promises about my otter," Jenny laughed weakly. "I don't think patience is her strong suit."

Something occurred to her. "You say 'Lynx' like it's capitalized. Not 'my lynx,' or 'a lynx,' but 'Lynx.' I haven't heard any other shifters say it like that."

"I grew up in a native village in Alaska, and our shifter lore goes back to old stories, about times when Lynx and Raven and Bear were spirits that roamed the world in their own skins."

Travis' voice caught a little as he spoke and Jenny realized that she had unconsciously started caressing his thigh.

Down girl, she told her otter, making her hand still. She wasn't quite willing to remove it.

"So you think of it as a spirit animal, or a totem?"

"Essentially, yes," Travis said.

Somehow, when she thought of her otter, it was too frivolous to be considered a serious totem animal.

One of us has to not take themselves too seriously, her otter replied with a sniff.

"Tell me about growing up in Alaska," Jenny said wistfully.

"I lived in a tiny village near the Brooks Range," Travis said. "You've never seen a land so beautiful and harsh. The summers are full of light and mosquitoes, the winters are endless twilight and cold so sharp it makes your nose hairs frost." He carefully covered her hand with his own, lacing his fingers into hers. She was glad the webbing hadn't come out in this shift.

Jenny and her otter both listened, enthralled, as Travis talked about a world so different from the mild-climate city life that Jenny had grown up in. His tales about the winter were an odd contrast to the warm, fragrant darkness they sat in now.

"Tell me about California," Travis suggested then.

Hesitantly, Jenny talked about growing up in the city-sprawl of Southern California. "I looked up to my dad so much. I always wanted to be a lawyer like he was. It was my whole goal in life."

"You must be pretty good at it," Travis said. "Laura said you were offered a partnership."

Jenny shrugged. "I'm not sure. I mean, I worked hard, but maybe it was just because my dad had been a partner..."

"I don't know much about law," Travis said, richly skeptical, "but I'm pretty sure they don't give partnerships just for your genes. Have you ever heard of imposter syndrome?"

"Yes, of course," Jenny said with a crooked smile she belatedly realized Travis couldn't see. "And yes, guilty." Thoughtfully, she added, "I feel like an imposter as a lawyer, *and* as a shifter."

"Give yourself time," Travis said. "You've only been a shifter a few days, really." He touched the side of her face tenderly, and Jenny wondered if he could see in the dark, too. It would make sense. His fingertips made her skin tingle.

Abruptly, Jenny decided it was time to be brave. "Earlier, you asked if you could kiss me," she said, voice hoarse.

He froze beside her, and Jenny could feel his coiled attention. Her otter was aquiver with anticipation.

"Even though my otter wanted to say yes, I was afraid. I was afraid there wouldn't be anything left of me if I did."

"I understand," Travis said, and Jenny could feel him fighting down disappointment. Was this what being a mate was like, more sure of his emotions than she was of her own? Could he sense her otter wriggling in need and lust the way she could sense his lynx? Did he think she was going to fight the creature instinct down again?

"I'm not afraid anymore," she said quietly. "We both want you to kiss us."

She ran a nervous tongue over her sharp teeth and swallowed. She knew he still wanted to, but would he like what he found?

CHAPTER 13

*T*ravis didn't need a second invitation.

With one smooth motion, he was gathering Jenny into his arms, and drawing her mouth to his for a kiss.

She gave a little whimper as she opened her mouth to him, hot and willing, and Travis dove in to claim it for his own.

Sharp teeth met questing tongue, and it only heightened his heat and desire. He slipped a hand along her neck, using his other arm to pull her close, kissing her with all his strength and focus.

"Oh, Travis," she said, when he released her and she could catch her breath. "I… didn't know it could be like that."

"It can be more," Travis said, sliding both hands up to cradle her face.

This time when he kissed her, it was more slowly, more demandingly, and he didn't release her until she was wordlessly begging for more, writhing against him wantonly. Was that her otter, or was it his Jenny? Was there any difference now?

Ours, Lynx purred.

He reached down and slid on hand up under her dress, cupping the outside of one thigh, one tantalizing ass cheek, and then found the thin fabric of her underwear.

He paused with one finger at the edge of the garment, giving her a chance to change her mind or draw away, and she whined and pressed closer in unmistakable invitation.

He drew it off of her, lifting her into his lap in one smooth motion. There was no way that she wouldn't realize now how badly he wanted her; he was harder than he'd ever been, and the fabric of his pants did little to hold his member down.

She gyrated on him, making him groan in need and desire, and Travis had to concentrate to keep from tearing her dress in eagerness as he slipped it off over her head.

She was not so gentle with him, and Travis heard a seam of his polo shirt rip as she clawed it off of him, kissing him hungrily whenever undressing gave them the opportunity.

"Pants," she said, breathing hard. Travis thought it was a slang expression of disgust, then realized she was actually concerned about his pants, fumbling with the button and belt. Travis stood, lifting her with him, and she gave a little gasp, giggling and grabbing around his neck.

Gently, he lay her down in a bed of flowers, kissing down her neck and arms as she reluctantly let go of him. He had never removed his pants so swiftly, returning to straddle her. She wore only her bra now, and it was everything that Travis could do not to simply let Lynx rut as he wished.

She wants us, Lynx insisted.

We can be a better lover than that, Travis countered.

So instead of burying himself inside her the way he so desperately wanted, he slipped a questing finger into her treasure.

She arched up to his hand, crying in pleasure and begging for release. He added a second finger, thrusting into her gently, slowly, making her squirm and gasp and snap her teeth in need. Her hands on his shoulders scratched and clawed, and when he coaxed a release from her, she sank her short claws reflexively into him.

"Oh!" She said in alarm, as the waves of pleasure ebbed away and Travis slowed his thrusting fingers in time with her breaths. "I must have hurt you!"

"It isn't pain," Travis assured her, and it wasn't. It was only sensation, glorious contact with his mate and an expression of his ability to make her resonate.

But he wasn't able to hold back his own need now, and when he pressed his hungry cock against her, she opened her legs eagerly.

She was so wet, so soaked in her own joyous juices, that Travis slipped in faster than he meant to, driving into her to the base of his shaft in one firm motion.

She cried out in ecstasy, rising to meet him and wrap her legs around his waist. "Yes, oh, yes," she gasped.

Her encouragement was all that Travis needed to begin thrusting in earnest, losing himself in the velvet of her skin, the smell of her sex, the sounds of her enjoyment. When she came again, clawing more gently along his arms this time, he made himself withdraw, panting and fighting hard not to come too quickly himself. He gently pulled her up, kissing her, then guided her over onto her knees.

She was intoxicatingly responsive, finding fresh delight in this new angle of penetration, and Travis finally let himself empty into her, his finally shuddering thrusts making her cry out in release one final time.

CHAPTER 14

*J*enny didn't realize she was dozing until Travis stirred beside her and she jolted into awareness again.

The delicious languor of sex still felt like it was weighing down her limbs, but familiar doubts were re-surfacing. Was this connection all otter and none of her own self? Would she continue to feel less human if she let herself fall further in love with this man?

The smell of crushed greens penetrated her thoughts, and Jenny realized that they were lying in one of the flower beds. She was delightfully sore in unexpected places, and felt guilty.

"Is Graham going to be angry?" she asked tentatively.

"Screw Graham," Travis said, drawing her closer into his arms.

Jenny chuckled into his shoulder.

"I should go," she said, finally pulling away and sitting up. "Once I find my clothes."

Travis sat up beside her, a hand on her thigh, caressing her gently in a way that made her blood stir even after all they'd already done. "I have a room in the staff house at the edge of the resort. You can stay the night there with me."

Jenny didn't want to admit that she had spent the night before as an otter. She found it impossible to sleep as a human, her thoughts too jumbled up and chaotic to give her any rest. Only slipping back into otter form had brought her peace, and she'd slept in a pile of leaves under a hedge. Gizelle assumed she slept nights at Laura's cottage, and Laura still thought she was rooming with Gizelle. Wherever that was.

"I... can't," she said, drawing away and scrambling to her feet. She found her dress with one foot, and yanked it over her head with determination. Her sandals were next to the bench, and she stuffed her feet into them.

Travis rose from the flower garden, a gorgeous slab of naked hunk even in the very faint, shivery light of stars and distant resort lights. "Jenny..."

This was the 'what happens next' talk, Jenny realized, and panic rose up in her throat, choking her. She didn't know *what* she wanted, even if she was now sure *who* she wanted. This was too fast, too much, it was all otter, not herself. She didn't know who she was.

"I'm sorry," she squeaked, and then she fled, not even bothering to find her underwear.

You're going the wrong direction! her otter told her shrilly.

Jenny stumbled over the path, her vision swimming as she battled otter inside her head for control over her limbs.

I didn't ask for you, she wailed at the creature in her head.

You needed me, the otter returned, fiercely.

You can't hold that against me forever, Jenny protested. *You saved me, great. But I want my life back.*

I'm not trying to hold anything against you, her otter growled back. *But I clearly haven't finished saving you. You still need me.*

I need you? Jenny was outraged. *I need you like I need a hole in the head. You want nothing but pleasures of the flesh, pursuing your own selfish agendas. You don't even care that you've ruined my life. I can't do my job! I can't read! I can't shift without claws, or whiskers, or pointed teeth because you won't let go of me!*

She thought that the silence in response was a victory, but her otter finally came back and told her softly, *Did you ever think that you can't shift completely human because you're afraid of losing me, that it's* **you** *not letting go of* **me***?*

Jenny's feet had taken her inexorably to the ocean, and she stood at the edge of the deserted beach now and considered her otter's uncomfortable idea without flinching. The chairs were all folded up and leaning against the beach bar. The stretch of empty sand was silver, with faint gossamer waves lapping against the shore. A sign proclaimed that no lifeguard was on duty.

She slipped off her sandals, and after a moment, her dress and bra, folding them neatly.

See? her otter gloated. *Naked is more fun.*

Jenny stepped into the sand, feeling the grains sift up between her toes like doubts. Was it true? Was she just afraid of being alone again?

She walked out to the edge of the water and turned to look back. The resort rose above her like a castle. Only the bar deck and a few stray windows were lit, and the underwater lights of the pool gave the underside of the palm trees an unearthly glow. Darkness undoubtedly hid her from anyone who might have been watching.

Jenny turned back to the ocean. She'd spent weeks out in that dark water, always an otter, always only barely aware of who she'd been. She waded out, feeling the pull of the waves at her ankles, then her knees. Sand slipped out from beneath her feet with the power of the water. Then she was swimming, with human arms and legs for the first time since her otter had come to her, and she sucked in a breath and dove under, eyes closed.

Water embraced her, and she felt the rush of the gentle currents around her. She drove forward, memorizing the feeling of her muscles with each stroke, the way her body moved when it was surrounded by water. She had to smile at the soreness that Travis had left her, and she broke the surface with a gasp for breath before breaking into an easy stroke along the surface, swimming out into the ocean.

It felt odd, after so much swimming as her otter. In some ways, she was comparatively awkward, not at all the lithe, graceful creature her furry alter-ego was. But in some ways, she was more beautiful as a human.

It was odd to find her otter in her head, enjoying the swimming as much as she was, reveling in the differences between them.

We're different, her otter told her, unexpectedly kind. *I'm not better.*

Jenny sighed. *I'm... sorry,* she told her. *I haven't been very understanding.*

She drew in a deep breath, dove under the water, and shifted.

It was a painless shift, executed between one breath and the time she would have wanted another, and she was the small, agile otter again, diving joyfully through the water.

The shift back was just as painless and smooth, and Jenny was breaking the surface and exhaling her stale air to take another breath. She didn't have to check to know that her teeth were only human-sharp, and that her fingers had no claws or webbing.

She rolled to her back, an otter motion that was less easily achieved by her human form.

I am better at that, otter scoffed, then added sweetly, *but you'll improve.*

I think you have always been in my head, Jenny mused. *You are every bad idea I ever ignored.*

*Maybe **you've** been every bad idea **I've** ever ignored,* her otter told her merrily in return.

Jenny chuckled, arms wide as she bobbed at the surface of the water.

I still don't know what to do about Travis, she said, after a moment of serene floating.

We'll figure it out, her otter told her carelessly. *He is our mate, and he'll be patient while you work through your issues.*

Jenny had to laugh. *It's like having the most unsympathetic psychiatrist in the world in my head with me,* she said wryly.

CHAPTER 15

"*I*t's insane," Travis admitted. "I'm on the world's worst roller coaster. Or the best, I can't decide." It was early enough that the sun wasn't up yet, but most of the staff was already getting ready for the day, gathered informally in the dated kitchen for breakfast.

"Yeah," Tex agreed with a drawl, leaning past him to get into the refrigerator. "Stick it out, man. She'll be worth the lows getting there. Her sister sure is." He shared a sly sideways grin as he came out of the fridge with a piece of pizza.

It wasn't often that the resort had such a pedestrian offering, and of course, it was a pizza with Chef's special flare: a mild, herby sauce with chopped basil, olives, and sausage crumbles, all smothered in white cheeses. Breck had brought all of the leftover pieces from the night before when he'd closed the dining hall.

Travis considered a piece for himself, but wasn't sure he wanted breakfast at all. Jenny had vanished after their evening tryst, and as much as he wanted to hunt her down and repeat the event, he knew he had to give her whatever space she needed. His chest hurt, and he was sure that food wouldn't fill the emptiness that her absence left in him.

"Guh," Breck disagreed vehemently. "Mates. Run while you can."

"You can't run from your mate," Tex told him. "And believe me, you won't want to."

"Oh, I can," Breck scoffed. "And believe me, I will." He elbowed past Travis, who was still camped out next to the fridge, and got his own piece of pizza.

"Breck finding his mate is going to be a train-wreck," Bastian observed, yawning his way into the kitchen. "Close your robe, Breck. No one wants to see that."

"Plenty of people want to see that," Breck smirked and leaned back against the counter as he ate, making sure the robe gaped just right. "This place *is* clothing optional."

"The *resort* is clothing optional," Bastian argued. "Not the staff house." He edged past Breck distastefully and moved Travis aside to grab two pieces of Chef's pizza out the fridge.

"I'm with Bastian," Tex agreed. "We need house rules that include a dress code."

"No Speedos," Bastian suggested. "Shoes off at the door."

"No nudity," Tex added.

"No cowboy hats," Breck countered.

"Hey now," Tex protested. "That's pretty specific."

"So is the nudity clause." Breck went for another slice of the pizza, making Travis realize that he was still standing too close to the door. He sighed, and got his own slice before the fridge door swung closed.

"There are more than two hundred guest beds in this resort," Graham announced, coming into the kitchen like a storm cloud.

The staff looked at him expectantly, and Travis looked up from taking the first bite of Chef's pizza-like delicacy to find that the brunt of Graham's glare was for him.

"And you had to use a *flower bed?*" Graham finished, biting off every word like it was dirty.

Breck, Tex, and Bastian all drew in theatrical breathes.

"Oh snap," Breck said. "See, I told you mates were trouble."

"You've smashed your share of flower beds," Tex reminded him.

"Hush," Breck said. "Travis is in trouble right now."

Travis made a sound that might have been a growl and might have been clearing his throat. "Sorry about the garden," he said, not feeling particularly sorry.

Graham stalked towards Travis, giving him a moment of concern, but opened the refrigerator instead, surveying the options before deciding on the last slice of the pizza.

He gave Travis a look chillier than the air escaping from the fridge and swept back out without another word.

"Dodged a bullet," Bastian laughed.

"I'm just glad we don't have to clean up any blood this time," Breck said, sounding faintly disappointed.

"Thanks for all the backup," Travis said sarcastically.

"No problem," Tex said cheerfully, clapping him on the back.

Travis left the house muttering, toolbox in hand, but he was smiling wryly.

The first thing he did was tear up the old decking from the porch at cottage twelve. It was cathartic to destroy it down to the structure, ripping up the previous boards with a crowbar or just his own hands. The next thing was to carry the new boards down from the other job site. With the bar still closed for the morning, Tex helped him haul them down.

"If I see Jenny, I'll tell her where you are," the bartender promised.

"Thanks," Travis told him, then lost himself in setting up the job site, leveling the sawhorses, and running the extension cord for the chop saw and the hose from the compressor.

He felt Jenny before he saw her, the hair at the back of his neck rising to attention as Lynx began to caper in eagerness.

Turning to see her was like a shock of electricity. She looked fresh and well-rested, and so breathtakingly gorgeous that Travis had to shift his hips to give his growing member space in his pants.

"Don't let me interrupt you," she said shyly. "I was just... looking for something to do. Some way to help."

Travis could think of something to do, but knew it wasn't what she meant. "I'd love your help."

She walked hesitantly into the work site, skirting around the chop saw cautiously. "I'm not sure how helpful I'll be. I'm... still having trouble reading words."

"Numbers, too?" Travis asked. He handed her a tape measure and noticed that her fingers had short, sensible nails, not claws.

She unrolled it a few inches and shrugged. "Apparently, I can read numbers."

Travis gave her ear protection and showed her how to hook the end of the tape measure on a board and mark the right number. "This porch is an easy job," he said. "All the boards will be exactly the same length. Some jobs, it's as much measuring as it is anything else; it can be tricky when every piece is a new length." He showed her how to place a speed-square and mark a line across the board. It was distracting, being so close to her delicious smell. He wanted to caress her, but kept his touches professional, even if he couldn't keep his lingering glances quite as reserved.

He caught more than one appraising glance in return, and several times, she licked her lips unconsciously and swallowed when their gazes crossed.

He cut the boards as she measured, and she grew easier with the task as they went, zipping out the tape measure and drawing the cut line with efficiency and confidence.

The last board, he took from her, then said, "Come cut it!"

"Oh, I couldn't," she protested. "It's so...loud. I'd cut off a finger or something."

"It's perfectly safe," Travis assured her. He showed her the cutting guard that came down to cover the blade, and put his hands over hers to show her where to safely hold the board and how to snug it up against the cutting guide.

He put her hands on the trigger and let her rev the blade up, letting her experience how quickly it would brake when she let go and what it would sound like, then stepped back. "Go for it!"

Jenny bit her lip, scrunched her whole face in concentration, and cut the board with one smooth, slow motion.

"Oh my gosh," she squeaked, when she had released the trigger and returned the chop saw to its upright position. "That was the most exciting thing I've ever done!"

Travis had to grin at her enthusiasm. He refrained from the obvious comment that her life must not be all that exciting.

She helped him carry the board to the bare deck joists and hold it in place while he screwed it into place. "Here," he said, passing her the tool.

She took it gingerly, then stared when he didn't make a move to take it back. "Wait, you want me to do this part? Oh, no, I'm no good at this kind of thing. I tried using a power drill once and couldn't even get one screw in. I chipped the drywall and still couldn't hang up my picture." She shook her head vehemently.

"Let me introduce you to the joy that is the impact driver," Travis said, covering her hands on the tool reassuringly. He showed her how to hold it, and what to do with the hose that snaked away from it to the air compressor. The screws had special heads that fit into a closed bit, and Travis demonstrated how to make sure the screws wouldn't wobble as they were driven in.

Then he moved back and let Jenny try her own. At first she was ginger with the screw, then bore down with more strength, and the screw shrieked into the lumber and left a little dimple in the board.

"Wow!" Jenny exclaimed, giving Travis a sunny smile. "That was so easy!"

Travis laughed with her. "My grandmother always said that no woman needs a man if she has the right tools."

Jenny look admiringly at the impact driver. "This is definitely the right tool," she said, nodding.

"My grandmother was a dirty old woman, and I think she was talking about something else entirely," Travis told her with a grin. "But it's still very true."

Jenny laughed, and it was the first time that Travis had seen her truly relaxed. "Can I do it again?"

He showed her how to adjust the resistance so that the screws went in just the right amount, then let her screw in the rest of the board. They brought the next piece, aligning it with spacers. He screwed in the first two, then let her go wild with the driver while he brought the next board over.

With two sets of hands, the work went very quickly, and in no time at all, they were screwing the railing back onto the new deck.

"I've never made anything before," Jenny said, standing back to admire their work. "What a feeling!"

"There's nothing like it," Travis said, but he wasn't looking at the deck.

She looked up to catch his gaze. "There really isn't," she agreed.

Travis didn't stop to ask permission this time, taking the invitation in her eyes as consent. He gathered her into his arms and kissed her with all the passion in his heart.

CHAPTER 16

*J*enny had read plenty of romance novels. She knew all the best descriptions for kisses and things more intimate. She was guilty of lingering over scenes of tenderness and the sweet nothings that the heroes would murmur as they caressed their lovers.

But romance writers, she realized in that moment, knew nothing.

It wasn't weak knees and gentle words. It was raw and animal, an utterly primal power that made every nerve ending in her body come alive with the touch of his lips on hers. It was need and strength, in the feel of his sweat-beaded muscles under her fingers. For a moment, she wished she still had claws, because she wanted to sink into that flesh and claim him as her own.

His fingers were impossibly strong, pulling at her shoulders, kneading at her waist, and Jenny wondered if she would have bruises that wouldn't show on her deep brown skin. She wanted bruises. She wanted marks of their lovemaking, and when Travis groaned and tried to gentle his hands, she pressed harder into him.

"The deck," she hissed near his ear. "I want to make love on the deck we built."

Her breath left her lungs as Travis lifted her effortlessly and carried her onto the new deck, laying her sensibly in the only bit of shade. The morning had gotten unexpectedly hot, and already, her entire body was moist with sweat.

It made every touch electric, and as wet as her body was, between her legs was a wetter place still. Travis peeled off her soaking underwear, and pulled her dress off over her head in one musical move. He was shucking off his own clothing with an eagerness that made him almost clumsy, and Jenny drank in the sight of him.

His cock sprang out eagerly, rigid and thick. Gold-skinned muscles gleamed with dappled sunlight and perspiration, a fascinating rippling effect that made Jenny flex her hands helplessly as she waited.

She did have long to wait, then he was straddling her, spreading her legs and thrusting into her without any of the preambles of the night before.

Their previous encounter had been lovemaking, this was just fucking, and Jenny loved every moment of it. She arched up to him, crying out and clawing at the boards they had so recently screwed in. He set a brutal, desperate pace to his thrusts, growling near her ear as she panted and met every stroke.

She came like an explosion, feeling the release ripple through her entire body right to her toes. Travis slowed his motions to let the decrescendo of her orgasm last longer, then slipped entirely out of her, gritting his teeth as he paused to delay his own release and prolong their fun. Jenny gave a cry of loss as he left her, but when he had recovered his control and made a motion to resume where they had left off, she sat up and pushed him back down.

She straddled him authoritatively, holding down his thick arms as if she had any chance of keeping him in place, and he grinned at her in delight and desire.

She teased him for a long moment, just touching the end of his quivering penis with her outer folds, letting him get only the head into her places of pleasure before retreating again. She leaned over to kiss his neck, sliding teeth over his collarbone and shoulders, licking, and letting her breasts, sensitive nipples fully erect, slide over his sweat-slick chest.

He groaned and thrust his hips at her, but let her continue to hold him down, though the muscles bunched up several times as if he wished to break free.

Then, finally, she buried him into her, letting his member fill her entirely, and then held herself there. The noise he made was half delight and half agony of desire, and he bucked against her. She locked around him, keeping him from retreating for a full stroke, and kept her motions to small, torturous gyrations.

She wasn't sure who finally gave in, whether she began the rhythmic strokes, in and out, or if he made it happen. His hands were on her hips, and she wasn't sure when she'd let go of his arms and put her hands on his shoulders; her world was reduced to the friction and pressure and throb of the pleasure he was raising inexorably in her.

When she came again, he did as well, and Jenny could feel the pulse of his release deep within her as all of his muscles turned to rock beneath her hands and her world reduced to light and completion.

When she could remember herself again, she was sprawled on top of Travis, both of them slick with sweat and other fluids, breath heavy in each others ears.

She felt satisfied. From the lobes of her ears to the heels of her feet, she was exactly where she wanted to be, her whole body feeling comfortably used.

"I think I have a splinter in my ass," Travis told her, and the laughter came through his chest into Jenny's ears and infected her until she couldn't do anything but giggle helplessly, clasp her sides, and gasp for breath.

"Let's go take a shower," Jenny suggested, sitting up at last.

"We should have the staff house to ourselves at this time of day," Travis said, rising to his feet and helping her up.

Jenny picked up her dress and looked down at her body. "I don't really want to put this on," she said.

Travis picked up his own clothing, but made no move to put any of it on. "Lucky you, the resort is clothing optional."

Otter cheered in her head.

Jenny's reluctance must have shown on her face, and Travis assured her, "I'll take you around the back way. We probably won't meet anyone."

Jenny stood up straight. "Alright, then," she said, putting her hand in the crook of his elbow that he offered. "Let's go get cleaned up."

CHAPTER 17

"...*A*nd then we gave the new decking a good load test," Travis said with a grin that felt like it was going to split his face.

Tex clapped him cheerfully on the shoulder. "Good for you!" he cheered.

"Dooooooom," was Breck's contribution.

"Details, man!" Bastian demanded.

But just then, Jenny appeared at the door to the kitchen, looking gorgeous and freshly showered. Breck and Bastian greeted her politely and excused themselves.

"Lunch rush is about to start," Breck explained. "As much of a rush as eight guests can be!"

"Going to grab food from the buffet and head to the pool," Bastian said with a wave.

The front door clicked shut behind them, but the open windows made their parting conversation carry clearly: "Damn, I need some of that mate action."

"Are you an idiot, man? Flex your muscles at one of the guests and get a room key or three, but don't ever wish for a mate."

"Good mooooorning," Laura sang as she and Tex came down the stairs behind Jenny, propelling her into the kitchen.

Travis finally stopped staring and stepped forward to give Jenny a quick, shy kiss on the cheek once she was in reach, hyper-aware of her twin sister and her mate at the kitchen bar behind him. Jenny grinned as foolishly at him as he knew she was at her.

"After lunch, I was going to go try to help Scarlet with that contract she was asking about," she said, accepting the plate Travis had already prepared and sitting with him at the kitchen bar. "I was able to read some of those magazines that I know you guys only have around for the articles, so I think I can probably make some sense out of Scarlet's contract now."

"Fantastic," Travis said.

"You never doubted for a moment, did you," Jenny said in wonder.

"Not for a second," Travis could say in all honesty.

"That makes one of us." Jenny was even beautiful when she ate, with graceful fingers, and a mesmerizing mouth. Travis realized he was staring and had to concentrate on eating his own food, glancing up to see that Jenny was watching him as avidly as he'd been watching her.

Their exchange of gazes did not go unnoticed.

"Oh, aren't they adorable," Laura said sweetly to Tex.

"Like a southern lemonade," he agreed. "New mates, you know. Can't keep their eyes off each other."

"You speak from such a position of superiority," Travis said dryly. "Being a whole week ahead of us at this."

"You know, I'm older than you by six minutes," Jenny reminded her.

"But not wiser," Laura said mockingly.

Travis thought it sounded like an exchange they'd had many times.

Jenny took her plate to the trash and brushed off the crumbs before putting her dishes in the dishwasher.

"I've got a bathroom to re-tile," Travis said, following suit.

"Tiling sounds really complicated," Jenny admitted, as they put their shoes on at the front door.

"It's pretty straight-forward," Travis said modestly. "I could show you how to do it."

Jenny's eyes danced with amusement. "I'll come by after I'm done with Scarlet, and we can test the final product."

"Get a room!" Laura laughed at them from the kitchen.

"Yes, ma'am!" Tex loudly and deliberately misunderstood her, and there was a playful shriek and the smack of a loud kiss.

Travis took Jenny's hand as they left the house, and it was incredibly delightful just to have to her hand in his, fingers entwined. He was reluctant to let her go when their paths diverged, and he drew her in for a long, lingering kiss.

"I'm looking forward to seeing you later," he said, when he finally released her lips.

"Me, too," she said breathlessly back.

He stole one final kiss, then turned his back decisively and marched away down the path, glancing over his shoulder to find that Jenny was walking backwards so she could smile after him. She gave him two thumbs up and mouthed "Great ass!" before turning and scampering up the steps towards the top of the resort.

CHAPTER 18

*J*enny was smiling and watching her feet as she wandered up the steps and steep paths towards the place where Scarlet's office perched at the top of the resort.

The building was empty.

Jenny waited a short while in the green, shady courtyard, wandering between the plants and reading the little tags that were in with each one. She fingered one of the flowers, but remembered Travis' warning about picking anything, and left it in peace.

After a while, she wandered back down to the bar deck, where Tex was polishing each of the bottles to a sparkling luster. Jenny walked to the railing to look below.

Magnolia waved at her from one of the deck chairs, and she waved back with a shy smile. The only other person on the deck was a tattooed man built like a small tank, who looked up over his sunglasses when Magnolia waved.

"Where's Laura?" she asked, returning to the bar and sitting on one of the bar stools. She'd rather go find Travis, but was hesitant to interrupt his work more than she already had. Despite his assurances, she suspected that laying tile was a tad more complicated than she was up for and knew she'd only slow him down. She waved off Tex's offer for a drink; she didn't want to freeload at the resort any more than she had to.

"Lydia is taking some time off, because the incoming storm has scared some of the guests off, so Laura offered to help out in the spa," Tex said. He showed her on the brochure where the spa was, circling it with a pen.

"Thanks," Jenny said, and she slipped off the stool to find her sister. She paused and turned back around. "Thanks for... being great for my sister."

Tex gave her a soft, crooked smile. "She's everything to me," he admitted without shame.

"I can tell," Jenny said thoughtfully. "And she adores you, too."

"Much like you and Travis," Tex said gently.

Jenny gazed back at him. She and Travis hadn't said anything about love, but she wondered if he felt it as deeply as she did. Tex seemed to accept it as foregone, but was it, really?

"Thanks again," Jenny said, taking the brochure that Tex had marked up.

She breathed deeply, wondering if she was imagining the strange feeling of pressure and rain in the air. It was sweltering hot and clear, and the path to the spa was steep, like most of the walkways in the resort, but a stiff breeze had sprung up.

Footsteps crunching swiftly in the gravel behind her made her turn curiously and find the hulking man from the pool deck following her. He didn't look like a good candidate for the spa, but they did animal grooming as well. Maybe he was going to get a good brushing. Jenny nodded politely and turned back to the path in front of her, scooting over so that he could pass her, as he seemed to be in a hurry.

Her otter screamed a warning at her too late for her to dodge the crushing blow that came from one of his large fists, and Jenny's world went to blackness.

CHAPTER 19

*T*ravis was kneeling in the work area, splattered to the elbows in grout and cutting one of the tricky corner pieces when Lynx yowled inside him, all claws and panic.

He dropped the tile, not even caring that it broke, and leaped to his feet.

Lynx couldn't lead him, only knew that something was wrong, that his mate was in trouble, that they had to do *something*. So Travis went to the bar, and he came in the back entrance just as Laura came sprinting from the side entrance. Not for a moment did he think she was Jenny.

"Something is wrong," he said, fighting down Lynx's blind panic.

"Something is very wrong," Laura agreed, eyes wild.

Tex put his guitar down. "What is it?" he asked, looking from one to the other in growing alarm.

"Jenny, she's gone." Laura tapped the side of her head.

"She's hurt," Travis added. Lynx snarled and Travis could feel him pacing anxiously.

Tex came out from around the bar. "I told her you were at the spa, love," he told Laura, reaching out for her hand. "Ten minutes ago, maybe fifteen."

"I didn't see her there," Laura insisted. "I just came from there, I would have seen her!"

Travis, finally with a direction to go, loped for the path to the spa, every sense alert for some clue to what had happened, and where his mate was. Laura and Tex were close on his heels.

"Hold up!" Tex said, coming to a stop behind him.

Travis turned to see Tex standing up with a discarded brochure that Travis had ignored, blown up into the hedge. The spa was circled in pen. "This is the brochure I gave Jenny."

Laura gave a little moan of worry and Tex put an arm around her. "We'll find her," he promised.

"Can you smell her?" Travis demanded. Lynx had hearing so keen he could tell when an engine was the smallest bit out of alignment, but he couldn't smell a cigar a meter away. Tex, on the other hand, had a bear's better-than-bloodhound nose.

Tex gave a sniff, walking in a circle around the area where he'd found the brochure. Finally, he shrugged and shook his head. "Guests, staff, Laura... I can't smell Jenny specifically, or tell where she is."

Travis snarled and balled helpless hands at his side. "Someone *took* her," he insisted.

The distant sound of the resort van coughing into life was clear to Travis' keen hearing. "And with no boat, there's only one way off this island!"

Travis bolted for the resort entrance.

CHAPTER 20

*J*enny woke when the van went around a hairpin curve and she slid into the side of the vehicle.

"Ow," she said out loud before she could stop herself.

"Dammit," a rough voice said. She realized after a moment that it wasn't addressed at her.

"No, I told you, I'm gonna need that plane now. I don't care if there's a storm incoming. This place is crawling with shifters. The lifeguard is a dragon, did you know that? Yeah. They're gonna come looking for her, I haven't got that kind of time."

There was a pause in the conversation and Jenny was able to lever herself up and peer over the back of the second seat back. The driver was the gorilla from the pool deck, wearing clothing now, and the throbbing in Jenny's head suggested that it was his fist that had caused her unconsciousness. Her hands were tied together, and just as she was considering whether she could shift her way out of the knots and escape, she met his eyes in the rear view mirror.

"Shit," he said. "And fuck you, too," he added as an afterthought into the phone. "It better be there when we get there.

That was the agreement." He hung it up as vehemently as he could with a tiny button on a tiny box that was dwarfed by his large hand.

"Don't try shifting," he warned Jenny. "I've drugged you with some fancy shit that should prevent you from shifting into a wolf or any other magic crap. Man, is your boss pissed at you right now."

Jenny was trying to wrap her head around why anyone at the firm would be this angry with her when the specific words from his statement sunk in. A wolf. They thought she was a wolf shifter like Laura. No, they thought she *was* Laura. This pleasant mountain of a man must have been sent by the mob that her twin sister had worked for.

Was he telling the truth about shifting?

Jenny reached for the otter within her, and was alarmed to find silence. She reached for Laura then, trying to use their odd twin bond to make some kind of meaningful contact. Silence met her again. Though her head throbbed, Jenny didn't think it was just a concussion. The mating bond... that was stronger than either of those things, wasn't it?

Travis...

Jenny scrunched her eyes together against the pain that bloomed behind her eyes at the effort.

"I'm not Laura," she said.

"Sure you're not," the man laughed gruffly. His voice went mockingly high. "You've got the wrong guy, mister! I swear!"

"I have a twin sister," Jenny said, offended.

"Oh, that's a good one," the man said flatly. "I've never heard that one before." His flat tone suggested otherwise.

The road they were traveling was full of tight corners and steep grades. Jenny found that her feet had also been tied, and it was a challenge to remain upright without being able to spread her limbs. She wedged herself against the window, and glared at the man in the rear view mirror.

"What are you going to do with me?" she asked.

"I'm just the collector," he said. "I deliver you to your boss in LA and get paid. Blacksmith said in one piece if possible, but he wasn't too picky. Guess he's not so happy that half his crew got nabbed by the pigs a few days back."

His phone rang then, and he nearly missed a curve answering it. "Wrench," he said sharply.

It took Jenny a moment to realize he meant it as his name.

He glanced back at her, listening to the phone intensely. He swapped ears, navigating another corner and a series of epic potholes. "I know," he said, clearly trying to keep his voice down. "I'm on a good job right now, I'll have the money real soon."

Jenny's otter senses weren't all gone; she could hear him without effort, even over the sounds of the van and the rising wind outside. The jungle was whipping alarmingly, and in the few places they drove through clear areas, she could see Wrench struggling to control the van against the wind.

"No, it's a sure thing. You can sign her up for the class, I'll make sure it gets paid."

Jenny could almost hear the voice at the other end, but not quite.

"Yeah," Wrench said ambiguously. It was night and day how different his voice was on this conversation compared to the last. "Can I talk to her?"

If his voice had been less gruff with this conversation, it was now an order of magnitude more gentle, and as quiet as Wrench could manage. "Hey, kitten!"

The chatter at the other end was even clearer, high-pitched and eager. Jenny could make out the words ballet, friends, music, and dancing. She watched Wrench in the mirror, re-evaluating him as he conversed with the girl at the other end of the phone. Even his face softened, and when he took off his sunglasses because the sky was growing dark, his eyes looked gentle.

Was this Stockholm syndrome? Jenny wondered. It wasn't that she didn't still want to kick the man in the knees, but it was hard to hate someone who would buy ballet lessons for a little girl. Even if it was with dirty kidnapping money.

"I gotta go, kitten," Wrench said at last, as they broke out of the jungle at the end of the little airstrip. Barely audible, he added, "Love you," before hanging up and glaring suspiciously at Jenny in the mirror.

Jenny pretended that she hadn't heard a word, and wondered if she'd imagined the gentleness.

Wrench parked the van at the end of the runway, and cursed when he opened his door and the wind blew it shut before he could get out.

Jenny considered struggling when Wrench came around the van to pull her out, but she knew at once that it would be futile and settled for stomping on his foot as he set her down. She tried again to shift to her otter shape, and the wave of dizziness that came with the effort made her almost fall over.

But she could tell that whatever it was she'd been given was weakening. Her otter was *there* again, growling and gnashing sharp teeth in frustration. Jenny played up her dizziness and slumped into Wrench.

Wrench cut the cords at her ankles, and hauled her to her feet. Jenny knew she had no chance of outrunning him in this form; she had enough trouble standing upright against the whipping wind.

Wrench's phone rang and he answered it with a growl of his name, turning away from the wind and repeating it louder when it wasn't heard the first time.

"He's nuts to try it," he shouted. "But we're waiting."

He hung up, and pulled Jenny into the dubious shelter behind the van.

Jenny looked at the way the trees were bending in the gusts. "You might want to make sure they know what to do with your money when you die in a fiery plane crash. Wouldn't want your kitten to default on her ballet lessons."

She was rewarded with Wrench's alarmed, embarrassed look. "You've got better ears than I thought," he snarled, not amused. "I'll be glad to hand you off."

The rumble of the approaching airplane was hard even for Jenny to hear over the wind, which was now roaring, crosswise to the runway. She pointed her bound hands in that direction. "Well, here it comes now."

Wrench looked, and they both watched in horror as the little plane was caught in a gust, twisted sideways and over-corrected, spitting back out over the ocean to crash into the waves offshore.

CHAPTER 21

Travis skidded to a stop at the top of the resort.

The van was long gone, down the winding jungle road that led to the airfield on the other side of the island.

He howled in rage, and Tex and Laura, panting, came up behind him.

"I thought that Costa Rica didn't get hurricanes," Tex said, staring at the sky and holding onto his hat. There were thick dark clouds gathering north of the island, and the wind was beginning to pick up with a vengeance.

"This isn't a hurricane," Breck said, coming out of the office. "Have you seen Scarlet? Did she take the van?" He looked from one to the other, picking up on the urgency of the situation. "What's going on?"

"We don't know who took the van," Tex said.

"But whoever it is, they've got Jenny," Travis told him, gnashing his teeth.

"I can't feel her," Laura said in anguish. "Not... not quite like before, it's a little different. Like there's cotton between us."

"Yes," Travis said, glad for her words to put what he was feeling into context. "That's exactly what it's like."

Breck looked from one to the other in growing alarm. "Kidnapped? Who would kidnap her?"

"Fred?" Tex suggested.

"He's still in prison," Laura said, shaking her head. "This feels more like the cartel's M.O."

"The cartel?" Breck asked in disbelief.

"It's a long story," Laura said.

"There was a last-minute guest who arrived yesterday who looks the part," Breck suggested. "Southern Californian for sure, lots of scars and tattoos."

"Mr. Muscles with the suitcases of lead," Tex said, snapping his fingers.

"Why are we not going after them already?" Travis asked, snarling.

"We couldn't catch them now," Tex cautioned. "They're halfway to the airstrip, and none of us are distance runners in either form."

"Who would send a plane in this weather?" Breck scoffed. "The regular charter got canceled. Anyway, take the Jeep."

The others looked at him with sudden hope. "It's running?"

"A little rough," Breck said with false modesty. "I've still got to rebuild the carburetor one of these days..."

Travis was already pushing past him to where it was parked. "I'll drive," he said.

CHAPTER 22

*T*he wings of the plane tore off as if they'd been made of paper when it hit the ocean. It made a terrible ripping sound even louder than the roaring wind, and the fuselage sank with a rush of bubbles and screaming metal.

Jenny and Wrench watched in astonishment.

"We should see if anyone survived," she said, finally. "They might need help."

Wrench squinted at her. "You do realize that they were here to drag you back to the cartel."

Jenny glared back at him. "I'm not saying that they aren't terrible people, but they are still *people*. Drowning is a horrible way to go, and I should know it."

Wrench tried to stare her down. "It's not like you can shift yet," he said.

Jenny closed her eyes and reached down inside of her. Her otter wriggled to greet her, eager to breach the prison she'd been trapped in.

If she concentrated... just like so... she could almost feel the barrier keeping them apart. And if she could just burn it away, she could shift again, and sense Laura again, and reach Travis. Travis.

She longed for his touch, his comfort. Even just knowing that he was there.

Something Gizelle had said to her bubbled out of her memory. Much of what she said was rambling and disjointed, and Jenny had learned to filter out some of the more absurd statements, but something the gazelle shifter had said about power stuck with her.

"There is power below you, if you can reach it," Gizelle had told her. "Sunlit caverns with no sky." She'd been talking about the power required for shifting, but Jenny had to wonder.

The sky above them now was dark and weirdly hard to see, even to Jenny's enhanced otter sight, and Jenny wondered if she imagined the power that crackled between sky and island. They felt… connected, as if the island itself had drawn the storm to it.

Jenny reached, and she wasn't sure if she was reaching above her to the storm, or below her to the depths of the island, only knew that she had to shift, and that she needed to break her otter out of her trap, and that the means were here, within her reach.

Power answered her, bright and clear and terrifying in its intensity, and otter sprang from her in the smoothest shift that Jenny had yet managed.

The restraints fell away from her small paws and Jenny was scampering away from Wrench as he cursed and grabbed for her.

She could escape, she realized, exactly as she realized with a wave of relief that Travis and Laura were back in her head with her, along with her otter self. All she had to do was get away from Wrench and hide.

Even as she thought it, she knew she couldn't turn her back to any survivors that might be out in the plane. She had the ability to lead them safely back to shore, and she had to try.

Jenny turned back to Wrench, to find a pitch black panther standing in a pile of shredded clothing. Perhaps getting free would not have been as easy as she'd first thought.

But he didn't pounce, and after a long moment of mutual consideration, Jenny turned her back on him and ran for the ocean, diving in without hesitation.

CHAPTER 23

"Jenny!" Travis said, nearly losing control of the Jeep around one of the hairpin curves.

"What the hell?" Breck yelled, clutching at the seat and glove box handles.

"She's okay!" Laura shouted with tremendous relief from the seat behind them where she was sitting with Tex.

"What was that?" Travis asked, twisting to look back at her.

"The road!" Breck hollered. "Please watch the road!"

"I have no idea," Laura said, looking as shaken as he felt.

It had felt as if their bond had been lit on fire, all the cotton burned away in a fiery blast.

Jenny, Travis thought fiercely, desperately.

And clear as a summer day, her voice came to him.

Travis! I'm alright!

Where are you? He asked, relief in every cell of his body.

The answer was wry amusement and a sense that it was complicated. *In the ocean. Rescuing the people who tried to kidnap me.*

Travis laughed out loud. Of course she was.

"She's free," he told the others. "But we need to get to the airstrip."

"On, James," mocked Breck, and Travis shifted gears as he drove around another tight corner, fighting the Jeep against the wind that was driving hard out the low, dark sky.

CHAPTER 24

*J*enny reached the wreckage in no time, swimming mostly underwater. She scanned the water for any sign of human survivors, diving under the surface to find any sunken bodies. She found that her otter had a strange vibration sense, and she listened for any motions in the water, someone swimming or struggling.

The water rippled with the force of the wind over top of it, but was quiet further down. The song of the ocean was still peaceful here, water buffering the power of the storm, and dampening the strange energy of the island. There were fish, going about their fishy business, and she almost went swimming after them before her human self reminded her firmly about why they were here.

It occurred to her again that she had no compulsion to return to the shore where Wrench waited. All she had to do was swim away, safe in her otter form from whatever the storm threw at her.

But that wouldn't keep Wrench from trying again, and perhaps getting Laura for real next time.

Jenny bobbed to the surface, looking for anyone clinging to floating debris. She nosed through pieces of fuselage, and parts of seats. Bits of unidentifiable plastic cluttered the surface, confusing her otter senses. Finally, she gave up, and she was just debating her return to the shore again when she found a floating briefcase.

While she didn't see anything special about it at first, her human gave a crow of triumph at spotting it, convinced that it had that spy movie ransom suitcase look. She swam over and wrapped her small forearms around it, then tugged herself onto her back to drag it to the beach.

Loaded thusly, her return trip was much harder and lengthier than her trip out, but Jenny doggedly continued, practicing her negotiation with Wrench in her head. He could have the briefcase, and would leave Jenny and Laura alone forever. Maybe he could convince the cartel that her sister had died when he tried to bring her in.

Just as the ocean floor rose beneath her to become the beach and the water turned to surf, she heard the comforting voice of her mate in her head. *Jenny! We're here!*

Before she could answer, there was a predator's shriek of rage from above, and Jenny was struck with outstretched talons, losing her grip on the suitcase as she was lifted into the air by something with wide, sweeping wings.

CHAPTER 25

Travis would never have driven so fast, on roads so terrible, for any other reason.

But his mate needed him, and he wasn't going to risk being too late to the scene.

When they finally broke out of the jungle onto the airstrip, he didn't even hesitate before gunning directly at the huge, naked man with tattoos and scars who was standing with his back to them on the far side of the field. He knew without a shadow of doubt that this was the man who had stolen his mate, and Travis had no qualms about running him down on the spot.

Breck, Tex, and Laura all yelled, and Travis wasn't sure if they were warning the man, trying to stop him, giving voice to the warcry in his own thoughts, or just screaming. At the last moment, the man leaped out of the way in a dark, shifting blur as the Jeep smashed through the place he was standing, and jostled down the bank of the narrow beach to stick fast into a pile of driftwood.

They spilled out of the Jeep and faced down the panther that glared at them from the bank.

Breck, who had already shed his clothing with the swiftness of consistent practice, shifted into a spotted leopard. Travis heard Tex and Laura growl beside him, still human, but flexing their hands.

The panther shimmered and stood up as a man again, hands spread. "I haven't got her," he said, not bothering to deny that he had once.

"Where is she?" Travis demanded.

The man pointed, out at the surf, where a tiny dark form was struggling out of the water, dragging a piece of debris. Further out, large pieces of smoking wreckage indicated that something had just crashed into the ocean.

Jenny, Travis thought at her. *We're here!*

Just then, an eagle shrieked and plummeted down from the stormy sky, talons outstretched, and plucked Jenny from the water.

Travis gave a cry that matched that of the predator bird and was hurling down the beach without thinking about it. He could feel Jenny's pain and shock as the talons gripped her mercilessly and hauled her into the air.

"Jenny!" Laura shrieked behind him.

The eagle struggled against the wind, nearly falling back into the surf before it gained enough lift to land with Jenny's limp form onto a tall tangle of driftwood. He put his beak around Jenny's throat and lifted her that way, flaring his wings in clear threat; he could easily break her neck.

Travis drew to a stop at the base of the driftwood, a snarling bear and whining wolf at one side and Breck's leopard at the other. "Let her go!" Only the need for human speech kept him from shifting.

"Hey now!" the man from the resort bellowed, muscling his way fearlessly between Travis and the bear. "That's not the right woman! We're after a wolf shifter!"

The eagle shrugged into a human form, deftly transferring his hold from beak to big hands. Jenny's otter neck was clearly no safer in one than the other — a single motion would break it easily. Jenny remained limp and unresisting, though Travis could feel her coiled energy through their bond.

"Let her go," Laura yelled, shifting into her human form and standing tall and proud despite her nudity. "He's right. I'm the one you want."

Tex shifted as well. "Laura..." he growled, almost lost against the wind.

"Boss won't care which of you he gets," the eagle shifter shrugged, with a cruel smile. "You've caused a lot of trouble in the organization, and either way, you'll pay for it."

The guest from Shifting Sands made a noise of protest that Travis wouldn't have heard if he hadn't been standing so close, then hollered, "You can't nab the wrong woman. She swam out there to try to save you."

The eagle shifter didn't look impressed. "Your vacation make you soft, Wrench? The boss wants revenge. Doesn't much matter how he gets it."

"I got a code," Wrench returned stubbornly.

"I got a code!" The eagle mocked in a falsetto. Then he returned to his usual voice. "Well, I got a job to finish."

"Let's make a call," Wrench suggested, as the eagle shifter raised his hand to make show of wringing Jenny's neck. "See what Blacksmith says direct."

Travis was done waiting for something else to happen. He bunched his muscles, preparing to shift.

Travis, be ready, warned Jenny, and Travis paused.

Wrench had all of the man's attention. "Make a call?" he taunted. "What are you in kindergarten calling your Mommy?"

Now! Jenny cried, and she twisted in the eagle shifter's hands and sank sharp teeth into the tender webbing of his thumb.

CHAPTER 26

*J*enny was not surprised when the eagle shifter dropped her and then missed at grabbing her again. His hands scrambled for her lithe, flexible otter body as she twisted and kicked away with clawed feet. While she struggled, she caught sight of Travis out of the corner of her eye, clothing shedding from him as he shifted, and leaped impossibly high into the air as a lynx to land on the driftwood beside her captor.

Jenny landed on her side with a thump in the sand that left her dazed, and scrambled to her feet, shifting back to human as she went.

Naked man versus enraged lynx was no match, but eagle was better suited for the battle.

Powerful wings battered at Travis, and sharp, wicked talons tore into his thick-furred shoulder.

Jenny bit back her cry of alarm, not wanting to be a fatal distraction at an inopportune point.

Travis shredded in return, using long, curved claws on powerful paws, sinking snarling teeth into the eagle's wing.

The eagle gave a cry of agony and rage, and snapped his strong, sharp beak at Travis, who was too fast for the assault.

Their battle sent them tumbling off the driftwood, and Jenny might have been knocked by one of the eagle's massive wings if Laura hadn't pulled her back out of the way.

Then there was a second big cat in the fray, and a massive brown bear waded in, snarling ferociously.

Jenny and Laura held each other and watched in alarm as claws and teeth flashed and feathers flew in the howling wind.

Knowing he was outnumbered, the eagle tried to shake them off and escape into the sky, but between the bleeding teeth marks in his wing and the wild, erratic wind, he was easily dragged back to the earth.

He was quickly overwhelmed, and shifted back to his human form with Travis' teeth at his throat.

"Mercy!" The shifter begged pathetically.

Travis, still a lynx, remained at his throat, growling, but didn't close his grip. The others backed away, but not far.

"You can't kill a man who's begging," the mobster whined.

Wrench had stayed back from the battle, but stepped forward now. "I thought you didn't have a code," he said scornfully.

Travis shifted back into human at last, and Jenny had to hold herself back from running to him. Blood oozed down his shoulder.

"Well, you're just lucky I do," he said, standing up and backing away.

Just then, the skies opened up and it began to pour.

CHAPTER 27

*I*t took all of Travis' self-control to back away from his prey, helpless and bloody in the wet sand now.

But he was aware of Jenny, behind him, and was so glad and relieved that she was unharmed that the fate of the eagle shifter swiftly became unimportant to him.

When Breck and Tex moved forward to secure the now-sodden shifter, he could finally turn away, and Jenny ran into his arms.

She was soaking wet, her sundress plastered to every gorgeous curve. Travis gathered her up in his arms, giving a little gasp as his shoulder reminded him that it had recently been pierced by eagle talons. It wasn't anything a few shifts and a couple of hours of healing wouldn't fix, but it was still bleeding sluggishly and Jenny exclaimed over it in concern when he set her back down on her feet.

It was a subdued party that returned to the Jeep, scavenging the parts of their clothing that they could. Tex and Travis, with the help of Wrench, were able to push the Jeep back out of the driftwood tangle that Travis had driven it into.

"Sorry I tried to run you down," Travis said cautiously to the big man.

"Sorry I tried to kidnap your girlfriend," Wrench replied in the same grave tone.

The eagle shifter was bound at the wrists using a roll of duct tape from the Jeep toolbox, and Wrench was left free.

"You aren't planning to try anything on the real Laura, are you?" Tex's tone might have been taken as teasing, but the way he bared his teeth at Wrench was serious. He was still holding the duct tape.

Wrench looked conflicted, then shook his head. "I ain't usually sent after people that don't deserve it," he said with a shrug of his shoulders. "But this time… I'm not gonna turn you over."

"What are you going to tell them?" Laura asked.

Wrench shrugged. "Failure ain't taken lightly by these guys, you should know."

"Oh!" Jenny said suddenly, and she turned and scampered down the beach.

Travis watched her go, thinking she looked sexier than ever and wishing that no one else was around. He wanted to lay her down in the sand and make love to her in the pouring rain, never mind his bleeding shoulder or the storm that was still crashing around them.

The heaviness of the driving rain nearly made her disappear as she waded into the heavy surf and she returned after a long moment, triumphantly carrying a briefcase.

She handed it to Wrench.

"That will probably pay for some dancing classes," she said mysteriously.

Wrench looked like he might cry, an odd look for a naked, hulking man covered in scars and tattoos. He cracked it open, and several American dollar bills fluttered out in a gust of wind before he could snap it shut.

"Or," Jenny continued, "You could turn it over as evidence against them and go the legal route and bear witness against your boss. You could get out of the business for good."

Wrench stared at her.

"I can't promise you wouldn't do time," she said. "But being cooperative would be very helpful to your cause, and I can recommend a good criminal lawyer."

"Doin' time again don't scare me," Wrench grumbled, scowling ferociously down at her. "But that don't fix the question of what I do afterwards. I like the idea of clean work, but no one good hires cons."

"Scarlet might," Travis suggested.

Tex and Breck looked at him, and Breck nodded. "She might," he agreed with a shrug. "Graham's done time."

"For what?" Tex asked in surprise.

"Murder," Breck said merrily.

"Murder?" exclaimed Jenny. "I didn't know that."

"Makes you reconsider having sex in the flower beds, doesn't it," Tex laughed

"Nah," Travis said, with a sideways glance at Jenny, who looked embarrassed, but rolled her eyes at him good-naturedly.

"Not for a minute," Breck added with a satisfied look.

"I'm soaking," Laura said firmly. "Let's go home."

"I'm driving the van back," Breck announced. "Travis almost killed us driving here, and it wasn't even raining then." He was fully dressed again, having stripped his clothing sensibly before shifting. Tex's clothing was rather worse for the wear; his staff uniform was equal parts shredded and soaking. Travis' clothing was in better shape, his lynx being smaller in size, but still badly ripped.

Laura's dress would be fine with small repairs, and Jenny, Travis realized with some surprise, had never lost her dress.

Part of him was selfishly disappointed.

CHAPTER 28

$\mathcal{B}$y the time they arrived at the resort, the worst of the storm had blown over.

There were several downed trees along the way, or at least big parts of them, and Jenny didn't mind watching Travis haul the ones they couldn't drive over out of the way with Wrench and Tex, marveling at his strength.

The resort itself was scattered with broken tree limbs and shredded flowers.

"I am going to hide from Graham for a week," Breck said, surveying the damage.

"We're going to have to repair several of the roofs," Travis said thoughtfully, looking down over the cottages. "I could use your help on that, Wrench."

Jenny thought Wrench looked touched. "I got no fear of heights," he rumbled. "But you'd have to teach me how."

"He's a very good teacher," Jenny assured him.

The rain had reduced to a faint drizzle, and the wind was almost nothing now.

Scarlet met them at the empty bar, looking a little wild-eyed, and as disheveled as Jenny had ever seen her.

"I trust you have an interesting story to share regarding the reason all of my primary staff have been missing for several hours," she said, looking at the trussed up eagle shifter with narrow eyes.

He responded with a string of expletives that made Tex tsk disapprovingly and slap a piece of duct tape over his mouth.

"We've got another charming character for the civil guard to pick up," Breck told Scarlet. "And some more paperwork for our friend Tony."

Wrench, recognizing her authority, handed her the briefcase, a little reluctantly.

"I'm willing to bear witness against the cartel what hired me," he said gruffly. "And I'd take a job, if you had one."

Scarlet looked at the briefcase distastefully, but took it. "I don't run a charity," she said crossly.

"I ain't afraid of hard work," Wrench assured her. "And I'm not too good to get dirty."

"We'll see," Scarlet said, her chilly voice without promise. "Let's put this guy in the usual place," she gestured at the eagle shifter, who was seething and working his mouth behind the duct tape. "Breck, catch me up on the details, and I'll call Tony." Her low heels clicked away across the wet tile decisively. "Have you seen Bastian?"

Breck poked the eagle shifter and marched him after her. "Not since this morning."

"Jenny!" Gizelle's hair was more wild than ever, and she looked as if she'd spent the storm cavorting in a field.

It occurred to Jenny that she might have done just that.

Gizelle ignored Wrench to skip to Jenny. "You're all wet!" she exclaimed, as if she wasn't equally soaked.

"Say," Laura said suddenly. "How'd you do that?"

Jenny realized Laura was talking to her. "Do what?"

"Shift your dress with you. You were dressed when you got free from that jerk with the wings."

Jenny looked down at herself. The sundress and her sandals had indeed shifted with her, without any conscious thought. "I don't know," she said in surprise.

"I'm a very good teacher," Gizelle said proudly.

"Can you clothing shift, too?" Laura asked her. "I thought it was only dragons and mythical creatures that could do that."

Gizelle blinked, then shook her head. "Nope," she said airily.

"Then how did you... never mind." Laura shook her head firmly. "Tex, I'd like a hot drink with a gallon of alcohol now, please."

Tex tipped his sodden hat to her. "Yes'm!"

Gizelle trailed after them to the bar. "Can I have some?" she asked innocently.

"I'll make you a hot chocolate, fawn," Tex told her. "Wrench, can I get you something?"

That left Jenny standing along with Travis, and she was glad when he slipped his hand into hers. The clouds above them had thinned, and though it was still raining lightly, the wind had died down and shafts of sunlight turned the wet leaves and gleaming tiles to jewels and treasure. Jenny suspected that if she looked around, she'd find a rainbow somewhere, but she didn't want to look anywhere but the smiling face of her mate.

"Hungry?" he suggested.

"Yes," she answered with a playful smile.

Oh, yes, agreed her otter.

He smiled back down at her. "Hot shower first?"

"Mm, yes," Jenny agreed, picturing his naked body in a cascade of hot water and foamy soap. "And then something out of the staff fridge would be plenty. Maybe Breck still has some cake stashed in there."

Travis bent down and kissed her. "I can think of something that tastes sweeter..."

EPILOGUE

*T*ravis put down his tools and stepped back to get perspective on their progress.

The last ravages of the storm had been all but erased from the resort. Graham had carefully pruned back the most obvious breakage and groomed the lawns, with help from Gizelle. An impressive pile of dead brush and branches had been stashed near the beach to dry for their next bonfire.

There were a few broken windows that were waiting for replacements from the mainland, but Travis and Wrench had repaired most of the roofs, mopped up the water damage, and started to fix the facade damage done to the spa. The man had proven himself quick to pick up on the things Travis taught him, as well as a hard worker. He seemed determined to make up for kidnapping Jenny, and Travis was inclined to forgive him. He'd coaxed enough parts of the man's story from him to be sympathetic, though he still didn't know who he would have been buying dance lessons for, or how he'd ended up in jail the first time; prying personal information out of him would require something stronger than an impact driver.

"Let's stop here and take lunch," he suggested, keenly aware of a certain item in his pocket and the hole it was burning there.

"We're getting to the hottest point of the day and there's still a few days worth of work here."

Wrench scowled. "I'm okay to work longer."

"Are you trying to make me look bad?" Travis laughed. "Seriously, the job will wait."

"Yeah, okay." Wrench looked past Travis and nodded understanding at the same time Travis recognized Jenny's presence behind him.

"I was just taking a break from my work and thought I'd come see if you wanted to take a picnic lunch in the gardens," Jenny suggested when he turned to grin foolishly at her. She was a vision in a simple silk wrap that made every curve look perfect. She had a basket over one forearm.

He suspected the picnic lunch she had packed was the second course to the meal she had in mind; merriment danced in her eyes.

"I'll pack up the tools," Wrench offered gruffly.

"How's the work going?" Jenny asked, twining her fingers with Travis' as they walked away. He remembered how embarrassed she'd been when she hadn't been able to shift the webbing between her fingers. She was so amazing, so capable, so in control now.

"We're waiting on some things from the mainland — it takes longer now that we don't have our own boat — but the rest is nearly all done. Just some cosmetic stuff at the spa to finish up. How's your work going?"

"It's quite a puzzle," Jenny told him enthusiastically. "I've never seen a contract with some of these specific terms, and there are references to some older documents. I'm having the firm run a search for the ones that may be relevant. At a glance, there are some weird loopholes that *would* allow Beehag's lawyer to legally take the resort lease out from under Scarlet, but the requirements are crazy specific. It's going to take some more research to be sure about any of it."

She was alive with excitement about the topic, eyes sparkling and her feet skipping eagerly over the gravel as they walked. Seeing her so happy made him feel a hundred feet tall and on top of the world.

It also made him want to kiss her, and slip the dress strap off her shoulder, so he was happy when they arrived at the garden and Jenny put the picnic lunch down on the bench and stood on tiptoe to slip her arms around his neck.

When Travis had finished claiming her mouth for his own, he suggested reluctantly, "Lunch first?"

"I'm having my first course now," Jenny answered. "The rest will keep."

He was hard against her, desperately hungry for the meal she offered, but he still drew back when she would have kissed him again, pulling his shirt from his pants.

"Wait," he said.

She paused, searching his eyes. "What's wrong?"

"Nothing in the world," Travis assured her. "Everything is perfect. Which is why I want to do this…"

He reached into the cargo pocket of his pants; it was a small box he'd been carrying around all day, since it had come express mail with the last charter plane.

Jenny looked at it curiously, then raised surprised and suspicious dark eyes to his.

Travis cleared his throat. "I love you, Jenny," he said without preamble. "I know you'll need to return to LA to give testimony in the next few months and I thought you might want to go up to Alaska afterwards and meet my family."

"Meet your family?" Jenny repeated, a slow, cautious smile blooming on her beautiful face.

"As my bride," Travis added. He popped the box open to display the modest diamond ring.

Jenny gave a wordless squeak, clasping her hands over her mouth.

"Crap," Travis remembered, hastily dropping to one knee. "I was going to kneel for that part."

He pulled the ring from its velvet casing, thinking too hard about other velvet casings, and offered it to Jenny.

Jenny gave him a trembling hand, nodding wordlessly, and Travis slipped the ring onto her finger.

"It fits perfectly," she breathed, smiling with her whole face.

"It's useful being able to quiz your twin sister for information," Travis confessed, as he stood.

Jenny grinned. "Oh, how'd Tex take that pressure?"

"Cussed me out for beating him to the punch like I didn't even know that cowboy was capable of."

"Did he mention the possibility of a double wedding?" Jenny asked.

Sensing a trap, Travis searched her eyes. "Do you want one?" he asked cautiously.

Jenny looked seriously back. "As a teenager who was sick of being a twin, I would have wanted to kill you for suggesting it. But now?" her face softened. "I sort of like the idea. I wouldn't have met you if I hadn't come to save Laura and Tex. And they wouldn't have met if Laura hadn't been pretending to be me. If Laura and Tex wanted to, I'd do it."

"We could have the ceremony in the gardens, a reception on the bar deck, if you wanted," Travis suggested.

"Ceremony on the beach," Jenny counter-offered. "I want this garden to be our place, alone."

Travis bent down to kiss her. "I'd be fine getting married by the dumpsters behind the kitchen," he said easily.

Jenny scrunched her face at him. "I would not be okay with that."

"So picky," Travis grouched merrily.

Jenny put her arms around his neck and kissed him soundly. He could not get enough of the taste and feel of her that close. He pressed his hard cock against her, drinking up the lush curves of her through her thin dress.

When she drew back after a moment, Travis felt it as keenly as if he'd lost something.

But she didn't go far, gazing into his eyes. "I love you, Travis," she said seriously. "I am so happy to be marrying you."

"I love you, Jennavivianna Rose," he told her just as seriously back. He had loved her full name from the first moment he'd heard it.

Her face lit up with mischief. "Want to crush a flowerbed?"

Travis gathered her back into his arms in answer, sweeping her off of her feet and back into the nearest bank of flowers, peeling her dress over her head as he lay her down.

She pulled his shirt off over his head and tugged at the waistband of his pants. "Why are you still wearing these?" she teased.

Travis was happy to facilitate their removal, and then his free member, thick and firm, was pressing at his lover's entrance, letting the anticipation build.

Jenny squirmed beneath him, and the flowers crushed beneath her were fragrant and green and Travis knew that he would never be able to smell this scent or walk through this garden without thinking of his gorgeous mate and the way that he loved her and wanted to protect her forever.

"Travis," she whined beneath him, arching and trying to take him into her.

"Jennavivian—" He didn't finish before she had succeeded in raising herself around him, and his world narrowed to the feeling of being in her, of joining with her as intimately as it was possibly for two souls to be.

"I love you," Jenny said near his ear, breathless and needy.

Travis fell into her completely.

TROPICAL DRAGON DIVER

CHAPTER 1

The last notes of her song were fading out of the room as Saina rose carefully from the foot of the bed.

The man at the other end of the bed remained still, one arm flung back on his pillow as he drooled on it. Saina nudged him with a finger and decided with relief he would probably sleep for a while. Her lullaby had done its work, and he'd fallen asleep without laying one of his greasy fingers on her.

If she was lucky, he'd be snoring for a few hours, and wake up not the slightest bit wiser for his little nap, every memory of Saina and her music nothing more than a distant fantasy. She gathered the skimpy dressing gown around her shoulders and drew in a breath, looking around.

It was a big room, for a boat, but it wasn't big enough to hide much in. The safe in the closet gave her a moment of pause, but she knew that what she was really after wouldn't fit in the shoebox-sized compartment, so she continued her hunt until she found the suitcase under the bunk. It was locked and too ridiculously heavy for its size to be clothing. The handcuff hanging open off the handle made Saina certain this was her goal.

She slipped her hairpin kit out of her dark, upswept hair and wriggled it into the lock, grateful that at least it wasn't a digital system. A few careful movements, listening diligently, and the tumblers fell away and clicked open. Saina unsnapped the clasps and tipped the lid back to expose bricks of pale gray, plastic-wrapped, just as it had been described.

This was it.

She sat back on her heels. She hated this whole job, every part of it was distasteful and wrong, even if the people on this yacht were all low-life smugglers who deserved no better. But her directions had been very specific and her Voice... her Voice *needed* her. No one else was going to come to her rescue, so it was up to Saina.

She went to the closet and got the lurid pink carry-on she had bought the week before, emptying its contents on the floor.

The bricks all but filled it, leaving room for one dress smashed on top and her evening purse with her phone and makeup. The rest of her clothing she stuffed into the handcuffed suitcase, shoving what was left to the very back of the closet.

Saina paused at the doorway and cracked the door, and was glad to see that the short hallway was empty. Sounds of carousing still came from the lounge towards the bow of the yacht, and she crept down the stairs towards the stern, pulling the luggage behind her as quietly as she could manage.

Two guards were standing outside the door to the back deck, smoking cigarettes and talking loudly.

Saina observed them through the windows and looked past them to the dinghy tied along the side of the boat. The sky was pitch black in the very early hours of the morning. The tropical air was warm and thick with humidity. Saina suspected that a storm was coming.

Saina chewed on her cheek for a moment, considering her options. There weren't many. She sighed, sucked her breath in, loosened her dressing gown, and sauntered out of the door like she owned it.

Her appearance arrested their conversation, and she heaved a dramatic sigh, nearly upsetting her breasts out of the skimpy lingerie she was wearing. "Good evening, boys," she singsonged.

"It's that lounge singer Anders picked up at Jaco yesterday," one of them said.

"And what a bore that guy was," Saina said, giving them both appraising looks. Anders hadn't gotten anything more from her than a nap, but they wouldn't know that. She put one hand on her round hip and inspected her fingernails on the other.

They stared, cigarettes hanging from the edges of their mouths, before exchanging looks. Saina immediately dubbed them Skeptical and Hopeful in her head, based on their expressions.

Skeptical eyed her overloaded rolling luggage curiously, while Hopeful couldn't stop staring at the cleavage spilling out of the frilly little number she was wearing. Saina turned her attention on Skeptical, humming lightly under her breath.

"You looking to give us a little private show?" Hopeful suggested gleefully.

Saina answered with a few bars of an appropriate pop song:

"Are you looking
For a good time?
Have you got yourself
A thin dime?"

By the time she hit the second chorus, they were both swaying in place, the smile on Skeptical's face as broad and entranced as Hopeful's.

She kept singing as she went to work, persuading them with her song that nothing out of the ordinary was happening. There was nothing to see, they were simply lost in a simple fantasy of their own imagination. It would have been easier to simply drown them than to keep singing, like any one of her sisters would have, but Saina couldn't bring herself to do that.

Not even to drug-running scumbag mercenaries like this.

She pulled the pink bag behind her to the stern of the ship and lifted the cowling off the inboard motor. It took only a few strong yanks to disconnect the fuel and easy-to-reach electronics, and Saina used a fire extinguisher to dent the ignition mechanism so it wouldn't be an easy fix. The last thing she wanted was for them to be able to follow her. A glance showed that the disruptions to her song as she worked hadn't broken the spell over Skeptical and Hopeful, but she knew she didn't have much time or breath left.

Hauling the dinghy down from its rack and getting it over the side of the boat was a Herculean task, and Saina wished, not for the first time, that sensible shoes fit with the image she was maintaining.

The dinghy splashed into the water, and Saina struggled to get the heavy luggage over after it, her song stuttering with the effort.

Then, as she drew in breath to get Skeptical and Hopeful back on track, her luck ran out.

On the deck above, there was a sudden shout and Saina looked up in alarm to spot another guard, this one with a girl hanging on his arm, dressed much as she was and looking vacant and tipsy.

Saina weighed her options. She wasn't sure that she could enspell the guard before others came to his alarm cry, and she wasn't sure how many more she would be able to sing insensible— she'd spent more of her energy than she anticipated. Instead of standing her ground, she kicked off her heels and vaulted over the edge of the boat into the wobbly dinghy. She flipped out the choke and yanked the tiny outboard to life.

The guard's shouts intensified and Saina heard others answer. Hopeful and Skeptical shook off the last of her song in confusion. Frantically, she pointed the dinghy away from the yacht and kicked it up into high gear, cursing its powerless motor and slow speed.

Still, the yacht and the shouting began to drop away in the darkness behind her and Saina breathed a sigh of relief. Maybe she would actually get away with this. Maybe…

Distant shots fired and bullets shattered the air around her. Saina dived to the bottom of the inflatable boat, covering her head and biting her lip against her cries of fear as they blasted around her for a length of time that seemed impossibly long. They couldn't see her in the darkness, so the shots were wild; she knew that was her only saving grace. As it was, the boat lurched sickeningly and she knew it had been hit. She could only hope that it had multiple flotation pockets, and that what hadn't been compromised was enough to keep her afloat until she could get somewhere safe.

The motor hummed blissfully on, pushing her further and further away from the disabled yacht, and the shots became more sporadic as the shouts got more distant. Saina's cries of fear turned to sobs of pathetic relief as she thought she might escape with her life.

She crouched again, leaning to one side as the boat, clearly deflating on the other side, tipped and sagged. She scanned the water ahead, hopeful for lights, but saw nothing.

Behind her, another few shots rang out, and she was driven forward, nearly out of the boat, as pain and fire bloomed to one side of her back.

CHAPTER 2

$\mathcal{B}$astian drew in a deep breath of salty air. It was already windy and he could smell the storm that was coming, though the sky above Shifting Sands Resort was still clear and sunny.

A sensible dragon would be taking cover, going to ground while the winds were too high to fly in. It was the sort of day to curl in one's hoard and count precious things, while the weather became wet and unfriendly.

But Bastian was no kind of sensible dragon.

In human form, he passed the pool, empty of swimmers, double-checking that the lounge chairs had all been secured and the towel cabinets were shut and latched. The bottles of sunscreen and lotion had all been stashed away, and the kickboards and pool floats were all behind closed doors. The sign declaring no lifeguard was on duty was already up, flapping noisily in the rising wind. Bastian grinned at it. A storm, rare here, meant a day off, and he was going to make the most of it.

He walked along the strangely bare deck. The few guests, like dragons, would be tucked away in their safe cottages, avoiding the wind and weather. As for the other staff, Bastian had no idea where they were, but he was just as glad not to encounter them and have to explain where he was going.

The steps down to the beach were littered with loose sand and Bastian shifted as he walked down them. One step was a sandaled foot, the next, a claw that spanned three of the white concrete steps. He may not be the largest dragon from his family, but he was far from the smallest. His scales gleamed green and gold, faceted like jewels.

Bastian paused at the lifeguard tower, taking a moment to appreciate the familiar view. The beach swept to either side, white sand stretching to meet sapphire water. The little beach bar was shuttered up, all the chairs safely inside. The dock was empty; the resort owner, Scarlet, had not yet replaced the boat that had been destroyed the week before.

He swiveled his head to look behind him. He was tall enough in dragon form to look easily onto the tiled pool deck, a useful trait as a lifeguard that enabled him to watch both swimming areas. Above the pool deck, the vacant bar deck looked down, and above that the restaurant deck. The steep structure of the Costa Rican island meant the resort was built in tiers, and it gleamed white in the sun.

The palm trees framing the pool were beginning to whip in the building wind. Bastian could see the dark clouds beginning to gather behind the crest of the hill above him.

A dragon face wasn't arranged for grinning, but Bastian's inner human certainly was.

He had the day for himself.

He had the wide ocean for himself.

He walked down by the dock, where the ocean fell away more quickly than the swimming and sunbathing area and he could wade in and begin swimming almost at once.

At first, the swimming was awkward, clawed feet and powerful legs were not arranged for paddling. Wings, even tucked tightly against his side, dragged on the waves and wind.

Then Bastian sucked in a deep breath and dived, pulling all his

limbs against his body and letting his massive tail propel him fully
under.

No longer divided between air and ocean, he cut through the
water as if he'd been born there, not a creature of fire, but of
saltwater.

He had to surface near the breakwater; it grew too shallow there
to stay beneath the waves, and he climbed over the rocks and
paused, shaking water droplets off his big head and spreading his
massive wings before he tucked them against his body again and
returned to the element he preferred.

Fish scattered before him, and a pod of dolphins gave him wide
berth, but Bastian paid them no mind. His human had eaten well
from the resort kitchen and he had no need for legless prey this fine
morning.

He was on a different kind of hunt, instead, and as he drifted
along the sandy ocean floor, still holding his breath, he closed his
eyes and let other senses take over.

At first, there was nothing, then, like distant musical notes, he
felt the first tingle of treasure.

His lungs cried out for air and Bastian oriented himself and
returned to the surface to refill. However he loved the water, he still
required air, like any dragon.

He dived down in the direction of the pull once he had sucked
in a big breath.

The bit of treasure gave itself easily up to his big claws, digging
down through the deep sand, and Bastian did a lightning fast shift so
he could tuck it into his human form's belt pouch and shift back
before he opened his senses to the next one.

Each time he returned to the surface for air, the waves and wind
were rougher and rougher, once even breaking directly into his face
as he was sucking in his breath.

He coughed and sputtered, thinking wryly that his family would
feel vindicated if he died by drowning. That alone made him stubbornly decide to stay out in the storm. He floated at the surface,
bobbing on the giant swells as he refilled his lungs and prepared to
dive again.

A sudden wave of treasure sense broke over him more strongly than the wave of saltwater had. It dwarfed the little tingles that had called him earlier and Bastian almost swamped himself responding to it.

There was a shark, he realized, as he dove back into the water; then he was surprised to sense another through the waves, until he realized that beneath the treasure sense was something else: blood.

He was not quite as fast as a shark, but Bastian put every ounce of his swimming strength into cutting the distance between his goal and himself.

By the time he got there, swimming up from beneath, there were three sharks circling what Bastian realized was a half-deflated dinghy, adrift without power and reeking of treasure and the iron tang of blood.

He could not roar underwater, nor flame the sharks, but he could growl, and the water took the vibrations of his claim to the interlopers.

The sharks circled one last time in confusion, then retreated some distance, continuing to swirl just out of his reach.

Bastian had no interest in them and considered them no threat. Even without flame, he was a dragon, many times their size and strength, and no stranger to the ocean. He had claws like swords, and his jewel-faceted scales were solid protection against their teeth.

He surfaced to inspect his spoils, refilling his lungs.

The sad, wilted dinghy had clearly taken a beating and it was being tossed on the wild waves, making it difficult to get close. Bastian's treasure sense was threatening to overwhelm him. There was something precious and rare indeed here.

When a wave washed over the dinghy, sloshing into the bed of the boat and what lay there, instinct made Bastian open his mouth and challenge the ocean itself with a roar. This was his, his treasure, his to crown his hoard with.

The uncaring ocean answered by slapping another wave at him, driving the half-limp boat up against his chest.

Finally, Bastian could look into the boat itself, and he dismissed the lurid pink suitcase that was deforming the bottom of the boat without a second thought; his treasure was not in the heavy luggage. It was the figure, a limp woman wearing something flimsy and soaking wet, plastered to every lush curve. Her long dark hair was loose around her shoulders like a cloak. She was face-down in the boat, barely breathing, and even in the storm-dark, Bastian could see that blood had dyed the water in the boat dark crimson.

He carefully rolled her over, using a dragon claw like a surgical tool, and her face was the most beautiful golden color that he had ever seen.

This is our mate, he realized in wonder.

His human added anxiously, *She's been shot!*

Bastian could see that she had a wound, still oozing sharp-smelling blood, just above her heart. His human was alarmed at the amount of the blood she must have lost so far, but Bastian only knew that she was every treasure he had ever sought, and that he must take her safely to his hoard and give her everything that he had.

Another wave threatened to rip the sinking boat away from him, just as the clouds above opened up and began to drench them in rain.

Bastian snatched the woman up into his forearms as the tortured boat began to sink, and his human helpfully suggested how to keep her above the water without jostling her injury further.

We don't know if that bullet is still in her, his human warned him, but Bastian didn't need a reminder to treat her gently.

He couldn't fly with her, not through weather like this, so he continued on his back, using his tail to propel them. Here, along the surface, their progress was agonizing slow, and waves broke over them several times, washing away the blood as they traveled. Bastian felt like he could hear a song at intervals, low beneath the roar of the storm.

It was hours of this unpleasant travel, feeling the weak beat of her heart against the scales of his chest, before Shifting Sands came into view once more. Bastian lifted her into one forearm as his back legs found purchase under him. The wavebreak was as tall as he was, but he wrapped his wings forward around her protectively and carried her carefully to shore.

The wind was finally beginning to die down as he got her up to the shelter of the bar. Tex was there, taking stock of the storm damage. If he was surprised to see Bastian away from the beach in dragon form, that was nothing to the surprise on his face when Bastian slowly lowered his prize onto the floor, bleeding and wet.

CHAPTER 3

Saina drifted through dreams of waves and wilderness. At one point, she thought she was being carried by a jeweled giant, but all the fairy tales faded into a hellish landscape of pain and misery with every jostle and wave. She tried to sing, desperate to convince the giant she was a friend, to spare her, but a storm ripped the words from her lips.

She woke later, hard tile beneath her. A shirt folded beneath her head smelled comfortingly of saltwater and sweat.

There was pressure at her shoulder, but the pain was pleasantly distant for the moment.

"She's stopped bleeding!" It was a voice that was both unfamiliar and familiar, all at the same time.

Someone was binding her up, she realized. She kept her eyes shut and her breathing shallow. The voice didn't sound threatening, but she knew better than to think that meant anything. She wasn't safe here. Assuming that she was would only lead to disappointment.

There were others nearby, too; she could hear their murmurs in a confused jumble: "Who would have shot her? Who is she? Could it be the cartel?"

"Bullet went through her," a rough voice with no welcome said. "Gotta be thankful for that."

"What is going on?" This new voice was a woman, sharp with authority and impatience.

"Bastian found a woman adrift in a sinking boat, all shot to heck." That voice was a Southern drawl.

"That is just what this day needed," the authoritative woman said, her voice closer. "What sort of boat?"

There was no attention being paid to Saina now, so she carefully drew in a breath and began to hum quietly. She was in danger here. Her only hope was to make them think she wasn't a threat. She wasn't sure if she was singing a seduction or a lullaby; she only knew that she was among strangers, that strangers were never benevolent, and she had to use the only defense she had to disarm them. Her shoulder was beginning to hurt in earnest now.

"It was an inflatable dinghy, out of gas and half-deflated." That was the voice she was thinking of as her savior. Bastian, apparently. "No markings, just a generic raft like you'd find on any yacht in the area. She was alone in it, with some luggage."

Her luggage! Saina breathed in a hopeful breath before resuming her faint, subtle song.

"Did you check the luggage for identification?"

"It sank," Bastian said apologetically, and Saina's heart sank with his statement. Her Voice would be gone from her forever.

Her song took a keen of grief that she didn't intend, and it drew attention she didn't want.

"Hey," Bastian said eagerly. "You're awake!"

Saina let her eyes flutter open. She couldn't tell how much of a spell she'd been able to cast; everything was distant and fuzzy with pain and confusion. Judging from the way he was gazing down at her, she'd been singing a seduction. She could expect the adoration to dissolve into confusion as her song faded, but there should be a short window of charity before it was gone completely.

What she didn't expect was her own reaction.

He was the most gorgeous man she had ever laid eyes on, with a jaw like a superhero, and arresting golden eyes. Sun-bleached hair was tousled over a tanned brow, and he had the most perfect nose she'd ever seen on a man. He was wearing a lifeguard uniform and she didn't have to feign a weak, grateful smile.

"My hero," she said musically, driving all her energy into the words.

The effort of it drained her to the bones, leaving her gasping as pain flooded over her.

"Shhh," Bastian said, gazing down at her like she'd unrolled the ocean. "Lie still, you're hurt…"

As he faded away into blackness, Saina found herself regretting the unconsciousness because she wouldn't be able to gaze back into those beautiful eyes any longer.

CHAPTER 4

"It's a mercy she's asleep again," the strange man with tattoos and scars told Bastian. "Bullet wounds hurt. But she's a shifter, sure as shit, because she's healing like one."

"Who are you, exactly?" Bastian asked, still feeling stunned by the woman's brief green-eyed gaze.

He had very mixed feelings about the man already; on the one hand, he'd been remarkably knowledgeable about bullet wounds, which was an area that lifeguard medical training hadn't been thorough on.

On the other hand, Bastian was the only one who should be touching his mate and he irrationally wanted to punch the stranger.

"Wrench," the man said briefly and unhelpfully.

"He kidnapped Jenny," Travis, the resort handyman, added merrily.

Bastian gave the handyman a quizzical look. The lynx shifter handyman certainly wasn't treating the stranger the way Bastian would have expected him to treat a man who had kidnapped his mate.

"To be fair," Jenny added, as the mate in question, "he let me go."

Scarlet made a displeased noise that was part sigh and part growl. "Let's get her inside somewhere and get to work cleaning up the resort. The Civil Guard will be here shortly for our other uninvited guest; we can have them take her back to the mainland with them."

"No!" Bastian said furiously, drawing his hands into fists.

The staff stared at him.

"Finders, keepers?" Tex, the Southern bear shifter bartender, teased. His own mate, Jenny's identical twin sister Laura, was standing next to him and she chuckled.

Bastian kept himself from growling at the innocent remark. "She's my mate. She stays on the island."

While the rest of the gathered staff gave exclamations of disbelief, congratulations, and surprise, Scarlet threw up her hands in disgust.

"That is just what we need," she said in frustration. "This is a business, not a dating club, and I've already taken one charity case today." She glared pointedly at Travis, Tex, and Wrench, who all sobered at her gaze. To Bastian, she said, "Put her in cottage eighteen and try to keep her from bleeding all over the sheets. And I don't want you mooning over her all day, we've got a beach to clean up. We have jobs, people!"

Her footsteps away across the open bar floor were angry and fast, and her absence left the bar feeling larger.

"I can keep an eye on her," Jenny offered kindly.

"I'm sure Lydia won't mind if we borrow one of her dresses," Laura added diplomatically. "They look about the same size."

Bastian realized that his mate was very scantily dressed, and that Wrench was trying very hard to keep from letting his gaze linger too long on the nearly-naked curves of her golden skin.

He managed not to bare his teeth at Wrench, appreciating his efforts, but when the other man offered to help carry her, Bastian simply gathered his mate into his arms and let Wrench and Jenny handle the doors and blankets.

As he settled her limp form into the bed, he smoothed her dark

hair back over the pillow and lay a single kiss on her perfect forehead. Everything was right with the world, now that she was here.

CHAPTER 5

Saina felt better the second time she woke.

The pain in her shoulder was considerably less, and she didn't feel as weirdly adrift and weak as she had before.

She was also in a much more comfortable bed, with big fluffy pillows under her head. A tropical print quilt was pulled up to her shoulders, and she found that the distasteful lingerie had been replaced by a simple, comfortable sundress.

"You're awake!"

A lovely, curvy Black woman was sitting at a desk next to the bed, holding a sheaf of papers open in a manila folder. She looked friendly enough, but Saina knew better.

Saina struggled upright, as the woman rose and tried to stop her. "You're hurt, stay still!"

But being upright gave Saina more breath, and she opened her mouth and sang a few notes of a love song lullaby.

"Easy nights,
Northern lights,
Open your heart,
The lines on your chart…"

The woman looked at her quizzically. "I'm Jenny," she said, completely unmoved. "You shouldn't be sitting up, but you do have a lovely voice."

Saina blinked at her. Her gift didn't tend to be as strong with women, but she hadn't met a person yet that a simple sleep song had so little impact on. Jenny didn't even yawn.

"I'm Saina," she said uncertainly, abandoning her plan to put Jenny to sleep and try to escape. Her shoulder hurt wickedly. "Thank you?"

"You should lay back," Jenny scolded her. "You don't want to open the wound again. Saina is such a beautiful name!"

"It's better," Saina lied, but she let Jenny fluff her pillows and tip her back onto them. "Saina is Hindi for princess," she added.

"We'll let Bastian be the judge of how much better you are," Jenny told her, unconvinced. "He'll be so happy to see you awake."

"Bastian," Saina tasted his name in her mouth. "He's the life-guard with the golden eyes?"

Jenny's smile was sparkling and oddly smug. "Yes. He found your boat sinking in the middle of a storm, lucky for you." She had an easy Californian accent and a kind smile.

Saina didn't trust it for a moment.

She looked around the room. She was in a small, beautifully appointed bedroom with big French doors opening out onto a little porch. "Where am I?" There were, at least, plenty of exits.

"This is Shifting Sands Resort," Jenny explained. "A shifters-only vacation resort off the coast of Costa Rica."

Saina's hands made fists in the tropical quilt. "Shifters?" she asked, as innocently as she could manage. It was unnerving not to have her music to simply make this woman automatically like and trust her. Maybe the pain of her injury was making it work incorrectly.

Jenny gave her an amused look. "You wouldn't be healing that quickly if you weren't one, too," she said. "You don't have to hide who you are here."

Saina gazed back in consternation, not admitting anything. "What kinds of shifters?" she asked suspiciously.

"All sorts," Jenny said with a laugh. "I'm an otter shifter." She said it with wonder, as if she weren't used to the idea yet. "My mate is a lynx shifter. My sister is a wolf, and her mate is a bear."

Saina wondered what Bastian was, with those bottomless golden eyes, but didn't want to ask. "Your...mate?" she asked, instead.

Jenny's face took a soft, distant look. "For shifters, there is one person, one perfect mate. They know each other at once, as if their souls recognize each other."

It sounded lovely. And romantically ridiculous. Saina wasn't even sure she believed in love, let alone love at first sight.

"You...don't know about mates?" Jenny added, coming fully back to the conversation.

Saina refrained from scoffing that it sounded like a fairy tale. "I'd heard of them," she admitted. She didn't have to add that she'd never thought they existed. It occurred to her that perhaps Jenny was under some other kind of magical influence, something that blocked Saina's own powers.

Jenny's eyes danced, like she had a delightful secret that she wanted very much to share. "I'll let Bastian tell you more," she said, gathering her papers. "I know he'll want to know that you're awake."

When she left, Saina slipped carefully out of the bed. The view from her porch was out over the resort, the roofs of other little buildings like the one she was in spread out below her. There was jungle to her right, ocean before her, and just visible through the trees to her left, a gleaming white fortress that must be the restaurant and bar. The sun was just beginning to set, turning the sky gold and rose.

Saina leaned against the deck railing and closed her eyes to listen to the quiet sounds of distant ocean.

"Saina?"

His voice gave her a crazy little thrill to her toes, and Saina knew before she turned that her lifeguard had returned.

He was standing in the doorway, looking nervous and excited. Saina was equal parts relieved that her magic wasn't entirely gone, and surprised. The effects of her song should have faded away by now, but he was clearly still utterly besotted with her. It made her feel unexpectedly guilty.

"Jenny said your name was Saina," he said, adoration in his voice. Then he scowled in concern. "And you should be in bed!"

"I'm fine," she said, with a practiced silky smile. "You don't have to worry for me."

His scowl melted. "Let me at least check it," he breathed.

Saina sat at the edge of the bed and let him peel the medical tape back and check under the swaths of bandage that covered her shoulder front and back. His gentle touch was surprisingly disturbing to her calm, sending tingles of sensation through her skin. Had she managed to enchant *herself* with her injury-addled song?

"Well?" she asked, looking up into his face.

The eye contact obviously unbalanced him. He gazed down at her and stammered, "It's, it's, looking, coming along nicely. Healing up well. It looks…good."

Saina made herself smile at him. Whatever the reason, she would have one unquestionable ally here, then. She had to remind herself firmly that this was in her nature, that she ought to be grateful for this unexpected enchantment, not feel guilty about it. Even though she didn't understand how she had managed to cast an enchantment like this at all. It was nothing like her usual siren magic.

CHAPTER 6

*S*aina.

Even her name was beautiful, as lovely and unique as she was. Her voice had a faint British-Indian accent.

Standing against the sunset, she was a dark silhouette, with long, loose hair to the middle of her back. She was neither short nor particularly tall, with lush curves in all the right places. Lydia's dress was flattering on her, a swish of embroidered white fabric to her knees, and Bastian wanted nothing more than to peel her out of it, lay her down on his hoard and claim her outright.

He wrestled his dragon back, checking her bandages, and was happy to find that her wounds were healing more swiftly than he'd expected.

"You must be hungry," he said, once he'd taped it all carefully back on, every electric touch tantalizing and tempting.

"I'm famished," Saina said, as if it hadn't occurred to her before.

His dragon was pleased with the idea of feeding her, but Bastian doubted she would want the cow carcass that *he* suggested.

"There's a buffet," Bastian said swiftly. "The best food. All gourmet. Chef is world-class, you won't be disappointed."

His dragon suggested feeding Chef to her if she found his food in any way lacking.

I doubt she's a cannibal, Bastian said chidingly.

We would love her even if she was, his dragon assured him.

Saina rose and accepted the elbow that Bastian offered her with her good hand.

"You're okay to walk?" he verified. "I could...carry you."

She laughed, and her laugh was like music. "I assure you that won't be necessary."

She had to walk carefully on the gravel path; it was getting dark, and once she stumbled and hissed in pain, her hand tightening on Bastian's elbow.

When they arrived at the restaurant, he put her at the best table. Scarlet didn't encourage the staff to sit in the restaurant, preferring that they take their food and eat it privately, but at that moment, Bastian would have faced down even *her* wrath. Saina was his mate, and he had every intention of feeding her in style.

There were only a few guests at other tables, and the white bandages, stark against Saina's golden skin, drew just a few curious stares.

Bastian's baleful glare put those to a swift end.

"Stay here. I will fetch you whatever you like," he said, settling her in the chair and not liking how strained her face looked.

"Oh," she said. "Some fruit would be lovely. Maybe some fish? I'm not picky, and it all smells amazing."

Bastian was reluctant to leave her and he piled her plate as swiftly as he could with a slab of baked fish, every kind of fruit the buffet had to offer, and a serving of fragrant saffron rice. He arranged it as pleasingly as he could, stealing a bit of garnish from the buffet display for the finishing touch. He was trying to work out whether he should put her dessert on a separate plate when his dragon growled in warning.

Dessert forgotten, Bastian returned to his mate's table at a trot, to find the head waiter, Breck, dancing attendance on Saina.

The leopard shifter was gazing at her in clear adoration, and Saina—his Saina!—was smiling back encouragingly.

His intended presentation forgotten, Bastian dropped the plate before his mate hard enough to make the food jump and muscled his way between Breck and the table, bristling with challenge. One of the chairs in his way toppled over backwards.

"Your work here is done," he growled.

Breck reacted with unexpected defiance.

"I'm here to take the lady's drink order," he said, not backing down.

"The lady is here with me," Bastian snarled.

"Maybe she shouldn't be..." Breck retorted, fists balled at his side.

He was dimly aware of the other guests in the room, some of them standing in alarm, some of them growling. He was going to tear Breck limb from limb, destroy the interloper, protect his treasure...

And then Breck was chuckling and putting up hands of mock truce, and everything was surprisingly fine. The waiter wasn't a threat, there was no threat, there was only peace, like the comforting rhythm of the ocean. His mate was standing, he realized, and she was singing.

Guests returned to their meals as if nothing had happened. Breck cheerfully picked up the knocked over chair, and said, "I'll have your drink right out."

Bastian watched him go, baffled, then turned to catch Saina, now silent, as she swayed and nearly fell.

"I'm confused," he confessed to her, lowering her carefully back into her chair and pulling up his own chair.

She was breathing hard. "I shouldn't have done that," she said, despair in her sea green eyes. "It was just a habit..."

"What did you do?"

"It was an accident," Saina said wearily, and Bastian couldn't bring himself to press her to explain. Instead, he lifted a fork and speared a triangle of pineapple. He could still feed his beloved.

CHAPTER 7

Saina hadn't intended to ensnare the waiter, it had just been a matter of a little musical note to strengthen her request.

It was the kind of thing her sisters did without thought, and though she didn't tend to do the same herself, she had been so baffled by her lack of influence on the otter shifter that she'd been curious to give her gift a test on someone else.

She had been gratified to see that her power was still intact, but the waiter had reacted more strongly than she'd expected. Bastian's reaction was even more over the top, a crazy-protective rush to defend her that Saina hadn't expected at all; her song hadn't been focused on him whatsoever. Saina couldn't decide if her magic was unpredictable in this place, or if she simply wasn't controlling it as well as she ought to because of her injury.

She could stop the chaos, of course, but it meant getting to her feet and singing a counterpart to the strife, a sweet, lilting lullaby that soothed everyone in earshot.

The conflict dissolved away to not even memory, and the waiter left to fetch her drink while Bastian sat and tried to feed her from her plate.

After just a few bites, she took the fork from him and insisted on feeding herself. Bastian watched her intently.

"Your chef is as good as you claimed," she said, several bites into the flaky fish. Some of her exhaustion faded with the food.

Bastian looked as pleased with her praise as if he'd cooked it himself. "We're lucky to have him."

Saina could see the questions in his eyes, behind the infatuated obsession she was still convinced she had put there, and she moved to divert Bastian from asking them.

"This whole place is simply lovely," she said honestly. "Tell me more about it! Jenny said we were in Costa Rica."

Bastian nodded. "The whole island is privately owned. Scarlet is the owner of the resort, she just leases the property. Most of it is wild jungle, but there's a private compound at the north end, and an airstrip on the east side. We get charters in a few days a week."

"You're the lifeguard?" It was a question with an obvious answer; Bastian was still wearing his uniform and had a first aid kit at his waist.

He nodded. "I keep an eye on the beach and pool."

"You'll have to give me a tour tomorrow," Saina said.

"I'd love to," Bastian said, a smile on his handsome lips.

Saina didn't want to stay longer than she had to, but it would be a day or two before her shoulder was completely healed. And the idea of a tour was strangely appealing, especially with Bastian as her guide.

She considered again the idea that she'd fallen under her own spell. Having him feed her had been unexpectedly erotic, and she found herself watching the way his hands moved, and the muscles in his jaw as he spoke. His hair begged for a hand to smooth it back, and Saina had to keep herself from doing it herself several times.

This was not how her magic was supposed to work. It was baffling enough that Bastian was still enchanted. *She* should be coolly indifferent, like a proper siren.

"I understand this resort is for shifters only?"

Bastian nodded, that unruly curl at his forehead bobbing with his earnestness. "There's been some talk about allowing humans to accompany shifter guests, but yes."

Saina glanced at the other scattered guests, all dining peacefully at other tables. She wondered what their forms were, what their ulterior motives were, and how they had gotten the kind of money it would take to vacation at a place this nice.

"It's good luck you found me," Saina said cautiously. "I'm very grateful."

Bastian's eyes glowed. "I don't think it was luck," he said, voice low and full of emotion. "I think it was destiny."

He would, Saina thought achingly.

She attempted to deflect the intensity. "Any other resort would have been quite baffled by how quickly I healed," she said with a light smile.

"Will you tell me what happened?"

He asked so respectfully that Saina found it difficult not to answer. She was actually surprised that no one had been more pointed about quizzing her over it. Did people show up at this resort half-drowned and shot up often?

She took a bite of a luscious scarlet strawberry to buy her a few moments. "It was a disagreement over ownership," she said evasively.

Bastian's eyes grew flinty. "Of you," he guessed.

Close enough, Saina thought. She looked at her nearly empty plate, flooded with guilt and shame, and couldn't answer. How could she explain to this earnest man that it was supposed to be in her nature to sow strife and chaos in her wake? And why did it feel so wrong?

Bastian's hand covered her own, and she tried not to flinch at the electricity that coursed through her at his touch.

It felt like home, having his skin against hers, and she wanted to crawl into his lap and cry out all her troubles. He wanted to protect her; would it be so awful to let him?

She bit the inside of her cheek. This whole feeling of connection was false. When her magic finally faded, she wouldn't be more than a puzzling gap of memory to him.

"If I could help…" Bastian breathed.

Saina drew herself up. There was no way he was as good and as selfless as he seemed. "You can't," she said with a practiced smile. "But you could get me a plate of dessert!"

Bastian was out of his chair and back to the buffet before she could even add a little pout at the end.

She had cleared the rest of her plate by the time he returned bearing a dazzling array of sweets on three different plates. "I couldn't possibly eat all that!" She laughed at him.

He seemed to find that reaction pleasing, and when she insisted he enjoy one of the plates himself, agreed willingly. Even the way he ate was sexy, and when he licked sugar off his lips, Saina had to pinch herself to stay focused.

Each dessert was more decadent than the last, and when she put her fork down at last, she had to groan. "I should have skipped the last cream puff, but it was sooo good."

Bastian preened. "I shall let Chef know that you liked it."

"Please do," Saina said sincerely.

She washed the last rich bite down with a sip of the juice she hadn't even noticed the waiter bringing her earlier.

With the sip, and the reminder of her true nature, the exhaustion that had been barely at arm's length came rushing back. Saina's shoulder ached again.

It didn't go unnoticed.

"You should rest," Bastian told her. "Let me take you back…" his hesitation was obvious. Saina waited for him to insist they go back to his own room, but he finished: "…to your cottage."

Could he really be that much of a gentleman? Saina had expected to have to sing him to sleep to keep her hard-won chastity. She was almost tearfully grateful for that grace, even while she was slightly disappointed.

"I'd like that," she said, not having to feign her weakness.

Every step back to her cottage jarred her shoulder painfully, and Saina was glad to have Bastian on her good side to lean against. When he picked her up to lay her into her bed, she let herself put her head against his broad shoulder for just a moment too long, and letting go again was more difficult than she imagined it could be.

He changed her bandage with swift, gentle fingers. "It's healing well," he said, sounding relieved.

"I'm mostly…tired," Saina said truthfully.

"That's to be expected. Sleep as long as you need," Bastian told her, tucking the light blanket carefully around her. "I'll know when you wake up."

Saina was too tired to ask how he would know, and let her eyes drift closed as she felt his lips chastely kiss her forehead.

This resort was like a guilty dream; people who didn't pry into her past or act like she was beholden to them, despite the fact that she owed them her life. No one obviously trying to hurt or use her.

Saina fell asleep wondering when the other shoe would drop.

CHAPTER 8

*B*astian returned to the staff house feeling like his feet had wings of their own.

His mate. His beautiful, graceful, glorious mate was here, and his life felt complete.

She had accepted his food, and suggested he give her a tour of his domain, sure signs of acceptance. She was healing swiftly, and Bastian expected nothing but a full recovery as his courtship started in earnest.

"The Menagerie? Or Animal House?" Breck greeted him as soon as he stepped into the door of the big house most of the male staff shared.

"*Non sequitur*, much?" Bastian responded, puzzled but amused. Their earlier altercation was still confusing, but forgiven.

"We're trying to name the house before Scarlet labels it something bland like Palm House or Cliff Columns," Travis explained. "I'm surprised you're back here for the night."

"I'm going to veto Menagerie," Jenny said from the far couch. "Too suggestive."

"But Animal House is way too National Lampoon," Travis added.

"The Furever House?" Breck suggested.

Jenny made a gagging noise and Graham, the lion shifter gardener, grunted negatively.

"It sounds like a pet rescue," Travis scoffed.

Breck blew him a raspberry. "You come up with something," he said. "Who wants a beer?"

Bastian settled into his usual chair with a bottle of beer, enjoying the camaraderie of the staff and the warm glow that still lingered from being in the presence of his mate.

"The Zoo?" suggested Jenny.

The others considered until Travis reluctantly said, "Too many memories of Beehag's zoo," and they all murmured in agreement.

Alistair Beehag, the previous owner of the island, had captured shifters, forced them into their animal forms, and kept them in a cruel zoo. The resort staff had helped free them, almost a year ago, but memories of the angry, sometimes damaged, victims were still fresh. A gazelle shifter named Gizelle for lack of a previous name had been imprisoned since she was a child and had no memories besides iron bars and torture. The odd, ageless woman was still skittish and sometimes outright incoherent.

"The Predators?" Bastian suggested.

"Jenny lives here now and an otter isn't really a predator," Breck said thoughtfully.

Jenny bared her white teeth at him. "Says someone who isn't a fish."

"Sounds like a team mascot, not a house," Travis said dismissively. "Anyway, with luck, Jenny and I will be moving to our own place soon enough. I'm going to ask Scarlet if we can renovate one of the houses up the hill."

Jenny cuddled into his side and purred, "What a beautiful idea!"

"Don't ask Scarlet this week," Breck warned them. "She's in a terrible mood. She was already on edge after the World Mr. Shifter event, and the storm did nothing to improve matters."

"Tooth Towers," Graham suggested unexpectedly.

"Hmm," Breck said.

"I like it," Travis said.

"Meh," said Jenny, less enthused.

"If we don't decide on something, it'll end up being Grouch Gables or something," Breck reminded them.

"Why *aren't* you with your mate tonight?" Jenny asked Bastian frankly. "She hasn't rejected you, has she?" Beside her, Travis took her hand and squeezed it.

Bastian didn't take offense to the idea, shaking his head. "Our courtship is just beginning," he said patiently.

"Guh," said Breck. "Dragons." Then he leaned forward curiously. "Have you found out what she is?"

Bastian shook his head. "It's not important," he said dismissively.

"Your family won't be happy if she's not a dragon," Graham said sagely.

A spark of anger lit in Bastian at the reminder of his family. "It's not their business," he said sharply. "And what do you know about dragons or my family anyway?"

Graham, unfazed, only shrugged in reply.

"Stick to plants," Bastian growled at him.

He didn't stay long in the common room after that, but slunk away to his room, stewing over the unwelcome memory of his family.

CHAPTER 9

ay dawned early in the tropics. Saina woke to sunlight sending fingers of light through the curtains over the big French doors to the porch.

When she gave her shoulder an experimental roll, it barely hurt at all, and she was relieved to find that she felt refreshed after the good night's sleep.

She remembered Bastian's last words about knowing when she would wake, so she was not surprised when there was a knock on the door.

She was, however, surprised to find that it wasn't Bastian, but a tall woman with shockingly red hair pulled back in an unruly bun. She buzzed with power to Saina's senses, the air around her crackling faintly.

"You are Saina," the stranger greeted her without preamble or particular warmth. "I am Scarlet, the owner here." They exchanged a perfunctory handshake with Saina's good hand, and Scarlet gave Saina a swath of fabric that proved to be a new dress and a pair of underthings still in packaging.

"I understand you'll be staying with us for a while," Scarlet said, not hiding her displeasure and giving Saina an appraising look. "Are you interested in working?"

Saina swallowed her protest that she wouldn't be staying, standing up straight under the woman's scrutiny. "I can, ah, sing. Perform, I mean."

The woman's gaze grew flinty. "This isn't a *Vegas* resort," she said dismissively.

Stung, Saina wondered if the woman assumed she was a Vegas-style escort. It would be a valid guess, based on the clothing she had arrived in, she realized with chagrin. "Of course not," she agreed firmly. "But I can earn my keep."

"Can you wash dishes?" Scarlet asked skeptically, looking at Saina's hands doubtfully. "Make beds?"

"I'm not above hard work," Saina replied defensively. "I can do any of that, or help trim hedges or pull weeds."

"We have a landscaper," Scarlet said flatly. "We'll try you in the kitchen. On a *trial* basis." She looked at Saina's bandage and her voice softened. "When you are feeling up to it, of course. I don't mean to rush your recovery."

Briefly, Saina thought that the concern was genuine behind her cool face and polite words, and the idea unsettled her.

"I will also expect incidents like last night to remain at a minimum," Scarlet added then.

Saina felt her eyes widen and she swallowed. "You heard about that?"

Scarlet smiled without humor. "I know everything that happens on this island," she said dryly.

"I will make sure that doesn't happen again," Saina said with a shy, tentative smile. Not all siren charms relied on magic, she reminded herself. She didn't like how unpredictably her magic worked here, and she didn't like how dirty it made her feel to use her magic on people who had offered her nothing but charity.

Scarlet made a noise that may have been polite or simply skeptical, and turned to leave just as Bastian came running up the gravel path.

Saina didn't like to admit how her belly fluttered at the sight of him, or how weak her knees suddenly felt. He was so gorgeous and athletic looking, with shoulders like a wall, and strong swimmer's legs, shown off to advantage by his lifeguard uniform.

Scarlet looked from one to the other and said dryly to Bastian, "I believe you'll be wanting the rest of the morning off?"

Bastian grinned and managed to look sheepish at the same time. "Yes, ma'am," he said hopefully.

"Fine," Scarlet said without smiling. "But we're getting a new batch of guests with the charter plane this afternoon and I expect our lifeguard to be on duty when they are ready to enjoy the swimming."

She didn't wait for Bastian's affirmation, but turned her attention to Saina. "If you are feeling up to it, we could use your help cleaning up after lunch rush in the kitchen."

She didn't wait for Saina's answer either, but turned on her heel and stalked away.

Her exit took a tension that Saina hadn't even recognized with her, like the pressure before a storm, and it left a new one in its place as she was alone with the man who had saved her.

He smiled at her foolishly for an awkward length of time, and Saina found herself doing the same, until she recognized it. "You mentioned a tour," she suggested.

"Yes, of course. I'd love to show you around!" Bastian offered his elbow chivalrously.

Saina nearly took it, then realized that she was still wearing the dress she had worn the previous day and then slept in. "Oh, could you wait while I take a quick shower? I promise it won't take long."

"Of course," he said with effort.

She was gazing up at his face, so she could see his impulse to offer to join her, and watch him wrestle with his desire to remain appropriate. No other man under any siren song had ever demonstrated that kind of restraint. By this point, she expected him to be demanding his way into her bed, and she'd have to sing him to sleep to make her escape. Once again, she wondered why her powers were behaving so abnormally; he certainly shouldn't still be enchanted, let alone acting like *this*.

She was faintly disappointed that Bastian hadn't made that kind of demand, and had to wonder if she wouldn't straight out welcome him under the sheets with her. It was an eye-opening revelation, as she retreated into the bathroom to wash.

She hadn't anticipated how exciting the shower would be, knowing that Bastian was just outside the door. Covered with bubbles, she couldn't keep her hands from drifting over her breasts a few extra times, and rinsing more intimate parts threatened to become a serious distraction as she wondered what he would look like out of his uniform. Then she imagined soaping those gorgeous shoulders, and her breath grew shallow and fast and she had to lean against the cool tile wall of the shower and get control of herself again.

Down girl, she told herself firmly.

She toweled off briskly, careful not to linger anywhere, then realized that she'd left her new clothing out in the bedroom.

Part of her wanted to saunter out naked and test Bastian's unexpected self-control, but most of her knew that would break her own tenuous restraint, so she cracked the door. "Ah, Bastian, could you bring me the clothes on the bed?"

"Of course!" He had been staring out the double doors over the porch and came swiftly with her request, slipping it through the door to her.

Any of her sisters would have given him a tantalizing tease, opening the door more than strictly necessary, but Saina only took the clothing and dressed efficiently out of sight. She didn't want to do more to the people here than she already had.

It's not real, she reminded herself firmly. *None of this is real, and you'll be gone in a day or two, so don't do anything stupid.*

Like fall in love…

CHAPTER 10

*D*ressed in a patterned golden sundress, freshly showered, with her hair loose and wet over her shoulders, Saina was the most glorious treasure Bastian had ever seen. The early morning light made her glow, and her green eyes were more radiant than any sea glass he'd ever seen. She had taken the bandages off in the shower, and Bastian made himself look at her shoulder professionally.

"I think we can leave the bandage off this morning," he said, trying not to sound as flustered as he felt. The wounds were barely puckered scabs, and the skin around them already looked healthy, with no signs of infection.

She rolled her shoulder experimentally, wincing only once in the rotation. "It's better," she agreed.

Then she tipped her chin up to smile at him. "I believe you'll be my tour guide for the morning."

Bastian shared the resort with her as if it was all his own realm, an attitude he was sure that Scarlet wouldn't appreciate, but one that she was not present to correct. They started at the top, where Scarlet's office presided at the top of the steep slope. From there, he pointed out the cottage roofs. "Tex and Laura are staying in that one, for now. The big one with the two porches, that's Magnolia's. She's one of our semi-permanent residents, you'll love her."

Saina made a small skeptical noise that made Bastian suspect she didn't have many female friends.

He led her down past the spa. Wrench and Travis were there, repairing some storm damage to the spa building finish, and Bastian was happy to show her off and introduce her to his coworkers.

"It's lovely to meet you," she said, and gravely shook their gloved hands.

He took a quick walk through of the garden and braved Graham's wrath by picking one of the red bell-like flowers for Saina's hair.

"There's a greenhouse, there." He pointed to the diamond-sparkle roof through the trees. "We grow a good portion of our own food. And the tall white house is where most of the male staff lives. The ladies' staff house is the green one beyond."

They walked past the utilitarian hotel building for budget guests, and Bastian pointed out his old room in the windows.

They walked down to the entrance of the restaurant, and snagged egg bagels dusted with green onions and flakes of wild Pacific salmon from the buffet before making their way down to the bar level. The bar was open air, as most of the resort was, tucked under the restaurant deck. The bar tables and chairs overlooked the jewel of the pool. Twin waterfalls toppled from this level, framing a grand staircase with columns down into the sapphire water.

Walking past the bar led to the event hall, where Lydia held her sunrise yoga and they hosted semi-weekly dance events. "You'll meet Lydia next week," Bastian told her. "She's back home visiting family in Mexico and doing some sort of massage training."

The pool deck had a few guests sunning themselves, and Bastian was pleased with Saina's reaction to the pool itself. "It's the biggest pool I've ever seen," she said in awe.

"We hosted the World Mr. Shifter event just a week ago. The photographers said it was one of the most beautiful places they'd ever hosted a shoot." Bastian was as proud of the resort as if it had been his own ancestral home.

"I can see that," Saina agreed, appropriately impressed.

Then he could guide her down the steps to the beach itself, and if she had loved the pool, she was clearly moved by the picture-perfect white sand crescent.

"This must be where you work," she said, standing by the life-guard tower. At some point over the tour, she had taken his hand, and they had fingers twined together.

"Well," Bastian said modestly, "I hardly ever use the tower. I'm usually in dragon form so I can see further, and keep an eye on the pool deck at the same time."

Her fingers in his turned to rock. "In what form?" she asked, frozen.

"Dragon," Bastian repeated, and he was surprised when she withdrew her hand and backed away from him, eyes wide and skin pale beneath her natural golden tone. "What is it?" He asked gently, suddenly afraid he'd done something wrong.

"You're a dragon," she said flatly.

"You didn't know about dragons?" Some cultures kept their dragons secret. Perhaps India was one of those. "I assure you, we are not simply mythological."

"I *know* about dragons," she spat, and Bastian felt as if his world was tipping unexpectedly.

CHAPTER 11

A dragon, Saina thought. She hadn't expected Bastian to be a dragon. This changed everything.

She had finally felt like maybe she could take this place at face value, had even felt badly for her first instinct to try to control the people here who had been nothing but kind and generous.

She turned away, more disturbed by this revelation than she ought to be. She shouldn't care. She shouldn't care in the slightest for this man, let alone should she care what his shifted form was.

But despite her care, he'd gotten under her skin, she'd trusted his boyish smile and softened to his chivalrous actions. Dragon honor could be a tricky thing, she should know.

"Saina?" Even his voice sounded innocent.

"What family are you from?" she asked, chin high as she looked out over the turquoise ocean that lapped along the beautiful beach.

He hesitated so long that she made the mistake of looking back at him.

His face was so terribly dear to her already, and the pain on it now made her want to comfort him.

"I am from the Santa Rosa dragon family," he said, and he said it with so much guilt that Saina knew he had to know. He *had* to know what his family had done to hers.

"You *knew*," she said. "You knew all along. Did Keylor send you after me? I'm such an idiot. I can't believe…"

"Keylor?" Bastian said in surprise. "You know Keylor?"

Saina paused in her rant. His disbelief felt genuine, however much that didn't make sense.

"Who are you to Keylor?" she asked, taking one angry step towards him. She put music into her words, and added:

"*T*ell the truth,
      Say it fair,
Speak it clear,
Don't lie, don't dare…"

*I*t was one of her strongest songs, and backed by her betrayal and anger, she could feel it bind Bastian like iron as she held the last note.

"He is—was—my brother," he gasped, as if he were being squeezed.

Saina let the last note go and he blinked at her in consternation. "I am not accepted as family any longer, and I am not allowed to claim kinship or mention their name."

Saina furrowed her brows at him. "Explain," she said firmly. She drew in a breath and held it, in case he needed a second verse.

Bastian sighed. "I am…mentally unfit for the family. I was cast out when my deviance was discovered. The only way I would be permitted to return would be to marry dragon royalty."

"Deviance?" Saina pressed.

Bastian gestured with a hand, out to the ocean. "Water. I am a fire dragon, a creature of air and flame and fortune. But my treasure sense is flawed and I have an aberrant love of water that my kin could not accept. Worst of all, though I come from a proud lineage of warriors, I wanted to save people, and learn healing. I am in every way a perversion of dragonkind; they could not allow me to pollute the purity of the family with my association."

Saina chewed on this. "And Keylor?"

"My younger brother," Bastian said. "A proper dragon of fire and temper. He took my place as heir when I was thrown out. I haven't seen any of them in three years."

Saina turned back to the ocean to digest these revelations.

"What was that?" Bastian asked quietly. "Saina? What *are* you?"

Saina turned back to him. She believed that he'd told the truth about his exile, and she knew that her song had been unnecessary. He would have been genuine without her magic, she realized, and it shamed her that she had used it.

"Haven't you guessed?" she mocked gently. "I'm a siren."

He looked at her blankly and Saina sighed. "A mermaid, Bastian. I'm a mermaid."

He continued to stare.

Did he have to be so handsome and innocent? Saina wanted to brush his unruly hair back from his high forehead and plant a kiss there. "Come on," she said. "I'll show you."

She took one unresisting hand and led him out into the water. She didn't bother undressing, but waded out with him until the swells were chest deep, then she fell into the saltwater and shifted.

CHAPTER 12

*B*astian let Saina lead him into the lapping waves, bemused by the depth of his own confession. He'd had every intention of telling his mate about his family disgrace, but he had hoped she'd have a chance to know him a little better before he divulged the extent of his exile and the depths of his depravity.

He certainly hadn't planned to tell her like that.

But he'd been as compelled as if he'd had Wonder Woman's lasso of truth wrapped around him, and she seemed to think that it was perfectly normal to be able to sing her will into anyone around her.

A siren, he thought in wonder. He'd been feeling so smug about how unknown dragons were, and she was something rarer and more mythical.

She is our treasure, his dragon said proudly. *There is nothing rarer or more valuable.*

Then, between one step and the next, she dived into the lightly lapping waves, and Bastian reached after her in alarm.

She surfaced beside him again, her long dark hair spilling back from her face, then swam beside him and flipped glimmering fins at him.

She was astonishing.

Her violet tail was more than just a simple flexible appendage; it was finery in jewel-faceted scales, longer than her legs had been by half. Feathery fins shimmered around her like veils and, when she moved, there were green and rainbow hues glittering beneath the patterned shades of purple.

Bastian had to swallow. Her breasts, bare, were as glorious as he'd imagined from all her various states of dress, and he had to remind himself repeatedly not to stare.

You should stare, his dragon urged him. *She is ours, and she is beautiful, and we should admire her.* (He was, not surprisingly, more impressed with her stunningly scaled bottom half than her curvy top half.)

"Come swim with me," she invited. Her voice was musical, but there was no compulsion to it.

"Don't sirens drown their victims?" Bastian said, trying to keep his voice light and the raging need in his blood from boiling over. He was grateful he was waist deep in the water now, because his erection would have been difficult to hide.

She raised an eyebrow at him, and while he was watching her face, flipped her fins to shower him with water.

Spluttering, he dived after her, to find that she had slipped further away, laughing and splashing.

Underwater, she was even more gorgeous than above, her graceful fins in mesmerizing motion, and she led him out to the wavebreak, and slipped over it into the surf.

Bastian hesitated only a moment before following her, and once past the reef, he shifted, diving fast and powerful through the water as the ocean floor fell away beneath them. She swam faster than a human swimmer, but not as fast as a dragon.

He was gratified by her wide-eyed surprise when he caught up with her.

She reached out as he passed, and her fingers were tantalizing brushing along his scales. He circled back to her, and she put wondering hands on his scaled nose.

You are so beautiful, she said in his head suddenly.

I was just thinking that, he told her, surprised and delighted to discover this new intimacy. Dragons could speak in this fashion with each other, but he had not known that he would be able to speak with mermaids this way, too. Was it only because she was his mate?

Take me deeper! she suggested.

She swam to the back of his head and held onto his horns. Bastian gathered his dragon body and kicked off with wings and legs before folding them back against him and letting his thick tail power them forward.

She was the barest tickle of fins at his head, but she was laughter and delight in his mind as they cut through the water, going deeper and darker below.

The wordless depths had been a place of peace before, but with his mate beside him, they became a new paradise. Schools of fish scattered before them, and a startled octopus darted away in a cloud of frightened ink.

It was several minutes before Bastian realized that he had unexpectedly had no need to return to the surface to breathe.

It's my gift, Saina told him. *Sirens can let anything breath underwater that they touch.*

I thought your voice was your gift, Bastian said bemusedly.

A girl can have more than one gift. Saina's mindvoice was sarcastic and dry.

Bastian's response was wordless gratitude and all the love and adoration in his big dragon heart.

He felt her withdraw from him, silent and non-receptive. Finally, she said, *Let's go back to the resort.*

There was an undercurrent of pain to her voice, and Bastian wondered if the swim had been too hard on her shoulder.

He took them back through the clear water, and rose out of the waves with her still clinging to his neck. She had shifted back to human form by the time he stepped onto the sand, and he shifted smoothly so that she was riding on his shoulders when he'd left the last lapping wave behind.

"Let me down!" she said, light laughter in her voice.

He crouched and turned to catch her as she slipped from his shoulders.

He put her down on her feet, but no power in the world could have made him let go of her then. She was human, and dressed again in the golden sundress. Her skin was warm velvet under his fingers.

When he bent to kiss her, she froze for a moment, lips just parted under his, then gave a sigh of surrender and put her arms around his neck and kissed him back.

CHAPTER 13

Saina couldn't figure out how something could be so wrong and so right at the same time.

Bastian's arms were the most wonderful place that she'd ever been. He smelled like salt and safety, and Saina wanted to stay here, kissing him, forever.

No, she realized after only a moment, she didn't want to stay here. She wanted to drag him somewhere private and peel him out of his wet uniform, and why shouldn't she?

He wanted her. There was no mistaking the urgency of the erection he was trying not to obviously press against her as he claimed her mouth.

And she wanted *him*. She wanted him more than she'd ever wanted anyone in her life, so badly that she ached with it. The pain in her shoulder was the merest tickle compared to the fire that was smoldering in her loins.

"My cottage," she said, between kisses.

She'd never felt someone smile *while* they were kissing her, but Saina immediately decided that it was one of her favorite things ever.

He swept her suddenly into his arms, making her squeak in protest and cling to his neck. Then he proceeded to carry her the entire way to her cottage, never pausing with his kisses.

He only almost dropped her once, during a particularly long, breathless kiss when he was climbing stairs at the same time, and Saina laughed and begged him to put her down.

"You are my treasure," he told her, and then they were at the door of her cottage and he finally had to put her down for lack of a free hand to open it.

She let him in almost shyly, and shut the door behind him as he shucked off his shirt and dropped the first aid kit he was wearing on a table.

He was so gorgeous, she thought, feeling weak. Her mouth was swollen with his kisses, and her heart was pounding.

His chest was like a sculpture, perfect tanned skin over muscles like mountains. Saina wanted to put her hands on it, but was suddenly, unexpectedly nervous.

"My treasure," Bastian repeated, looking adoringly at her.

Saina wanted to be that treasure he saw, she realized. She wanted it so badly.

And it was utterly wrong.

She didn't know how or why her enchantment had taken such a hold on him, but it had to be her magic that made him look at her that way. If she slept with him now, she was no better than any of her siren sisters...and he made her want to be better than that.

She stared at him, wrestling with the fire in her belly that urged her to do what they both wanted so badly, and the little voice that told her she would regret it forever.

He was waiting, invitation and tension in every plane of his amazing body, and she was just staring at him in growing consternation.

"Saina?" he said gently when she didn't come to him.

"I can't do this," she said miserably.

He swallowed hard.

Saina opened her mouth. This was where she would sing him to sleep and make her escape. She could swim again; her shoulder barely ached at all.

Then she closed her mouth again.

That was the easy way. The siren way.

But it wasn't the *right* way.

CHAPTER 14

Bastian watched Saina struggle, fascinated and heartbroken by the array of emotions that crossed her beautiful face: guilt, pain, resignation, frustration, fear. He wanted to close the distance between them and gather her into his arms, to assure her that whatever crisis she was facing, he was hers. But something told him that would only make things worse, so he waited, leashing his desire and protective instinct to the best of his ability.

"I'm sorry," she said achingly. "I'm sorry you found me. I'm sorry I am who I am. I'm sorry I let you think this was something more than it was for so long. I'm just… so sorry."

Bastian blinked. "I'm not sorry I found you," he said at once.

"Don't," Saina breathed miserably. "Don't be so perfect."

Perfect? She thought he was perfect?

"Saina…" Something occurred to Bastian. "Have you ever been with…er, am I your *first?*"

Her face was a kaleidoscope of emotion.

It wasn't an obvious guess. She was lushly curved and exuded sexuality like a cat in heat to Bastian's senses. She had perfect flirtations that she could turn on in an instant, and she clearly knew exactly how to walk and smile for just the attention that she didn't seem to want. The clothing she had arrived in suggested that she knew exactly how to play the seduction game.

But Bastian believed her when she sighed and admitted, "Yes. You would be."

She dropped into the chair and Bastian settled on the bed opposite from her.

"This would be much easier if I were like other sirens," she said in frustration.

"What are other sirens like?" Bastian asked, already disliking them for not being like her.

"Oh, you know," she said mockingly. "Seducing sailors, drowning people."

Bastian was fairly sure she wasn't really joking; there was too much bitterness in her voice.

"Tell me," he told her without judgment, wishing he could touch her.

She looked back at him unflinchingly, then lowered dark lashes over her sea green eyes. "I wish I were kidding," she said in a flat voice. "But every mermaid I've ever known but one was out only for themselves. We...don't have families like you do. Siren women form a loose pod, but our loyalty to each other is usually not strong."

"And the men?" Bastian had to ask.

"There are no male sirens," Saina said stiffly. She swiftly added, "Children of trysts are raised in the pod if they are girls, and abandoned on land if they are boys. None of them ever find our pod."

"Can all sirens sing like you?" Bastian asked, putting an unconscious hand to his throat as he remembered the compulsion of her song on the beach and the way she had defused the unexpected tension in the restaurant the night before.

She stiffened. "No, not all of us," she said, and her voice was full of grief and regret. "Most of us can sing a simple seduction, but not all of us have more complicated talents."

Bastian didn't press her and Saina gathered herself and went on.

"My grandmother was a singer like me. She used to tell me that the magic we could do came from our hearts, that sirens were meant for greater things. And when she was lost... I realized that she was the only reason our pod had stayed together as long as it had. Without Our Voice, we were lost. My sisters all left, free to pursue their own baser desires."

"Your Voice?" There was a significance to the title that Bastian couldn't define.

"It is the title for our matron, our leader if you like. I went after her, made a deal for her freedom, but it went badly."

Bastian had wondered how she ended up with a bullet hole, adrift in the middle of the ocean, and this started to explain it. He made a sudden connection. "Keylor. That's how you know Keylor."

"He swore he would free Our Voice if I did a job for him. A simple job, for someone with my gifts. And I got what he was after, too. But it sank with the dinghy. I'll never get it now and I don't know another way to satisfy his demands."

Bastian could feel the fire of rage rising inside his chest. "He blackmailed you. He kidnapped your grandmother and blackmailed you for her release."

"He took her as a matter of debt," Saina elucidated. "I don't know the details, but he considered himself wronged and took her to satisfy his honor."

"He wouldn't harm her," Bastian assured her, knowing it was a pitiful assurance.

"Of course not," Saina agreed. "I know a little about dragon honor." She said it with disgust. "It's no wonder you all make such amazing lawyers."

"I would make a terrible lawyer," Bastian confessed.

Saina smiled at him, a crooked, genuine smile. "That's why I like you so much."

Bastian felt like his chest expanded seven times when she said it. "I want to show you something," he said impulsively, standing up.

CHAPTER 15

Saina knew where they would go even before Bastian led
her to the staff house. A paper taped to the front door
read "Bachelor Barn." This was crossed out and beneath it, in
different handwriting: "Crew Quarters." This was crossed out with
a side-note: "No Star Trek references!"

The common room was empty, sunlight streaming in through
the open curtains. The decor was decidedly dated and 80s style, but
everything was clean and tidy, and the couch looked comfortable.

Bastian's room was at the end of a short hallway on the top
floor; Saina guessed that this had originally been the master
bedroom from the floor plan. Rather than a standard bedroom lock,
it had a sturdy hasp with a keyed padlock on it.

Bastian unlocked it, then hesitated, one hand on the doorknob.
"I don't want this to be a surprise," he said awkwardly. "I'm not sure
how to explain it."

"I've known a few dragons," Saina said. "I know about their
hoards."

Bastian looked more uncomfortable, if possible. "It's not a
normal hoard," he said, and he looked so anxious that Saina

wanted to give him a hug. She squelched the uncharacteristic impulse.

He probably had a puny hoard, by dragon standards. Saina braced herself for a few sparse jewelry boxes and a couple of brass goblets. Maybe the walls would be tapestries that weren't embroidered in gold.

She started to hum out of habit, wanting to ease Bastian's tension, and made herself bite her cheek to stop. She was done singing her way out of awkward places of her own making.

Bastian took a deep breath, and opened the door.

Saina sucked her own breath in and stepped into his dazzling nest.

There were no tapestries on the walls at all, only fine fishing net bleached white, covering every wall and each inch of the ceiling. It was even over the windows, and sunlight glowed through the treasure that hung on it, turning the room into a rainbow.

There were a few golden necklaces and rings laid out on the dressers—the sorts of things that Saina had seen in other dragon hoards. But most of it was treasure from the ocean: sea glass, shells, shards of mother-of-pearl, pieces of brilliant coral. A tall brass vase stood in one corner, pitted and crusted with barnacles. An entire anchor filled another corner, more treasure displayed on it. There were sea stars and sand dollars, and old gold and copper coins, polished clean.

It had all been selected for beauty, not value, and the effect was utterly magical. Each piece had been placed as carefully as it had been collected; the room was completely in harmony with itself. It made a song rise up in Saina's throat that she had to stuff back with determination. She felt as if she had just come home.

Saina walked into the room in a daze. The floor was a fluffy, thick white carpet; her toes felt worshipped just wriggling in it. She couldn't help but wonder how awful it would be to vacuum sand out of it, and she hoped her feet were clean.

The bed was a monster of comfort, with about a hundred throw pillows in sea themes, and a glittery comforter that Saina recognized from a Bedding and Bathing catalog. It had been advertised for little girls' rooms; she hadn't even realized it was offered in a King size.

Bastian was watching her anxiously.

"Do you...like it?" he asked, as if he were being forced to and was dreading her answer.

Saina laughed, and couldn't keep her magic entirely out of the sound. "I love it," she admitted, trying to rein in the effect.

It was no good, Bastian was looking at her with that dazzled look she knew too well, worshipful and adoring.

He cleared his throat. "It's our tradition to gift our mate with the most valuable treasure from our hoard," he said formally.

Saina stared. His mate? She'd only tried to make him feel well-disposed to her, to be her ally in a strange place. Instead, he'd fallen harder for her than anyone she'd ever enspelled.

Bastian was holding a necklace made of massive gold links and rubies that didn't match with the rest of the hoard at all. "This was my coming of age gift," he said. "It is worth more than anything else here."

"Oh, oh, no," Saina said.

He blinked, looking at the necklace. "I know it's not very... elegant, but these are very rare rubies and it's all solid gold."

"No, no, no," Saina repeated, trying to retreat to the door and nearly tangling herself in the fishing net beside it instead. Sea glass chimed reproachfully at her.

Bastian looked crushed and stared at the necklace in distaste. "You're right, it's not good enough. I'll get something else, find something...it's all wrong." He looked around at his room in shame and disgust.

Saina couldn't bear the way her chest felt. She had caused that terrible look on his face. She was the reason he was embarrassed of his beautiful hoard. She had cracked the confidence of a man as good as he was gorgeous.

She reached out to him automatically and put a hand on his arm. The touch was electric. "I love the hoard," she said. "It's the most amazing hoard I've ever seen. But you can't give it to me, not any of it. Not to me."

"There is no one else in the world for me," Bastian assured her, putting the necklace aside.

Saina felt saltwater in her eyes unexpectedly.

She'd heard plenty of professions of devotion before, been at the receiving end of adoring acts of compelled generosity, but this was the first time she had gone so far as to make someone *love* her before, let alone think she was their mate.

Worse, this was the first time she wanted it to be *real*.

While she struggled to regain her composure, Bastian gathered her up in her arms and kissed her.

CHAPTER 16

*B*astian couldn't disbelieve Saina when she said she loved his hoard. There was no falsifying the admiration in her eyes, no way that her words could have been lies.

She didn't want the gift from his hoard, which confused both Bastian and his dragon, but perhaps they'd only chosen the wrong piece; his treasure sense was haywire and he doubted his own understanding of value.

But she wanted *him*.

He knew it in the way she kissed him, and the way she looked at him when she thought he didn't notice.

It wasn't her practiced smiles or her careful eyelashes, it was the other look—the puzzled, tender look she had when she thought he wasn't looking. The crooked smile when something truly amused her. The way she hummed happily to herself when she liked something.

That was the Saina he kissed.

And to his heartbreak, she still pulled away. "I…I can't do this," she said.

"We can take it as slow as you want," he assured her, letting her retreat.

"Oh, Bastian, you deserve so much better than this."

There were tears in her green eyes.

"I'm not your mate, Bastian. Sirens don't *have* mates. It's just my magic, you only think you feel this way, and when I leave, you..." she gave a little sob. "You'll look back at these few days and it will feel like a dream, because that's all it is. It's just a happy little fantasy that I *never* should have indulged in. I'm so sorry. There isn't anything here, between us. It's not...real. It never was."

She turned and fled through the door. Bastian let her go, too baffled to stop her.

After a moment, he left his lackluster hoard, locking the door behind him.

He walked to the pool deck in a daze, and stared at the "Lifeguard Off Duty" sign for a long, confused moment. He almost took it down, then reconsidered, and realized what he had to do.

Tex called down to him from the bar deck above, but Bastian ignored the bartender and stalked to the beach, not pausing at the little beach bar or the lifeguard tower. He walked straight into the water, shifted, and swam out the same way that he'd gone the day before.

It took several hours of swimming to reach the spot he'd found Saina. There were no features above the waves once the island was out of sight, but beneath the water, he could follow the landmarks of the ocean floor, and if he concentrated very carefully, he could feel a faint tingle of his treasure sense, leading him back to her sunken luggage.

While he swam, he tried to sort out his confused feelings. Saina was his mate. She was his everything. It didn't matter what she said, he knew to the core of his heart that she was his, meant for him in every way.

He loved the charm she could easily turn on, and the vulnerable confusion she so rarely let him see. He loved the way she moved and the way she swam.

He missed the way she let him breathe underwater and surfaced to suck in a breath of air. The ocean looked like a different place today, smooth and sparkling cheerfully. It wanted to play, today.

He dived again. The ocean floor was hundreds of meters down here; his chest protested the pressure and his tail ached with the effort. It was dark, too, but between his luminous eyes and the faint tug of the treasure sense, he knew he could find his target.

Confidence swelled in him again, tingling through his limbs as he approached the treasure.

She was wrong, he thought, with increasing resolution. He wasn't under her spell. He was too strong and powerful a dragon to be caught in any web of enchantment.

He was too magnificent to be snared by magic, he thought as his treasure sense flared and began to burn with more intensity than it had except for the time he had found Saina.

He was stronger than any siren, his will was harder.

There must be some other reason she was refusing his hoard, but it was of no consequence. He was a dragon, and she was his mate. He would make her the prize of his nest; she would be his finest treasure. There would be no more running from him.

If he had the air to spare, he would have roared, because there, half-buried in shifting sand, was Saina's suitcase, its lurid color washed away by the murkiness of the depths.

He put a claw around the handle and kicked off from the floor of the ocean, making a swift, determined beeline for the surface.

He was not built for water liftoffs; he needed to kick off with his strong hindlegs from something solid to get enough lift to get him into the air, but knowing that he'd never been able to before didn't stop Bastian from believing he could now as a strange resolution crept over him.

He darted for the surface, and just as he broke through it, spread his wings and gave a tremendously powerful beat that took him into the air.

A triumphant laugh turned into a roar of celebratory fire as he escaped the distasteful draw of the saltwater and returned to the air where he belonged, his prize safe in his claws.

He soared through the salty air, snapping at seabirds who dared get in his way, and flew back to Shifting Sands with sure, strong wing strokes.

He circled the resort twice, gratified when the people sunbathing below looked up to admire his big, gleaming body. Then he landed at the back entrance to the kitchen, closest to where he sensed his mate.

Saina! he roared, calling her.

Saina! I have your tribute! You will be mine!

Obediently, as she should, Saina came to the door, Breck and Chef right behind her, staring curiously. Chef was holding a wicked knife, and Breck had a dish towel. Neither of them was any threat.

Bastian dropped the sodden suitcase at his mate's feet. *I have won you*, he snarled.

Her spoken voice was sharp and unexpectedly clear. "You have done nothing of the sort, you idiot."

He opened his jaws and roared flame into the air.

CHAPTER 17

𝒞hef proved to be a large older man with a twinkle in his bright eyes, a white mustache, and biceps the size of winebarrels. He welcomed Saina into his kitchen domain with the open-hearted kindness that she was beginning to accept was a genuine part of this odd resort and showed her the tasks that needed attention.

"Are you sure you are up to this?" he asked sincerely.

Saina rolled her shoulder, turning her head to look at the fading puckered scab. "It's almost all healed," she promised before diving into a soapy sink of dirty dishes.

He continued to regularly check in with her as he moved around the kitchen with busy authority, praising her attention to detail and generally encouraging her in an unexpected way. He sang as he worked, and it was surprising to Saina because it was without method or motive, just for the joy of it.

She joined him, because his pleasure in the music was so addictive. She was careful to keep her magic dampened, and to keep her grief from coloring the counterparts she sang. It helped that Chef seemed to like happier tunes, skipping from Italian arias to folk songs as the mood struck him. Most of them weren't songs that

Saina knew, but she could improvise a harmony to almost anything, and after a few choruses could usually pick up on lyrics. Breck joined them for a few lines, as he moved in and out of the kitchen bussing tables and restocking and refreshing the buffet.

She was chopping tomatoes for that night's dinner, singing the soprano to "Tonight" from West Side Story and forgetting for a while that she would be leaving very soon, when Bastian broke through her reverie.

Saina! He called her. *Saina! I have your tribute! You will be mine!*

Saina dropped the knife, snatching her hands out of the way in time to avoid disaster, and left it on the counter to answer the call. Judging by the way that Chef and Breck also startled, they'd heard Bastian's imperious words, or perhaps just his roar; they were at her heels when she came out of the back kitchen door to find a gigantic green dragon perched at the retaining wall.

Her pink rolling carry-on case fell with a sodden thump at her feet.

I have won you, Bastian said, and his golden eyes were shot with glowing red.

Goldshot.

"You have done nothing of the sort, you idiot," Saina could not stop herself from saying, and she saw Bastian flinch and then rear his head back in anger to flame into the air.

She recognized his irrational anger and the unnatural glow to his eyes and scales. She didn't for a moment fear for her own self, but she knew that Bastian would lose his real self if she didn't do anything, and she cast desperately for something she could do to free him as she opened her mouth.

Her grandmother's words came back to her, and she drew power not from her belly, but from her heart. She focused all of her unpredictable magic into the idea of leaching the personality-altering drug from his system. She had to draw out the poison, sing it from his very veins. Not sure it would work, she poured her magic into her song.

Let it go,

Let it die,
Let it out,
Let it fly…

When the last note died away, Saina waited to see if it had worked.

Bastian remained perched on the retaining wall, swaying slightly, and she panted, every muscle in her body aching from the effort.

Chef and Breck looked from one of them to the other, baffled.

Bastian shook his big head and just as Saina was drawing in breath to try another song, he blinked and the remaining red in his eyes faded away. He seemed to draw into himself, suddenly much smaller and less glittery, but there was only a brief moment to observe his dragon before he shifted into a man. Then he was Bastian, vaulting down from the retaining wall to kneel at her feet.

"Saina," he said. "I…don't understand what happened. I'm so sorry."

"You should be," Saina said furiously. "You don't own me and you never will, but more than that, you are an utter fool."

He looked up at her in consternation.

"Do you have any idea what is in that suitcase?" she demanded.

He started to reach for it, and she quickly said, "No, don't touch it!" She crouched next to it and unzipped it, flinging the lid back to reveal a sodden, dissolved gray mass in a slurry of half-empty plastic wrappers. "This is goldshot."

Bastian, poor sweet, innocent Bastian, looked across the luggage at her with no understanding at all.

"Goldshot is what got that French dragon eliminated from the World Mr. Shifter contest," Breck supplied, snapping his fingers with the memory.

"It's a drug," Saina added. "A terrible, expensive designer drug that only works on dragons. You probably absorbed several doses of it getting that close to the stuff dissolving underwater."

"I was a real dragon," he said achingly, standing up and wrapping arms around himself. "For a little while I was a *real* dragon. A dragon of *fire* and *strength*."

"You *are* a real dragon," Saina told him firmly, standing to face him. "And I love you just the way you are, the way you really are, not the trumped up ball of muscle and ego that the goldshot makes you."

He squinted at her, like he was struggling through the worst hangover of his life. He probably was.

"You love me?" he said plaintively.

Saina sighed. "Yes, dammit." It hurt to admit, and felt good at the same time, like pulling off an old scab.

Bastian grinned at her lopsidedly through his pain. "You *are* my mate."

"I'm not," she insisted, but weakly. She wasn't entirely sure of anything anymore. "You shouldn't trust your feelings for me."

"This is not a spell," Bastian insisted. "I know what false confidence feels like now, and that is not what I feel for you."

"I should have brought popcorn," Breck told Chef. "This is better than the Spanish soaps!"

"That's only because you don't speak Spanish," Chef hissed back. "And you're too lazy to read the subtitles."

"What would convince you?" Bastian asked, ignoring them.

His question was meant seriously, Saina realized, he wasn't just speaking metaphorically about having her set an impossible quest for him to complete.

"Time," she said thoughtfully. "Time *away*. My magic wears off if I don't renew it. But..." she swallowed. "I don't trust myself not to cast again, without meaning to. I have never loved anyone before. I don't know how to do it without magic."

Chef and Breck both made suspicious sniffling noises, and Saina glared in their direction.

CHAPTER 18

*B*astian would have preferred to have this conversation without an audience, and without a headache so terrible it seemed to sink into his very bones. But fate seemed determined to cross him.

"I was curious as to why I didn't have a lifeguard on duty, and I also believe there were promises about this not happening again if you were to stay here, Saina," a new voice cut in.

Scarlet's arms were crossed and she was standing by the gate to the kitchen garden, looking as if she'd been there for some time.

"The plot thickens," Breck said in a stage-whisper to Chef.

Scarlet turned her icy stare to him. "I believe you have somewhere else to be," she suggested.

Chef helpfully took the head waiter's elbow and dragged him back into the kitchen, shutting the door firmly behind them. Bastian almost laughed, picturing them leaning with their ears against the other side of it. Almost laughing made his head hurt worse.

"I'm sorry," Saina said in small voice.

"It was my fault," Bastian added quickly.

"I'm sure it was," Scarlet said without quarter, looking down at the seeping suitcase. "I want this removed before it gets into the soil," she said in disgust.

Bastian automatically bent to pick it up and Saina swiftly said, "No! Don't touch it again!"

She knelt beside the bag and zipped it up, at least slowing the leaks. "I will leave," she said in a small, brave voice. "I am sorry for the trouble I've been."

"No," Bastian said. "You stay here. I have...business I need to attend to." He turned to face Scarlet's wrath. "I need five days off."

Scarlet's face grew chillier. "You realize that we have a new batch of guests and no other lifeguard on staff."

"I can certify Saina," Bastian said swiftly. "Like I did with Neal a few months back. It's just a swimming test I know she can pass, and a few safety and first aid lectures I can pack into an afternoon."

"You don't have to do that," Saina said.

"He might," Scarlet countered dryly.

Bastian turned to Saina. "You told me you need time. Time away from me." The idea of it hurt to his already aching bones. "I'll give you that time."

To Scarlet, he said firmly. "I'm sorry not to give more warning, but this isn't optional."

Scarlet met his gaze without wavering. "How do I know she can control her magic?" she asked, as if Saina wasn't standing right beside them. "I can't have our guests accidentally enspelled because a little girl gets emotional about some setback or imagined slight."

Bastian bristled, wanting to snarl at her for the insult but at the last moment recognized it as bait.

"I can't promise it won't happen again," Saina said calmly in reply. "But I *can* promise that I mean you, your guests, and this place no harm, and I will see that none comes to it while you employ me. I am happy to work here in whatever capacity I can until Bastian returns."

"And then?" Scarlet prodded.

Saina drew in a breath. "I don't know. If he still thinks I'm his mate, I...would like to stay. If he doesn't, you'll be rid of me."

Scarlet considered this for a long moment while Bastian watched Saina's carefully serene face.

"I am satisfied with this," Scarlet finally said. "Bastian, I hope you find what you need. If there is any change to this arrangement, I expect to be notified. I am attempting to run a professional establishment here and I need to be able to rely on my staff."

"Yes, ma'am," he and Saina said together.

Scarlet gave a harrumph in reply and stalked back the way she had come, muttering about dating services and schedules.

CHAPTER 19

Saina watched Scarlet go with a sigh of relief. The woman made her uneasy, raising the hair at the back of Saina's neck. The power that seemed to bleed out from her was something she had never felt before and the air was easier to breathe with her gone.

"So, I guess you've volunteered to teach me to be a lifeguard," she said, turning to Bastian. "Can you really do that? Legally, I mean?"

Bastian, still looking like he had a terrific headache, shrugged and gave a lopsided grin. "I'm certified to train lifeguards. I know you can swim, I just have to quiz you on first aid and ocean safety, which I'm also sure you won't have any trouble with, and there's a temporary certificate I sign and a form I mail in to the Civil Guard for the permanent certification."

"Let's go make me a lifeguard," Saina said, and she took Bastian's offered arm and dragged the luggage that had changed her life so drastically behind her.

She dropped the bag at her cottage, wrapped in a garbage bag to keep the ooze from spreading, while Bastian got his lifeguard manuals from his room. They flipped through them together at the pool. "You know CPR?" he asked

"Sure," Saina said.

Bastian flipped a few more pages. "Name the first three things you do with a drowning victim."

"On land or in the water?"

"Assume you've gotten them back to land."

"If they aren't breathing, turn their head to the side so the water drains out, start mouth-to-mouth, and steal their wallet."

Bastian chuckled. "Close enough. Describe two kinds of drowning behavior."

"Well, there's the struggling sort, and the bobbing sort. Plus the being dragged under by tentacles sort, but you hardly ever see that this close to shore."

"What would you do with a hysterical swimmer in the water?"

"Sing them to calmness before I even attempted to get close."

Bastian flipped a few more page. "We can skip that part, then. And the bit about how long you can hold your breath and dive."

"Do we get to practice the mouth-to-mouth?" Saina asked, feeling suddenly mischievous.

She regretted the joke as tasteless as Bastian looked up too quickly and then winced as his head caught up with the motion.

"You need an aspirin," Saina told him.

"About seven of them," Bastian agreed. "But let's get this finished."

Together, they flipped through the rest of the manual, and Saina convinced him that she knew the material well enough.

She demonstrated basic swimming strokes in the pool and showed him rescue carries with a floating mattress.

"You're qualified," Bastian said at last, closing the book and flinching at the sound of it. "I'll sign for it."

Saina dried herself off with one of the fluffy pool towels and frowned at him.

"Let's go get you that aspirin," she said.

She led him down the path to the staff house, where the sign on the door had been further annotated "House of Hooligans" and "Stud House." Both were crossed out.

By the time Saina got Bastian up the stairs, he was staggering badly.

"You poor thing," she said as he fumbled with the lock. "Let's get you into bed."

"I like that idea," he said in a low rumble.

Saina paused in the doorway. "I…I can help you," she offered. "But only if you want me to."

"How do you mean?" Bastian asked sensibly.

"I can rub your shoulders," Saina said hesitantly. Could she really do that without wanting to touch more? "And I can try to sing more of the goldshot from you."

"I'd like that," Bastian said gravely.

Saina made him take four aspirin with an entire glass of water, drew him down onto the bed and kissed his forehead, then took his shirt off carefully.

It was hard not to linger over the muscles of his arms, she wanted nothing more than to kiss down his chest, but Saina made herself stay to her goal. She sat chastely behind him on the bed and began kneading the knots from his shoulders and neck.

He groaned in pleasure as Saina found all the tightest places and applied siren-strong fingers to unwinding them. She hummed as she worked, cautiously letting her magic loosen all the tension from his body and leach what she could of the remaining poison from his blood.

When she was done, he turned abruptly and gathered her into his arms.

"You're supposed to be relaxed now," Saina protested with a squeak.

"You missed a spot," Bastian murmured near her ear. "But my headache is gone."

Saina could not keep her hands from continuing to stroke the tanned lines of his shoulders. "What if…what if you're wrong?" she asked quietly. "What if this is just enchantment, like I said?" She didn't want to stop touching him, she wanted his skin against every inch of hers. It didn't feel like song-fantasy. It was so beautiful and right-feeling, just being with him, held in his strong arms.

Bastian put a hand at her chin and gently tipped her head back so he could look into her eyes. His eyes were all gold now, glimmering like distant treasure. "I will take a moment of enchantment with you over a lifetime without you."

But it wasn't her magic looking back at her, it was Bastian. Not Bastian-on-goldshot, not Bastian-entwined-in-her-spell, just Bastian.

Bastian, who loved her without magic.

Bastian, who wanted her as much as she wanted him.

Saina opened her mouth, and it wasn't to sing.

CHAPTER 20

*B*astian hadn't been honest about his headache; it still lurked behind his eyes and in the pit of his stomach.

But it was nothing compared to the joy of having his love in his arms, her sea green eyes tender and her fingers lithe and clever over his skin.

When he kissed her, he forgot the pain in his head and the hunger in his belly, happy to lose himself in the taste and feel of her against him.

Her dress slipped easily off over her head, his shorts followed swiftly, and for a long, delicious time, they simply touched each other, hands over exposed flesh.

Bastian didn't want to rush her, and held himself to worshipping each plane and curve of her body. He kissed and sucked and nibbled. She did the same in return, cautiously, then eagerly. Mutual fingers traced every sensitive place, looking for the spot that drew the hiss of breath and flush. Her hair tickled him as she kissed his chest and cupped his ass. He licked her neck and traced the small of her back.

Breath grew ragged and Bastian couldn't tell where hers began and his ended; he wondered if her magic would help him breathe without air out of the water as well as it did under it.

Urgency mounted and the touches grew more intimate; he slipped a questing finger into her wet entrance and kissed her neck as she arched into him. She put her fingers around his eager cock and stroked him until he was ready to cry out loud.

He lay her back on the pillows, loving the dark hair spread on his pillows as it took a hundred hues from the gleaming sea glass he had called treasure before he'd known his true prize.

He slipped into her slowly, with the same deliberate care he had explored her body, and she moaned in pleasure as she spread her legs in welcome.

Bastian was careful, gentle, pausing when she tensed, and she made a little noise of need and pressed herself onto him in a rush.

She was his shield, his holt, he thought. Being deep inside her was the safest place he could imagine.

For a moment, an ugly, unwelcome need interrupted, urging him to be the dragon he'd been so briefly again.

Then Saina cried out as the muscles in her body clenched in orgasm, and that need was forgotten, washed away in cleaner desires.

He returned to his mate, not ready to sate himself and end their bliss, and let her pleasure wash away in a slow, controlled wave.

When she returned to herself, they rolled across the bed so that she was straddling him, and she moved with the same slow, deliberate strokes, drawing him deeper, and deeper, like they were swimming together on a fathomless ocean floor. His senses constricted; he was pressure and slick skin against hot velvet. Her touch, her little sounds of joy, were all that anchored him.

He was ocean and fire, she was the tide and the fuel. They moved in perfect symmetry and as she cried again in release, he lost himself in the only magic he needed from her.

CHAPTER 21

*A*fter bringing her to unknown heights of delight, Bastian collapsed next to her. Saina didn't have the breath left to hum him to the sleep she knew he needed after his exposure to the goldshot.

She was glad that by the time she had gathered herself, she didn't have to do anything. He was asleep, one strong arm splayed over her belly possessively.

Saina closed her eyes and enjoyed the moment as long as she was able to.

Then, unbidden, doubts crept back.

Had she sung out in the moment of her pleasure? Had she unknowingly cast another seduction spell? Had she been wrong about Bastian's love being untainted of her magic, sure of what she saw because she wanted it so badly?

No, she was sure there had been no enchantment left, but what if distance dampened his ardor and he came back from his trip and looked at her without that same affection?

Saina's chest hurt worse than her shoulder ever had.

She could imagine nothing worse than Bastian looking at her

with indifference. The idea of it staggered her, and filled her with fear.

It would be better not to know, to hold this one perfect memory and flee, she realized, looking up at the sea glass glittering over the ceiling. She could be gone before he returned, and she would never have to face that possibility. And she still needed to figure out a way to free her Voice, something she could not do in the safe haven of this resort.

She slipped out from under his arm and wriggled back into her clothing. He was so beautiful, sprawled on his big bed, looking innocent and exhausted in sleep.

Before she left, she circled the room, dragging fingers over the beautiful things he had collected from the ocean she loved. She made the sea glass chime and considered taking just a piece of it, to remember him forever. She paused at the necklace he had tried to give her, so out of place and awkward in his beautiful collection. He had, technically given it to her, but she knew that it had been under false pretense, still thinking she was his mate.

Sirens don't have mates, she reminded herself.

Even if he loved her, some day his true mate would come into his life and he would know that the gift had been an error. She would leave this, even if she disagreed that it was the most valuable part of his hoard.

Would his real mate think so? Would she know how perfect his unusual hoard was, or appreciate the beauty of it?

She supposed the hypothetical partner would have to, if mates were really as perfect as advertised.

She ached at the idea of someone else bringing Bastian joy, but sadly realized that she would rather he was truly happy with someone else than falsely happy with her.

The sun outside the open windows was beginning to plunge to the ocean, turning the sky golden and bleaching the green and blue from the sea glass glinting in the window.

Saina put fingers to a particularly fine piece of glass, a shard as big as her palm that was swirled green and blue and ground by sand

and salt to a soft-edged plate. Then she pulled her hand back. She couldn't disturb his hoard.

She had memories to take with her; that was enough.

She crept down the stairs as quietly as she could, hoping to leave unnoticed, but she was greeted at the bottom by Travis, who was just coming up. "Hi, Saina," he said cheerfully, as casually as if she lived there and was already an established part of the staff. "How's the shoulder?"

"All better," she said in surprise. She hadn't thought about it all day.

"I hear you're going to be our lifeguard while Bastian's gone a few days," he continued, friendly.

Saina nodded slowly, surprised by how fast the news had traveled. "I am," she said. And she'd be gone before he returned, she reminded herself.

"Let us know if you need anything," Travis continued, then he was moving past her up the stairs.

It was odd, being the object of friendliness with absolutely no sexual expectations behind it. They accepted her as Bastian's mate, not as something potentially their own.

Even Graham the landscaper, who hadn't said so much as a word to her the few times they had crossed paths, gave a nearly friendly nod from the common room as Saina passed it to get to the door.

She would miss this place, she realized as she shut the door behind her.

Not just Bastian, who was going to leave a hole in the heart she had never believed she had, but the resort had grown on her as well. Her magic felt odd here, but she liked the quirky, big-hearted staff. She even thought Jenny might even become a good girlfriend, something she had never enjoyed before.

She looked out over the cliffs at the rosy-colored ocean.

How completely unexpected.

CHAPTER 22

*B*astian woke just before the sunrise, knowing at once that something was missing from his hoard.

A thread of anger and hunger rose in the back of his throat before he recognized that Saina was gone. He could still taste her in his mouth, but the bed was cool beside him.

The headache was gone, but the desire remained. He wanted badly to be back the way he'd been with the drug coursing through his veins. He struggled, hating how he'd been to Saina, but loving how simple and powerful it had been to be a complete dragon, strong and sure and single-minded.

Bastian-with-goldshot had known who he was and where he belonged. He could do anything, stronger and faster than Bastian-without. Bastian-without was adrift, caught between two worlds, unsure of his path.

Bastian-without rubbed his eyes and rolled from the bed.

For the first time in a very long time, he did not dress in his life-guard uniform, regretfully putting it aside for a light silk shirt from the back of his closet and a pair of tailored gray slacks. Tooled leather shoes were dredged from beneath the bed and a fine wool suit jacket went over his shoulders. If he was going to battle, he was going to do it well-armored.

It was odd to turn from the staff house door to walk towards the cliffs instead of towards the heart of the resort. He shifted and fell from the cliffs to spread wings and catch the wind in his dragon form.

He felt small and fragile, compared to Bastion-with.

Then he thought of Saina and his wing beats steadied. Whatever kind of dragon or perversion of dragon he was, he would earn his mate. He had none of her doubts regarding the truth of their bond, but he knew he had one more thing to do before he could completely claim her.

He flew through the sunrise, and through most of the day, following the coast of the mainland Costa Rica. He might have enjoyed the flight, and the pods of dolphins and whales he passed, but he dreaded his destination.

Midafternoon, he arrived, turning inland at the end to climb into the coastal mountains. The compound he arrived at was castle-like in its grandeur, with towers intended to imply the royalty he knew his family craved.

He circled the structure once before landing in the secondary courtyard, folding glinting green wings back neatly as he set claw to the stone he thought he'd left behind forever.

He was not surprised when a second dragon, darker green, back-winged into the courtyard moments after.

Mother and Father have no desire to see you, the newcomer said in his silky mind-voice. *You are no longer family, brother-not.*

I didn't come to see them, Bastian replied evenly. *I came for you, Keylor.* He was concerned to see that Keylor seemed significantly larger than he had been mere years ago. Bastian had always been the big brother in both years and mass, but that was no longer the case.

What do you want with me? Keylor sniffed.

I am here to treat with you, Bastian said, drawing himself up to his full height. *I'm here for Saina's Voice.*

CHAPTER 23

*S*aina's first stint as lifeguard went smoothly. Bastian's uniform didn't come close to fitting her, but Scarlet provided a staff polo shirt in her size and a pair of nondescript shorts. With the orange high visibility first aid kit strapped at her waist, Saina looked the part, and the swimmers accepted her authority without question.

She found the work easy and enjoyable, bantering with older women on the pool deck who reminded her achingly of her Voice and showing a pair of younger men the basics of the paddle boards at the beach. She reminded pale-skinned people to reapply sunscreen at appropriate intervals, and handed out cold bottles of water and sunhats to guests who weren't used to the intensity of the heat in the tropics.

When the sun began to set and people abandoned both pool and beach, she wasn't sure what to do with herself. After she put all the beach chairs back at the beach bar structure and straightened the now-abandoned pool deck, she wandered up to the bar.

Jenny was sitting at the bar, holding hands with a bartender in a cowboy hat, which puzzled Saina until she realized it wasn't Jenny, just a woman who looked exactly like her.

"I'm Laura," she said, offering a hand as Saina approached the bar. "You met my identical twin sister, Jenny."

"Saina," she answered, accepting the hand for a polite shake.

"You're looking considerably better than the last time I saw you here," Laura teased gently.

Saina realized that Laura must have been present when Bastian brought her to the resort. "Well," she said dryly, "I imagine it's not too hard a bar to beat, given that I was unconscious and bleeding all over the place at the time."

Laura laughed.

"What can I get you?" the bartender asked, after introducing himself aptly as Tex.

"Is staff supposed to drink here?" Saina asked cautiously.

"As long as you don't make a habit of getting falling down drunk on the expensive stuff or get in the way of serving the guests, Scarlet gives us free rein and encourages us to eat and drink well," Tex said. "The profit shares have been pretty non-existent, so she wants the room and board to be a fair trade for our work."

"Seems like a sweet deal," Saina said wistfully. It was getting harder and harder to think about turning her back on the resort. "Can I have something light and fruity, just a little alcoholic?"

"Yes, ma'am," Tex said, putting his fingers to the brim of his hat.

As he bent to mix her drink, Laura gave her a sidelong look and a grin. "So. Bastian."

Saina was glad her golden-brown skin didn't show a blush easily, and she had to use all of her willpower not to squirm in her seat. How could she explain that she wasn't Bastian's mate, that she'd just enspelled and deluded the poor man and then had the poor grace to fall in love with him? Whether he loved her without magic or not, they were not mates.

She didn't want to talk about Bastian.

"Is that a karaoke machine?" she asked desperately, hoping to deflect the topic.

"It is," Tex said, setting the umbrella-topped drink in front of her. "Care to fire it up? Usually it doesn't see a lot of use until the evening drinking crowd really settles in."

Most of the guests were on the deck above, eating Chef's fine food at the gourmet restaurant, but a few were nursing before-dinner drinks here in the bar, scattered between the tables in the open air bar and out on the uncovered deck, where stars were just beginning to appear in the purple sky.

Saina took a sip of her drink, eyeing the little stage hesitantly.

"I'm dying to hear you sing," Laura admitted. "Jenny says you have the most gorgeous voice."

Saina gave her a hard look, trying to determine if she'd heard about the things Saina could do with her voice, or if it was an innocent request.

The mischievous look on her face suggested it was not innocent.

Saina's eyes narrowed. She wondered if Laura would prove as impossible to enchant as Jenny had.

"Of course, I could quiz you about Bastian, instead," Laura suggested breezily.

"Hush, love," Tex chided her. "It's not always easy at first, and we should know. Give her space and let her enjoy her drink."

Laura pouted good-naturedly.

Saina was puzzled. This wasn't the mean-spirited kind of teasing she was used to in the siren pod. They were smiling, not only at each other, but inclusively at her. They would give her space if she asked for it, and she thought that they would lend her willing and understanding ears if she wanted to talk about Bastian. She wondered what they could tell her about him, and then remembered that she was planning to leave before he came home. She didn't need to know more about him, as badly as she wanted to.

Suddenly singing seemed like the much simpler choice.

CHAPTER 24

*K*eylor slithered to one side, flaring his wings. *So, you've met Saina the siren. Did she enchant you into coming to fight for her?*

I am not enspelled, Bastian said, calmly confident. He remained seated, wings neatly at his back, not returning Keylor's posturing. *You have done her family wrong*, he said reproachfully.

Is that what she told you? Keylor scoffed, drawing himself up. *Made herself out to be the innocent victim of a cruel dragon deal?*

Bastian reminded himself not to rise to Keylor's baiting. *If there is a debt, let me pay it and call it done. Release her Voice!*

Slights of honor cannot be repaid with gold. At least not the amount of gold in your ridiculous hoard.

Bastian chewed on this.

Sirens lie, Keylor told him. *They thrive on power and control. They backstab and weave fantasies as a matter of nature.* He paused, and gave Bastian a sly sideways look. *If she said she loved you, it was a falsehood.*

Bastian wanted to mantle his wings and hiss fire at the idea that Saina's love was untrue, but he kept himself controlled.

Oh, brother-not, do you really believe you love her? You are a bigger fool than I ever knew.

This is not about me, Bastian snarled. *This is about releasing her Voice.*

Her Voice is mine now. She has a debt to repay and I do not choose to release it. I gave Saina a chance to buy it out, but she must have failed, if you are here now.

Then I challenge you for that contract, Bastian said.

Keylor laughed derisively. He spread his wings and drew himself up, demonstrating beyond a shadow of a doubt that he was indeed larger than Bastian now, and his scales had a deep, healthy glimmer to them that suggested greater strength. *You think you have a chance against me?*

Bastian was privately thinking he probably didn't, but he wasn't about to admit this, keeping his head high and proud.

Then he realized that Keylor's eyes, which had always been the same golden as Bastian's, were glowing red. As he furrowed his dragon brow, his human realized, *Goldshot!* Keylor was dosing on goldshot. Pieces of the puzzle fell into space. Keylor had sent Saina to get more of the drug, not for its value, but for *himself.*

If Bastian had goldshot himself, he would be even mightier, he thought grimly. He would be stronger, faster...

I accept your challenge, Keylor roared, and he pounced, claws outstretched.

CHAPTER 25

Saina took one last sip of her drink and then stood, leaving the lifeguard first aid kit behind her on the counter.

The karaoke machine had the usual selection; mostly pop music and classic rock.

Saina picked a love song at random and settled herself behind the microphone as the opening bars of music played.

The first line, she kept her magic dampened, relying only on the clear sound of her voice to set the emotional tone.

That got some of the attention in the bar, a few people turning their chairs so they could watch her. She knew she wouldn't be as eye-catching as she usually was, in her understated staff polo shirt and unremarkable shorts, but she stood as tall and confidently as if she were wearing an evening gown and when the chorus came around, she leaned into the song.

> You are my star
> However far
> I will wish on you
> I will always miss you…

She hadn't intended to pick a song with a sad undertone, but when she heard her own voice singing the words, she could only think of Bastian, and how she would never see him again.

By the second round of the chorus, everyone in the bar was completely enraptured, and drinks were forgotten on their tables.

Saina could feel power resonate deep beneath her, like the resort itself was on a pocket of magic that was leaking out of a dozen cracks in the earth. She could tap it, she realized. She could rule this place, she thought, giddy with the strength of it. She could worm her way into every heart and force them to love her; it could drown out the gaping place that Bastian would leave.

She reached out with her voice, held their hearts, and squeezed.

The urge was like a whisper in her ear, tickling at the back of her mind.

She was a siren and they would obey her.

They were hers, all hers, and she could force them to feel anything she wanted. And with this army of shifters to command, no one could keep her from her goals.

She poured her agony and loss into the last stanza, then suddenly thought, *Bastian wouldn't want this.*

She remembered his quiet confession that he had wanted to save people and heal them, despite coming from a family of warriors.

She didn't have to be like other sirens, either, always seeking control and self-satisfaction.

She looked out over the audience, their tear-streaked cheeks and agonized expressions, and she let the last note release them, holding it while she keyed up the next song, a cheerful pop song that swiftly devolved into happy nonsense.

Instead of reaching down to the great pools of magic below, Saina let it lie, and kept her spell light and easy, an invitation, not a command. Be happy, she suggested with it. Be joyful and love each other.

Bastian would have wanted that.

These were his people, his place. As badly as she wanted for it to be her own, it was his. She didn't know where she fit in the world without him, but it wasn't here, knowing she wasn't wholly his. And it certainly wasn't at the head of a shifter army. Where had such an idea even come from? She had no desire for that kind of power and control. If that made her a poor excuse of a siren, she could accept that.

CHAPTER 26

$\mathcal{B}$astian and Keylor battled as only dragons could, claws drawing along hardened scales, fire singeing, crashing into courtyard walls and stair railings as they beat wings at each other and slashed with tails at sensitive eyes and undersides.

Keylor was stronger, longer-limbed, and faster.

But Bastian was smarter, and he had unexpected endurance from his years of diving.

He could hold his breath when Keylor ignited the air around him, when Keylor had to suck hot breath in, and stagger back as the heat scorched unprotected throat and lungs, or pull his head back out of the flame, leaving himself exposed to slashing claws and gnashing teeth.

They tumbled, wings tangling, and tore scales from each other.

Keylor fought like a thing possessed, confident in his superior strength.

Bastian fought like he swam, making the best use of his advantages and compensating for his weaknesses.

He also had more to lose; if he lost this challenge, he knew he would lose Saina's Voice, and with her, Saina.

So he poured everything into his fight, ignoring the bites and the wing tears when it allowed him to slip past Keylor's defenses.

When Keylor leaped onto one of the walls, trying to increase his advantage with height, Bastian gathered himself and leaped after him, and Keylor took the battle to the air with strong wing beats.

Come and get me brother-not, he taunted.

This was a new disadvantage for Bastian, whose strength was not so concentrated in his wings. They swept upwards, then tumbled and dove, slashing and flaming at each other

Bastian tried to use fast, sniping techniques, only to find that Keylor was faster, and still stronger, and met every attack with confidence and cunning.

They battered at each other, angry and mighty, and red blood stained green scales as they fought.

Bastian wanted to protest that this was not an honorable fight; they would be evenly matched if Keylor were not dosed with gold-shot. Or, he thought lustfully, if he were also dosed.

I concede! he finally said when they broke apart at last. Fair or not, this would be Keylor's fight. Bastian had failed Saina.

Keylor paused to pose with an egotistical roar. *Win! Smite! Flame!*

I conceded! Bastian protested, darting aside at the last moment as Keylor shot a column of flame where he'd been.

Fight! Kill! Dominate! Keylor's eyes were brilliant red, glowing in madness and bloodlust.

Stop! Brother! Bastian had to dive aside as Keylor came for him, claws-first. He rolled barely in time, and claws scraped across hard scales.

Brother-not! Keylor replied derisively, flaming in his direction.

Bastian began to concentrate on escape, winging upwards while holding his breath. Keylor caught him easily, wings more powerful and more used to flying. Bastian bit and flamed, then darted away through the clouds, trusting his nose.

Keylor was not going let his prey go willingly now; he was out for blood, not just victory.

Bastian desperately winged through the low coastal clouds, twisting away from Keylor's teeth and claws, slashing with his tail as he climbed into the sky and dived away. Only the fact that he wasn't flying in a predictable dragon pattern kept him safely ahead of the glinting weaponry…and it didn't last long.

Prey! Claw! Kill! Keylor slashed him with a swipe of a lucky claw at his underbelly, and when Bastian's wing beats faltered in pain and shock, Keylor caught him with his tail, and put claws to his chest as his own strong wings kept them aloft.

There is no honor in this, Bastian roared, flaming directly into Keylor's face to drive him back.

Honor is a dead thing, Keylor replied, and he flexed his claws into Bastian's chest, piercing the finer scales around his heart.

CHAPTER 27

*S*aina sang the last bars without the slightest hint of magic, and the bar broke into applause.

Above them, the restaurant, which had frozen to listen, also cheered, and there were even whistles and stomps. Saina replaced the microphone and stepped down from the little stage, and everyone went cheerfully back to their meals and drinks, exactly as she'd meant them to.

Tex and Laura, however, stared at her when she returned to the bar.

"That was…interesting," Tex said diplomatically.

"Beautiful," Laura was quick to add. "You do have a gorgeous voice."

"Yes, ma'am," Tex agreed.

"But I thought I was going to enlist in some crazy zombie army for a few moments there," Laura confessed.

Saina looked at her in consternation. She shouldn't *remember* that fleeting compulsion.

She looked over at Tex thoughtfully. They both looked rattled, but not enchanted.

"I wonder if it is because you are mates," Saina said suddenly. "Most people don't have clear memory of siren manipulation."

Tex and Laura looked at each other and shrugged in unison. Their connection was so tangible and beautiful. Saina allowed herself a pang of envy. That was what Bastian thought they had. It was a more lovely fantasy than anything she could have woven for him.

To her surprise, they did not seem to be afraid of her after that. Tex handed her drink back across the bar, and Laura gave her a twinkling smile and went to take drink orders from the newcomers to the bar, and do a quick round to make sure everyone else was still satisfied. A pair of giggly girls took the karaoke stage after her, teasing each other as they made their song selection from the menu.

"Saina?"

Saina froze at Scarlet's familiar voice and turned slowly to face her.

Scarlet looked no more enchanted than Tex and Laura had. Did she have a mate, too? She looked more put together than she had the last time they'd met, her bright hair pulled tightly back without a single strand escaping.

"Yes, ma'am?" Saina said with a crooked smile, trying to look brave.

"A word, if you don't mind." Scarlet did not wait for her response, but turned and clicked away with her sensible business shoes into the darkness past the bar deck to the stairs down to the pool deck. Saina scrambled after her, feeling shabby and chastised in her cheap flip-flops.

At the bottom of the steps, Scarlet continued down the pool deck, pausing only to pick up a towel that Saina had missed, draped at the foot of one of the lounge chairs.

At the dark end of the pool, where the deck wrapped around to overlook the beach, she finally stopped so that Saina could catch up with her. The chatter from the bar and restaurant faded to a hum and the chorus of night frogs and insects made a pleasant drone against the waves lapping the beach below.

"That was an impressive show," Scarlet said, her voice carefully neutral.

"It wasn't what I...expected," Saina said honestly in return.

How much did the resort owner know about the pool of power underneath the resort, Saina wondered.

"You showed restraint."

Well, she knew something, then.

Saina lifted her chin in challenge. "I'm a siren," she told Scarlet frankly. "Restraint may not be something we're known for, but I promised no harm to your resort."

Scarlet smiled in the faint light. "I'm pleased to see that you recognize the gravity of a contract," she said. Then, unexpectedly, "I was impressed with your performance as a lifeguard today, but I was perhaps unnecessarily dismissive when you told me you were a performer earlier. If you choose to stay here at Shifting Sands with Bastian, I would be pleased to put you on our entertainment schedule."

Saina suspected that was as close to an apology as Scarlet would get, and it was gracious. She was touched. "I would love that," she said in an uncharacteristic rush—then she remembered that she would be leaving in a few days and the familiar pang of regret squeezed her chest. "But I...won't be staying."

Scarlet's expression was not surprised. "You plan to leave before Bastian returns," she said dryly.

Saina pursed her lips, not exactly answering. "He's not my mate, though he thinks he is. And I have unfinished business to take care of. I don't mean to waste your time."

"I have no patience for drama," Scarlet warned her.

"Yes, ma'am," Saina started to say, then she staggered in place, clutching her chest and gasping for air.

Everything was black pain, then Saina was aware that Scarlet had her by the arm, looking her anxiously in the face.

"Bastian," she choked helplessly. "Bastian, you idiot!"

CHAPTER 28

*B*astian fell, tumbling without purpose.

He was distantly aware of Keylor's roar of triumph above him as he tumbled through the clouds. He'd failed Saina, lost his bid to free her Voice. There was nothing left.

Bastian, you idiot!

Saina's voice flared in his mind, sharp and angry.

I had to try, he told her, apologetically.

You have to come back to me, she said fiercely. *Now!*

Bastian was tired, and fighting with her seemed like more work than twisting, folding his wings against his back and diving into the ocean surface that was rushing up at him. He had, at least, been able to lead their fight out over the water.

As he broke through the waves and was once again cradled in the comfortable saltwater he knew so well, he thought belatedly that he should have brought the fight here, to his own element. Keylor, even with goldshot coursing through his veins, wouldn't have stood a chance against him here.

Air, Bastian. Go up and breathe now. Saina's voice in his head was all that could make him move again, and he obediently broke the surface again, pain blossoming in his chest as he drew in a heavy breath. *What did he do to you?* Bastian couldn't tell what was her agony and what was his.

Kicked my ass, he said. *Sideways.* He had to add defensively, *But only because he was dosed up on goldshot.* Did it sound like an excuse?

I could have told you that he would be, Saina said in exasperation. *Bastian, you have got to tell me your stupid plans beforehand so I can talk you out of them.*

I will, Bastian said meekly.

Go breathe again, Saina chided him. Bastian hadn't even realized he'd gone beneath again, half drifting rather than swimming. Swimming hurt.

He broke the surface too close to a ship. He squinted at it in tired confusion. They wouldn't see him, of course. He was masked in the way that dragons naturally were, and only other mythic shifters would see him in this form.

Slowly, as it bore down on him, he realized it was a container ship, chugging south at a steady clip, faster than he'd be able to swim in his current state. It should pass Shifting Sands in just a day or so. He dove just as it came upon him, and rolled, shuddering at the effort, to come up alongside it, hooking one forearm into the docking clips and letting it drag him forwards.

Clever Bastian, Saina said in his head. *I will come meet you.*

Am I clever, or an idiot? Bastian found the energy to tease, shifting his grip to ease the pain in his chest. *Make up your mind.*

You're both, Saina said. *My dear, clever idiot.*

CHAPTER 29

"*I* have to go to him," Saina told Scarlet, as she realized the red-haired woman was still holding her up with one arm. "He's hurt, he needs me."

She could stand again and Scarlet let go of her carefully.

"Is there anything you need?"

Bastian, Saina thought achingly. *I need Bastian.* She shook her head to clear it, and Scarlet took it as an answer.

Scarlet sighed. "Our boat has not been replaced or I would offer you the use of it. Our usual alternative would be to have Bastian himself do an airlift, but that is of course not possible. I could check the guest list and see if we have any other dragons at the resort currently who may be able to take you, but I don't recall any."

Saina suspected that the offer was only a courtesy, that Scarlet had the list memorized. "I will swim," she said firmly. "He has caught a ride on a freighter headed this way, so it won't be long until I can get to him." She looked down at herself. "I should get the first aid kit." She would be able to shift anything she was wearing with her, and it might come in handy. She remembered that it was resort property. "Er, may I borrow it?"

"Yes," Scarlet said promptly. Then she added, "Saina?"

Saina braced herself to meet any argument against her departure.

"We're all very fond of Bastian," the owner said gently. "Bring him back safely."

"I will," Saina promised firmly.

She had to.

CHAPTER 30

*B*astian let the ship drag him in a daze through most of a day, exhausted muscles cramping and wounds stinging from saltwater as they continued to ooze precious blood.

He could dimly hear sailors arguing over the poor performance of the vessel he was clinging to and knew he must be slowing it considerably.

Saina remained close in his head, teasing him, reminding him to breathe if he let his head slip beneath the surface for too long, even singing to him when the pain grew unbearable.

His strength felt like it was coming to an end when Saina finally told him, *Let go. I'm here.*

He opened gleaming eyes, not even aware that he'd closed them, and groaned, slowly let his cramping forearm release the ship. It was full night, and he could not see her at first, but her hands on his nose let him breathe freely as they sank to the bottom of the ocean.

Saina, he said weakly, drifting down.

My treasure, she said sweetly, her loose hair tickling sensitive scales on his dragon face as she leaned into it with her arms wrapping around him.

They reached the bottom of the ocean with a lazy, gentle

landing in soft sand. A stingray that had been hiding there high-tailed away from his monstrous shape.

Bastian drowsed as she swam the length of his body, making angry, concerned noises over the cracked scales and wounds, gentle hands exploring the damage.

You aren't bleeding badly anymore, she said at last.

Just need to rest, heal, Bastian said, fighting to stay conscious. *Sleep.*

You sleep, she said fiercely, laying a kiss on his big head. *I will watch and let you breathe.*

Bastian had never felt safer.

CHAPTER 31

*B*astian groaned as he settled into the sand, wrapped his tail over his feet, and closed his giant eyes. It was darker with them closed, but Saina was relieved to hear his breathing grow steady as he fell into sleep. She found that he continued to breathe easily as long as she was within arm's length and she inspected the scaled length of him again.

Satisfied that nothing else could be done to make him more comfortable, Saina curled into the hollow by his neck, where his tail made a perfect resting place.

Nothing dared to disturb them, but Saina didn't allow herself to sleep. She did sing, a wordless, watery song of comfort for Bastian, tangled with a warning to anything that might encroach.

As dawn began to send tendrils of color into the dark water, Bastian stirred at last.

I'm here, Saina told him at once, letting her voice rest.

I failed you, Bastian sighed.

That's the first thing you think of? Saina scolded him.

You are the first thing I will always think of, Bastian responded. *And the last thing when I sleep.*

Saina couldn't reply for a long moment, and she suspected that she would have been crying if she hadn't already been bathed in saltwater. *How do you feel?* she was finally able to ask.

In answer, Bastian unwrapped his tail and stretched his body, creaking and wincing as he uncoiled. *Better*, he said in surprise. *Better than I expected.*

We're still a ways from Shifting Sands, Saina told him. *Can you make the trip, or is it better to stay here another day?*

Let's go home, Bastian said.

Alright, Saina agreed reluctantly. She would have liked to see Bastian gain more strength first.

They were almost halfway back before Saina recognized that she had unthinkingly accepted Shifting Sands as her own home as well.

They swam at her speed, which would have been ridiculously slow for Bastian at any other time, but it was a terrible effort for him now.

When they reached the reef protecting the beach of Shifting Sands, Saina convinced Bastian to shift to human.

"I'm a lifeguard now," she reminded him. "You should listen to me."

She pulled him gently the rest of the way to shore, using the very carry they had practiced in the pool.

They rose from the surf on the resort beach in human form, Saina wriggling up under his arm so that some of Bastian's exhausted weight was on her as they waded through the waves up onto the sand.

Sunbathing guests greeted them with surprise, and someone offered a bottle of water from the little beach bar. Saina realized that Bastian was dressed in a fine silk suit, absolutely destroyed by blood and saltwater where it hadn't been ripped and torn. His human skin showed bruising that had been masked by his dragon scales.

Tex met them at the bottom of the stairs to the beach and took Bastian's other arm over his own shoulder to help them up the steps.

"His room," Saina gasped. "His hoard will help him heal fastest."

Bastian was staggering and made a noise that might have been protest. He wouldn't want anyone else seeing his hoard, she realized, and then Travis was taking the rest of his weight from her. She fought down a pang of jealousy as the two helped Bastian across the pool deck and up the next flight of stairs.

Scarlet was waiting on the bar deck, but to Saina's relief, only looked concerned, not the slightest bit angry.

The owner did not move to delay them, only surveyed the activity and exchanged a wordless nod of greeting with Saina as they went past. Guests openly stared, and Scarlet walked across the tile to personally reassure them that everything was under control while Tex and Travis manhandled Bastian through the staff door.

Saina wondered what Scarlet would tell their audience.

Laura or Jenny met them there, Saina honestly wasn't sure which. She was wearing the white apron of the spa, her hands still in plastic gloves as protection from whatever she had been working on.

"Is he...?" she asked.

"He's going to be fine," Saina said truthfully. "He just needs to rest and heal up."

There were so many stairs. Narrow steps that the three men didn't even fit on together past the staff gate, broad steps along the main path, then three flights of stairs within the staff house. Saina didn't pause to find out what house names they were currently considering.

At the door to his room, Bastian gathered himself. "I can do this," he said, shrugging off Travis and Tex and reaching into a battered pocket for his key. Lifting his arms up to the lock made him groan, and Saina took the key from him without protest.

"*I* can do this," she said firmly.

To the other two, she smiled her gratitude. "We've got it from here, boys," she said lightly while Bastian clung to the doorframe. "I can get him into bed."

"No doubts there," Travis said archly.

"Yes, ma'am," Tex said more diplomatically, elbowing Travis in the ribs.

As they turned away and tromped back down the stairs, Saina unlocked the room and helped Bastian limp into the room to fall face forward into his bed.

CHAPTER 32

astian swam back to consciousness, found blissful contentment in Saina's presence and the harmony of his hoard, and went immediately back to sleep.

The second time he came awake, she was sitting cross-legged on the bed beside him, and he recognized that the smell of the food she was holding was what had woken him.

She smiled when he stirred.

"I thought that something tasty from Chef might coax you back to the waking world," Saina said.

Bastian groaned as he sat up. His wounds had all healed into fresh scars, but he felt very much as if he'd been tenderized by something large and unfriendly.

And he was famished.

Saina fed him the first few bites and he felt his energy begin to return, rising with his appetite. It was some sort of creamy, herb-flavored pasta, with thick, homemade noodles.

He took the fork from her and fed himself when she seemed too slow.

"You slept for two days," she told him, handing him a tumbler of cool water to wash it down with. "But you certainly look better for it."

Bastian downed the water and handed the glass back. "I should have known better than to challenge Keylor."

Saina balled up a fist and hit him in the shoulder. "Damn straight."

It didn't hurt as much as Bastian had feared.

"And what was with having a knock-down, dragon-out fight? I thought you dragons just listed your hoards to each other and the winner was the one worth more!"

Bastian snorted. "Maybe that's what those anemic European dragons do, but New World dragons have never had to worry as much about collateral." He looked around his hoard, feeling ashamed. "And I would have lost that fight, anyway."

"Because Keylor has *gold*?" Saina scoffed. She ran her hand along the sea glass that hung above the bed, making it chime. "Your hoard is *tuned*."

She touched a shell nestled in the netting above the headboard. "You have a perfect unbroken ammonoid shell."

She rolled off the bed and danced across the room to the anchor. "This anchor is from the *Morning Star*, lost north of Australia in 1814. The wreck was never found!"

"Keylor wouldn't even know what to do if I started listing these," Bastian laughed. "He'd sprain something laughing."

"His loss," Saina said with a shrug, returning to the bed.

"You are the crown of my fortune," Bastian said, reaching for her.

She came willingly into his arms, tickling his neck with her kiss.

"Do you accept that you are my mate now?" He had to ask.

She drew back and gazed into his eyes. "I don't know about mates," she confessed. "It seems like a far-fetched fairy tale to me. But..." she placed her hand on Bastian's chest. "I cannot deny that you are a part of me. The very best part."

Bastian put hands on either side of her face and kissed her. "My treasure," he said happily.

He kissed her until his muscles ached, then drew back. "What are we going to do about your Voice?" he asked soberly.

Her eyes grew shadowed. "I'll think of something," she vowed. "I have to."

Bastian brushed her hair back from her face. "We'll think of something," he said confidently.

Saina's eyes narrowed thoughtfully. "Your parents, they are very strict, and honorable?"

"There's a reason that draconian is a term for being harsh and exacting," Bastian said dryly. "I think that the only thing my parents value more than honor is the nobility they lack."

"They aren't royalty? I sort of assumed that because of their edict for your return, they were trying to keep their lines clean."

"Rich, of course, but neither has ever really forgiven themselves for their own low origins. I guess they hoped to gain some sort of royal stink for themselves if I married into it."

"Intriguing," Saina said. "But I'm not sure how to work that to our advantage. Now, when you were disgraced, did you forfeit your hoard?"

Bastian gave a dry bark of a laugh. "I would have, but no one wanted it."

"That's more useful," she said thoughtfully.

"What do you have in mind?" Bastian asked suspiciously.

"I'm not sure yet," she said slyly. "But I think we may need Chef's help."

CHAPTER 33

*A*fter assuring Bastian that he could not help with the first phase of her plan, Saina reluctantly left him. Even with a rainbow of bruises and a crushed ego, he was the most intoxicating man she had ever met. She wondered if he didn't have a little bit of siren in him somewhere, the way he enchanted her.

Chef was on the restaurant deck. It was the end of the breakfast service window, and a few guests were lingering, enjoying a last cup of coffee or relishing a last sweet pastry or piece of fruit. Chef often liked to come out at this time, or whenever the kitchen wasn't busy, and mingle with guests. He was a charming mix of friendly and professional and Saina wondered if he ever broke out in song as he did in the kitchen.

He was standing by the table of one of the largest women that Saina had ever seen.

"I insist you sit," the woman was saying, indicating the opposite chair with an imperious fork. "I cannot make informed decisions with you hovering around like a common servant." Her words were kind, but brooked no argument.

Chef sat, looking unaccountably as if he would prefer to kneel.

Saina tried not to fidget, and Chef caught sight of her over the woman's shoulder.

"Saina," he said, rising again with impeccable politeness. The seated woman gave a noisy sigh. "How is Bastian doing?"

"He's awake," Saina said, moving into the social ring of the table as the woman looked around at her. "Ma'am," she said in polite greeting.

"This is Magnolia," Chef introduced, bowing in her direction.

"And you must be Saina," Magnolia said, giving her an openly appraising look. "I cannot count how many hearts you must have broken by being Bastian's mate. Our lifeguard has been coveted by many!"

That was not the fashion in which sirens usually broke hearts. "I...ah, yes, I'm Saina," she said, caught off-guard.

Magnolia offered a hand of round bejeweled fingers to delicately shake. "A delight to meet you. I am looking forward to hearing you sing. I have heard so much!"

That wasn't usually a good thing, Saina thought wryly.

"What can I do for you?" Chef asked. "You look like a woman on a mission."

Saina glanced sideways at Magnolia. "I came to ask for a favor."

Her cautious look did not go unnoticed. "Whatever mischief you are planning, I will find out eventually," Magnolia said arrogantly. "And if you two don't sit, I shall become cross."

Saina and Chef both sat obediently and Saina gave Magnolia as frank an appraisal as she'd received. Violet eyes looked back from a serene face ending in unabashed extra chins. Gorgeous auburn hair was perfectly styled down past the seat of her groaning chair.

Her gaze was sharp and intelligent, and warm with friendliness.

Finally, Saina smiled. "Here's what I need..."

After Chef approved of her plan, Saina walked down from the restaurant deck past the bar towards her cottage.

She waved at Tex, behind the bar, and Laura, who was clearing tables, and winced at the 'No Lifeguard on Duty' sign beside the pool below. Scarlet hadn't said one word about their delinquency, but Saina knew that this tolerance wouldn't last indefinitely.

As she went to the gate that would take her home, a wild-haired figure stepped in front of her.

"My friend doesn't trust you," the young woman said.

Saina took an automatic step back. "Who is your friend?" she asked in alarm. She had heard of Gizelle, and spotted her several times in her gazelle form from across the lawn, but had never spoken to the shy girl.

Gizelle stood up tall, unexpectedly as tall as Saina, every bone in sharp relief under her pale skin. "I'm friends with the stars in the sky and the sunlight in shadows. But the ocean eats the shore."

Saina started to speak, and fell instead.

She was standing in a strange field, sunlight illuminating grass endlessly in all directions, but when she slowly lifted her head, moving as if she was in an ocean of molasses, the sky above was black and featureless.

She opened her mouth to cry out or sing her way back, and was surprised to find that she was entirely mute. It should have alarmed her, but everything felt impossibly heavy and meaningless. She wanted to lie down and sleep, but even that much motion seemed like too much effort.

Then she was blinking in the brilliant tropical sunshine again.

"Gizelle, honey, what are you doing?"

Saina shook her head and staggered a few steps away. She felt drunk and tingly, as if all of her limbs had been asleep. She recognized Tex's voice, and then Laura's.

"Are you alright? Saina?" There was an odd clicking sound, and Saina realized that Laura was snapping her fingers in front of Saina's face.

"I, ah, what happened?"

Gizelle was still looking at her, but from behind a curtain of her salt-and-pepper hair now, a shy smile blooming on her face.

"Gizelle, sweetie, you're not supposed to do that to people," Tex was scolding her gently.

"It's okay," Gizelle told him, cocking her head at him. "I like her now."

Then she was scampering away.

"This is a very strange place," Saina said in confusion.

"You've only seen it on its slow days," Laura said wryly.

CHAPTER 34

*B*astian's head hurt.

The sunset sent stabbing rays of light into his eyes and he squinted at it with a draconic scowl. The last of the beach sunbathers and swimmers were packing up their bags and returning to the resort for their dinners and drinks, and he was glad to see them go.

He shifted to human to collect the chairs and the minor litter they'd left behind. The beach bar was briefly straightened, and Bastian bundled up the trash to take with him. It felt impossibly heavy.

Saina was waiting for him at the top of the beach steps, and his heart lifted.

In the last rays of the sun, she was a dark-haired, golden goddess, all curves and swirls. She took the bag of trash from him and took his hand in her own. Her fingers were strong and his skin against hers was like the touch of a unicorn's horn in tainted water; he could feel the headache ebb away and the black mood that had haunted him faded.

"How are you feeling?" she asked, after she had tossed the trash and helped him pick up all the towels on the pool deck and reorder the chairs.

"Better," Bastian said stoically.

"Liar," Saina scoffed.

"Why'd you ask if you knew the answer?" Bastian sulked. They were standing at the far end of the pool deck, looking out over the dark beach, and he leaned down on the railing.

Saina answered with a kiss on his cheek. "Being grouchy is totally normal for goldshot withdrawal," she said with understanding.

"It's awful," Bastian admitted. "I have never felt so weak and useless and hungry."

"Dinner is being served now, but we could grab something from the staff house or the back of the kitchen."

"That's not the kind of hungry," Bastian complained.

Saina put an arm over his shoulder, pressing herself against his side. "I'm so sorry," she said, leaning her head against him. "This wouldn't have happened if it weren't for me."

"I'm not sorry," Bastian said swiftly. "I mean, this is awful, but I will get over it eventually. I would take this a hundred times over for the chance of meeting you."

"I'm not worth it," Saina said bitterly. "Sirens are never worth their ticket price."

"You are," Bastian told her sincerely. "I would take goldshot hangovers for a century to spend one day with you."

She looked at him in wonder. "You really mean that."

"Dragons are always honest."

"Mermaids never are," she retorted.

"I will always trust you," Bastian said firmly.

"Then you're a fool," Saina said, with her crooked true smile.

Bastian smiled at her and reached to smooth a lock of hair back from her face. "A glad one."

She kissed him, then, wriggling between him and the railing to put arms around his neck.

Her lips were healing, chasing the last vestiges of pain from his head.

When he drew back for breath, he had to ask, "Are you sure about this plan?"

"I'm only sure of one thing in this world," Saina said gravely. "And that's you."

CHAPTER 35

Saina wasn't sure how this had turned into such a production. The little conference room behind the kitchen was crammed with people and suggestions. Her pink suitcase was open on the table on a plastic trash bag. The goldshot sludge had dried to a brittle crust.

Travis had brought an array of plastering tools and a bucket of gypsum. Chef had bins of flour and sugar.

"I don't want to kill him if he actually takes it," Saina said firmly, looking skeptically at Travis' bucket. "It just needs to fool him for a little while."

Laura picked up a crust of goldshot with a gloved hand. Jenny, like a double-image beside her, poked a piece with her pen. "Are you sure it's safe to touch?"

"It won't have any effect on you unless you're a dragon," Saina promised.

Jenny's face quirked into a smile. "Well, I don't think so, but I didn't know I was an otter for the longest time, so who knows!" She kept her bare hands well away.

Chef boldly plucked a rind of the substance off and held it up to the light. It had a slight iridescent sparkle to it. "How heavy did you say the cakes were?"

"Maybe 3 kilos apiece," Saina guessed, showing the size with her hands. "Denser than you'd think."

Half the staff looked at her blankly while the others nodded. "A little more than 6 pounds," she added for the Americans and English.

"A quarter of a brick of gold," Breck offered. Saina wasn't even sure why the waiter was there, or how he knew the weight of a brick of gold.

"Fruitcake," Graham suggested dryly. Even the dour landscaper had shown up for the meeting Saina hadn't known she'd called.

Chef looked thoughtful. "I could do a dense cake and we probably have enough here to frost one over with the real stuff." He crumbled the piece in his hand and tested how well it pressed back together. "I'll have to make a binder. Sugar, probably. That will match the sparkle and set up nicely."

"Will he smell the difference?" Tex asked. "I've known some drinkers who could tell the watered-down stuff from across the bar. And they were just human."

"It will be wrapped in plastic, and the suitcase is so saturated with the stuff, I imagine it will mask the weakness of the rest," Saina guessed. "Bastian should be able to give us an idea of how well it will work."

"And if he does eat it?" Tex queried. "You don't offer a shot to a recovering alcoholic."

Saina had wrestled with the morality of every aspect of their plan. "I am bound not to work magic on him, or I could try to sing it out of him. Fortunately, goldshot works itself entirely out of the system within a few weeks of being clean, so all we have to do is see that he doesn't get a supply for a while."

"I'm not sure there's even a full dose here," Chef said. "It's enough to frost a brick, and maybe fool him, but I'm not convinced it would actually be a fix."

"We'll need to clean the outside of the suitcase," Jenny suggested, lifting the open lid with her pen.

Travis scraped a shard of the goldshot off the suitcase with one of his tools. "I can color match this. We can pack the suitcase with fake bricks and one real one."

"Almost real," Chef corrected.

"What if he grabs the wrong brick to inspect?" Laura asked.

There was a moment of silence, then Wrench, standing in the back with his big arms crossed, suggested, "Take the right one out and put it on top of the suitcase when you open the negotiations."

There was a chorus of approval for the idea.

Wrench gave a dry laugh. "It's like you've never been in on a drug deal before."

"This is a fascinating conversation to walk in on."

Scarlet stood in the doorway; none of them had even heard her open the door.

The staff froze in a tableau of guilt.

"I'm sure this proposed drug deal has everything to do with the fact that *only* my lifeguard is on duty right now, in the middle of a busy afternoon," she said mildly, looking straight at Saina.

Saina cleared her throat to formulate an explanation, but Chef beat her to the punch.

"We're all helping Miss Saina get her grandmother out of a bit of a pinch," he explained simply.

"And it's not really a drug," Travis added. "Most of it will be gypsum."

"And technically, she isn't even dealing for the false drug," Jenny added. "It's really just a standard contract negotiation with a red herring. It might not hold up in a real court, but it doesn't actually have to."

"And it's her *grandmother*," Laura insisted.

Breck joked, "We've got to get her voice back from the sea witch before the sun sets on the third day!"

Tex elbowed Breck.

"Well, she got her true love's kiss already and that didn't work," Breck protested.

Saina, still locking gazes with Scarlet, shut her mouth. She wasn't even sure how the others had gleaned so much of the story from her, but she was touched by their quick protection, if not the Disney references.

"I have something that may help you," Scarlet said mildly.

In her hand was a syringe.

CHAPTER 36

*B*astian back-winged into the familiar courtyard carefully. It had been a week since his last visit here, and he was significantly healed from his last encounter with Keylor, but he wasn't entirely sure he was ready for this. Saina's gentle hand on his neck reminded him of his purpose and he opened his mouth and roared a dragon challenge.

The courtyard still had some of the damage from his last visit, he was rather glad to realize; if it had been entirely repaired, he would have felt less effective.

Keylor did not keep them waiting long.

I am surprised to see you alive, he said derisively. *But I should have known the ocean wouldn't finish you off as it would have a* real *dragon.*

Bastian lowered his neck to the ground and let Saina hop off, dragging her heavy pink suitcase behind her.

Ah. You are only here as the siren's lackey. Keylor snorted a trail of dark smoke in derision and ignored Bastian to look greedily at Saina.

I have something you want, Saina said, her audible voice humming lightly in counterpart. She unzipped the suitcase and put a single, plastic-wrapped gray brick on the top of it.

Don't attempt to enchant me, Keylor said, drawing his head back.

I already agreed once not to, Saina said, *and I keep my promises forever.* Whether she wanted to or not, she couldn't break the contract she'd made.

Keylor sniffed. *I thought by now that you had failed in your goal.*

I don't fail, Saina said loftily. *But I've had a better offer in the meantime. I'm here to see if you're willing to change the terms of our agreement.*

Bastian was sizing Keylor up as they treated. He was less impressive than Bastian remembered, and his eyes were more orange than red. Saina had been right about his access to the goldshot—he was running out. Which was why he was eyeing the suitcase with such lust.

I still have your Voice, Keylor sneered. *You dare to ask for more?*

Keep my Voice, Saina laughed. *I have my own song. What use would an old woman be to me?*

Keylor drew up. *What is it you wish to trade, then?*

The crown of Viracocha, Saina said smoothly.

Keylor's snort of laughter had flame, and Bastian, unable to stop himself, crouched to protect his mate.

Well-trained, brother-not, Keylor mocked. *Or well-sung, I should say.*

Saina let her hum raise into an aria, and snapped her fingers at Bastian. He settled back on his haunches as if against his own will.

Can we deal? Saina pushed. *Or are you wasting my time?*

You want me to steal from my parents' hoard. That's a bold request from a half-fish.

I'm a siren who knows what she wants, Saina said, inspecting one of her hands as if her nails were a hundred times more interesting than two gigantic dragons posturing at each other. *And I have other buyers if you aren't willing.*

Keylor gnashed teeth the size of her forearm, casting longing looks at the suitcase. The smell was deliciously tantalizing to Bastian, too, but he fought back the desire, reminding himself that it was only false.

Keylor's eyes narrowed then. *Why would you send my brother-not to challenge me for your Voice, if you did not desire it?*

I didn't direct him to do that, Saina said with the unmistakable ring of truth. *He's the fool who came up with that idea. The suitcase for the crown,* she repeated. *Is it a contract?*

Yessssssss, Keylor hissed angrily.

Then Saina stopped singing.

You would enter a contract to steal from our hoard?

The illusion that Saina had been holding dropped with her song, revealing two dragons, one a deep navy blue, the other a forest green, perched on the highest of the courtyard walls.

Keylor, recognizing the trap, tried to protest, *Father, I wouldn't.*

The blue dragon leaped down into the courtyard. *You entered a contract you didn't intend to keep?* He asked fiercely. *I don't know which is worse.*

Keylor, the smaller green dragon sitting above them said reproachfully.

Keylor writhed, and Bastian was not a big enough dragon not to feel smug about his discomfort.

Do you disinherit this dragon? Saina asked pointedly.

Both of his parents turned from Keylor and gave Saina their full attention. To her credit, she didn't so much as squirm.

Who are you? his mother asked, not gently.

I am Saina. Do you disinherit this dragon? she repeated.

Bastian's father glanced in disgust at Keylor, who was still belly down in the courtyard trying to formulate a defense. *Yes,* he said reluctantly, clearly angry and betrayed.

Father, no! Keylor protested. *It was not such an offense.*

Saina ignored him. *Then his hoard is forfeit to you and I will treat with you in his stead. I seek the release of my Voice.*

You will offer us this vile contraband in trade, and come here with lies expecting us to treat with you? his father protested with a snort of flame.

Neither, said Saina. *I have been entirely truthful. I told him I had my own song and asked what use she would be. I told him I had a better offer. He drew his own conclusions.*

You can't do this, Keylor snarled.

Then what do you offer? Bastian's father ignored Keylor.

The truth, Saina said. *I gave you the truth about your son.*

Bastian met his mother's luminous eyes briefly. Her glance slid away quickly.

Keylor, as furious at being ignored as he was at this unexpected turn of events, gathered himself and just as Bastian was going to risk interrupting the negotiation in warning, he leaped—not for the suitcase drenched in goldshot, but for Saina, his claws outstretched.

CHAPTER 37

*T*his *might actually work,* Saina thought privately, hardly
daring to hope. Dragons kept promises, but they were
masterful at loopholes; that was why they made such terrific lawyers.
She kept her chin high and was careful with her words. Dragon
expression was hard to read, and she was watching Bastian's father
carefully.

She didn't see Keylor's attack until silver claws were slashing
at her.

Before she could so much as stagger backwards, Bastian was
diving between them, driving into Keylor with a roar. *That is my
mate!*

Saina fell back against a fountain as the two tumbled in a flurry
of beating wings and lashing tails. Her hand came away from her
chest bloodied, but it was quickly obvious that it was little more than
a surface scratch.

She couldn't hear what Bastian was saying—it was private to
Keylor only, and Keylor's responses were similarly narrow-banded,
but the fight intensified. Over and over, Keylor attacked, and
Bastian drove him back and released him, withdrawing and giving
his brother a chance to surrender.

Keylor wanted no part of surrender.

Keylor sank teeth into Bastian's shoulder and held on like a pit bull while Bastian shook him, staggering and dragging him along a stone balustrade.

Why won't you stop them? Saina shrieked at their parents, who were both watching the fight with detachment, stepping back delicately whenever the battle grew too close.

Neither of those are our sons now, Bastian's father said coldly.

Saina balled her hands at her sides. She wanted to run over and pound her fists on his uncaring blue scales, but she knew too much about dragon honor to believe that it would make any difference.

Bastian rolled over the cold stone and Keylor finally let go of his shoulder. Saina was alarmed at the amount of blood, dark against his green scales. *I just put him back together*, she thought crossly.

The two dragons circled each other, snarling and flaming. Bastian limped slightly on his injured shoulder, but otherwise seemed faster and stronger than his brother.

Then Keylor paused, his attention caught by the forgotten pink suitcase. Saina saw that he was trembling, and knew that he must be feeling the withdrawal from the goldshot fiercely now.

Take the bait, she willed him, but she couldn't put any magic in it because she had promised not to.

Fortunately, she didn't have to. Keylor led their circling closer to the suitcase, and dashed at the last moment in, to snatch the plastic-wrapped brick from the top and swallow it in one fast gulp, smashing the suitcase aside.

Bastian darted forward, trying to take advantage of Keylor's distraction, but Keylor dodged him and leaped to the top of one of the walls. For a moment, Saina thought — hoped — that he would simply abandon the battle and flee. Bastian roared at him, but didn't follow, glancing back instead to assure himself that Saina was safe.

Keylor, his eyes already starting to swirl more red, snarled and jumped down upon him, wicked claws spread.

Bastian reared to meet him, wings beating for additional forward momentum as they clashed.

Saina bit her lip as they tore and flamed at each other, then ducked and took cover behind the fountain as the battle raged closer. Bastian just had to last a short while, but Keylor was stronger and faster now, Bastian's advantage gone now that Keylor had the goldshot coursing through his system.

Keylor's attacks grew stronger and he pinned Bastian, striking dizzying blows at the side of his brother's head. Bastian flamed and writhed, wrenching free just as Keylor moved to bite him in the already wounded shoulder. His actions became more and more defensive as Keylor stepped up his attacks, darting away at the last moment to slash as he leaped out of the way.

Saina's nails cut crescents into her palms as she watched through the smoke-hazed courtyard. Each escape was narrower, each attack more enraged, and she had no idea how long Bastian would need to keep dodging.

She couldn't sing her magic into Keylor, but she could into Bastian, she realized.

She planted her feet and opened her mouth to sing:

> Stronger than you've ever known,
> A king lacking only a throne.
> You will always be
> Royalty to me.

Saina couldn't direct their battle, but she could remind Bastian of his strength. *Your hoard is better*, she whispered at him. *Your heart is truer.*

Bastian crashed with Keylor into another wall, and they were a snarling, tail-lashing, wing-beating ball of dragon together.

Did Bastian look stronger? Saina sang louder, desperate to help him, wincing at every blow and slash.

Then, just as Keylor turned to bite Bastian's briefly exposed neck, he shifted, and for one ridiculous moment, was dangling as a human from Bastian's scales, holding on only by wholly inadequate human teeth as his limbs flailed.

CHAPTER 38

*B*astian knew he'd made an error of exhaustion, just as he turned too late to protect his neck and saw Keylor lunge for him, teeth bared.

Then, finally, the substance they'd put in the goldshot brick that Saina had scraped together from her sodden suitcase took hold and Keylor was an ineffective human, surprised and dismayed by his unplanned shift.

As Keylor fell from the height of a dragon, Bastian twisted to catch him in one clawed foot.

The temptation to squeeze the life from his brother was as painfully keen as his desire for the goldshot that he still reeked of. Keylor had tried to hurt his mate, and had held her dearest relative hostage. He deserved death. He deserved painful death.

But Bastian uncurled his claws and put Keylor on the ground, then shifted to face him.

"What are you doing, brother-not?"

As a human, Keylor was less impressive than he was as a dragon; a pasty, thin man with an unpleasant sneer and a tremor in his voice.

"I have no taste for your death," Bastian said gently. "I know that goldshot can make you do vile things, and you have already been stripped of your hoard and your family. I know how that feels, too."

Keylor gnashed his teeth, hunched himself over miserably, then launched himself desperately at Bastian's face with an incoherent cry of rage. His eyes were still red with the goldshot, even in human form.

Bastian, with the human muscles and reflexes of a swimmer, easily backhanded him away into a wall, where he crumpled into unconsciousness.

Saina's voice had died to a cough; the courtyard was filled with acrid dragonsmoke.

Bastian turned to limp towards her, and glowing eyes appeared through the smoke above her curvy form.

Finish your bargaining, Bastian said to them. *Saina's Voice shall be returned to her safely and we will leave you in peace.*

He wondered at the authority in his own mindvoice. His parents had always awed and intimidated him, but now he found that they occupied no place in his thoughts. Only Saina mattered, and he wanted nothing but to turn his back for the final time on the place that had taught him only his weaknesses.

What did you do to Keylor? his mother asked. Was there concern in her voice? Did she love her children, or were they only parts of her own glory, little more than an extension of their hoard, to be judged for their value and nobility?

He wanted a drug, we happened to have one that would constrain him to his human form for a time. Bastian had no desire to explain that the drug had been liberated from the zoo prison of an insane shifter collector who had been hell bent on adding Bastian himself to his collection.

Trickery, his father rumbled, and Bastian found himself bracing for the pang of guilt he should feel for disappointing his progenitor. It was oddly missing. Perhaps he was more tired than he realized.

All an aside to the deal at hand, Saina swiftly interceded. *I offered you my exposure of your son's true nature in exchange for my Voice.*

They returned their attention to her as Bastian staggered the final steps to her side and took her hand in his own.

Riches are a more standard exchange for dragons, his father told her coldly. *There is no value in your part of this exchange.*

I base my offer on your past behavior, Saina said with no kindness. *You cast out your eldest son for something as trivial as compassion. Clearly you value your family reputation above any treasure.*

You are blackmailing us, his mother exclaimed. *You are threatening to tell people about Keylor's dishonor!*

Bastian felt Saina's grim smile. *Blackmail is such an ugly word.*

He tightened his hand in hers. This was the part of the plan with the most uncertainty.

You are a remarkable woman, his father said thoughtfully, and Bastian relaxed. They were impressed by Saina, as they should be. *It is a pity you are not a royal dragon. That would simplify this situation considerably.*

There is a story that sirens were once dragons, his mother added, cocking her head at Saina as she lowered her face to inspect her more closely. *Are you royalty among your kind?*

Saina looked back at the dragons without flinching or stepping back, despite her small comparative size and their impolite crowding. *We have a similar origin story,* she conceded. *But sirens do not have royalty.*

Then she laughed dryly. *But my name does mean 'princess' in Hindi.*

Bastian's parents exchanged a significant look and a private exchange, then turned to Saina.

We would accept this as fulfilling the terms of the contract, his father said proudly.

Bastian had been trying to decide which of his shoulders hurt worst, and whether he could gracefully go sit down on the bench to recover for a moment while his parents treated with Saina, then realized where the conversation had unexpectedly moved.

He blinked up at his father. *You...you'd take me back?*

Even as he tried to wrap his tired mind around the idea, Saina spoke.

You can't have him.

She was drawn up to her full height, tiny against his monstrous parents and she brought them to silence with her statement.

Bastian is **mine,** *by bonds more powerful than family blood or title,* Saina snarled. *He is better than any of you, by any standards of human or dragon or siren, and you* **may not have him.** *He has a family of his own making, in a place that accepts him as he is, where he has a hoard that puts your gaudy pretension to shame, and if you try to take him from me and from his true family, I will hunt you to the ends of the earth and sing the sky down on you.*

Her words echoed in their minds and in their ears. Bastian was not sure when she had started singing the words out loud, but the magic in the courtyard was tangible and full of anger.

She took two firm steps forward. *I came here to treat for my Voice, taken from me by your dishonorable son, and you try to take from me the treasure that you discarded in foolishness. I will give you one chance and only one to redeem yourselves.*

Bastian's parents gaped at her.

Give. Me. My. Voice.

CHAPTER 39

"*A*re you sure about this?"

Bastian's parents had flown away with Keylor's limp form once the deal had been struck. Saina had even managed to make them promise to see him through his withdrawal, using every non-magic negotiating tool that she had.

Saina and Bastian stood alone in the courtyard at last.

"I'm sure," Bastian said firmly, leading her up the steps to the grand entrance.

"I don't want you to feel tricked," Saina insisted. "It isn't fair, and you shouldn't have to."

Bastian drew up at the top of the stairs. "The only thing that isn't fair about it is that they beat me to the punch and robbed me of the chance at a deeply romantic speech that I'd undoubtedly have forgotten in the panic of the moment anyway. You were saved the awkwardness of having to accept a ring from someone who looked like a beached fish with stagefright. As grievances with my parents go, this is fairly far down on the list."

Saina twisted the pearl ring on her finger and smiled foolishly. This was not the bargain she had expected to drive, but she was delighted with the outcome. The rings the dragons had produced from their hoard were surprisingly compatible with their tastes; Bastian's was a simple gold band and hers was a pearl cradled by four diamonds. It was likely that his parents felt like they were ridding their hoard of items too pedestrian to keep.

"Let's go find your Voice," Bastian told her, when all she could do was smile at him.

He took her hand and they walked together into through the modest man-sized door set within the larger door.

Keylor's lair was dragon-sized at the front, but more human-sized to the rear, and a quick search revealed a set of cozy rooms. Saina's heart caught in her throat as an elegant silver-haired figure in a plush chair turned to look at them.

"My Voice!" Saina cried, and rushed forward.

"Heavens, child, it certainly took you long enough to come get me," her grandmother chided her as she rose gracefully from the chair. "And wearing that? Gracious, I hope no one sees us leaving together. I do assume you have come to free me?" The teasing, skeptical tone of her voice was achingly familiar.

Saina flung her arms around the slim figure, catching her in an impulsive embrace.

"Yes, yes," her grandmother said, patting her with exaggerated awkwardness. "I'm sure you're happy to see me."

"We *are* here to free you," Saina said, withdrawing to arm's length. "Your contract with Keylor is dissolved." She had to ask, "Was it terrible here?"

Her Voice sniffed. "The food was dreadful, and the service so spotty. Who only has maid service once a week? The internet connection was barely tolerable for streaming television, and you know how drafty and dry a dragon's lair generally is."

"We'll get you back to the ocean, my Voice," Saina told her, trying not to laugh at the glimpse of amusement in her grandmother's twinkling eyes. "But I want you to meet Bastian first. This is my grandmother, my Voice, Gita."

Bastian came forward from where he'd been lurking in their door for the reunion. He gave Gita his most winning smile and offered a hand. "Ma'am."

Gita looked him over carefully, and did not take the offered hand. "You may address me as your Voice," she conceded. The ring on his finger did not go unnoticed. "I suppose you think you are marrying my granddaughter."

Bastian's smile froze on his face. "Yes, your, er, Voiceness," he stammered. "It was part of the agreement for your release."

"Oh Saina, how dreadful for you!" Gita patted Saina's hand in pity. "I had the perfect man chosen for you. You could have drowned him afterwards, for all I cared, but he would have made beautiful little baby girls."

"My Voice," Saina said gently, covering her delicate hand with her own. "Bastian is my mate. I *want* to marry him." She wasn't sure how much of what her grandmother was saying was in jest, but she answered gravely, serious to the bottom of her soul, and thought she saw a flash of pain in Gita's face.

"Sirens don't have mates, my darling! And sirens certainly don't *marry*." Gita gave Bastian a sweeping look. "And if you did, Saina, sweetheart, I'm sure you could do better."

Poor Bastian looked like a beached dolphin, opening and closing his mouth as he struggled to find something to say.

Saina realized she was humming out of habit when Gita turned to her sharply. "Are you trying to enchant *me*, girl? You *have* learned a lot of bad habits while I was away."

"You!" Gita said imperiously to Bastian, leaning her magic into the musical word. "You may fetch the bags I have packed up in the other room."

Bastian looked befuddled, exchanged a look with Saina, and then politely nodded and walked to get her bags.

Gita watched him go. "Well, isn't that curious. A bit more to him than meets the eye."

"I told you, my Voice, he's my mate. You can't influence him."

"That sounds like a challenge," Gita murmured. "But no matter! Tell me what happened with our pod when I left. Why didn't one of the others come get me, if you were going to take so long about it?"

"Our pod dissolved when you left," Saina said sadly. "They fell into bickering and infighting, and I was the only one who cared to come free you."

"Ungrateful, the lot of them," her Voice sniffed. She patted Saina's hand again, more slowly this time, and Saina thought she saw a glimpse of sorrow in her sea green eyes before she straightened her shoulders. "I suppose you want me to come live with you, in whatever beach hovel that lifeguard will put you in?"

"You'd be welcome at Shifting Sands, my Voice," Saina said, though as she spoke, she wondered exactly how welcome she would actually be. She tried to imagine Gita working for Scarlet and it was nearly as impossible to picture as Scarlet being happy with Gita's presence.

"Oh, that's a shifters-only island resort, isn't it?" Gita said dismissively. "I've heard it's alright, if you don't have real standards."

"The food is very good," Saina said neutrally. She didn't precisely want to encourage the idea.

Gita waved an imperious hand of dismissal. "You two just take me to the ocean and *abandon* me there. I'll find a cruise ship that will take me. I need a little rest and pampering after my long imprisonment."

Saina looked around the well-appointed room, but held her tongue.

Bastian returned, laden with matching suitcases.

"Well, you are a strong one," Gita conceded. "Did you fetch the case from the bathroom?"

"Yes, Ma'am," Bastian said, holding it aloft.

"Maybe you'll do for Saina," she said with faint approval. "As long as she has heavy bags to lift."

They walked together to the courtyard. The smoke had mostly cleared, and the evening sun through the jungle sparkled on green leaves. Somewhere overhead, a toucan cried.

"Where's the car?" Gita asked, once they had reached the bottom of the entrance stairs.

"Ah, we didn't bring a car," Saina said. "I rode here on Bastian."

"I don't need dirty details like that, girl," Gita scolded.

"Bastian is a dragon, my Voice," Saina explained cautiously. "He can fly us wherever we'd like."

"A dragon?!" Gita took an unsteady step backwards, looking at Bastian with new cautiousness. Saina took her arm when she might have stumbled back on the last step.

"A dragon," Saina said firmly. "My dragon."

Gita sniffed. "This day is turning out to be more and more disappointing."

CHAPTER 40

"*A*re you sure we can just leave her here?" Bastian asked, trying not to sound as hopeful as he felt. He'd heard of nightmare in-laws, and even suspected he came with some, but nothing had prepared him for the casual condescendence of Saina's grandmother. He wasn't convinced it was all in jest.

"My Voice will have no trouble finding whatever she needs here," Saina assured him. While they watched, a pair of deckhands leapt to their feet to gather Gita's luggage, practically tripping each other to follow close at her heels. Further down the dock, a man who'd been stacking crates abandoned his task to sweep the deck in advance of her approach.

Bastian could hear the faint strains of her song as she walked away—for good, he could not help but hope.

"Oh gosh," he said insincerely. "I don't know how we'll get in touch to invite her to the wedding."

Saina looked at him sideways. "There's going to be a wedding?"

"We did promise to get married," Bastian reminded her.

Saina blinked, heavy eyelashes over sea green eyes. "I guess I figured we'd just do a walk-in wedding somewhere. They have those in Costa Rica, don't they?"

"We could go through a wedding lawyer," Bastian said, feeling oddly disappointed. "Fill out some paperwork, show your passport and birth certificate. He rounds up some witnesses and it's done. Er, do you have a passport or birth certificate?"

Saina shrugged. "I can wave a piece of paper in front of him and convince him it's one."

"You don't...want a real wedding?" Even Bastian could hear how wistful he sounded.

She smiled at him, her true, crooked smile full of warmth and amusement. "Do *you* want a real wedding?"

Bastian scuffed a foot in the sand. "I do. I want to watch you walk down an aisle towards me. I want all our friends there to witness our vows. I want a giant reception with every fancy dish that Chef knows how to make."

Saina narrowed her eyes. "You want to outshine Tex and Travis' double wedding."

"I guess there's a little dragon competitiveness in me," Bastian admitted. "They're planning to marry early next summer after their court stuff is settled, and I was sort of thinking about an early spring ceremony."

"We'd have to invite your parents," Saina reminded him.

Bastian froze, imagining his parents at Shifting Sands. It was almost as horrifying as the idea of her grandmother. "I've changed my mind," he said swiftly. "It was a terrible idea. Wedding lawyer it is."

"I don't know," Saina teased. "Now I really like the idea. I could throw a bouquet and we could have a fancy dance. Everyone would know I was yours, and boggle at our elegance and beauty."

"Hrm," Bastian said, unconvinced.

Saina moved closer into his arms, sliding her curves along him. "You could peel me out of a fluffy white cupcake dress afterwards."

Bastian swallowed, his imagination doing plenty to fill in the picture. "I'm not sure..." he said.

"Maybe your parents wouldn't come?" Saina suggested, slipping her arms up around his neck.

Bastian kissed her, hands at her waist. "Is that a chance we're willing to take?"

"I'll risk it," Saina purred in his ear.

When he put her down at last, drawing away with bruised lips, Bastian remembered something she'd said. "My parents said that they had a story that sirens used to be dragons, and you said that you had heard a similar origin story."

Saina laughed. "It has significant differences. We say that dragons came from sirens. They were sirens—siren men—who preferred war to love. They could not reconcile their natures, and changed to shifters with two forms, one of scales and violence and one of humankind. I don't have a mermaid voice within me, not like you have a dragon. I am a siren, it's just who I am. Sometimes I have legs and sometimes, I don't."

She tapped the middle of his forehead. "It must be crowded in there."

"That's not where my dragon is," Bastian corrected, catching her hand. He pressed it against his chest, feeling the flutter of his heartbeat against her palm. "He is here, deeper, and it still felt empty before you came."

She looked at him with glowing eyes.

"Marry me," Bastian said, falling to one knee.

"We're already engaged," Saina reminded him, showing him her ring.

Bastian slipped it off her finger. "Pretend we're not," he suggested.

Saina left her hand extended. "Bastian, my love, I will marry you. I pledge my life to you."

Bastian eased the ring back onto her finger. "I love you, Saina," he said, standing up and sweeping her into his arms.

When he'd kissed her breathless, he set her back onto her feet. "Let's go home."

EPILOGUE

> Someone to love,
> Someone to hold.
> A prize of silver,
> A treasure of gold...

*S*aina let the words and the magic with them fade away in the low-lit bar. She gestured for the audience to join her in the final refrain, and they did so eagerly, needing only the tiniest thread of encouragement from her magic. She convinced them that they each sounded amazing.

> Someone to love,
> Someone to hold.
> A prize of silver,
> A treasure of gold!

Saina stepped off the little stage to a round of gleeful applause and a chorus of requests.

"Fight Song!" someone yelled.

"Take Me Down!" someone countered.

"Part of Your World!" Breck hollered down from the restaurant deck above.

There was scattered laughter from the audience members who got the joke. Sania flipped the bird in Breck's direction and gave the rest of the audience a more decorous wave.

They returned to their chatter and drinks cheerfully.

"We might have to get Wrench to provide nightly concert security," Tex joked. "They adore you."

Bastian met her at the bar with a kiss. "They'd let you sing until tomorrow morning," he observed.

"I'm on the schedule for tomorrow at dawn to do a morning meditation," Saina said. "Lydia's doing some kind of certification or training until next week, and Scarlet thought I could probably fill the gap with a morning song-and-stretch sort of thing. If I don't cut them off now, I won't get any sleep first."

"Sleep is overrated," Laura said, from the far side of the bar where she was helping Tex fill drink orders. "And just try to convince me that you'll be getting any tonight. You're just looking for an excuse to head back to your room."

Saina grinned at her, aware of Bastian's arm, which was still around her waist possessively. She was wearing the evening dress that had been salvaged from her sodden suitcase, washed thoroughly clean of the last traces of goldshot.

"I am so glad you're taking over the dawn class," Jenny said, putting a tray of empty glasses down on the bar. "I am incapable of doing yoga at that hour. We spent ten minutes in the child pose this morning before I could even think of anything else to do."

Saina fabricated a yawn. "I may not do much better," she joked. "My only hope is that I won't accidentally sing a lullaby and put us all back to sleep."

She took Bastian's hand and left the cheerfully lit bar behind them as they crossed the bar deck to the staff gate.

The white gravel path past the staff gate was a ribbon ahead of them as they walked, hand-in-hand. The staff house ahead of them, aglow from within, was the home that Saina had never had, that she'd never known she wanted. She could feel the safety and harmony of Bastian's hoard from the doorstep.

The sign on the door had a dozen names crossed out, and Saina read them curiously, then left a puzzled Bastian at the edge of the kitchen to get a pen from the cup on the fridge.

She returned to the front door and in the final space at the bottom of the page, wrote, "The Den."

Bastian, watching over her shoulder, laughed. "It's perfect."

Saina returned the pen to the cup. "It is," she agreed contentedly, and she meant all of it. The name, the house, the resort, the island with its mysterious pool of magic, and most of all, the man beside her.

She turned to take his hand, and could not resist standing up on her tiptoes to kiss him. "Let's go to bed," she said.

"Bed sounds great," Bastian agreed.

Neither of them mentioned sleep, and by the time Bastian had unlocked the door to his hoard, most of their clothing had been already peeled off of each other.

Saina led him by the half unbuttoned shorts to the bed and pulled him into it over her. "My dragon," she breathed. "My mate."

Bastian managed some sort of acrobatics to remove his shorts without losing any skin contact, and was strong and firm along her as he pushed her hair back and kissed her neck. "My fish," he teased in her ear.

"Reptile," Saina countered, drawing gentle nails along his erect member.

Bastian flickered his tongue out at her, and she laughed until he kissed her again, drawing her close.

When he entered her, she knew she'd been wrong. *This* was home, not knowing where he ended and she began. *This* was home, being held in his strong arms. *This* was home, his kisses hot on her neck and his breath ragged in her ear as she arched against him. *This* was home with her mate.

TREASURE SENSE

Bastian's book, Tropical Dragon Diver was one of the novels I was looking forward to writing from the moment I started the series. But I never really answered the question of how he came to the resort in his book, and when I sat down to write this story, I only knew it would start in the sea...

The interface between sky and sea had always fascinated Bastian.

Some days, the ocean was a faintly rolling bolt of silk, and some days it was a roiling cauldron, with foaming peaks and churning valleys.

Mostly, when the sky was stormy, the ocean was wild, but some days, like this one, it was still and blue above, but some distant weather system was causing deep currents and tall, curving mountains of waves.

Bastian swam near the surface, letting the agitated water wash over his scales.

It had been years since he first slipped into the ocean, unable to resist its siren call as a child. His younger brother, Keylor, had flown down and scooped him out, sent by his parents, who were sure that his presence in the water was some kind of childish mistake, or a clumsy misstep.

Bastian tried to explain to his frowning father and his worried mother and his scornful little brother that it wasn't an accident. He had wanted to be in the ocean, had deliberately gone out in it, swimming cautiously with limbs made for fighting and flying.

He became accustomed to their looks: skepticism, concern, worry—not for him, but that other dragons might hear about his abnormal interest and judge the *family*. They were not *sea dragons*, after all. Their honor as fire dragons was as pure as their blood and must be kept unquestionable.

Young Bastian learned to keep his swimming secret, staying deep enough that he wouldn't be spotted from above as long as his lungs would hold out. Further and longer and deeper he learned to dive, and it was never enough.

While his brother followed his healthy, strong treasure sense and began the approved practice of amassing a hoard, Bastian found bits of seaglass and parts of fishing nets, lost ship bells, and particularly fine shells. He didn't dare take them to his rooms in his family's grand halls, so he hid them in a beach-side cave that could only be reached underwater.

He took his fighting lessons with ill grace and even less talent, and no one was sorry when he spent more and more time…not there.

And every day, Bastian ranged a little further, and a little further, until he sometimes spent days at a time in the water.

This was a fine day for flying, with a brisk, steady wind and a blue, cloudless sky. It was a less fine day for swimming, with the ocean feeling fickle as it plucked at his wings and tried to toss him to the surface.

Then, suddenly, there was an unexpected twang in Bastian's head, like his broken treasure sense, but more urgent. He wasn't expecting to find anything of value; he already knew well enough to mistrust all of his senses and instincts. But he knew that he couldn't turn away and went diving deeper to escape the turbulent place between ocean and air and swim faster towards the disturbance.

It was a person, he realized as he rose again under the weakly struggling figure. Not a human, but not a dragon. A shifter, he recognized, as it finally lost its grip on the pitching paddle board.

Who would come out on the ocean on a day like this? The sky was clear, but the water was so angry…

Bastian couldn't let stupidity be fatal, and he breached the surface with the limp figure cradled carefully in claws.

It was an unaccustomed awkwardness, trying to keep the poor creature's face in the air and keep a body meant for flight from swamping in the cresting swells. He rolled onto his back and found a way to swirl his wings and keep himself afloat with the shifter on his belly.

But the man wasn't breathing.

CPR, Bastian thought in panic. He should administer CPR. Floating on his back as a dragon in the middle of the ocean.

He'd never had any training, but the man still hadn't taken a breath, and Bastian knew that even a shifter could not last that long without air. He put a claw gently on the shifter's chest and pressed. The second time, he pressed harder, and he continued another few palpitations out of desperation for anything better to do.

To his shock, the shifter twitched, gave a great cough, and spewed a fair amount of salty water down Bastian's side.

Relief and triumph flooded through the dragon as the shifter sat up, coughing and clutching at Bastian's scales.

"Mother of…what the hell are you?"

Bastian gave a rumble of laughter, knowing his speech wouldn't be understood by the common shifter.

The shifter clung to his rumbling belly. "Sorry I asked," he said with a hiccup of hysterical laughter. "Ugh, my mouth tastes like ass and I feel like I've been hit in the head with the world's nastiest water balloon. That is the last time I try paddle boarding to impress a girl."

Bastian swiveled his head, looking for the closest land, and it was nearer than he feared.

There was an island to the west, a green jewel on the shimmering ocean. This was undoubtedly where the erstwhile paddle boarder had come from.

"I don't suppose you happened to grab the paddle board?" the man asked plaintively. "Cause Scarlet is going to murder me if I return without it and you may as well have let me drown."

The paddle board was not immediately apparent, and Bastian gave a shrug that disrupted his delicate balance and nearly swamped them both.

"Or not!" the shifter said, frightened. "Don't worry about it. Really."

The shifter was quiet as Bastian figured out how to move through the water without knocking the man off his belly. Once he'd figured out a good rhythm, the man spoke up. "So, um, thanks for getting me out of the drink. I appreciate the save."

When Bastian didn't answer, he went on. "Well, my name's Travis. I've just been hired over at the island. They're opening a fancy resort there, we're just starting to patch up some of the buildings and get things operational. It was built in the 80s, but it's just getting off the ground now. It's in good shape, considering it's been abandoned for so long. Scarlet—she owns the place—she's a good boss. Sort of... scary, but fair, you know. Like, don't cross her, but she'll give you the shirt off her back if she decides you deserve it."

Bastian glanced behind him, surveying the coast. There was a reef protecting a golden beach, and above it, he could see white buildings nestled into brilliant green jungle. There was a dock at the near end of the beach, new wood so fresh it was still yellow. There was a dark-haired woman standing on the dock with a paddle board and paddle, watching their approach with concern. Was that Scarlet?

Bastian angled himself to meet the dock, and drew up beside it neatly to let Travis scramble off his belly. The woman reached a hand to help him.

She said something in Spanish, sounding alarmed. "I thought I'd lost our carpenter for good when I saw you go out on that riptide. Scarlet would have much to say about losing you, and no one could get a signal to call the Civil Guard. I certainly did not expect to see you coming back in on a *dragon*."

Bastian reached one forearm out over the dock and shifted as he went, standing from a crouch on two feet. "I'm Bastian," he said, rather bashfully. Would they judge him for swimming in water like some kind of sea creature? But more important than that: "Are you alright?"

Travis reached out and shook his hand vigorously. "Never better. I owe my life to you. I'd given up the fight when he found me, Lydia. I would have drowned for sure."

"*Maravilloso*," Lydia said, staring at Bastian in awe, as she offered her own hand. "I am Lydia. I didn't know dragons were real."

"Neat trick shifting your clothing with you," Travis said admiringly. "That would certainly come in handy at times."

"You can't?" Bastian asked, surprised.

Travis and Lydia both laughed and shook their heads. "No shifter I've ever known could do that," Lydia said.

"Haven't you ever met shifters?" Travis asked. "Other than dragon shifters, I mean."

"No," Bastian said briefly. His family thought simple shifters were beneath their status as dragons and rarely spoke of them. They certainly never associated with them.

"There are many here," Lydia said kindly. "Scarlet is building Shifting Sands Resort only for shifters, a safe place where we can be ourselves."

Bastian looked from one to the other thoughtfully. "That sounds...nice," he said hesitantly. "Are you all the same kind of shifter?"

Travis laughed. "Not at all," he said easily. "I'm a lynx. Canadian lynx."

"Black swan," Lydia said. "We have all types here. The chef is a wolverine. The landscaper is a lion. I don't know what Scarlet is, do you, Travis?"

Travis shook his head. "Something big," he guessed.

Neither of them had expressed any disapproval or fear of his form, or any hesitation at the fact that they'd caught him swimming like a common sea creature. His parents had insisted that other shifters were terrible speciesists and jealous of dragons, but it was Bastian who caught himself feeling jealous.

There was an easy friendliness between them that Bastian had never witnessed before, a camaraderie that defied their different shift forms. Lydia hadn't once belittled Travis for losing control of his paddle board, and Travis didn't seem the slightest bit ashamed of his display of weakness.

It was...unnatural, Bastian decided.

His dragon unhelpfully added, *I like it.*

"I should go," Bastian said stiffly. "If I see your paddle board, I will return it." Was that an admission that he would be swimming again, that they hadn't simply caught him taking a fluke dip in the sea? Perhaps he should have specified that he'd been flying overhead at the time; Travis had certainly been in no state to tell anyone otherwise.

But they didn't seem to care.

Indeed, Travis smiled warmly when he shook Bastian's hand. "Thank you again," he said sincerely. "I owe you."

Bastian felt the iron clang of an oath in the words; dragons were particularly sensitive to promises and vows, and this had all the solemnity of such a thing.

Lydia actually hugged him, while Bastian stood frozen in shock, and then dropped a brief, friendly kiss on his cheek. "Thank you for bringing Travis back." Then she turned to Travis. "You should have some water," she scolded him. "Fresh water. And sit down for a while."

Bastian walked to the end of the dock and pushed off as he shifted, his strong wingbeats churning the water to foam beneath him. As he circled curiously back, Lydia was walking arm in arm with Travis up the steep resort. Their body language was not romantic, but it was...affectionate, Bastian decided.

～

*H*e ate that night with his brother and parents, observing their interactions with new eyes.

There was no affection there. Even among family, it was a jostle for power, always watching one another for weakness, for a chance to gain status.

To his surprise, they were watching him, as well. Usually, his family preferred to ignore him, because there was nothing to gain from him. Now, however...

"The king of Borya is looking for a husband for his only daughter," his mother finally said.

His parents had enviable hoards. They were rich beyond most people's capacity to imagine. They were admired as fierce fighters and had impeccable bloodlines. But there was one thing that they'd always coveted and never achieved: royalty.

It wasn't enough to be powerful members of dragon society, they each got a gleam of jealousy and desire at the mere mention of a crown, at the hint of a title. With nobility, they thought they might finally find satisfaction and happiness.

"It would be fitting for the oldest son of the Santa Maria dragons to be a prince," Bastian's father said, with a casual tone that fooled no one.

A prince? They expected *him* to marry them into nobility? Keylor was glaring at him.

Bastian almost laughed and turned the sound into a cough, instead, taking a bite of his steak in order to escape having to say something. The tiny, dragon-ruled country of Borya was an inland desert country; he could imagine no torture worse than being trapped there.

"We could host an event," his mother said thoughtfully, neatly cutting her meat. "Arrange for them to meet."

His father frowned and gestured Keylor to pass a bowl of roasted potatoes. "We'd have to increase his hoard between now and then. He's been so slack in gathering treasure."

"And he'd have to stay away from the ocean for a while," his mother added with distaste. "I can smell the salt water and fish on him from here."

"I saved someone today," Bastian said defensively. He resented being talked about as if he wasn't there.

Everyone stared at him, and Bastian hastily added, "A shifter lost control of his paddle board and got caught up in a riptide. He was unconscious when I got there." He didn't specify *how* he'd gotten there. "I performed CPR." Sort of.

"A dragon shifter?" his mother asked swiftly, hopefully. She was clearly wondering if a daring rescue of someone important would add to their social profile.

"No. A lynx shifter."

Both of his parents gave a sigh of disgust.

"Why didn't you let him drown?" Keylor asked. "You could have added his *paddle board* to your hoard."

Something about his brother's emphasis on the paddle board made Bastian suddenly suspicious. Did Keylor know about Bastian's second, shameful hoard?

"I didn't want to let him drown," Bastian said. "I wanted to save him."

"You can't save everyone," his father said dismissively. "It's usually best to let nature take its course."

"I don't want to save everyone," Bastian said, angry. "I just want to save the ones I can." He didn't know how to explain to his cold, power-hungry family how good it felt to rescue someone. He'd never had a feeling of pride like he had when Travis came back to life on his belly. He'd never guessed that it would feel so fulfilling, or that he would finally figure out what it was that he wanted from life.

"We should see if the Valtyra royalty will attend an event here," his mother said, ignoring the topic entirely. "They're only *bears*, but they are royalty. Perhaps that would set the right tone, show Borya what might happen if they don't find a good dragon family to marry into."

Bastian let the conversation go on without him, finishing his food, and excusing himself as quickly as he was able to.

He didn't even bother returning to his room, simply lifted from the courtyard on dragon wings as swiftly as he could.

There was a full moon that night, and the sky was mostly clear, so the surface of the ocean was clear, with silver ripples. Bastian found the place he'd rescued Travis from overhead, fighting his desire to search from below. He was better suited to see the paddle board from above, he reminded his dragon.

He found the paddle itself, but not the board, and with that clasped in his claws, he circled outward in a sweeping spiral, watching the waves and tracking the currents. The ocean was calmer now, almost apologetic for its earlier ire.

The night grew thin and deep, and the moon sank into the water.

Bastian admitted his defeat, and returned to his hoard. His *real* hoard.

He had to dive to enter the underwater cave, and when he did, he knew at once that it had been disturbed.

More, the object of the disruption was sitting smugly in the center of the cave. *No wonder you hide this hoard,* Keylor scoffed. *Broken glass and sea trash. It is proof of your mental weakness.*

Bastian's blood boiled as he rose from the water and mantled his wings. He was larger than Keylor, and stronger from his hours of swimming.

Leave! he commanded. *This is mine!*

Keylor spread his wings in challenge, but only for a moment, clearly sizing Bastian up with new understanding.

You're an aberration, he said, folding his wings back as if Bastian wasn't worth the trouble. *No one will even want this hoard when you are disowned. I will bring the family glory. You bring it only grief.*

Then he dove down into the water with an expression of disgust on his long, scaled face, and was gone.

Bastian put the paddle against a broken column, then moved it, then rearranged the fishing net and the treasures hung on it, until the hoard had a sense of balance and harmony again. He curled into the middle of it, feeling hollow and uncertain.

Keylor had said nothing he didn't know. Bastian's treasure sense was faulty. He loved water. He wanted to save lives.

He didn't belong here. No part of him fit with his power-hungry family. They were fire, he was water.

He drowsed unhappily until morning, then swam from the cave and returned to the family manor.

He was not surprised to find his parents waiting in his rooms, his mother looking grieved and his father looking thunderous. Keylor lurked behind with a knowing smirk.

His father started as Bastian expected: "You have been *swimming*. You have been hoarding inappropriately."

"We could get you help," his mother interjected.

"I don't want help," Bastian objected.

"Then you want no place in this family," his father snarled.

He was bluffing, Bastian thought, with sudden clarity. They wanted him to conform, to be a happy, productive member of the family, to renounce his irregular hoard, and marry obediently. They thought they could bully him into being normal by threatening to remove him from the family.

But he didn't want to be a part of it.

It was a realization of mixed emotions. He desperately wanted to belong, even as he knew that he never could. But he didn't want to belong here, he wanted to be somewhere he could be *himself*.

He thought longingly of the friendliness of Travis and Lydia, of their enthusiasm for their work, and their fondness for each other.

"No," Bastian said slowly. "I don't think I *do* want a place in *this* family."

It hurt. It cut deep to admit it. He had failed in all of his efforts to fit in, and his dragon pride smarted.

But for once, he thought there might just be something *better*.

"The princess of Borya..." his mother hissed, ever focused.

"If he marries a princess, it would undo his disgrace," his father growled. "It is the only way I would take him back into the family now." To everyone's surprise, there was a resonating feeling of oath promise to the words. "Leave this house, forfeit your hoard."

"No one wants his *real* hoard," Keylor mocked him, holding up a set of golden chalices. "But I'll take these."

"Behave," his mother scolded Keylor. "Those are your father's, now."

Bastian was cut loose. He was a tangle of emotions as he backed away. He felt like he ought to thank them for his freedom, and part of him wanted to fall at their feet and beg forgiveness and lenience, because this was all he'd ever known.

He wandered out of the manor, into the courtyard, and flew for the coast. He paused at his hoard to get one item, then flew for Shifting Sands Resort.

~

*B*astian landed in the clearing at the top of the resort and tossed the paddle he'd been holding in his claws to himself as he shifted into human form.

He was facing outwards, looking down the road that led to the airstrip on the other side of the island, and when he turned to face the entrance to the resort, he was somehow not surprised to find a woman standing in the doorway.

"I see you found our paddle," she said serenely. She was tall and slim and it was not hard to guess how she had come to be named Scarlet; her hair was brilliant red and pulled back into a tidy bun.

"I haven't found the paddle board yet," Bastian admitted, holding it out to her.

"I would rather lose a board than an employee," Scarlet said, gravely taking the paddle. "I am in your debt."

Bastian felt the caress of the promise, and was emboldened to say, "Then I am in a good position to ask for a favor."

There was the tiniest hint of a smile on Scarlet's serious face. "I invite you to ask."

"I am...seeking employment." Bastian could imagine the blast of disapproval that his request would have caused his family. Bad enough that he chose questionable hobbies and hoarded worthless things. But to actively seek to contract himself for common work? It was unspeakable. "I don't have many applicable skills, but I can learn fast and work hard."

Scarlet gazed at him from leaf-green eyes, and he couldn't read her expression. He could understand why Travis thought her shift form was something *big*; she had a powerful, confident presence. "Travis could use some assistance, and something the size and strength of a dragon could be useful in our rebuilding efforts," she said thoughtfully. "But for something more long term, I have been considering hiring a lifeguard."

"A lifeguard?" Bastian said, eyebrows rising. An excuse to swim? A chance to *save* someone again? "I don't have any certifications…"

"I can send you for training on the mainland," Scarlet said dismissively. "Having a lifeguard on duty *would* lower my insurance. Travis and Lydia spoke highly of you, and I trust their opinions." She handed the paddle back to Bastian. "I expect my employees to work hard and take initiative. Your work would include cleaning the pool deck and beach. Your pay would be in room and board plus yearly bonuses based on the resorts profits; there is a top corner room in the hotel that we've got set aside for staff that should be appropriate for your hoard."

My inappropriate hoard, Bastian thought, bemused.

"See Lydia in the spa about some resort staff clothing," Scarlet said, looking him down to the toes thoughtfully. Bastian was aware that his fine silk suit was not exactly *appropriate*, either. "The paddle goes in the storage room at the pool."

"Yes, ma'am," Bastian said. She seemed to think this was a done thing, and Bastian had no reason to deny her.

Scarlet thrust a hand at him. "My name is Scarlet Stanson," she said formally.

Bastian paused a moment. Usually, for official occasions like this, he would use his full name, but he'd lost that. "Bastian," he said solemnly. "Just Bastian."

"Welcome to Shifting Sands."

～

*A*fter a busy day of helping Travis plaster walls and run wires and haul supplies, Bastian found himself invited to a motley table of shifters to eat the simple dinner being offered in the half-finished restaurant.

"I didn't realize what I've been missing all this time," Travis said merrily, introducing him around the table. There was Graham, the dour landscaper, Breck, a hire as new as Bastian was who would be working in the restaurant in charge of waitstaff once it was complete, and a handful of other general laborers.

"There is nothing quite as useful as a dragon when you've got a lot of stuff to get from point A to point B," Travis raved. "I can't believe how much we got done today. If we can keep this rate up, we'll be done in time to open next month."

To Bastian's surprise, they all praised him, and welcomed him to the team, not one of them acting jealous, or denigrating his shift form, or expressing disgust that he was going to be a lifeguard. They didn't seem to bear any ill will to any kind of shifter; one of the laborers was a mouse shifter, and they all remarked admiringly on how useful she had been in getting a fallen wire end from inside a finished wall.

She blushed and wriggled her nose and looked terribly pleased.

His parents, Bastian realized as he served *himself* the plain, hearty fare, were the speciesist ones, and he was able to look beyond his fresh shame of disgrace to feel relief in leaving them behind.

It was something new and different, to have pride in what he did, instead of pride in what he was.

Or shame in what he wasn't.

But one thing that dragons did was keep their debt balanced, so after the diners had dispersed, Bastian found Travis.

"We don't have to work through the night," Travis teased Bastian. "You're allowed to take it easy sometimes."

"I wanted to thank you," Bastian told him gravely. "And settle your life debt."

Travis looked alarmed, so Bastian went on quickly. "It is paid in full. You have shown me a new life, a better one, and I do not want you to feel that you still owe me anything."

"Ah, sure," Travis said, smiling cautiously.

Bastian could feel the oath compulsion ease. "You are free."

"It's not a balance sheet that's ever going to be exactly zero sum," Travis told him, cocking his head to one side curiously. "You just...help each other out when someone needs it," he said sincerely. "And if someone helps you out and you can't help them, then maybe you can help someone else. It's called paying it forward. That's what we do here."

Something in Bastian's chest loosened. This was how things should be, not constantly vying for status. This was having *friends*, not trying to one-up enemies. It was foreign and uncomfortable... and felt so *right*.

"Thank you," he told Travis sincerely.

Instead of returning to his new housing, or even flying back to his shore-cave hoard to begin moving it, Bastian went to the beach, slipped into the water and swam out past the breakers over protective reef.

Out in the great swells of ocean, Bastian turned and looked back at the resort, lit like a palace of white light in the dark jungle.

His treasure sense would never be considered normal, but he thought that for once, it had served him well.

What he'd found here was worth more than anything in his hoard. It was more valuable than anything in *any* hoard, he thought, with satisfaction.

He'd found a place to be himself.

TROPICAL PANTHER'S PENANCE

CHAPTER 1

"Wrench," Travis said.

Panther shifter Warren "Wrench" Martin looked at him blankly for just a moment before he realized that the lynx shifter handyman was asking for the tool, not initiating a conversation. He dug into the toolbox between them and handed Travis the requested tool with a grunt.

He watched as Travis opened the problematic trap, and dumped the sludge out of it into a waiting five gallon bucket.

"Ahah!" Travis said triumphantly, fishing a scrap of cloth out of the drain above. "I don't know what possesses people to put these things down drains, but I've found some odd stuff down here."

The handyman reattached the trap. "Did you see how that worked? The most important thing is not to yank on it too hard. With a wrench and shifter strength, you can deform the pipe before you unscrew it if you aren't careful."

Wrench grunted an affirmative as Travis emerged from beneath the sink, wiping his hands.

"Let's give it a test drive," he said, and Wrench flipped the tap open.

Water poured cleanly down the drain without so much as a gurgle of protest or a drip.

Wrench wondered if the job always felt so rewarding; he had worked a long time in the shadowy persuasion business, and as well as it paid, it had never felt as victorious as any single repair he'd done with Travis.

"That did it!" Travis said with clear satisfaction.

As messy as it could be, this was clean work, and Wrench felt more fulfilled than he had in a lifetime of building a reputation for retribution and destruction.

"That's our last job for the day," Travis said putting the last of the tools back in their place. "You've got a few hours of daylight left if you want to hit the beach for a swim or something."

Wrench raised a skeptical eyebrow at him. "I ain't a swimmer," he said, picking up the toolbox before Travis could. He had done little enough of this job as it was. "But I was thinking…"

He paused, hesitant to continue, and Travis closed up the under sink cabinet and then looked at him curiously. "Spit it out, man!"

"There's a lot of broken roof tiles from the storm we're just going to piss away."

"Not much you can do with them," Travis shrugged. "You can't really repair them."

"You could… break em more." That wasn't too bad, Wrench thought. He was good at breaking things.

"And then?" Travis prompted as they closed up the cottage behind them and started hiking up to the mechanical room where Travis kept his tools.

"They'd make a nice… art piece. Like those things with tiny tiles that make a picture."

Travis blinked. "A mosaic?"

"Sure," Wrench shrugged. "It's just an idea."

"Well, yeah," Travis agreed thoughtfully. "You could just press it into wet thinset over stucco if the pieces were small enough. You got a picture in mind?"

"I dunno," Wrench growled, embarrassed. "Like a flower or a butterfly or something. They're kinda orange."

Travis did an admirable but insufficient job of hiding his amusement. "Yeah, we could do that," he agreed.

"It's something I could do," Wrench said offhandedly. "Wouldn't take more of your time."

"You ever done anything like that before?" Travis asked candidly.

"Nah," Wrench admitted, scowling. He was regretting voicing the idea.

"Let's do a little piece of the courtyard behind the spa, see how it goes, before we do it anywhere lots of people will see it. Pretty much only Lydia uses that space."

Wrench grunted, happier with Travis' agreement than he wanted to admit. "I could do that now," he suggested. "I ain't got anything else going on."

Travis's thoughts were clearly off somewhere else. Wrench looked up along the resort above them and saw one of the twins waving from the deck above. That would be Travis's mate Jenny, by his distracted grin and return wave. "Sure," Travis said. "Knock yourself out. The ratio of water for the thinset is on the bag. Use one of the gray buckets."

"Got it, boss," Wrench said automatically.

"Not your boss, Wrench," Travis reminded him as Jenny disappeared above them. "I'm just showing you the ropes."

"Well, I'm real grateful for your helping me get this work," Wrench said gruffly. "Especially after that, er, professional misunderstanding."

He had been hired to bring Jenny's twin sister Laura back to the cartel in Los Angeles, but had mistakenly taken Jenny instead. He still wasn't entirely sure how he'd been convinced to turn on his employers for a plea bargain, but he felt like for the first time in a long time, his life had some sort of real potential.

The biggest problem he had working here at this tropical resort was the island time they seemed to be on, with long periods of leisure that didn't fit with his need to be constantly busy. He didn't want the time to think about the pending sting or court date, and he had no interest in the luxury beach entertainment the resort offered.

Travis punched him in the shoulder and Wrench had to hold himself back from turning and pounding him into the ground in return. "You've been a great help," the lynx shifter said merrily. "And you say probably twice as much as Graham does."

Wrench grunted.

"There's that chatty nature," Travis teased.

Jenny skipped down the stairs towards them. "Scarlet is thinking about having an impromptu beach bonfire tonight, if you think the storm-downed wood has dried out in the sun long enough."

"Will you dance around it nude?" Travis asked with a grin.

"Keep dreaming," Jenny told him, but she was smirking in return.

Knowing that they were aware only of each other now, Wrench left them without further comment.

CHAPTER 2

*L*ydia Moreno looked out the small window, down at the crinkly ocean and the island growing below. She was more excited about returning to Shifting Sands Resort than she had ever been before.

"Isn't it lovely?" the little white-haired woman sitting next to her chirped, leaning over to look out the same window. "Have you ever seen such a gorgeous little island?"

"It's more beautiful every time," Lydia said with a gentle smile, sitting back so the woman could get the best view.

"Oh, you've been before?" the woman said with an appraising glance.

Lydia knew her simple clothing didn't make her seem like someone with the kind of cash to travel multiple times to a luxurious tropical resort. "I work there," she said without shame.

"What a gorgeous place to work!" the woman said with an overly friendly pat to Lydia's knee. "My goodness, you must love it! Tell me what you do!"

Lydia smiled. "I run the spa," she said proudly. "I also teach salsa and do many of the meditation and yoga classes."

"I simply must take your classes," the woman said too eagerly. "What do you like most about your work?"

"I enjoy meeting all the new people who come here," Lydia said simply. "My work is very varied, and although it is sometimes busy, I never get bored."

"Do you like the people you work with?" The woman was over-the-top nosy. "Do you get new people in very often?"

"Turnover is high," Lydia said agreeably. "Not everyone can handle the isolation. But we have a really excellent core staff that is like family."

She was glad when the woman finally turned to converse with the woman across the aisle from her, and she could politely return to watching the island grow below her.

Every time she returned from visiting with her family or renewing her certification, she felt more and more like she was coming home.

But this time was different.

This time, her mate was there.

She had always known where he was, like a faint compass pull; most swan shifters had a mate sense. The tug had always been weak enough that she'd never felt compelled to drop her life in progress to find him. Even as she got older and her younger sisters and brothers went seeking their own partners as their mate sense matured, she had waited in the wings, trying to be patient and trust that things were happening as they should.

Now, her patience would finally be rewarded, and she could not help squirming with nervous excitement.

What would he be like? A guest at a shifters-only resort, so he was a shifter, and probably well-to-do if he could afford Shifting Sands' exclusive pricing. Would he be young? Old? Blonde? Tall? Short? Would he sweep her away in a romantic dance at the next formal? Or go swimming with her at the beach at midnight?

Lydia put a finger to the cross at the base of her throat. She had to believe she would love him no matter what. She just had to trust that this was her path to happiness and have faith that they were going to be perfect for each other.

The hot tropical air that greeted her when the plane doors opened smelled amazing and charged with energy. She let the guests disembark first, struggling with their overstuffed carry-ons and exclaiming over the humid, scented air.

By the time she was off the plane, the resort van had already departed with the first batch of guests, leaving her with the second group and the extra luggage.

The white-haired woman had secured a seat on the first van trip, and the few remaining guests were sitting in the little open shelter that was the only structure at the landing strip. They seemed to be an equal mix of patiently enjoying the tropical view and feeling slighted that they were having to wait. A middle-aged brunette woman immersed a book sat between a bored-looking blonde wearing impractical heels and a young Swede. The Swede was trying to explain over her head to the blonde that he was a professional hockey player. She didn't look impressed.

A grim-faced man completed the group, and he scowled at everyone and then walked to the far end of the structure to light a cigarette. He didn't look like the sort to book a solo vacation at Shifting Sands, but they did get all kinds.

When Travis, the resort handyman, returned with the van, she enfolded him in a warm, brief hug, and then helped load the luggage in the back.

"We've got stories," the lynx shifter told her, a merry twinkle in his eyes. "So many stories!"

"I can't wait to hear them," Lydia said eagerly. He looked different, somehow, though he'd been so overworked and stressed out when she left that perhaps it was only that he'd finally gotten a decent night of sleep.

The road back to the resort was noticeably worse than it had been when she left, thanks to the storm that had just swept through, and the jaw-chattering trip was too rough for conversation, or much of anything except clinging to the side rails in the van trying not to end up on anyone else's lap.

Graham, the lion shifter in charge of landscaping, met them at the resort entrance to help unload the luggage and Lydia caught him for a quick hug as well. He gave her a dutiful kiss on the cheek and said gruffly, "Welcome back." Then he picked up more of the giant suitcases than looked possible and vanished down into the greenery.

The resort owner, Scarlet, was checking guests in and paused in her task to flash Lydia a quick welcome smile. "Meeting at three!" she called, and Lydia waved and carried her own small bag to the top of the path down into the resort.

She paused for only a moment, to soak in the familiar view. Her mate was down there, somewhere tantalizingly close, and she longed to drop her bag and fly to find him.

But she'd waited this long to meet him and she could wait a little longer. She knew that her spa would soon be busy with all the new arrivals and duty called first.

CHAPTER 3

*W*rench was used to crowds. The bigger the crowd, the easier it was to get lost.

But he was used to city crowds, crowds that would elbow you aside without a glance, crowds that didn't care.

He wasn't used to resort crowds.

They came all in a flock, chatting and gaping around the place like the tourists they were, asking anyone in earshot how to find the thing right in front of them. They smelled like airplanes and booze, and they all had the terribly unnerving habit of looking right at him with wide, curious eyes instead of pretending he didn't exist like people in crowds ought to.

"This is the rush," Tex told him, when Wrench found himself backed up to the bear shifter's bar trying to avoid a grandma maneuvering a monstrous plaid thing on wheels. "When the charter plane comes in full, there are always a few hours of chaos as everyone tries to figure out where things are and everyone wants to try everything. It'll ease up in a few hours."

"Can I help?" Wrench asked with dread.

Tex, without pity, suggested, "You can go offer to help that lovely old lady with her suitcase."

Wrench drew in his breath and tugged the ill-fitting polo shirt into some semblance of neatness. At the moment, chasing down a rogue gang member and teaching him manners with a pipe seemed like a far easier assignment, but he was keenly aware that he was under evaluation for staying to work at the resort.

And he'd never been to a place that he wanted to stay at so much.

It wasn't the easy tropical weather—he'd already been through one of the worst storms he'd ever seen on this island. It wasn't the upscale lodgings or the gourmet food—if anything, that made him more uncomfortable than the poverty and squalor of the streets where he'd grown up.

It was the way this place felt like it was willing to give you a shot.

It didn't matter if he was schooled or not, Travis was teaching him all sorts of stuff about building and repairing.

Scarlet, for all of her toe-tapping and terrifying frowns, had been willing to give him a chance, despite his criminal record and his inauspicious arrival at the resort to kidnap one of her staff.

Jenny, the otter shifter he'd kidnapped, had turned out to be a lawyer, and was even trying to get him a plea bargain in return for testifying against the cartel that had hired him. Wrench was absolutely sure that if the deal fell through, they'd all look the other way while he hopped on a plane somewhere with no extradition laws rather than turning him in pitilessly.

The rest of the staff seemed to care more that he was attempting to pull his own weight than that he didn't have highfalutin manners or much social polish. They drank beers with him in the evening like he was a long-time buddy, and they didn't pry at him with questions that he obviously didn't want to answer.

They accepted his desire to go straight without question or doubt. He wasn't sure why, or why it mattered so much to him, but it did.

"Hey, lady, er, ma'am." Wrench tried not to hulk. "May I help you with your bag?"

She looked up, and up, and up at him. "Goodness, aren't you a… thing." She didn't seem particularly bothered by his thing-ness.

"One of these wheels does have a habit of sticking," she said, handing him the handle. "And gravel paths! I didn't think I'd have to drag this down a gravel path."

Wrench followed her as she unfolded her brochure and pointed out her cottage on the little map. She had peeled off a sticker nametag that said 'Dot' and put it on the brochure. "I'm in cottage twenty-three," she said, and then she led Wrench off at a fast trot.

Wrench followed her dutifully, carrying the bag by its awkward long handle rather than even trying to roll it. It was surprisingly heavy.

"Is it always so hot here?" Dot chirped curiously as she led the way, pausing only briefly at the signpost pointing directions. "Goodness, it is quite a lot hotter than the Midwest this time of year. Of course, my kids all think I can't handle the cold anymore, so this is their early Christmas gift. I think they're hoping I like it so much they can convince me to move to Florida. I'd as soon eat my socks as move to that alligator-infested swampland. You could be an alligator, son. What's your shifter form?"

Wrench cleared his throat. "Panther. Ma'am."

She sniffed. "Big cats. I'm a fox, thank you very much, and when I was younger I was quite the fox in either form."

Wrench caught what might have been a wink.

"Yes, ma'am," he decided was safe.

"You got family?" the woman prodded.

"Sister," Wrench said briefly, surprised into admitting it. "Niece."

"That's lovely," Dot said cheerfully. "I have two brothers, six kids, and three grandkids. Nothing is as important as family, now, is it. How old is your niece?"

"Eight," Wrench ground out.

"That's a good age," she said approvingly. "Not so old they're in the talking-back stage, but old enough to have a conversation."

Wrench grunted politely.

"Do they live here?" the white-haired woman pried.

"No ma'am," Wrench said miserably.

Her cottage was fortunately not far, and he carried her suitcase just inside the door. "That will do," she said, and she began to fumble in her purse.

"No tips, ma'am. It's all inclusive," Wrench reminded her.

She came up with a mint that had clearly traveled further than Dot had. "Take a mint, boy."

Wrench dutifully took the mint and fled back to his mosaic.

CHAPTER 4

The spa was all the familiar chaos that Lydia had missed. She exchanged enthusiastic embraces with each of her assistants and dived in to get guests set up with pedicures and facials. When two of the guests were chattering together in Russian, she was able to get more of the gossip from Laura.

"Kidnapped!" Lydia exclaimed as the tale unwove.

"My fault, really," Laura explained. "The cartel I worked for took offense to my desire for retirement, and they thought Jenny was me, and sent Wrench to bring me back."

"Wrench?"

"He's really an okay guy," Laura was quick to explain. "He let her go when he figured out it wasn't me, and when we gave him a chance to give testimony against his boss in a plea bargain, he took it."

"That sounds a little overly trusting," Lydia suggested. "Good people don't go around kidnapping innocent people."

Laura shrugged, patting off her client's foot with a towel. "You could argue that good people don't end up working for the cartel, but it's hard to turn down a job when you're in a tight place. He made the right choice in the end. Gave up a suitcase of money, even."

Lydia pursed her lips. "You're right of course," she said, not wanting to paint Laura with the same brush; she liked the curvy wolf shifter. It was hard to picture her working for a mob organization. "And if Scarlet thinks he's worth giving a chance, I have to trust her judgment."

Laura's smile was bright and grateful. "But that's not the only gossip you missed. Bastian found his mate, too!"

At the reminder, Lydia was aware again of how close her own mate was, tantalizing and exciting. She wanted to share the news, but almost as much, she wanted to hold the knowledge close, to savor the anticipation privately a little longer. "Bastian! How delicious! Who is she?"

"Her name is Saina. She's a siren, and she'll be singing tonight in the bar if you don't see her before then."

"A siren!" Lydia exclaimed. "An actual mermaid? I didn't know they even existed."

"That's a story I'll let them tell you," Laura teased her. "But come hear her sing tonight."

"I was only gone a few weeks, and you had a storm, and kidnappings, and a whole raft of new staff!" Lydia exclaimed. "There you are," she said to the owner of the foot she was pampering. "Can I get you a little polish for these happy toes?"

"Oh, yes, please," the guest said in her thick Russian accent. "It's been ages since they've been shown off in sandals. I want them to look their best!"

Lydia let her choose a color and bent to apply it. "Where is Angela?"

"Ran off with Mr. Brazil after the World Mr. Shifter competition," Laura giggled.

"Good for her," Lydia laughed in return.

"And have you seen Mr. *Professional* Hockey player from Sweden? A looker, but man, he's got to lay off explaining to everyone he meets that he's a *real* hockey player. You know, *expert*?" Laura's false Swedish accent was amusing.

"I had the honor of watching him explain that to everyone on the plane," Lydia said, rolling her eyes.

They put the finishing touches on their clients and helped them out of the chairs.

"Scarlet said there was a meeting at three?" Lydia said, looking over the schedule. It was always ridiculously busy shortly after the charter planes came in, then died to an irregular, easy workload.

"Senior staff only. It's starting to slow up for now. I can keep an eye on things here," Laura promised, looking at the clock. "Have you had a chance to unpack yet?"

"I don't travel with much," Lydia said. "I'll head down a little early and catch up with the others. It sounds like a lot of congratulations are in order." And her own would follow soon, she knew, but she kept the excitement from bubbling over out of her mouth. "I'll be back right afterwards!"

Laura gave her a last swift hug before she left; they hadn't known each other long, but Lydia had felt an immediate kinship with the woman when they met. They had bonded over hospitality horror stories and coffee, and Lydia was well-disposed to any mate of Tex's.

A large part of her wanted to turn the direction she knew her mate was, but Lydia made her feet walk down from the spa to the conference room behind the kitchen where Scarlet held the staff meetings.

Breck, the leopard shifter who ran the waitstaff, was already there, and he abandoned his futile teasing of Graham to rise and wrap her in an enthusiastic embrace. "Lydia, my love, come save me from this dour grouch and the terrible contagion of mates in this room."

"I've heard!" Lydia exclaimed with a laugh, returning his embrace with a sisterly kiss on the cheek. "First Tex, now Travis and Bastian!"

"It's awful," Breck said, dropping into a chair beside her. "I'm afraid to drink the water."

Lydia patted his leg reassuringly as she sat beside him. "It wouldn't be so bad, would it?" she teased.

"I'm not done sampling all the beautiful people the world has to offer," Breck said firmly.

"You won't want anything else," Tex, the bartender and bear shifter, told him, pulling up a chair on the other side of Lydia. She leaned over to give him a sitting half-hug.

"Maybe you didn't," Breck said skeptically. "But you weren't gifted with a libido like mine."

Travis gave a friendly laugh as he took a seat across the table with Chef and Bastian. "No one in the world has been 'gifted' with a libido like yours."

"On other topics," Scarlet interrupted firmly, "we do have business to cover." The resort owner tolerated Breck's extracurricular activities with guests and staff alike provided it didn't cause any drama, but she didn't exactly approve of it.

Lydia listened politely as Scarlet outlined the bullet points of the resort business. Comment cards had come back from the World Mr. Shifter event, and most of it was positive. They were having unfortunate supply problems following the storm that Lydia had missed, and their lack of a boat was complicating their ability to restock.

"The insurance company doesn't really have a leg to stand on," Scarlet explained. "But they are using all the delay tactics at their disposal. We're going to have to purchase the boat and roof repairs out of pocket and wait for reimbursement. Most of the profits from the Mr. Shifter contract went to pay off some of our outstanding debts, and we're going to have to reopen credit at some of our suppliers. I had hoped we would be able to operate in the black after that windfall, but it doesn't look like we'll be quite that lucky."

"No Christmas bonus," Breck muttered to Lydia in an aside.

Scarlet's sharp ears didn't miss it. "A minimal bonus, at the most," she said frankly. "I'm having the accountant go over my numbers again. Last year's unexpected housing situation put us at a fairly large deficit going into the fiscal year."

She was referring to the fact that they had fed and housed, free of charge, a large number of refugees from the shifter zoo that had been kidnapping people from all over the world that had been on the other side of the island from the resort. None of the staff had protested the act of charity, but it had dented the operating budget of the resort rather severely.

"On the upside," she continued, "we do have a busy schedule for the remainder of the year and well into the first months of the next. As we had hoped, the World Mr. Shifter competition gave us a great deal of positive press in the shifter community. If the insurance company stops balking and this trend continues, we should be back in the black early next year."

"And if nothing major breaks," Travis added cautiously. "I'm not sure how much longer the air conditioner in the hotel is going to keep grinding on."

Scarlet grimaced. "Cross your fingers," she said. "We're well stocked in duct tape, at least."

The rest of the staff went around the table and updated each other on plans and problems. Lydia gave the okay to put her morning yoga, meditation, and dance classes back on the schedule. "I'm also certified in acupuncture now, so we should add that to the list of services!"

"Congratulations," Scarlet said, with a warm smile as she noted it down on her clipboard. "And welcome back! You missed some exciting weeks."

Lydia could only smile secretly. She knew that the most exciting week of her life was just ahead of her.

CHAPTER 5

*W*rench held the shampoo bottle at arm's length, squinting at the butterfly on the label as it compared to the butterfly he had plastered onto the wall.

It was better.

Having a reference had helped. The first butterfly, down in the corner of the wall was awkward and cartoony. The second was not much better, but this one, larger, had a more correct form, and a more pleasing placement on the wall.

"Oh."

Wrench turned in alarm to find that a woman had come into the private courtyard while he was inspecting his work.

And not just any woman.

She had a healthy, unadorned beauty, from the crown of her straight, shoulder-length dark hair to the curves of her tanned skin. She was standing like a dancer, poised to fall into motion at the slightest hint of music. Her body was a lush combination of strength and softness, and Wrench might have stared at the generous expanse of her cleavage if he had not been entirely captured by the gorgeous planes of her face and the eternity in her brown eyes.

"Oh," he said in return.

Oh yes, his panther said, stretching in his head.

For a lengthy moment, they stood there, just staring at each other.

"You must be Wrench," she finally said.

"Yeah," Wrench was able to say gruffly. "You're gonna be Lydia."

He was torn. Most of him wanted to gather her up in his arms and lay her down on the tiles of the courtyard right then and there. The rest of him, humiliated, wanted to cover the work that he'd done on her wall. It was insufficient. It was unworthy. It was painfully amateur.

"So," she said softly. "You're my mate." She was toying with a necklace.

"Yeah," Wrench agreed, at his panther's urging. "I guess so," he added.

Her eyes flashed with something. Pity? Wrench hated pity worse than being touched.

"This is awkward," he said swiftly, scowling. "It's gotta be a disappointment. I mean, ah, not you. You're not. Just...." *Me. I'm the disappointment.* He was the kind of guy you wanted to scare off door-to-door salesmen and tax collectors. He wasn't the kind of guy a nice woman like this dreamed of for a mate. Any other day of his life, he would have been just fine with his role, but for the first time, he wished he were someone else. Someone she'd actually want.

Panther lashed his tail in displeasure. This was not how their meeting was supposed to be going.

"Oh!" she said swiftly. "I'm not... ah, it's not. Of course not." Then her gorgeous face quirked into a brilliant smile. "I'm just caught by surprise," she said shyly.

Wrench was not sure he should believe her.

She looked past him then, and appraised the wall of her courtyard. "*Mariposa*! I like it," she said.

"I can take it down, plaster over it or whatever," Wrench said swiftly, before he registered her words. "You do?"

Lydia moved like a dancer, too, with graceful, purposeful steps, until she was standing close to him, looking at the wall. She smelled like tropical flowers and soap.

It was intoxicating.

Panther thought it was better than catnip and Wrench had to squelch his impulse to rub himself on her hair. He took a half-step away.

"It's cheerful," Lydia said approvingly.

"The first few weren't right," Wrench said honestly. "But I found this to look at." He waved the shampoo bottle at her. "This one's better."

"Will you do more of them?" Lydia gave him a glance from beneath thick, dark eyelashes.

Wrench would cheerfully have taken the roofs off of every cottage in the resort to break into pieces to make mosaics on every wall she walked past. "I guess." He shrugged.

"I'd like that," Lydia said, biting her lip.

She was looking at him as appraisingly as she'd looked at the mosaic. "What now?" she asked hesitantly.

Panther had decided ideas about what came next, and Wrench had to swallow and shift his erection in his pants as discreetly as possible.

When he didn't offer any ideas out loud, she suggested, "Do you want to join me for a cup of coffee? Get to know each other?"

"Coffee," Wrench echoed stupidly. Panther's imagination was vivid and involved no clothing, so very little of his blood was getting to his brain.

"It's a drink made from caffeinated beans," Lydia explained. A playful smile lurked at the corners of her mouth.

She was actually trying to put him at ease, Wrench realized, and he was painfully grateful for her efforts. He drew himself up and tried to mimic Tex as he said, "I'd like that. Ma'am." He reached for his head before he remembered that he wasn't wearing a hat, and turned it into an awkward rub at his bristle-short hair.

"Lydia?" One of the curvy identical sisters was standing at the door to the courtyard. Wrench wasn't sure if it was Laura or Jenny, but he wanted to snarl and throw something at her, even if the moment she was interrupting was awkward and awful.

Lydia turned away from him to answer. "What is it?"

"We've got someone asking about a deep tissue massage, any chance you're free?" Her look at Wrench was curious and puzzled, and Wrench scowled back at her.

"I'll be right there," Lydia said.

Laura-or-Jenny scampered away, and Lydia turned back to Wrench. "How about after dinner?" she suggested.

"Coffee?" Wrench repeated helplessly.

"Maybe something not caffeinated," Lydia suggested. "We could meet at the bar."

He knew he was making her do all of the heavy lifting here, but Wrench was desperately out of his depth and adrift. He couldn't stop imagining what she must taste like, what her skin would feel like, what she'd sound like when he... "Yes," he choked. "Bar. After dinner. Not caffeinated."

She reached out like she might touch him, and Wrench couldn't quite keep himself from flinching away.

Her look was puzzled, and a little hurt, Wrench thought, but she gave him a little smile before turning away.

It wasn't until after she had glided away that he realized she was going to want to *talk* to him at the bar that night.

CHAPTER 6

*L*ydia's heart was pounding in her chest as she left the tiny courtyard behind the spa.

Her mate.

She'd met her mate.

And he was nothing like she'd expected.

She'd followed the tug of her mate sense with nervous excitement, eager to meet the man she would spend the rest of her life with... and been surprised to find a great wall of a man who could only be Wrench.

He was far more handsome than she'd expected when Laura had described him; the tattoos and scars had been part of a much greater package, and not nearly as jarring as she'd expected. The ill-fitting staff polo shirt could not mask the fact that he was built like a tank, every muscle rippling under his adorned skin.

He undeniably raised all the feelings of desire and lust that she had anticipated, but Lydia had never thought it would come in such a confusing package. He barely had a dozen words to string together, though to be fair, if he was feeling as gobsmacked by the meeting as Lydia was, it wasn't really a wonder that conversation was a distant secondary concern in his head.

Maybe meeting for drinks was an error. Many confusions could be sorted with a simple roll in the hay, and as much as Lydia had secretly hoped for a little courtship, a slow burn, even a friendship first... maybe that wasn't going to work.

She banished her thoughts as she entered the massage room, a private little alcove with a few high windows to let a cooling breeze in.

"Good afternoon!" she greeted the client, the slight little woman with a mane of white hair from the plane who was already undressed and face down on the table. "Dot, right? You requested a deep tissue massage?"

She always confirmed, never trusting the schedule or second-hand requests when it came to client preference.

"Really get in there," the woman said firmly with no hint of recognition. "Don't hold back because you think I'm old. It was a long flight!"

"Yes, *Senora*," Lydia agreed with a laugh. She could not help adding, "I have worked a long while at a resort for only shifters. I know that appearances can often be deceiving."

She considered her own words for the length of the massage, wondering how it applied to her own situation.

CHAPTER 7

*W*rench wasn't used to being nervous.

He was the decisive sort. He got job offers and he accepted them, or he didn't, if the money wasn't worth the risk or regret. He didn't spend a lot of time tying himself up in knots over maybes or might-have-beens, and he sure as spit didn't waste his energy worrying about things before they happened.

But there was no contingency plan in place for Lydia, or her impossible brown eyes, or the way she moved.

The idea of facing her over a table, of 'getting to know her,' or worse, letting her know him, was more nerve-wracking than entering a bar already knowing that it was going to explode into a gunfight.

He pulverized a broken roof tile before he recognized that he was in no state to try to continue the mosaic. It had been enough pressure before, but knowing whose wall he was working on now made it seem like an impossible task.

He was glad to see that the thinset was nearly gone; he'd have to mix a new batch to work further anyway, and it would be best to stop now and rinse the bucket before it hardened.

There was a spigot in the courtyard, and Wrench filled the

bucket at it and scrubbed harder than was required to wash the tools and thin what was left down to something that could be rinsed away and dumped into the bushes.

He was giving the bucket a second swirl of nearly-clear water when someone behind him growled, "What are you doing?"

Wrench looked around to find Graham, a trowel in one hand and a bucket of dirt in the other, glowering as if he'd just stepped in shit.

Panther snarled in his head. This was Lydia's courtyard, his *mate's* territory. He didn't need another alpha male mucking around, and Wrench definitely didn't want anyone to see the hash he was making of the wall.

"Just cleaning up here," Wrench growled in return, moving to empty the second bucket in the greenery after the first.

"You can't just dump that in the plants!" Graham's outrage touched every raw nerve in Wrench's head.

"What are you gonna do?" he challenged, and he deliberately finished tipping the bucket onto the broad green leaves of the underbrush.

He and his panther both took a deep amount of satisfaction from Graham's snarl of challenge, and he threw aside the bucket in time to brace for the landscaper's angry attack.

Wrench was more of a knives and gunfire fighter, preferring to take any advantage over an enemy that he could. But there was a certainly gritty pleasure to bare-knuckle fighting. Even as he dodged Graham's fist as it came flying at his face, he caught himself grinning.

This made sense to him, it fit in his world order. A mate was confusion and levels of emotion that he didn't want to face. A fight, though. A fight was a simple give and take. Dodge and strike, absorb the blow if it gave him an advantage, use his greater size against Graham's greater speed.

The lion shifter was clearly a grade of fighter better than Wrench; the blows he landed were pulled, Wrench was sure, but still carried enough power to stagger him, which was no small feat. Wrench started by pulling his own return strikes, but Graham seemed unfazed, even when Wrench scored direct hits, and they stepped up their conflict, testing each other.

Graham was grinning, too, Wrench realized, and after they had each tallied several good punches, they slowed their circling and finally lowered their fists. Graham wiped blood away from the corner of his mouth. Wrench blinked and realized his vision in one eye was hazy from a good hit. He wondered if the black eye would be gone by the time he met Lydia. Not that a black eye was going to make or break his image of refinement.

One of his teeth was loose.

"I thought I was going to have to spray you two down like two fighting tomcats," Travis said in disgust.

Startled, Wrench looked around to find that Travis and Breck were standing at the entrance to the courtyard.

"What is *wrong* with you two?" Travis scolded them. "You'd better get cleaned up before Scarlet sees either of you. You're still on probation," he reminded Wrench. "And I'm the one who vouched for you."

He directed a chiding glare at Graham. "I was here to see if Wrench could give me a hand with some burst pipes in cottage five."

"And I'm here to see if Graham can cram his surly self into a waiter's uniform and help with the dinner rush," Breck added. "We're up a few guests and down a waiter."

Graham shrugged an affirmative and followed Breck out of the courtyard.

Wrench cleared his throat. "I'll be right there," he said, bending to pick up the empty bucket and the scattered tools.

"Are you guys okay, then?" Travis asked in concern.

Wrench gave a rough laugh. "Never better," he said sincerely.

CHAPTER 8

"$\mathcal{W}$hat can I get you?" Tex asked as Lydia drifted up to the bar, butterflies in her stomach.

"A quiet table for two," Lydia said, eyeing the crowd skeptically. There were a lot of people in the bar for dinner time, and she could hear the steady buzz of conversation from the restaurant deck above.

Tex looked at her quizzically, taking in the tight red dress she'd chosen, and the matching flower in her hair.

Lydia looked back, biting her lip. She was practically bursting with the need to tell someone—anyone!—her news.

"You could take a candle down to one of the tables at the far end of the pool," Tex suggested. "It's as quiet as you'll get, but the drink service will be slow." His face was alight with curiosity, but he didn't pry.

"I'm meeting Wrench," Lydia blurted, even though he hadn't asked.

Tex blinked, and gave her a cautious smile. "I wouldn't have guessed he was your type," he said in neutral tones.

"How about a glass of wine?" Lydia said plaintively.

Tex grimaced. "Anything else? We're out of white and nearly

dry on the red, too. It's been hard getting restocked since the storm, with no boat of our own."

"Anything," Lydia said, sinking down onto a barstool. "Not too strong. Well, maybe strong."

"I'll whip you up something perfect," Tex promised, filling a glass with ice cubes and reaching for bottles. "And you tell me about your date."

Lydia misheard *date* as *mate*, and said, "How did you know?" before her ears caught up with her brain. "Oh, you said... *never mind.*"

Tex wisely kept his mouth closed while Lydia twisted the hem of her full dress in her hand. It was a dress she often wore for the formal dances held once a week, and probably overkill for this meeting, but it was what she had always pictured herself in when she had thought about her mysterious future mate. Probably the dancing through a garden and the poetry she imagined he'd whisper to her weren't going to happen.

"Your mate then?" Tex prodded, putting the drink down in front of her.

"Don't tell anyone yet," Lydia begged.

"My lips are sealed," Tex said gravely. "Nervous?"

"He's not what I expected," Lydia confessed. "He's... so..."

She didn't know how to finish the sentence. Her swan wanted to dwell on his strength and handsome face, but Lydia couldn't put aside the things that Laura had told her. He kidnapped people and did who knows what else for terrible men. He wasn't anything like the suave billionaire philanthropist she had always fantasized about.

"Complicated?" Tex suggested.

"That's a start," Lydia said hopelessly, taking a sip of her drink. It was light and fruity, with just a promise of warming alcohol behind the subtle fruit and bubble. "*Bueno.* This is good," she said, determined to concentrate on the best before her.

"I'll name it after you," Tex said. He pushed a candle across the bar to her and lit it. "Now you take this and your drink to one of the tables on the pool deck and when Wrench shows up, I'll send him your way."

Lydia smiled. "Thanks, Tex," she said gratefully.

"You're going to be fine," he assured her. "Mates always find a way to muddle through."

"There might be a lot of muddling," Lydia said faintly, remembering the way he had flinched away from her touch.

Someone down the bar called for Tex and he turned away to attend to them.

Lydia gathered up her candle and went to find the perfect place for an imperfect meeting.

CHAPTER 9

"What are you grinning about?" Wrench growled, pulling at the starched collar of his suit.

Tex didn't pause in his mixing, giving a bottle an unnecessary flip as he topped off the concoction he was working on. "You clean up nicely, that's all. Lydia's going to be impressed."

Wrench scowled at him. "What do you know about that?" he asked.

"I'm a bartender," Tex said cheerfully. "I know everything." He passed the glass across the bar to the waiting guest and turned to give Wrench an appraising look. "Yup, she's going to find this quite acceptable."

"So glad you approve," Wrench said dryly. "Where is she?" He had scanned the crowd, but none of the milling women, despite the curious and interested stares he was receiving, held the slightest hint of interest to him.

Tex pointed, along the bar, out the deck. "Down on the far end of the pool deck. Take your own drink, the service is going to be lousy there. Pour you a beer?"

Wrench's heart did a little flip flop in his chest. Past the cheerful lights of the bar, he could only make out the vaguest impression of a figure sitting at a table lit by a single candle.

Ours, his panther purred. *Only ours.*

"Whiskey," Wrench told Tex. "On the rocks. Make it a double."

He stared into the darkness at Lydia while Tex poured it. "Good luck," he said, and Wrench couldn't doubt his sincerity... or his need for all the luck he could get.

The walk was agonizingly long. He elbowed his way through the bar crowd without really registering them, then faced the long staircase down to the pool deck. The splash of the pool water features turned the sound of conversations to a distant hum, and as he walked the length of the pool, the thrum of the ocean surf muffled both.

By the time he'd made his way past the lounge chairs to the end of the deck overlooking the beach, his eyes had adjusted to the dim light and he could make out Lydia, sitting at a round table with a candle in a jar, watching the flame. She was wearing a red dress, and her dark hair was swept back with a red flower. Candle light warmed the planes of her perfect round face. The dress was long, but slit up one side, and a long, strong leg ended in a high-heeled shoe.

She drew herself up as he approached, and Wrench almost faltered as she turned to look at him, before stomping to the far chair. It squeaked across the tile as he dropped himself gracelessly into it and put his untouched whiskey on the table.

"Hi," Lydia said shyly.

Wrench made himself reply, "Hi."

There was a silence that deserved no adjective but awkward.

"Great suit," she finally said.

Wrench realized that he should have said something about how beautiful she looked, but the moment was long past. "I was supposed to be here as a guest," he felt obliged to explain. "And sometimes I do bodyguard work at fancy affairs so I gotta be able to clean up and put on the penguin suit."

"It looks good," Lydia said warmly, and Wrench was astonished by how good her praise felt. Panther purred louder.

"So, what do you do when you aren't doing bodyguard work?" Lydia asked, fingers toying with the condensation on her glass. Even her fingers were sexy, and Wrench had to focus with determination to stop imagining how they'd feel on his skin.

"I fix stuff for people. Independent hire for…" Wrench tried to figure out a delicate way to explain his work. "For when you gotta scare someone or need a guy who's good in a fight."

Lydia looked disturbed by the idea. "Did you… hurt people?"

"Yeah," Wrench said, hating the way she flinched. "But I had a code, you know. I was careful no one on the side got hurt, and I was pretty picky about jobs. Not, you know, indiscriminate." He hoped he used the word correctly. The line of her neck was distracting him, and the way her hair curved along it. Had it been straight before? Now it was in big waves.

Lydia took a hearty swallow of her drink, clearly not eager to pursue this line of conversation. "So, do you have any family?"

Wrench took his own sip of whiskey. It was warm enough that the ice had melted, watering it down just a little. "Sister," he said briefly. It certainly wasn't sisterly feelings that he was having now, watching the bounce of her dark hair on that tantalizing arc of her shoulder.

Lydia perked up at that. "Oh, what's her name? Younger or older?"

"Renna. Younger. Foster sister, actually. Ended up in the same house when I was ten and she was eight. We looked out for each other. They were going to split us up after a couple of years, but I was big for my age and people were already paying me to, you know, walk 'em down the bad blocks and remind people of their promises. It helped that I was a panther shifter. So we skipped school and took off on our own."

"You lived on the streets?" Lydia's expression in the flickering light could have been horror or pity.

Either emotion was unwelcome. Wrench wasn't sure why they were talking so much about him. He supposed he ought to be asking her these kinds of polite questions.

"You got family?" It didn't sound as polite when he said it.

Polite or not, Lydia grasped the effort like he'd thrown a lifeline. "I have six brothers and sisters, all younger. My mama and her two sisters live on the same block, so there have always been a passel of cousins and aunts and uncles around. Holidays and weddings are always madhouses, and there's not a month that goes by without some occasion for celebration."

Wrench stared. "That's a lot of family."

"I can't imagine growing up without them. Even when they drove me absolutely crazy and made me long for the tiniest piece of privacy."

She had relaxed when she spoke of them, and leaned forward to the table to include Wrench in her enthusiasm. He was helplessly enraptured by the way her whole face smiled, and the golden candle light over her generous cleavage. Then she reached across the table and put her hand over his and Wrench startled back, nearly spilling his whiskey as he scrambled up.

She rose to her feet and he stared across the table at her.

Every emotion she felt was bare on her face; she hadn't spent a lifetime trying to shutter those thoughts from the world. Wrench could see her frustration, confusion, and hurt as clearly as if she'd spoken them out loud.

"I'm making a mess of this," he said regretfully, and her face softened.

"Maybe we shouldn't be talking," she suggested, moving around the table towards him.

Her breath was ragged, Wrench realized. Could she be wanting him like he was craving her? The scent of her, the rustle of her skirt, it was like a net of feminine enticement.

"Wrench…" she said, then paused; it was a ridiculous name from her mouth. "Do you have another name?"

"Warren," he said, and the name was as unfamiliar to his ears as it was to his mouth.

"Warren," she tested it, and when she said it, it sounded respectable. "Warren," she repeated, and then she was standing right before him, so close he could have bent down and kissed her if he dared.

"Do you dance?" she asked.

"Nope."

"A shame," she said. "I find that things are simpler when you dance." She put a hand on Wrench's chest. "I could teach you."

"I doubt it," Wrench said. Her hand felt like a brand, hot through the layers of his suit. The evening was comparatively cool, but he was sweating. She was so close, her toes almost even with his own. Even in heels, she had to look up from about the height of his shoulder.

"Warren," she said warningly.

It didn't feel like his name.

"You're going to have to kiss me eventually, you know."

He was dying to. He was ready to. Panther was panting and pacing and lashing his tail. Lydia was looking up at him with expectant eyes, her hand still on his chest, her red lips just parted. He had to know what she tasted like.

Then his phone rang.

CHAPTER 10

*I*t wasn't terribly surprising that a man named Wrench was exceedingly good at swearing.

Lydia took her hand back as he dug into his suit pocket, blistering the air with his displeasure. She grimaced as he found the offending phone and thought for a moment that he was going to throw it directly into the pool. But his eyes fell on the message on the screen and his face went from angry to grim. "Renna," he said apologetically. "I have to take this. She wouldn't call. Not unless…"

Lydia waved at him to take it, hoping she looked more patient than she felt. She walked back around to her seat at the table, wishing she had more of her drink left.

She watched as Wrench paced around in the shadows just out of earshot, clearly agitated. He raised such a tempest of feelings in her. She'd been wildly attracted to him when he was flexing muscles in the sun of her courtyard, but in a suit, she'd barely been able to catch her breath. He walked like he owned the very ground he passed over, like he had a place to go, and the place he had to go… was to her.

Their conversation had been deeply confusing. She didn't know how to reconcile his rough speech with a man who could use 'indiscriminate' and looked *that* good wearing a suit. Even if it did look faintly like he had a fading black eye.

When she'd talked about her family, his face had been so hungry and full of longing behind his scowl. But when she imagined bringing him to meet her family, she balked. He was just so rough around the edges. Her sisters had brought home lawyers and doctors. She would be bringing home... a felon?

Footsteps along the pool caught her attention.

Laura's arrival with a tray bearing a second drink for her was a welcome distraction.

"Tex says that if you need him thrown in the pool, he's happy to oblige," the curvy woman said with a knowing wink.

"I don't think it will come to that," Lydia said gratefully, taking the drink.

"He's on the phone," Laura pointed out. "During your date."

"It was really important," Lydia said swiftly, surprising even herself with her quick defense.

Laura didn't pursue the subject. "I'll take your empty glass," she offered. "If you need anything, or you change your mind about having him dumped in the pool, just wave."

"Thank you."

Lydia watched her walk away down the long edge of the pool, and turned to find that Wrench had hung up and was dropping into the seat opposite her.

"Everything okay?" she asked tentatively.

Wrench raked fingers through his cropped hair. "Not really. Renna's been put in witness protection."

"Witness protection? What happened?"

"Blacksmith happened." Wrench's face was a deep scowl that Lydia could sense held a world of worry.

"Blacksmith?" she prodded. The name was familiar.

"The cartel. The one I'm supposed to testify against. They tried to blow up her car."

"She's okay, though?" Lydia knew that something else was causing Wrench's distress. "She didn't get hurt?"

"She's okay, but she doesn't trust the people in the witness program," Wrench growled. "Says there's probably a mole, and she doesn't want them to know about Ally."

"Your niece?"

"She was with her dad this week, hasn't been entered into the system, and Renna wants to keep it that way. She wants Ally to come stay with me here." Wrench stood, pacing to the edge of the pool.

Lydia could almost feel his agitation, and could imagine his panther's tail lashing. She stood and followed Wrench.

"Her dad can't keep her?"

Wrench snorted. "Her dad couldn't protect her from a wet piece of toilet paper," he said derisively. "And he travels a lot. I gotta go back. If I can't bring her here, I gotta go take care of Ally myself."

"Would *you* be safe? If someone is after your sister…"

"Doesn't matter," he growled. "Got no choice."

"There has to be another option," Lydia said, exasperated.

Wrench stopped and pivoted to face her. "It's not that I want to go," he said mournfully. "I finally felt like I had a chance here, and you…"

"Have her come here," Lydia said impulsively. "Wait, Jenny's going to LA tomorrow to do something at her law firm for a few days, she could bring Ally back with her."

Wrench stared at her, looking suddenly hopeful. "Would Scarlet be okay with that?"

Lydia frowned. "Probably not. She doesn't want kids at the resort because it's clothing-optional."

All the hope that had started to light up his face drained out.

"She doesn't *have* to know," Lydia suggested.

Wrench looked dubious.

"Ally can stay in my room. I have a private bathroom, and no one else uses my courtyard. It wouldn't be for long, would it?"

"Jenny said that she'd heard from Tony that they were still prepping for the big sting. It might be before Christmas, but that's not for sure."

Lydia frowned. "Well, that's just a month away. And she could come here while we worked out something long term, if it ends up taking longer."

"I ain't got money for the plane ticket," Wrench growled.

"I've got airline credits," Lydia said swiftly. "They bumped me off my last flight home and I've got enough to get her this far."

"Why would you do this for me?" her mate asked wretchedly.

Lydia had been very careful about reaching out to him, seeing how he avoided it. She liked to touch people when she was talking to them. She was used to standing close to people and would frequently pat them, or even put her arm around them if they were friends. She couldn't resist now, sliding her hand into his carefully and twining her fingers with his. He stiffened, but didn't pull away.

"You are my mate," she said simply. "I would move the stars for you."

The feel of his fingers against hers made her shiver. He was so strong, his fingers calloused and rough against her skin.

He stared and her, then slowly squeezed her hand, using it to draw her nearer, until she was close enough that he could put his other hand at the small of her back and bend down to kiss her.

CHAPTER 11

*L*ydia's lips were everything Wrench had suspected they'd be, her hot mouth opening at his touch. He was not sure how her fingers had slipped from his, but both her arms were somehow around his neck. She was stronger than she looked, and if Wrench had wanted, he was not sure if he could escape her.

He had no desire to escape.

He did have other desires, and when she pressed herself against him, he knew she could not be unaware of the need he was feeling. His erection was not in the slightest way disguised by the suit he was wearing, and when Lydia slid against it, he wasn't the only one whose breath hitched.

She was more woman than he'd ever held in his arms, more eager, more alive. Her hands were at his neck, his shoulders, sliding along his jaw. Her tongue was demanding, and when he finally had to break away for breath, she was panting.

"That's more like it," she said, sounding raggedly delighted.

Wrench wasn't great at conversation, but he was better at this, so he kept silent, and when Lydia tugged at his tie, bent willingly to kiss her again.

This kiss was brief and relatively chaste. "I don't know what time Jenny will leave tomorrow," she said warningly. "If we want to talk with her about it, we should catch her tonight."

Wrench couldn't quite keep from growling in displeasure, both at the interruption, and at the reminder about Ally. He nodded, and reluctantly let go of Lydia, first one hand, then the other, giving her shoulder one last caress.

She fixed his tie and rubbed her lipstick from his mouth, to his bemusement, then turned and marched down the pool deck, her heels clicking commandingly on the tile.

Wrench followed, moving silently behind her.

The guests gave them no more than a glance, but Tex and Laura, behind the bar, both smirked knowingly at their approach. Wrench suspected they'd been watching, and glowered an unspoken challenge at the bartender.

"Is Jenny here?" Lydia asked firmly.

"At The Den with Travis," Laura supplied, turning serious. "What's up?"

"Is she still planning to spend a few days in LA?" Lydia asked.

Laura nodded. "As far as I know. She's planning to leave on the charter tomorrow morning."

Lydia exchanged a look with Wrench. "She may be coming back with a... visitor."

Laura and Tex both leaned in eagerly. "Who?" Laura asked avidly.

Wrench would have kept them out of the mess, but Lydia clearly had other plans. "Wrench's niece, Ally."

That earned him surprised looks. "How old is this niece?" Tex asked suspiciously.

"Eight," Lydia explained, and both Laura and Tex made little noises of protest. "And she's in trouble, with the same lovely people who brought you to us in the first place." That was to Laura, and Wrench had to smother a smirk.

His lady was no dummy.

Laura's look of pity and guilt was immediate. "Blacksmith?" she said quietly.

Wrench nodded an affirmation. "My sister's in witness protection. I need Ally out of his reach."

"Just until we figure something else out," Lydia added quickly.

Laura and Tex exchanged worried looks.

"Scarlet won't approve," Tex warned.

"She doesn't have to know," Lydia said firmly. "Ally can stay in
my room and never leave my courtyard. We just need a little inter-
ference."

"It would be easy enough to smuggle in food for her," Laura
said thoughtfully. "And Scarlet doesn't come to the spa much."

"Not that you'd guess it by her nails," Lydia said with a sideways
smile.

"Blacksmith is bad news," Laura said with a shake of her head.
"Tony says that they are pretty close to making their move against
the cartel. Maybe even before Christmas, thanks to the extra
evidence Wrench was able to give them." She sighed. "I'm in. You
know it."

Tex looked sideways at Laura. "It's an eight-year-old damsel in
distress. What's a cowboy to do?" When he extended a hand across
the bar to Wrench, Wrench shook it heartily.

"Scarlet can't fire all of us," Lydia said merrily. "Not right
before the Christmas rush!"

Wrench wasn't as sure, but he followed his mate as she led the
way back past the pool steps and up through the garden to the staff
house known as The Den.

Travis and Jenny were cuddled together at the couch, watching
Graham and Breck play a first-person shooter video game on the
TV screen.

Wrench would have left Graham and Breck out of the plan, but
Lydia didn't pull the others aside like he thought she would, sitting
instead on the other leg of the L-shaped couch. Wrench settled
awkwardly next to her and Travis and Jenny sat up to give them
their attention.

"What's up?" Travis asked.

"You're going to LA tomorrow?" Lydia asked as an opening.

Jenny nodded, looking from one to the other. "That's the plan," she said. "I've got a few things to do in person at the law firm."

"You know Blacksmith, the charming individual that is the reason Laura and Wrench are both here?"

"Can't say I've actually met him," Jenny said wryly. "But we do have some history." She smirked at Wrench, who kept his expression carefully shuttered.

"He's put Wrench's sister in witness protection and his eight-year old niece is in danger."

The silence that met that statement was amplified by Breck or Graham pausing their game to turn and listen more obviously.

He scowled at them indiscriminately.

"That's terrible!" Jenny said in horror.

"What can we do?" Travis asked.

Realizing that the lynx shifter's hand was twined with Jenny's made Wrench aware that Lydia's was similarly resting on his; he took a moment to marvel that it felt so natural that he hadn't even noticed when it happened. It took all his willpower not to pull it away once he was aware of it.

"Bring her back here from LA with you," Lydia said.

Jenny didn't even hesitate. "Yes, of course."

"Are you sure?" Travis said at the same time. "No kids allowed at the resort."

"Scarlet doesn't have to know," Lydia said.

"Scarlet knows *everything*," Breck interjected.

Graham's growl might have been agreement.

Wrench had a feeling this was going to be a harder sell than it had been to Laura and Tex. Laura at least had an idea what Black-smith was capable of.

Lydia's skirt rustled as she leaned forward earnestly. "Ally is eight. She's old enough to understand that she needs to stay out of sight. But we need to keep her off the radar of the cartel."

Lydia was not just smart, Wrench realized. She was masterful. It was hard not stare at her beautiful profile and want her.

"I'll bring her back," Jenny said firmly. "What will I need?"

"I'll get the plane ticket sorted," Lydia said. "Give me your

phone number and we can stay in touch as we work out the details."
She produced a phone from somewhere impossible within her dress.

"I dunno," Breck said skeptically as the girls exchanged
numbers. "I'll do what I can, but Scarlet doesn't fool easily."

"She's got a lot on her plate right now," Jenny said soothingly.
"She'd probably just rather not be bothered."

Travis smothered a dry laugh. "If by that you mean she is totally
fed up with lawyers—present company excluded—and insurance
company bean counters, and we should all just stay completely out
of her way anyway, that's probably true."

"I thought she seemed tense," Lydia said knowingly, as she sat
back again. "That's settled then. Thank you."

Wrench added, gruffly but sincerely, "Thank you."

He was rewarded with smiles from all but Graham.

They stood up, and Wrench gave firm handshakes all around.

"Now then," Lydia said, standing and brushing out her skirt. "I
believe we were in the middle of a date?"

Wrench frowned and stood at attention. "Yes, ma'am."

This earned them a round of smirks and knowing looks, which
Wrench chose to ignore as Lydia slipped her hand into the crook of
his arm. Head as high as it went, he led her out of The Den and
back into the darkness that was just theirs.

CHAPTER 12

"You are amazing," Wrench said gruffly to Lydia, once they were out of earshot of The Den.

It was astonishingly meaningful. Lydia looked up at his face, already so familiar. "I couldn't do anything less," she said simply.

He stopped, and Lydia drew up in front of him. Just as she had hoped he would, he gathered her gently into his arms. "Thank you," he said. He looked like he might want to say something more, but only repeated, "Thank you."

Then he kissed her again, and Lydia put her arms around him, wherever she could reach, and kissed him back.

His shoulders were ridiculously wide under her hands, and his mouth was insistent and strong on hers. His hands seemed to hold her entire torso with no effort, big thumbs making patterns along her muscles. Every nerve in her body was alive with hunger.

"My room," Lydia breathed, when they broke apart for a moment of air. Wrench's hands gripped harder, then he let her go free with visible effort. She made herself let go as well, stepping back. She smoothed her mussed hair back, then took his elbow again.

They maintained a decent charade of self-control all the way up the gravel path, breaking it only as they came to the front entrance of the spa. Lydia wasn't sure who reached first, but they fell into the doorway pulling at each other's clothing, desperate for the feel of skin against skin.

His plain gray silk tie came untied with a whisper and was flung to the tiled floor. Lydia's fingers were trembling with need as she unbuttoned the tiny buttons of the shirt beneath, and she had to pause to run her hands up underneath the crisp material.

Wrench's hands were trying to make sense of her dress, baffled by the lack of zippers or buttons, while his mouth was distracted on her neck and at her collarbone.

Lydia finally took mercy on him and backed far enough away to get her dress off over her head.

The way he looked at her, amazed and longing, made Lydia pause, wearing nothing but her heels and underthings.

"You are so beautiful," Wrench said breathlessly.

Lydia realized that he wasn't going to move again without help, and stepped into his waiting hands. "You're wearing too much," she told him chidingly.

Moving much faster than a man of his size ought to, he sent the jacket spinning across the room, shortly followed by the shirt. Lydia wasn't sure if he managed the buttons or simply tore them off, and didn't find that she cared either way, as his free hand was touching parts of her like they'd never been touched before. When she moved up against him, she was keenly aware of his erection between them, pressing in tantalizing places.

He lifted her up onto one of the chairs, kissing her neck and running big hands down her thighs. He toyed with the lace of her underpants, but didn't offer to remove them, making Lydia sigh in delicious frustration.

"You're still wearing too much," she pointed out.

It was quickly obvious that the chair wasn't wide enough for their intended activity, and Wrench growled near her ear, then lifted her up as she wrapped her legs around his bare torso. He refused to be distracted by her kisses, and carried her to one of the curtained alcoves. He sat her on the massage table and returned swiftly to his attention to her breasts, barely contained in her bra.

Lydia unclasped his pants and ran the zipper down slowly, thoroughly distracted by his stubbly kisses on the delicate skin of her chest. She reached questing fingers into his underwear as he let the pants slip down, and freed the member that was waiting impatiently there.

His hands were definitely not his only large feature.

When his fingers made their way down from her ribcage this time, they didn't skip over her lacy underpants. He removed them like they had offended him, lifting Lydia and slipping it out from beneath her in one smooth motion. They shifted as necessary to line up, and then Lydia was moaning out loud as he spread her at last and drove into her.

"Yes, oh, yes," Lydia told him. "My mate, my one."

Wrench may not have been exactly as she'd fantasized, but this was more than her imagination had been broad enough to anticipate.

He didn't just enter her, he owned her. Every nerve was afire. Every touch was electric. When he drew back, she was bereft. When his stroke drew him in deeper, she was complete. Her entire consciousness narrowed to how he filled her and lifted her and the crest of the orgasm he built in her.

When she fell from the heights of her release, she expected... she wasn't sure what to expect, but it wasn't to have Wrench kissing her neck and using his clever fingers at the small of her back and his hips to soothe and calm her as he slowly—so slowly!—continued to stroke into her.

She could do that again, she realized in astonishment as he steadily began to increase his pace, licking her collar bone. One of his hands moved into her hair, which was loose now. Lydia had no idea where her flower clip had gone.

It didn't matter. Her world diminished again, to his hands on her skin, to his member filling and satisfying her bone-deep hunger for him. She was feather to his fur, and she was a vessel of pleasure and completion.

As she came a second time, she felt the steady rhythm of his strokes become more frantic, and his hands clawed at her flesh in desperation.

It was unsurprising that he swore when he came, blistering the air with his release as he filled her at last.

Lydia dissolved into breathless laughter, somehow not at all bothered by it through her own bliss.

Wrench came to a panting halt, holding her tight against him and staying, pulsing, in her for as long as flesh allowed it.

"Did I hurt you?" he asked, hands careful where they'd been clawing only moments before.

Lydia drew his face down and kissed him, carefully and deeply. The urgency was past, but all the tenderness remained. "Not at all," she assured him.

"Lydia," he said, looking back into her face.

Lydia waited for him to continue, but he didn't.

He didn't resist when she kissed him again, opening his mouth to her tongue willingly. Lydia was astonished that desire woke at the pit of her stomach again already, and she kissed him with the unspoken promise of 'more' and 'soon.'

Then she pushed him back. "Come," she said. "We've got to find all of our clothing or I will never hear the end of it from my staff."

Her dress was an easy find, and all the parts of his suit except two buttons. Her hair clip had vanished.

"Lydia," Wrench said again, standing naked and befuddled with his clothing in his arms.

Lydia added her dress to his pile. "Come," she said again.

She led him past the storeroom to her room, tucked away at the very back of the spa. To her surprise, someone had snuck in and lit candles, and her bed was scattered with rose petals. "Well, this would have been lovely," she laughed, and Wrench cracked a smile.

On her bedside table, her usual reading material had been tucked away and there was an ice bucket with a bottle of champagne and a handful of condoms arranged in a rosette.

"Champagne?" she offered Wrench with a laugh.

"Not really my bag," Wrench said apologetically.

"Not mine, either," Lydia agreed. "Anyway, we've got a lot to deal with tomorrow, and I've got sunrise yoga to lead."

Wrench dropped their clothing on a chair. "That sounds suspiciously like it happens at sunrise."

Lydia removed the bra that hadn't made it off her during their eager lovemaking, enjoying the way it made Wrench's breath hitch when she released her breasts. "That is how it works, yes." She yawned, blew out the candles, and slipped under the light blanket on the bed, scattering rose petals. "Come on, Warren," she said, patting the bed beside her. The name didn't sound quite right to her ears, but she couldn't reconcile 'Wrench' as a name in her head.

He glowered for a moment, then sighed and slid down under the blanket with her.

Lydia scooted to curl up with him, worried for a moment that it would be awkward and restless to sleep next to someone after so long in an empty bed.

But he felt perfect in her arms, like they were both exactly where they belonged, and she was asleep before she could do more than sigh in contentment.

CHAPTER 13

*W*rench was good at waking up without betraying that he had, staying still and keeping his breath even while he got his bearings.

There was a naked woman in his arms, and memories of the night before came flooding back in vivid detail.

Lydia.

It took all of his willpower to continue not to move. His brain wasn't the only thing that had identified his situation, and his morning erection felt thick and hard between them. It was increasingly difficult not grinding himself against her as he registered that his hand was on a lush, perfect breast.

He opened his eyes. He was going to have to do the right thing.

He had no idea what the right thing was.

Marriage. Marriage was pretty typical, wasn't it?

Wrench squeezed without intending to, and Lydia stirred and murmured in pleasure.

He pulled his hands off of her and rolled away as she woke up, resisting his other desires. He was supposed to be helping Travis this morning, and he slipped out of the bed and began pulling on his clothing.

"Oh crap," Lydia said, looking at the clock beside the bed as she stretched. "I didn't set the alarm." The faintest hint of sunrise was creeping in the high windows. She scrambled out of bed and began dressing as quickly as Wrench was.

"I'll do the right thing," Wrench said firmly.

"Excuse me?" Lydia was pulling on yoga pants, hopping around on one leg and jiggling very distractingly.

"We gotta get married, I guess," Wrench said. "I'll do it."

Lydia froze in an impossible position, and nearly fell over. "*Excuse* me??" she repeated.

"I ain't got a ring or nothing, but I'll have someone pick one up, and we can find a priest or whatever if you don't want to do a court-house thing."

Lydia's look of surprise turned stony.

"Or a church," Wrench said faintly. "We could do a church if you wanted." Probably he wouldn't burst into flame.

"This is your idea of a marriage proposal?" Lydia said coldly.

Wrench pulled on his shirt, and found that several key buttons were missing. He wasn't entirely sure why Lydia's reaction was so chilly, but he knew that he'd better get it figured out in short order. "White dress?" he guessed desperately. "Um, do I need to ask your dad?"

Lydia yanked a tight shirt down over her head and started flinging things into a bag: a rolled up piece of foam, and what looked like a tiny gong.

"I'll do what I have to," he promised.

"What you have to?" Lydia stared at him. "I don't want you to have to do anything. Screw that. Screw *you*. It would... just have been nice if you had *wanted* to."

Then she was dashing out the door, while Wrench was trying to figure out where his shoes had gone.

The shoes proved to be under the chair holding their clothing, along with Lydia's red dress and high heels. He picked the dress up, remembering the feeling of the fabric over her skin. Without her, it was just a lifeless shell.

Like him.

That was... sort of a poetic idea, wasn't it? Wrench thought about writing it down for Lydia, but knew it would come out awkward and stupid.

He wasn't a romantic person. But Lydia deserved better, so Wrench lay the dress neatly over the back of the chair and picked up his suit coat.

He was going to need help with this.

CHAPTER 14

*L*ydia wasn't terribly late, and there were only a few guests waiting in the event hall where they held classes and the weekly fancy dress dances.

She apologized sincerely and hastened to roll out her yoga mat. The music was waiting for her in the disc player, and she took the guests through a series of stretches and warm-ups automatically.

The time they spent silently holding each pose was agonizing. She kept remembering Wrench's reluctant proposal to marry, and his scowling resignation. She also kept remembering how he'd felt, moving inside of her, and the way he smelled, and the way his hands felt in the small of her back.

"Let's ease into child's pose," she squeaked, not remembering for a moment what she usually did next. "Extend your arms, palms down, and let your forehead rest on the mat. Feel your back relax and soften as you stretch. Allow the tension in your shoulders to leave your body through your arms, into the floor."

Her tension wasn't going anywhere.

After they had held that for a count that Lydia forgot to keep, she took them through increasingly challenging poses, automatically talking about centering and embracing the day.

After the session broke up and she said her final *namastes*, she remained, cross-legged in the empty hall, trying to find the peace that she had espoused.

"I keep swearing to myself that I'm going to get up early enough to actually catch this class one of these days."

Lydia opened her eyes to find Laura, dressed in workout wear. She had a cup of coffee in each hand and a sly smile on her face.

Lydia sighed as Laura took a seat opposite her, and accepted the coffee she offered.

"You don't look as happy as I expected," Laura said candidly. "Are you wishing you'd taken Tex up on that offer to tip Wrench into the pool?"

"A little," Lydia said wryly, sipping her coffee. It was sweet and creamy.

"What did he do?" Laura demanded.

For a blinding moment, Lydia could only remember how he'd taken her on the massage table, setting every nerve on fire. "He proposed," she said, attempting to leash her body's reaction.

Laura squealed. "Ooo! You go, girl! And you said yes?"

"It was the most awful proposal I've ever even heard of," Lydia said frankly. "He made it sound like the worst kind of torture. Like he had to make a proper woman of me or something. 'I guess I gotta,' he said."

Laura nearly spit out her coffee. "'I gotta?' He said that?"

"He said he'd get someone to pick up a ring, like it was some grocery order from the mainland," Lydia snarled.

Laura gaped at her. "What did you say?"

"I told him, 'Screw you.'" Lydia rubbed her forehead. "I was late for class already and just left."

"That's kinder than I would have been," Laura sniffed. "What a jerk."

"He's not a jerk," Lydia said, surprising even herself with her quick defense. "He's just… just…" she floundered. "He's trying," she said achingly.

Laura reached out and took her hand. Lydia squeezed back.

"He's not what I expected," she confessed. "I had my mate built up in my mind. He was this... ideal. And Wrench... Warren..."

"He's not ideal," Laura said sympathetically.

Even though she'd been thinking the same thing, Lydia had to restrain herself from hissing defensively, and her swan flared strong wings in protest. "He's so handsome," she protested. "And when he kisses me, it's all the magic I could ask for."

Laura grinned wickedly. "A good lover is a good start," she suggested.

"But is it too much to ask for a little wooing?" Lydia couldn't help complaining. "I mean, maybe I'm not going to get him to write poetry for me, but could he pick me flowers, or tell me I'm pretty or *anything*." She gave a windy sigh and slumped forward over her knees. "I sound like a whiny teenager."

"It will work out," Laura promised. "He's your mate, and you're perfect for each other."

He's perfect, Lydia's swan agreed serenely.

Lydia drew in a deep breath, turning her fold into a deliberate stretch. "You're right," she agreed. "I just have to have faith that we'll get where we're going, and I won't strangle him on the way there. I'm too old for silly girl dreams, anyway."

"I wouldn't give up on those dreams just yet," Laura said with a knowing smile. "He might surprise you!"

"Speaking of surprise," Lydia said, glad of another subject to distract herself with. "When is Jenny leaving? I'd like to see if I can get her flight numbers so I can coordinate Ally's flights."

"The charter comes in mid morning," Laura said, rising as Lydia did. "She's packing now, I think."

"I'll go catch her now," Lydia said, then stopped. "Or maybe just a little later." She knew unerringly that Wrench was also at The Den right now, and she wanted nothing less than to run into him and let everyone witness their ridiculous awkwardness. "After breakfast."

*W*rench stripped out of his suit with distaste. He always felt ridiculous dressed up. There was no point putting a diamond collar on a junkyard dog.

Someone had snuck into his room, much as they had Lydia's, and tidied the place. The champagne was in a vessel of meltwater, and the condom rosette made Wrench scowl. Rose petals bruised underneath his feet, making the room smell too sweet.

The Shifting Sands staff uniform felt considerably more comfortable, and Wrench stomped down to the kitchen to find breakfast and advice.

Jenny and Travis were kissing in front of the fridge, which did not improve Wrench's mood.

They broke apart when he cleared his throat, and laughingly gave him passage to the food.

Tex was pouring himself coffee, and Bastian and Saina were sitting together on the couch. Saina was reading a wedding magazine and Bastian was sorting his first aid kit on the coffee table.

Wrench took a plate of fancy egg pie and a thick slice of bacon, and went to the little island, altogether too aware of the amused and curious looks he was receiving.

"Does he look satisfied?" Jenny asked Travis in a stage aside. "I can't tell."

"Who could? He doesn't do anything but glower."

"Lydia never signaled us to come dump him in the pool, so presumably he didn't blow it," Tex added, leaning against the counter.

"I'm right here," Wrench growled. "And I have ears."

"No expressions, though," Jenny teased.

"I asked her to marry me," Wrench confessed.

From the couch, Saina actually applauded, and the rest of the staff gave a chorus of congratulations until Travis thought to ask, "What did she say?"

"She... didn't seem real happy about it."

There was a moment of silence, then Bastian demanded, "What did you *do*?"

"I told her, we had to, I guess, and she... wasn't really pleased."

The men in the room all groaned.

"Did you say that?" Jenny asked in disbelief. "'I guess,' and 'We have to?'"

"Sweet daisies," Tex said, shaking his head.

"I think that's worse than my proposal," Bastian said in a stage whisper to Saina.

"You didn't propose," Saina whispered back. "Your mommy and daddy made you promise to marry me. And this is even worse than that."

Wrench stabbed a fork into a fancy egg. "Look, I know I screwed up," he said. "I ain't no poetry man or whatever Lydia was looking for. You can all be assholes, or you can actually fucking help me."

There was a moment of silence, then Tex cleared his throat. "What kind of help are you hoping for?"

"I'm not writing poetry for you," Travis said swiftly. "Ask Jenny, I'm terrible."

"It was sweet," Jenny protested.

"I wanna know how to do my own sissy stuff," Wrench said. "I'm not gonna ask someone else to do it."

"It doesn't matter what you do," Saina said, putting aside her magazine. "It will just matter that you try."

"It's just showing that you care," Jenny agreed.

Wrench might not have expressions of his own, but he was good at reading them on the faces of others; the men in the room did not agree.

"Flowers," Tex suggested neutrally. "There's a reason they're a classic."

"Just don't pick your own without asking Graham," Travis reminded him firmly.

"He could take her on a walk out to the waterfall," Bastian mused.

"Oh, that's a gorgeous walk," Jenny agreed. "Take a blanket."

"Just don't fall down a cliff and collapse a lung," Travis added.

Jenny sighed. "You could just bring Travis, he's a wet blanket."

Saina rose to her feet and walked into the kitchen. "You guys are amateurs. You have to figure out what it is she'd specifically enjoy," she said. "The more personal the gesture, the more it's going to mean. When Bastian was courting me, he went and got me the one thing I needed more than anything else in the world."

"You called me an idiot," Bastian protested.

"You were," Saina told him with a dazzling smile. "But it was very sweet of you. What does *Lydia* like?"

The things Wrench first thought of were wildly inappropriate. He struggled to remember what she'd had in her room. "Yoga? Piles of rocks?"

Tex smothered a laugh. "That's not much to work with."

"She likes music," Jenny said. "Can you play an instrument?"

Wrench gave her a skeptical look.

"Okay, maybe not."

"She likes pretty things," Bastian offered.

Everyone carefully *didn't* look at Wrench.

"I could figure out her favorite dishes and you could cook her a romantic dinner here at The Den," Saina suggested.

Wrench snorted.

"Maybe we should narrow this to things Wrench can do?" Travis suggested. "What are your skills?"

"My skills ain't applicable," Wrench said dryly. "Unless she needs a drain unclogged or someone *persuaded*."

"She likes dancing," Tex said thoughtfully. "Breck still says he can teach anyone to salsa."

"Nope." Wrench stuffed another fancy egg bite in his mouth. "Not happening."

Jenny looked at her watch. "I'm going to have to get going. The charter is coming in about an hour. Who's driving the van?"

Travis offered his elbow. "I'll be conducting your chariot, lady."

Jenny took his arm. "Thank you kindly, sir."

"Will you need assistance with your luggage?"

"You may carry my bag, James," Jenny said with laughter.

"Is this the kind of crap Lydia wants?" Wrench asked Tex desperately.

"Afraid so," Tex said with a laugh.

Wrench groaned. "I'm so fucked."

CHAPTER 16

"He's trying," Jenny told Lydia when they met near the resort entrance. "He really is!"

Lydia didn't have to ask who. She tried to help load the luggage into the van, but Travis waved her off and she stepped back with Jenny to watch him finish putting the luggage into the van. "I suppose everyone has heard about my charming marriage proposal."

"You aren't really angry about it, are you?"

Lydia sighed. "No, I'm not mad anymore. It's just that I wish... I wish it had been from the heart, you know."

"It was," Jenny insisted. "It's just that his poor heart is all shriveled up and starved for affection, so it came out stupid and backwards."

Lydia had to laugh at the image of Wrench's heart, prune-like, in that magnificent chest. "It's not so small as all that, or he wouldn't care what happened to his sister or his niece," she pointed out.

"So there's hope for him!"

"There's hope," Lydia sighed. "He's my mate and of course we'll make it work."

"Travis probably felt just as frustrated with me," Jenny reminded her. "It was days before I could even talk with him. I was so sure I was going to lose what was left of my human self if I let myself love him the way I wanted to."

Lydia looked at her thoughtfully. The otter shifter certainly looked content now. "How'd you work things out, then?"

"I finally trusted that he'd love me, even with all my flaws and foibles. And he helped me realize that my otter was really a part of me, and it was safe to let go of my fears."

"I'm not afraid," Lydia said hesitantly, and then wondered if she really was. She was afraid of disappointment. She was afraid she was being judgmental. She was afraid she had missed her chance at perfect happiness.

She could feel her swan's cluck of disapproval. *We did not miss our chance*, her swan said chidingly. *This **is** our chance.*

Maybe she *was* a little afraid, because the idea irrationally made Lydia want to turn and run. She'd spent so many years longing for this, hoping and dreaming, waiting for her mate bond to bloom from the faint direction sense to the beautiful, perfect calling as it had for her brothers and sisters. And now that it was here, and nothing was the way she'd imagined it would be, she was acting like a spoiled little brat.

Had Wrench ever imagined her?

She tried to picture growing up on the streets, protecting one of her younger sisters, never even knowing if she'd ever find her mate, not just wondering when.

Jenny was giving Travis a lingering embrace and kiss.

"I'm going to miss you, Whiskers," he was teasing her lovingly.

Lydia abruptly remembered her original purpose in finding Jenny. "Your return flight numbers," she said. "I need to get Ally's ticket!"

Jenny quickly pulled them up on her phone and they exchanged all the numbers that Lydia could imagine they'd need.

"I'll work out the custody details with the police in LA," Jenny promised as the guests in the van began to grow impatient. "I've got a friend at the firm who specializes in weird custody cases."

Lydia gave her an impulsive embrace. "Thank you for every-thing," she said sincerely. "Have a safe trip."

She waved at the van, then returned to the spa to make sure that everything was ready for the next wave of guests.

It definitely wasn't. Some of the wiser guests had decided to schedule services before the rush, and one of Lydia's assistants was panicking that they didn't have enough hands or supplies.

"We'll make do," Lydia said firmly in Spanish. It was her new motto.

She got to work, turning the last jugs of product on their lids so they could squeeze as much out of them as possible. "I'll take the massage," she said. "Call down to see if Laura can come do mani-pedis."

She took the guest, the middle-aged brunette who'd been reading a book at the airstrip, back to the private alcove.

Memories of the night before swam back and Lydia had to catch her breath. Maybe they should concentrate on what worked for them, and the rest would come later.

Her swan settled serene black feathers against her back, pleased with this resolution.

Lydia was glad for the mood lighting as she went through her questions about injuries and the massage request with the client; she knew she was blushing like a schoolgirl.

By the time the spa had caught up, the next rush of visitors had arrived and were beginning to drift in.

Lydia only had time to eat an energy bar for lunch, and when the salon finally slowed for dinner, her hands were aching and her shoulders felt like she'd been lifting weights for a week.

"I'm going to need to get my own massage," she laughed with one of her assistants, rolling her shoulders back and stretching. She wondered if Wrench would be any good at massage; he had those big, clever-looking fingers, but he seemed so nervous about touching her.

Small wonder, she thought, if touching her did the same things to him that it did to her.

But it gave her an idea.

CHAPTER 17

*W*rench plodded through his day, muttering over the list that Bastian, Saina, Tex, and finally Laura had talked him into. Take an evening walk on the beach. Don't talk about beating people up or how he got scars. Compliment her clothes. Laugh when she made jokes. He added himself, Don't think too much about Renna or Ally, though he couldn't keep himself from checking his phone a dozen times for a missed call, or a text with any news.

"You look lovely in that," he practiced, over and over again. "Your hair looks great."

The others had vetoed 'You smell good,' because they said it made him sound creepy.

"She does smell good," he had protested.

"It's best to pretend there is no other way they could smell," Tex had corrected him.

Wooing a woman was clearly a minefield.

He made his way to the spa as the dinner rush was starting, glad to find that the front of the spa was not crowded. One of Lydia's assistants was sweeping up, and she nodded towards the back with a knowing smile and a spatter of swift chatter in Spanish.

Wrench went back through the storage area and went out Lydia's back bedroom door, where he finally found her.

Lydia was in the little courtyard behind the spa, folded into an impossible shape and balanced on one leg.

Wrench drank her in. As much as he dreaded the whole prospect of courtship, he felt better in her presence. Everything seemed somehow softer, without being weaker, and he could feel his panther settle.

Was this what peace felt like?

Lydia unfolded herself and bent her head over her tented hands, then looked up at Wrench expectantly. "*Hola.*"

Every practiced phrase was gone from his head, but Wrench realized he was holding a flower and thrust it at her. A compliment. He was supposed to give her a compliment.

"You're bendy," he growled.

To his great relief, Lydia laughed tolerantly and accepted the flower. "Did you ask Graham about this?" she asked, drinking in the smell of it.

"Got his blessing," Wrench said with a nod. What was he supposed to do next? "Walk on the beach?"

"Is that an invitation?"

"Yeah." Belatedly, Wrench remembered the advice about polite invitations, and the playful interaction between Jenny and Travis. "If you wish, my, uh, lady?"

That earned him a quizzical look. "Well, that sounds lovely, my, uh, lord," she said. Wrench decided that it was mocking, but not unkindly.

Wait, was this a joke? He was supposed to laugh at her jokes. "Huh huh huh," he attempted badly.

Lydia mopped off her forehead with a towel. "Mind if we swing by the kitchen on the way? I'm famished. We can make a picnic of it!"

"Great." Eating food on a sandy beach in the dark sounded like a new level of torture, but Wrench was here for Lydia, and he'd accepted every level of discomfort that came with her. Gritty, ill-lit food was a small price to pay for a mate like her.

She tossed her towel back into her open door into the basket that waited there, and Wrench had to swallow at the way her lush body wiggled with the motion.

"Why don't you go see what you can gather up for us from the kitchen," she said. "And I'll take a quick shower and put the flower in water."

"I can do that," Wrench agreed, though he'd much rather stay and observe the shower. The others had been adamant that he go along with her ideas if she countered with anything.

When he got to the kitchen, he wondered if he'd already erred; the place was bustling like a beehive. He stood near the back, wondering who he'd need to bother.

"You've betrayed me," Breck hissed at him, elbowing past with a tray full of dirty dishes.

"What are you on about?" Wrench growled, dodging another server with a tray of clean cutlery who was dashing out.

"I don't know what's worse," Breck said, shaking his head. "Whether it's the fact that you had to up and find your mate and steal a perfectly gorgeous woman from the open market, or that you would ask those buffoons at The Den about romance." He made a rude noise with his lips. "Those rookies were all but celibate before they met their mates, and what they know about courtship would fit in a greased flip-flop."

He deftly unloaded the tray into the sink for the busy dishwasher as he continued to berate Wrench. "Seriously, courtship? If you're going to do Lydia right, and I certainly hope you will, you need good advice, knowledgeable advice, not the bumbling attempts of those idiots. They probably gave you a line about saying how pretty she looked and suggested a walk on the beach."

"I need a picnic basket," Wrench said.

"I *know*," Breck said, rolling his eyes. "You suggested a moonlit walk before she'd had a chance to eat dinner, of course she's going to counter with a dinner on the beach."

Wrench blinked. "Well, yeah…"

"And they probably gave you a bunch of compliments to give

her and tried to come up with thoughtful gifts that cost no money or some kind of ridiculous camp craft you could make."

Wrench frowned. This was also true.

"Amateurs," Breck said scathingly. "Compliments from you will never sound anything less than painfully rehearsed, and Lydia doesn't want a crappy paper mache heart. Play to your strengths and keep your mouth shut. She'll happily carry the conversation if you let her, so ask about her family, her spa, and her dancing, and let her do the talking. All you've got to do is listen when she's talking and fuck her brains out when she's done."

That sounded far more useful to Wrench than anything the others had been able to tell him.

"Order up!" Chef hollered from deeper in the kitchen.

"There's a basket by the door," Breck said hastily.

As Wrench looked around for it, Breck added, "Cottage two is right off the beach and set up for you. Shower outside if you're covered with sand." Then he vanished with his tray to swoop up a pile of full plates to deliver to tables at the restaurant, leaving Wrench to gape after him.

Wrench found the basket, right by the back door and gave a grunt of surprise when he went to lift it; it was not the empty basket he expected to have to fill at the buffet, but already packed to the rim. He flipped open the lid to discover a blanket at the top, covering whatever wonders had been loaded into it.

"Thanks," he said gruffly, but Breck was already long gone.

CHAPTER 18

*L*ydia was surprised how hard it was to watch Wrench walk away, even when she knew it would only be for a brief time. There was something about his presence that put her at ease, even while it made her restless and full of longing—this odd dichotomy that somehow completed her.

She showered swiftly, hopeful to meet him at the kitchen to save him the walk up to the spa. But as she was toweling off, she felt him start his return trip unexpectedly and she paused. Had something gone wrong? He couldn't have picked food from the buffet so quickly, could he?

She finished drying with alacrity, and applied a touch of quick lipstick that probably wouldn't survive the meal anyway.

Wrench came around the narrow path to the courtyard rather than through the spa, and Lydia was delighted to see that he was carrying a heavy basket. Her stomach growled in anticipation.

"Breck packed it," Wrench said abruptly, as if he was worried she'd think he was trying to take credit for it.

"Right now, I'd eat a rake," Lydia admitted. "I'm ready." She slipped shoes onto her feet and put her hand at the crook of Wrench's elbow. "Let's go down the back way."

She led him out the back entrance of her little courtyard, down to the far side of the kitchen complex, past the hotel and down to the dark side of the pool deck where their first disastrous date had been.

From there, they could take the steps down to the beach. Lydia wriggled out of her shoes and put them on the grass where the sand began. Wrench untied his shoes awkwardly and peeled off his socks to put next to them.

"I know a place," she said, and she slipped her hand into his, thrilled by his touch.

He was clearly not used to walking in sand; stomping did not work, and though his balance was excellent, he floundered through it with brute force rather than grace. Lydia led him down to where the water had hardened the sand, and the walking was easier.

They passed one other couple braving the moonlight, then had the sand to themselves.

Across the crescent of pale sand, away from the lights of the resort, Lydia took Wrench up the bank to a place under the trees, right next to a downed trunk. A pile of discarded beach treasure had been accumulated in a heap nearby: broken shells and bits of coral and colored rock.

Wrench looked up sensibly. "Should we worry about coconuts or something?" he asked.

"Not here," Lydia assured him. She went to take the basket from him, nearly dropping it due to its unexpected weight.

Then she spread out the feast.

A blanket went down over the scrubby sand, corners weighted by bottles of beer (for Wrench) and a bottle of ginger ale (for Lydia). "They don't usually let people bring glass to the beach," Lydia said to Wrench appraisingly. "But there are perks to working here."

"You break it, you rake it," Wrench repeated Bastian's familiar warning.

He pulled out a little electric lantern and set it up while Lydia unpacked the food. There were sandwiches for each of them—Wrench's was almost entirely red roast beef and hers was a leafy vegetable and hummus concoction drizzled with truffle oil and red wine vinegar. The bread was thick and fresh and fluffy.

Chef's twice mashed potato coins were as good cold as they were hot, and were paired with a lightly fermented cabbage salad with carrots and beets. There were two generous slices of a spicy pecan pie for dessert.

"Oof," Lydia said, once she had inhaled everything and licked all the last crumbs from her fingers. "That was amazing."

"Better than I expected," Wrench agreed, his own food gone just as fast.

She scooted a little closer to him on the blanket, so they were both leaning against the downed tree trunk. "Well done, Warren," she told him. "This date's already got an A, and there's still a chance for extra credit."

Wrench gave a guffaw of laughter that surprised them both. "Long as you ain't going to ask me to move again for a bit," he said. "I ain't put down a sandwich that size since I was a teenager."

This would have been the point where anyone else would have put an arm around her, but Wrench didn't offer to. Lydia wondered if he would move away if she scooted closer. The heat that radiated from his side was magnetic.

"I plan to go nowhere for a while," Lydia agreed. Before them, the moonlight reflected in shimmering ripples off the ocean surface. Frogs and insects made a familiar drone in the air. If it weren't for the new need growing in her core, Lydia would have been utterly content to spend hours here.

Then there was an odd rumble, and the ground beneath them gave a buck and a growl and shook like a dog coming out of water.

Lydia and Wrench tried to stand, and failed, each ending up on their knees as the motion finally subsided. Wrench wrapped his arms around Lydia, holding her tight and tucking her under him as big leaves and small fruit pattered down all around them.

CHAPTER 19

A resident of Southern California, Wrench was no stranger to earthquakes.

It still left his knees feeling like water and his jaw clenched like iron, and he was reluctant to let go of Lydia until she squirmed in protest.

"Well, Warren, I'm awake now," she said shakily as he slowly let her go.

The lantern had fallen over, as had Lydia's ginger ale, soaking the blanket. "Good thing that wasn't an old fashioned oil lantern," Lydia said, setting it upright. "Even if that would have been more romantic."

"Lydia," Wrench said, as she started to gather their picnic back into the basket.

"My heart's still racing," she laughed lightly. "What an eye opener!"

"Lydia," Wrench tried again.

"I don't suppose that was part of your date plan?" she said, with a sly sideways look. "Got my blood to rise, certainly."

Wrench finally caught her arm and pulled her up close. "Lydia," he said, and this time she looked back at him, her eyes bright in the darkness.

"I ain't Warren," Wrench said seriously. "I ain't this picnic. I ain't the kind of guy who's going to write you poetry or sing you love songs. Believe me when I say you wouldn't want me to. I'm just Wrench."

"War—Wrench," Lydia said softly.

"Lemme say this," Wrench said desperately.

Lydia was silent, but her hands crept up his arms and gave him courage.

"I love you, Lydia," he said in a rush.

She didn't say anything and Wrench scrambled to fill the silence. "I'm just Wrench, and I ain't got fancy learning, and I've done a lot I ain't proud of, but I'll do my best for you."

Just as Wrench feared he'd have to come up with more to say, Lydia rose up on her toes and kissed him.

Kissing Lydia was like fighting—all adrenaline and excitement. And at the same time, it was like floating in a pool, and a shot of whiskey, and that moment you wake up before you remember that you have to get out of a comfortable bed and stop dreaming.

She tasted like pie: spice and molasses.

And her tongue was alive in Wrench's mouth.

He picked her up into their kiss, one hand cupping her sweet ass and the other arm across her back. She slipped her arms up around his neck and held on, kissing him back.

"My room?" she said when she had breath for it.

Wrench shuddered as Lydia slid herself along his body, catching on the erection that was bulging through his shorts.

"Got a better offer," he told her, kissing down her jaw and tangling his fingers in her loose hair.

The rest of the picnic was stuffed back into the basket willy nilly; the blanket had no chance of fitting back in and Lydia gathered it up in her arms as Wrench took the basket and led them back towards the resort, then stopped at the high privacy hedge. "Cottage two?" he asked Lydia, and she took point, leading him by the hand to the second path up from the sand.

Cottage two proved to be one of the fancier rentals, with its own covered hot tub on a porch, and steps up to big sliding doors—one of them still missing glass and boarded up from the storm that had recently passed through. The doors opened onto a well-appointed living area between two luxurious bedrooms. The larger of these bedrooms had a trail of rose petals, but there was no champagne this time, and the condoms were down to one.

Wrench was almost offended. Did they think he and Lydia would be slowing down? he wondered, amused.

Breck's fine advice matched his panther's plan perfectly, and Lydia was clearly done with the talking part of it—she was stripping off her clothing wherever Wrench wasn't touching her. It was challenging to keep his hands off of her long enough to get his own clothing off, but she tugged at it insistently, running clever fingers up under his shirt and down into the waistband of his shorts.

"Wrench," she sighed, as he wriggled short pants down over her hips.

The name sounded right from her lips.

Almost as right as she felt under his hands.

She was strong and curvy and her breasts filled his hands perfectly.

Her hair was silky and loose, like a dark curtain to her shoulders, and it whispered over him when she pushed him over on the bed and straddled him like a goddess.

Wrench felt like a starving man at a buffet, not sure where to look or what to touch, because everything felt like the fulfillment of a wish he'd never known he made.

And Lydia rose to every touch, shivering and gasping when he found the place where waist met hip with both hands, closing her eyes and moaning when he put a hand at the back of her neck under her hair, crying out when he explored the inside of her thigh, keeping his touch careful and light.

She was wet on his fingers, and she pressed herself around them when Wrench hesitated. He stroked her gently, drinking up her delighted reaction as he deepened the touch and brought her higher and higher.

He was harder than he'd ever known was possible, and every time she writhed, his cock rubbed against the velvet skin of her thigh, driving him mad with desire.

Then she was drawing off his fingers, and before Wrench could decide what to do, she was impaling herself, and he made a roar of triumph before he could stop himself.

"Yes, oh, yes," she said, as he arched up and drove deeper into her, holding her on by her glorious hips.

He worried briefly that he might hurt her—he could not hold her on himself as hard as he wished, then she was rolling, and pulling him over on her across the broad bed.

Crushed rose petals scented the air and he found that he could press into her harder this way, fingers clenched into the coverlet with one hand and wrapped around her shoulders with the other.

"Yes, please, *yes*" she cried, polite even in the throes of the orgasm that Wrench could see in the way her muscles all tightened, leaving only her gorgeous breasts to move freely.

"Fuck yes," Wrench replied with less civility but no less sincerity.

As she cried out in release, he came as well, any hope he'd held onto of prolonging their act washed away in the way her orgasm dragged him into his own.

"Yes," she repeated, laughing as she fell from the heights, still arching into his last strokes. "Fuck, yes."

CHAPTER 20

*L*ydia had enough of her mind left when Wrench had finished unmaking and rebuilding her world to set the alarm on her phone, so morning didn't catch her by surprise this time.

It was still very challenging to untangle herself from his big arms and rise in the dark.

She had never wanted so badly to stay under the covers; usually when she woke, she found no point in remaining in bed and didn't really understand the more usual impulse to pursue sleep longer.

But listening to Wrench's breath near her ear, feeling the steady thrum of his heart through his chest—there was nowhere Lydia wanted to be more.

She felt safe here, and with sudden clarity realized that this mattered to her far more than any of the romance and courtship that she'd once imagined.

She was safe.

She was filled with trust and contentment.

There was an erection, thick and demanding, pressing against the small of her back.

For the fun of it, Lydia pressed back, and was rewarded by Wrench's hands tightening against her and muttering as he woke.

She wanted him again, as badly as she had when she'd first seen him, standing in his courtyard.

It was hard to remember why she'd been so disappointed when she realized who he was. So he wasn't a doctor or a lawyer—he was a hundred times more. He was thoughtful, gentle, caring. The way he'd reacted to his sister's danger and his niece's need betrayed a heart that didn't match his gruff exterior.

And damn, he looked great in a suit.

It was with great reluctance that she pulled away. Wrench rolled out of the bed after her, despite her murmured reassurance that he could sleep longer if he wanted.

"No point in staying in bed alone," he said, giving her a look that suggested she could easily change the conditions.

His unclothed body was like a dream; his big body rippled with muscles.

"You're going to have to tell me about those tattoos someday," Lydia said, pulling on her clothing. She had just enough time to scamper up to her room for a quick shower before her sunrise class.

Wrench shrugged. "Not a lot to do in jail. One of the guys was a good artist. Short story."

Lydia had to chuckle. "And that scar?"

Wrench looked cagey.

"What?" Lydia asked, pulling her hair back into a quick ponytail.

"Tex said not to talk about how I got scars," Wrench confessed.

"You've been talking a lot with those guys in The Den," Lydia said suspiciously. "What else did they tell you?"

"Give you compliments," Wrench said. "Don't talk about work or how I got scars. Learn to dance." He said the last with absolute dread in his voice.

"War—Wrench!" Lydia stopped gathering up herself. "You don't have to do any of those things!"

He glowered at her in disbelief.

"You don't have anything to prove to me," Lydia said firmly, wishing she'd said so sooner. "You don't have to be something you aren't. You are everything I need, everything I never knew I wanted. If I ever gave you the impression that I wanted more, I was wrong."

She remembered his face in the moonlight when he'd told her he loved her. He had been ashamed that he wasn't the poetry and picnic.

"When I said we should get married—"

"I don't want to be something you have to do," Lydia cautioned. "Not ever."

"You're not," Wrench said simply. "I've never wanted anything more."

Lydia could not resist looking at his erection, which had not so much as stuttered in intensity while they talked. She could not doubt that he wanted her, and he was refreshingly unabashed about it. She had no idea whether he was still talking about matrimony, but she stripped her shirt back off.

She could rinse off in the shower here and still be to class on time.

Wrench was reaching for her as swiftly as she was reaching for him.

And then Lydia didn't even care if she made it to class at all.

CHAPTER 21

"Got a load of roofing supplies coming on the next charter," Travis said loudly with a smile at Wrench that lacked both secrecy and subtlety. "I'll need your help getting it up here, Wrench."

Wrench gave a deliberately slow glance in Scarlet's direction, but the red-haired resort owner was frowning over her phone, oblivious to their conversation. They were gathered at the back of the bar, where outgoing guests were getting their last drinks and Wrench was carrying their luggage up to the courtesy van.

"Fine," Wrench said gruffly, putting down the giant rolling bag he'd carried up from one of the lower cottages. He knew that neither his expression nor his tone would betray his own nervousness; this was the flight that Jenny would be returning on, his niece Ally in tow.

He hadn't seen either Ally or his sister in months, and probably Ally's last memory of him was promising to pay for dance classes that he'd never been able to deliver. She was eight now, so grown up compared to the adoring little niece he remembered bouncing on his knee and carrying on his shoulders.

What if she hated him? What if she blamed him for her mother being put in witness protection?

Wrench certainly blamed himself.

"It'll be in about eleven," Travis continued loudly as Scarlet tucked her phone away and returned her attention to her staff. "I'll bring a load of guests and luggage up, then I'll need your help for a second load."

Wrench was just wondering how much more suspicious things could look when Tex came to the rescue. "Get you a drink, Scarlet?"

"I might need one," she said unexpectedly—Wrench had never seen her with anything stronger than a glass of water. "That ass Benedict Beehag has the nerve to tell me he's showing up tomorrow afternoon in a helicopter with some new interested buyers that his lawyer found for him." Beehag was the owner of the island, and he had been threatening to sell it out from under Scarlet for several months now.

Tex winced. "In the middle of the new guest rush?"

Scarlet's face was as angry as Wrench had ever seen it, and Wrench thought he could hear her teeth grinding. She turned to Travis. "Tell me Jenny made her connecting flight." Her voice dared him to have a different answer.

Travis replied cheerfully, "She did! She'll be coming up with the second load in the van. With the roof supplies. That I need Wrench to help carry—ow!"

"Sorry," Wrench said insincerely as Travis stepped back to nurse his trod-upon toe. Had the man never lied about anything in his life?

This plan to hide Ally was looking more and more unlikely.

On the other hand, if there were already unwanted visitors coming, that was the kind of chaos that would do an excellent job of masking one small girl's secret occupancy.

"I am going to fight this with every legal advantage we can get," Scarlet said fiercely. "Jenny said she'd found some language in the contract that we might use to block a sale, and at least stop these unscheduled visits."

"Surely they aren't all going to end in a hostage situation," Tex said lightly.

"They might," Scarlet said savagely. "Each set of buyers seems worse than the last. I can't imagine where Benedict's lawyer is even finding these monsters."

"Surely 'monsters' is a little harsh," Tex said peacefully.

"I'm not sure it is," Scarlet said suspiciously. "These buyers are the dregs of bad people. Not just self-centered rich jerks, but... drug dealers and slavers." She looked over at Travis thoughtfully. "What's up with you?"

Wrench swallowed hard, watching sweat bead on Travis' forehead.

"Up? With me?" the lynx shifter asked, brown eyes wide with desperate innocence.

"Why aren't you getting the last batch of guests to the airstrip?"

Wrench gathered up an armload of luggage. "Off we go," he rumbled, pushing Travis in front of him before he could open his mouth again.

"Off we go!" Travis echoed obediently, taking a load of his own luggage. Guests downed their last drinks and straggled out after them as they headed for the tiny parking lot at the peak of the resort.

"Whew," Travis said, as Wrench helped him stash the luggage in the back of the courtesy van. "That woman, I swear. She just looks right through you sometimes."

Wrench refrained from pointing out that Travis' performance might have been a tad suspicious. It had worked for the moment, now he just had to wait.

And he knew just how to fill the hours he had to kill now.

CHAPTER 22

*L*ydia frowned, surveying her spa.

"Someone left a jar of honey treatment open overnight," Laura told her, looking a little wild around the eyes.

"Let me guess," Lydia said with a sigh. "Ants."

"Ants," Laura agreed.

Two of the assistants were clustered by the door, refusing to step any closer to the stream of wriggling invaders.

"Go get a mop and bucket," she told them, striding into the room. Their little island off the coast of Costa Rica had absolutely wonderful weather, perfect humidity, and any rain was short-lived and warm, but it *was* a jungle, and a jungle that came with bugs. The resort rule about food in private cottages was strict for a reason.

The sugar ants, though tiny, made the cosmetics shelf look like it was alive in their relentless march for food.

"We're going to need to clean them off of all the product bottles," Lydia said, surveying the scene. "And wipe up their trail all the way out the door. Use the spray bottle in the cabinet that is marked 50% alcohol."

As they went to work, Laura elbowed her. "Made the earth move, did you two?"

Lydia smirked sideways back. "We didn't move the earth until after the earthquake, thank you," she sai, mock-primly.

The infestation was small, at least, both in tiny species and in total number, and Lydia and Laura were able to seal up the object of their interest and kill them in swaths. Lydia's distaste for causing pain had made her choose to switch to vegetarianism years ago, and she found that ants were not entirely beneath her regret, even if she did accept their deaths as necessary.

Was this how Wrench felt? she wondered, then had to laugh at herself for comparing pest control with Wrench's checkered past of freelance thug work.

She heard the quiet beep-beep of the courtesy van as it arrived with the next wave of guests just as she was shaking the last inter-lopers from the cushions.

"Go let the check-in station know that the spa is open again," she said to Laura. Across from the bar was a bulletin board that had sign-up lists for all the classes and events for the week, as well as major status updates. The staff had their own version of this board by the mechanical room where they could list housekeeping prob-lems and negotiate shifts.

Ally would be on this charter plane, Lydia suddenly remem-bered, but she guessed that Travis and Wrench would have to make a special trip to get her and smuggle her in. She didn't have to even concentrate to sense Wrench passing close by, using the outside entrance around the outside of the spa to head for the van. He had been back by her room, probably making sure it was ready for Ally, and undoubtedly worrying.

Though the big man was good at shuttering his expressions, Lydia was coming to realize that this didn't indicate that he wasn't feeling things.

Quite the opposite. She had caught him checking his phone frequently, hoping for an update from his sister, and when he spoke of her, it was gently. And when he thought she wasn't looking, his expression softened. Lydia had some hope that she might even make him laugh someday, and she looked forward to that.

She was giving her third pedicure, laughing and chatting with a new guest when Wrench returned and she sensed him slipping back to her private courtyard.

She bit her lip, not wanting to rush her job. "A polish?" she offered, hoping for a negative.

Not unexpectedly, the guest accepted a coat, waffling an agonizing time between two similar shades of pink.

Lydia applied it expertly, but made herself slow down and continue the conversation, making suggestions about the best things to do at the resort, and the foods not to miss. "Chef's cinnamon brittle at the dessert table," she said firmly. "If you like sweets or cinnamon even a little."

A guest wanted to feel pampered and important, she reminded herself. That was her first job.

"No tip?" the guest said hesitantly, admiring her new nails as they dried.

"Oh, no," Lydia said. "Everything is included. If you feel moved, you can leave a general tip on your way out, because everyone here pulls together and I couldn't do my work without the handyman who keeps our plumbing going, or a dozen people you may never even see!" She thought tenderly of Wrench.

Finally, the guest left, and Lydia could wash her hands and go meet Ally.

CHAPTER 23

*A*lly was exactly as Wrench remembered, all pink cheeks and blonde curls, and nothing like his own dour, dark-haired self. She bounded off the plane into Wrench's open arms. "Uncle WRENCH!"

"You know you're going to have to be more quiet than that here," he scolded her, enfolding her into a hug that lifted her off the ground.

"The plane was REALLY LOUD," Ally protested. "My ears are all numb."

Wrench held onto her longer than she wanted and Ally squirmed free and dropped back to the ground. "THANK YOU!" she hollered at the stewardess who was helping to fold up the stairs, waving enthusiastically.

While Wrench helped Travis load supplies into the van, she tripped back and forth with them, carrying the lightest items, sometimes with hilarious results.

She continued to be exuberant for the entire trip back, shouting over the road noise and exclaiming over all of the lush greenery and ridiculous road conditions.

Graham met them at the top of the resort. "Scarlet's at the bar," he told them briefly, and Ally came up from underneath the tarp she'd been crouched under. "You're clear for now."

"Are you the gardener?" Ally asked, looking at the wheelbarrow he'd been pushing.

"Groundskeeper," Graham growled at her.

"Can you tell me what all the plants are?" Ally asked eagerly, pulling her purple speckled suitcase out from under the tarp and letting it fall down the steps behind her as she scrambled out from the van.

Graham glared down at her until Travis laughed at them. "If Wrench hasn't been able to scare her, what makes you think you could?" he asked. "Come here, kitten, let's get you down to Lydia's."

Ally tried to take point, even not knowing where she was going, and nearly led them into Scarlet's office.

"No, no," Travis and Wrench both said together.

"Never in there," Wrench added.

"I'll lead," Travis said, and they shushed Ally as they passed above the bar to the spa.

She squeaked and then covered her mouth as they walked into Lydia's courtyard. "It's so pretty," she whispered.

"Did you do this?" Travis asked in amazement.

"Had a few hours," Wrench said, disproportionately pleased by their reactions. "Not done yet."

The mosaic had grown. He had returned to the spot of his picnic with Lydia and gathered up the broken shells and rocks that had been collected and abandoned to add to his materials.

The first few butterflies were still awkward, but as the image moved from lower right to upper left, they had improved, and the addition of shimmering mother-of-pearl and dark lava rock had given Wrench the extra colors he'd wished for. He'd begun experimenting with size and rotation, and the effect, as he'd hoped, was that they gained life and motion as they spilled out of the original corner.

"Can I do some?" Ally asked eagerly, eyeing the bucket and the bag of thinset.

"Sure, kid," Wrench said.

"It's a good way to keep her busy while she's lying low," Travis said with approval. He was still appraising the mosaic. "Can you do one of these on that wall on the restaurant deck? That one that's just painted cement? I've been thinking I'd tile it one of these days, but this would be better."

Wrench shrugged. "Sure."

"Oh, maybe we could wrap a couple of columns with this stuff," Travis suggested gleefully.

But the lynx shifter's opinion had ceased to matter, because the one person he really wanted approval from came out of the spa drying her hands on her apron.

"You must be Ally," Lydia said to the girl, then she looked up at the mosaic and her jaw fell open. "Oh, Wrench! It's gorgeous!"

"Are you my uncle's girlfriend?" Ally asked suspiciously.

Lydia looked at Wrench like a drowning woman. "I, ah…"

"She's my mate," Wrench said, in what he hoped was a squashing voice.

It was usually effective on grown men, but less so on little girls.

"Oh, are you an Australian?" Ally asked with interest.

Lydia smothered a laugh. "No, dear, I'm from Cabo San Lucas, Mexico."

Ally looked disappointed. "Well, I've always wanted to meet someone from Australia. Do I have to live with you?"

"I hope it won't be as bad as all that," Lydia said tolerantly. "Let me show you your room."

Ally perked up at that. "I get my own room?"

"It's technically my closet," Lydia admitted. "But it's big enough for a cot, and I've moved most of my clothes out so we can make it yours." She offered Ally a hand, which was accepted after just a moment.

"It's a good thing you're doing," Travis said, when the two had slipped into Lydia's room.

"Not much else I could do," Wrench grumbled.

"We'd better get cracking on those roof repairs," Travis said. "After that big deal we made about getting the supplies in."

Wrench grunted, and was kind enough not to point out the big deal had been all Travis.

CHAPTER 24

*L*ydia was relieved by Ally's impression of her new bedroom. "It's CUTE!" she said in glee. "Like a fort!"

Lydia had given the room a little extra glow with a string of Christmas lights she'd borrowed from the holiday supplies, and found a mosquito netting to drape the little cot in. Every spare pillow she could find went in to make the bed more homey, and she'd draped it with one of the fancier cottage quilts; they had plenty of extra bedding, at least. Her own hanging clothing had been mostly put in boxes under the cot, the few garments she knew she'd need were pushed to the back.

"Oooo, can I wear the dresses?" Ally asked.

Lydia hesitated. She didn't want to say no, but… "Only when I'm here, dear. Some of them are tricky to get on and some are a little fragile."

"They are PRINCESS dresses!" Ally said, not dismayed by Lydia's decree. She pulled her little suitcase over and began dumping her clothes—scruffy jeans and t-shirts, mostly—willy nilly into the drawers that Lydia pointed out as hers. "Are you an actress?"

"I run the spa," Lydia explained. "And I teach dance classes."

"I was supposed to take ballet," Ally said wistfully. "Can I take your class?"

"Yes," Lydia said, then regretfully, "No. No one is supposed to know you are here, of course! But I can give you a special class."

Ally gave an ear-splitting squeal of delight and threw her short arms around Lydia's hips. "I'm so EXCITED!" she said.

Lydia shushed her, and Ally clamped a hand over her mouth. "THORRY!" she said, not at all quietly from between her fingers.

"I have to go work in the spa soon," Lydia said. "I'm afraid I don't have much here for kids, but we've tried to find some things for you that would be fun." She opened up a drawer and shared the few treasures that the staff had scrounged together: Travis had brought a carpenter's pencil and a notebook, Tex had supplied a pack of cards. Bastian had supplied a little bag of shells. Even Graham had brought by a wholly unexpected stuffed kitten which looked quite well-loved.

"It's okay," Ally said softly, but she said it bravely. She lifted up the notebook and pencil, and sat down on the little bed. "Can I draw in this whole thing?"

Lydia failed her attempt to resist patting Ally on the top of her curly head. "The whole thing," she assured her.

"*Senora*!" There was an anxious whisper from the doorway, and Lydia turned to find one of her assistants, Anna, wringing her hands. "It's *Senora* Scarlet!"

"She must have heard about the ants! I'll be back as soon as I can," Lydia promised Ally in a whisper, and she pulled the closet curtain closed and rushed after Anna.

Sure enough, Scarlet was scowling at the product shelf.

"We've got the ants all cleaned up," Lydia said with a broad smile that she hoped didn't look too guilty.

A single lost ant, smaller than a fingernail, attempted to make a liar out of her by crawling up a bottle of massage oil.

Scarlet picked it up and let it flee around her finger in little ant terror. "Hmm," she said, before she flicked it onto the ground out of the open door. "I was actually here to talk about which products you were running low on that were most critical. We're going to have to airmail them over, so I want to make sure that we're only ordering what we need for now."

"Oh, ah, of course." Lydia felt her cheeks heat. "Well, we're nearly entirely out of the hair conditioning spray, and there are three key colors of foundation the Mr. Shifter competition ran us out of. We don't have to restock all of the colors of polish right away, but we do need the clear coat rather desperately."

Scarlet took careful notes as Lydia showed her each of the nearly empty bottles and cosmetic trays.

"We've got another week or two worth of most of the massage oils, we can do without as many choices as usual, and we've got the most important unscented oil in case someone has allergies." Lydia hoped she wasn't talking too quickly or nervously, and made herself take a deep breath and try to center. "Most everything else will last a few weeks, so we don't have a lot of buffer, but it should get us through."

"What did the ants get into?" Scarlet asked, giving Lydia a hard look.

Lydia knew that she was doing a terrible job of looking innocent, and wished desperately that she had a fraction of Wrench's poker face now. At least she had a story to fall back on.

She sighed. "Someone left the honey facial treatment open. We had some sugar ants this morning, but I got them all cleaned up before the rush started." They were standing far enough away from the guests being pampered that the sound of the dryer was enough to keep her careful words from carrying.

"Hmm," Scarlet said, looking over the shelf.

"They do love the sweet things, you know. Just can't resist it." Lydia had to stop herself from babbling further.

"Speaking of things you can't resist…" Scarlet trailed off, giving Lydia a skeptical sideways look.

She knew, Lydia realized. She didn't know how, but Scarlet knew about Ally.

"I know what goes on in my resort," Scarlet reminded her mildly, confirming her guess.

"We couldn't do anything else," Lydia said defensively.

Scarlet's smile was unexpected, if a little exasperated. "You don't generally get a lot of choice in the matter," she said with amusement.

Lydia blinked at her in confusion. "I don't mean to put you out," she said apologetically. "And it's only temporary."

Scarlet's smile cooled. "Temporary? Are the two of you planning to leave Shifting Sands, then? Or are you thinking of a honeymoon?" She looked as confused as Lydia felt.

"Honeymoon?" Lydia squeaked.

Scarlet raised an eyebrow at her. "With Wrench?"

Lydia stared, trying to put the pieces together. "Wrench," she repeated.

"Your mate," Scarlet reminded her.

She didn't know about Ally, Lydia realized in a rush. She'd found out that Wrench and Lydia were mates, which, to Lydia's astonishment, was so natural and perfect as to be unremarkable in her own head now.

She put a hand over her eyes and laughed weakly in relief. "It's been a crazy week," she admitted to Scarlet.

"I'm so happy for you," Scarlet said warmly.

"We haven't made long-term plans," Lydia said faintly, remembering Wrench's reluctant proposal.

Scarlet put a hand on her arm. "Are *you* happy?"

Lydia blinked at her in surprise. "So happy," she blurted without thinking. "It's been..." what word had Tex used? "Complicated." The word failed to capture the nuance. "But I'm... really happy." She laughed, and felt a little shocky. "*Really* happy," she repeated, with emphasis.

And she was.

Wrench made her feel complete in ways that Lydia had never even known she was missing.

He hadn't come with the romance that Lydia had expected, but she couldn't imagine her life without him any longer. And the life she imagined for them together filled her with joy and contentment.

Scarlet gave her a swift, warm hug, a strangely familiar gesture for the resort owner.

"I'm glad," she said simply.

"I'm sorry if it's been any disruption," Lydia said contritely, thinking of her several late classes.

Scarlet waved her off. "No one has complained. I'll get this product ordered, and if you need time off, please give me some warning."

"Of course," Lydia agreed. "You'll know my plans as soon as I do."

As Scarlet left, Lydia heaved a sigh of relief.

A burly blonde man replaced her in the doorway. "I am here for a massage, yes?" Lydia recognized him as the Swedish hockey player, now tanned to a new shade of bronze.

"This way," she said courteously.

CHAPTER 25

*W*rench headed back to Lydia's courtyard, drenched in sweat. Roof work was hot work, and it had been a sweltering morning of it. The pool, as he walked past, was as busy as he'd ever seen it, with many dozens of guests seeking relief in the cool water as the sun reached its peak. The conversation still buzzed with talk about the earthquake, which had apparently originated very near their little island.

"Another morning of roof repairs should do it," Travis told Wrench cheerfully. "It goes pretty fast with two sets of hands."

Wrench grunted.

"We'll have new glass in next week and get the last two cottages back up and running. Scarlet says the boat she ordered should be ready by then, too, and we can start managing our own deliveries again. That's a relief."

Wrench grunted somewhat more positively.

"Bright and early tomorrow at cottage eight," Travis told him, not at all bothered by Wrench's surly silence.

Wrench managed an affirmative grunt.

"Say hi to Lydia and Ally for me!" Travis trotted off towards The Den as Wrench continued upwards towards the spa.

Ally. Wrench quickened his pace. Who knew what kind of trouble she might have gotten into if she was too bored. What if she and Lydia hadn't gotten along?

He drew up at the edge of the courtyard, just beyond a screen of green hedge.

Lydia and Ally were standing together, and both of them were wearing colorful dresses with full, fluffy skirts. Ally's was clearly too big, and pinned to fit, but the smile on her face was exactly right. A little boom box was playing tinny Latin music.

"Now we're going to do the side basic," Lydia said mysteriously. "Watch me first, then we'll do it together."

She did something simple with her feet that made her hips do something amazing, counting as she went. "One, two, three, pause, five, six, seven, pause."

The second time, Ally mimicked her, watching her feet.

"One, two, three, don't watch your feet! Seven, eight, fantastic!"

Ally squealed, clapping her hands and spinning. "This is so FUN," she said in delight.

Something tight in Wrench's chest released a fraction.

"Show me the back and forth again," Lydia commanded, and she counted out, "One, two, three, heel, five, six, seven, heel."

Ally scrambled to keep up, stepping forward when she should step back, but Lydia patiently led her through it again, facing her so that she could lead her through the movements.

"Everything else builds off these two steps, so once you've got them down solidly, we'll move on," Lydia told her.

"Can I wear heels like you?"

"It's best to get the basics down before you get add the complication of heels," Lydia advised.

Ally pouted dramatically. "How old were you when you got to wear heels?" she asked suspiciously.

"Your age," Lydia said without apology. "But I had already been dancing for three years. Don't rush your way to a broken ankle, dear. Let's do the back and forth and I'll show you how to go from one to the other."

Ally's pout vanished as they went through the steps together several times.

When they finished, Lydia turned towards where Wrench was watching. "You may as well come out," she said in exasperation, voice carrying. "I know you're there."

It took Wrench a moment to realize that she meant him. She must have one of those keen shifter senses. He hoped it wasn't smell, because he knew he was filthy from the hot work on the roofs.

He stepped out and gingerly accepted Ally's enthusiastic hug. "Have you heard from Momma?" she asked quietly.

Wrench's heart fell for her. "Sorry, kitten. But no news isn't bad news in this case. She's safe, and she won't call unless there's a change."

Lydia's soulful, sympathetic brown eyes met his over Ally's curls.

"Let's get out of that dress, sweetheart," she said to Ally. "I'll undo your safety pins."

Subdued, Ally let Lydia unfasten the dress and went into Lydia's room to change back into her shorts.

As Wrench was wondering if it would be appropriate to bend down and kiss her, someone behind him cleared a throat and they turned in alarm to find Scarlet standing at the courtyard entrance.

She gave an appraising look at Lydia's dance wear and the boom box as she came into the courtyard. "I came looking for Wrench."

"Oh, Scarlet," Lydia said too loudly. "I was, ah, teaching Wrench a few salsa steps," she scrambled to explain.

Scarlet nodded approvingly. "I presume you will be joining us at the next dance night," she said, to Wrench's sinking stomach.

"Yes, ma'am," he growled unhappily, hoping Ally was smart enough to stay in Lydia's room when she heard that they had visitors.

"You don't need to call me ma'am," Scarlet reminded him. "I prefer to be Scarlet."

"Yes, er, *fine*."

"I need your assistance," Scarlet continued without apparent offense. "We've got some unsavory visitors and I'd like to give them an official escort. I've got Graham getting changed and I'd like you to join him." She eyed him critically. "After a shower, if you don't mind."

"Yes, ma'am, er, yeah. *Scarlet*." Wrench could see Ally appear in the doorway over Scarlet's shoulder, and just as he was wondering how to keep Scarlet's attention, the girl sensibly vanished back into the shadows of Lydia's room.

"Meet me at the office as soon as you can," Scarlet said, and without so much as a glance towards the open door, vanished back along the outer courtyard entrance where she'd come from.

"Oh," Lydia said, weakly laughing and leaning into Wrench. "I swear, she *never* comes here." She began to laugh in earnest against his chest. "You know what this means, don't you?" She teased.

Wrench groaned. "I'm actually gonna have to let you teach me how to dance."

Wrench let himself kiss the top of her dark head, then reluctantly pulled himself away. "I gotta go change."

Lydia stopped him with a hand at his collar and drew him down for a proper kiss. "Come see me after you've chased them off," she said when she had released him.

Wrench felt like his face was somehow unfamiliar, and it was a moment before he realized he was grinning at her.

CHAPTER 26

$\mathcal{L}$aura sidled up next to Lydia, who was standing in front of the buffet trying to decide if Ally would prefer a white lasagna or a Spanish rice. "I hear you'll be teaching Wrench to dance after all," she said archly.

Lydia smirked. "I'm looking forward to it," she said.

They shared a moment of amusement, then Laura sobered. "How's Ally doing?" she asked quietly

"We've had some close calls with Scarlet," Lydia admitted, looking around carefully.

Breakfast had been cleared away for some time, and lunch was generally a lazy buffet affair, with people drifting in and out as they grew hungry. This late in the afternoon, most people were saving room for Chef's culinary dinner masterpiece, and there were only a few people sitting, mostly in pairs, throughout the spacious room. Across the room, Breck was setting the empty tables for dinner, and one of the other waiters was sweeping.

"She's a dearheart," Lydia went on. "And she misses her mother awfully, but is being so brave. I've started teaching her salsa, and Wrench gave her a space in the mosaic to work on." She chose the rice as the most likely to make the journey back to her room without incident.

"Mind if I come up and meet her?"

"It's starting to look suspicious," Lydia said regretfully. "My room has suddenly been the staff's social meeting place the last few days." She slipped a roll into the purse she'd started carrying for the purpose, and followed it with a few pieces of fruit. Then she froze, sensing the unexpected approach of Wrench. Was he still with Scarlet?

Not noticing her sudden discomfort, Laura laughed. "She's the most interesting thing that's happened here since Bastian came home with a shot-up mermaid."

The air in the restaurant grew somehow denser, a neat trick for an open-air building, and both women looked around to find that a contingent of people, each looking more dangerous than the last, had walked in from the back entrance. Scarlet was flanked by Graham and Wrench, who both somehow made the unassuming Shifting Sands polo shirt look military. Neither of them held quite the same menace as Scarlet's stony face.

The other party, led by Beehag's pasty heir Benedict, somehow managed to look sleazy and dangerous, with less veneer of civilization than Scarlet's company. One of them was a fat man in a suit worth more than all of Lydia's clothing put together, and there were three men who had the courtesy not to carry large automatic weapons, but looked no less warlike for that restraint.

"Oh, sweet daisies," Laura whispered at her, clearly from Tex's influence. "They're like a *caricature* of bad guys. I honestly am expecting to hear the score to an awful movie right now."

But Lydia was watching Wrench, observing the tension in his neck and the line of his eyebrows. "Something's wrong," Lydia said, hands clenching on her tray.

"I'll say," Laura agreed. "Scarlet looks like she's going to grind her teeth to nothing."

Benedict was pointing out the spacious area and gesturing to the view. "It's a state of the art kitchen and service facilities," he was saying, barely within hearing distance. "Two walk-in fridges and two walk-in freezers."

"*Three* freezers," Scarlet corrected him frigidly.

"No," Lydia said quietly. "Something else is wrong."

Then one of the goons stepped forward into view from behind his buddies.

Laura sucked in her breath audibly and nearly dropped her tray. Shifter reflexes helped her catch it at the last moment, but the silverware rattled, and she turned away so quickly that the water in her glass sloshed over.

"What is it?" Lydia asked, torn between watching Wrench and comforting her friend. "Who is that?"

"Blacksmith," Laura hissed. She slipped behind one of the columns, out of easy view.

"That's Blacksmith?" Lydia gasped, following Laura.

"No, it's not him," Laura whispered. "But it's one of his regular hires, Bruno. I think. Usually does dirty work."

Like Wrench did, she didn't say, but Lydia added it in her own mind.

She shuddered. "Are they here for Ally?" She wanted to drop her tray and rush up to her rooms to check on the girl.

"They shouldn't know about Ally, but they could be here for me," Laura said. "Or Wrench. Or possibly Jenny. Take your pick. Plenty of us have pissed him off, and if he's gotten wind of the sting..."

Then Jenny strode in, by way of the side entrance, and Lydia had to glance at Laura just to confirm that the other woman was still at her side.

Jenny had lawyered up—she was wearing heels and a fine linen suit, and had her hair back in a twist. She was carrying a leather portfolio, and she had reading glasses she probably didn't need perched on her nose.

"Excuse me," Jenny said, approaching the company fearlessly.

The man that Laura had recognized started just slightly. If Lydia hadn't been watching him when Jenny walked up, she never would have noticed.

Scarlet turned to greet Jenny, introducing her to the group. "This is my lawyer, Ms. Smith."

Benedict and the buyer both look slightly unnerved by the presence of a lawyer, and they exchanged wary looks.

Jenny gave them a dismissive nod. "I'm sure you'll be interested in knowing that I've been reviewing the lease for the resort." Her back was to Lydia now, but there was confidence in every line of her body.

"You can't block this sale," Benedict started to whine immediately.

"Of course not," Jenny said firmly. "But there are very specific terms for showings, which include two weeks of written notice, and mandatory payment of lodging and services at regular market cost."

The buyer was frowning, and looking at Benedict with distrust and skepticism.

"It's not too uncommon to overlook such details in such a *lengthy* document," Jenny said sweetly to the buyer before turning to Benedict. "And I would love to have a chat with your lawyer about some binding references to a previous contract that we don't appear to have on file."

"Believe me, you'll be hearing from my lawyer," Benedict snarled at Scarlet.

"I'll be sure to give him the contact information for *my* lawyer," Scarlet told him serenely. "In the meantime, let me show you back to your helicopter pad, where we will conclude this tour."

Wrench and Graham each took a coordinated step forward, and Benedict took a cowed step back, nearly colliding with the muscle behind him. "This isn't over," he threatened. "You'll get your written notice and I'll be back. You can't stop me from selling this cursed island. You can't!"

Clearly, Benedict was reluctant to give Scarlet an opportunity to sue for breach of contract, and they left with more haste than they'd come, the buyer shaking his head and muttering under his breath.

Laura didn't relax with their exit. "This isn't over," she said darkly. "It wasn't a coincidence that Blacksmith's thug was hired for this job."

CHAPTER 27

*W*rench was thinking along very similar lines. It wasn't chance that Bruno had been hired for this visit. It couldn't be.

There weren't coincidences in this business.

They knew he'd squealed, and there was payback in the works. The biggest question in his mind was, did they know about Ally?

He'd kept his sister and niece secret for so long, and now the very worst sort of people knew about them.

Ally was here, within reach of a man that Wrench knew first hand had fewer morals than even he had ever had.

"What's the problem?" Graham asked gruffly, pitched so that only Wrench would hear.

They were standing at the edge of the pad at the top of the resort, watching as one of the heavies got into the helicopter and started it. Scarlet, arms crossed, was clearly intent on staying until every last one of them was gone from her resort.

This suited Wrench just fine, because he knew that he would not be able to relax until he knew that Bruno was off the island.

"An old associate," Wrench answered Graham in a similar tone.

Graham grunted his understanding.

But watching them fly off wasn't the relief that Wrench was hoping for. So soon after Ally had arrived, Bruno's visit could be nothing but a warning. They must know she was here, just as they knew that hurting her was more of a threat than anything they could threaten him with.

If he chose to continue on his plan to testify, he was jeopardizing Ally, as he'd already risked Renna.

Could he go back?

All he had to do was turn in Laura. It wouldn't be hard to get a phone call back to his contacts with Blacksmith. The staff at Shifting Sands trusted him now; it would be ridiculously simple to merely complete his contract, and deliver either of the sisters to satisfy the terms. Ally and Renna would be safe—as safe as the double-edged protection of the cartel could make them.

Which was a helluva lot safer than a rag-tag resort staff on a tropical island could keep them.

But Lydia… Lydia thought he was better than that.

He was used to disappointing himself, but he could not for a moment bring himself to disappoint her.

A terrible thought occurred to him.

What if the cartel found out about *Lydia*?

He rubbed his brow crossly as Scarlet turned to dismiss them. "Thank you for your assistance, gentlemen. I will return you to your regular duties."

She looked tired for a moment, then her usual expression of confidence returned as she tipped her face up to the sunlight. The oppressive heat did not seem to bother her. Though Graham and Wrench were both sweating, she looked as cool as ever as she left them to stride back through the resort entrance towards her office.

"You okay?" Graham asked.

Wrench knew that a shrug or a one-line response would get Graham to leave him alone, and before this week—before this crazy resort of people who actually cared for each other, or the unexpected discovery of his mate, that's exactly what he would have done.

But instead, he surprised even himself by asking Graham, "You ever feel like you're only really good at awful shit?"

Seeing Bruno had reminded him too keenly that however hard Wrench tried to fit in here, his real skills were violence and mayhem.

Graham gave him a long thoughtful look. "Yeah," he said at last. "When I was a kid, I did underground shifter matches. They pay good money if you can fight, and I *can* fight." He said it with the same sort of confidence that Wrench knew too well. "But it's a... bad scene."

It was more words than Wrench had ever heard from Graham, and he was surprised to recognize the faintest hint of a British accent.

"It isn't the violence that's the problem," Graham continued. "Fighting, guns, they're each just another sport. But you draw money into the mix and you start to get people that make money their goal and don't care who gets hurt."

Wrench stared at him.

"What?" Graham asked.

"That was unexpectedly fucking deep," Wrench said. "You don't talk like a groundskeeper."

Graham shrugged. "Unplumbed depths, man."

CHAPTER 28

*I*t wasn't just that Wrench didn't like casual touches, Lydia was realizing. He bordered on actually being touch averse.

"We will stay with open position," she suggested, taking both of his hands firmly and demonstrating. "Elbows up just a little, good. You want to keep energy in your arms, don't let them just droop."

Ally, beside them, held her own arms up in a passing imitation. "Like this, Uncle Wrench," she said cheerfully.

"You're leading," Lydia reminded him after a brief smile for Ally. "You step forward first, claim your space, then draw me back in. Count it out: step, shift, back, pause, step, shift, forward, pause. One, two, three, pause, five, six, seven, pause."

Wrench staggered through the steps as she patiently led him.

"You're not good at this," Ally said critically.

Lydia's swan hissed defensively and Lydia was swift to gently say, "You've had two whole lessons more than he has, remember? You'll have to help him get better like you have, Ally!"

She paired them up, standing beside Wrench while he stepped backwards and forwards to the count she kept. "One, two, three, pause, five, six, seven, pause."

"Good job, Uncle Wrench," Ally said in lackluster encouragement, as Lydia caught her eye.

Lydia continued counting as Wrench got more comfortable with the stepping pattern. "It's just muscle memory, pause," she said to the rhythm. "Train your feet to fall back to this pattern, good, pause." The music ended then, and Lydia demonstrated an ending flourish that Ally mimicked in delight.

"You don't have to do anything more complicated than this step, if you don't want," Lydia said comfortingly. "Perfectly competent dancers just do this around the dance floor for whole songs. Just guide your partner around using your hands and you don't need to do anything more complex."

Wrench looked relieved behind his poker face.

"Show him the side-to-side one!" Ally said with enthusiasm.

Lydia traded spots with the little girl, automatically stepping into the closed position. The muscles in Wrench's neck turned to stone as he froze, his hand where Lydia had placed it on her waist.

He swallowed.

Lydia, far from unaffected by his hot closeness, stepped back. "We'll continue in open position," she said lightly, going back to arm's length. For a moment, dizzy from his closeness, she forgot what she was planning to teach him.

"Side-to-side," Ally reminded her.

Lydia cleared her throat. "Right. Now, this follows the same pattern of pausing on the fourth beat and eighth, but instead of back and forth, we'll simply be going side to side."

Trying as hard as she could, she could not stop thinking about how the dancing rhythm would translate to sex.

CHAPTER 29

*I*f it weren't for Ally's presence, Wrench was not sure how far into the dance class they would have gotten.

It was hard enough to keep track of his feet and keep count and figure out where the beat was in the music, but with the addition of the impossible grace and beauty of Lydia's gorgeous body as she wiggled through the steps, his brain immediately went off in very different directions.

With luck, this meant that what he was stubbornly learning would stick in his head, despite future distractions.

He paraded side to side with her, doing his weak best to follow directions like, "let your hips loosen" and "relax your shoulders."

Paired with Ally again, Lydia drilled them through the steps until the girl began to complain, "My arms hurt and I'm hot!"

Lydia chuckled. "You're making your muscles strong," and let the little girl retreat to the cool sanctuary of her room.

Alone in the courtyard, Wrench wasn't sure what to do with himself. Most of him wanted to sweep Lydia into his arms and see what other actions could be done to the seductive rhythmic pattern of salsa.

She sashayed back into his arms as if she were thinking the same thing, but was then cruel enough to take his hands in the dance position again. The arm's length position, not the closer one, to his disappointment.

"Just a few more," she said coaxingly as the next song came from her little boombox. At least, Wrench assumed it was the next song. They all blurred together, since he couldn't understand a single word they were singing.

They did the front and back thing, then she talked him through switching to the side-to-side, then they went back to the first step, and Wrench actually felt remotely competent at it for the first time as Lydia praised him and she twirled away and then back into his arms where she belonged.

"See, you're getting it," she said breathlessly, smiling up into his face. "But you're supposed to let me go, now."

Wrench realized that he hadn't let go of her to return to the dance position. "Do I have to?"

"Salsa is about the courtship, not the catch," Lydia said with mock reproach.

He was bending to kiss her when someone behind them cleared their throat.

"Sorry to break up the moment," Travis said apologetically. "But I also know that it's all moments during the honeymoon, and we've got some work to do."

Wrench froze, but Lydia rose up on her toes and brushed her luscious lips against his. "I have to go lead a mediation class anyway," she said regretfully.

Wrench knew what he'd be spending the next several hours meditating about.

CHAPTER 30

*L*ydia was toweling her hair off after her shower, listening to Ally prattle about... she honestly wasn't sure what most of it was actually about and had to keep reminding herself that Ally didn't have anyone else to talk to. It was unending, though, and breathlessly exciting to the little girl.

"And I had to EAT the lunch ANYWAY because otherwise I would have had to buy HOT LUNCH and... UNCLE WRENCH!"

Wrench had stopped at the buffet on his way up to Lydia's courtyard, and he had a tray with two plates heaped in food. "Told 'em I was bringing you a picnic," he said sheepishly to Lydia as Ally squealed over the offerings.

"I'll get a PICNIC towel!" Ally suggested, disappearing swiftly into Lydia's room. "We can sit in the GRASS!" she called from inside.

Wrench grimaced in what Lydia had learned was supposed to be a smile and put the tray on the small table by the house. He looked like he wanted to bend down and kiss her, and she tipped her face up invitingly, but he hesitated, and then Ally was back with a beach towel, spreading it onto the grass imperiously.

"You sit HERE, Uncle Wrench," the girl directed. "I'll sit next to Lydia, here. There are only two glasses of lemonade!"

"I have a bottle of water," Lydia chuckled, realizing she was going to have to steal her own kisses if she wanted them.

We want them, her swan assured her with a sigh of regret for the missed opportunity.

She settled into the place that Ally pointed out for her once the food was laid out to the girl's satisfaction, and raised her bottle of water to toast with. "To picnics," she said.

"To PICNICS!" Ally agreed. She turned and did it again with Wrench. "To PICNICS," she repeated.

"To family," Wrench said, and he tapped his glass against Lydia's bottle with a thoughtful look.

Ally fell into her food, while Lydia and Wrench did the same more sedately and reminded her repeatedly not to talk with her mouth full.

"But I think of things to SAY when I'm eating," the girl protested, around a bite of sandwich that Lydia wasn't even sure she *could* chew.

Then Ally's mouth fell open and she struggled to say something, eyes wide in alarm.

"Swallow first," Wrench growled good-naturedly.

Lydia glanced at him, then screamed, "Look out!" as the snake behind him coiled up to strike.

CHAPTER 31

*W*rench dived to one side at Lydia's shrieked command without hesitation, and heard the snap of strong reptile jaws just missing his neck.

He rolled to his feet and crouched, facing the giant cobra that had been lurking behind him.

The thing must have been seven feet long, its muscled body a hand span in diameter at least. It hissed, showing wicked fangs, and flared its hood in anger at its missed prey.

Ally had apparently managed to swallow, because her scream was clear and high and loud.

Wrench was shifting without conscious thought, clothing ripping from his panther's sleek body as he twisted to charge at the snake, snarling in challenge.

The snake moved in impossible ways, slithering out of reach of Wrench's grasping claws and somehow coiling itself to strike again at the same time.

Wrench dodged its snapping jaws and lunged forward to try to bite at its hooded neck.

Again, it wasn't where he was expecting it to be, and his teeth closed on air as coils of thick scaled muscle tangled his feet. He snarled and spun, and suddenly Ally was dashing forward wielding a fork like a weapon, whooping in challenge.

"Ally, no!" Lydia cried, and then she was shifting into a tornado of black wings and wading into the fray.

The snake seemed to be everywhere, its snapping fangs seeping venom and its scaled body looping underfoot.

Lydia hissed back at it, trying to get between it and Ally while the girl bravely tried to stab it with the fork clutched in her hands.

Wrench finally got claws into the snake, flexing wickedly into its flesh, and it gave a weird shriek of pain as it moved lightning fast to bite deep into the offending paw.

Wrench howled in agony, venom burning painfully into his blood.

Lydia beat at it with her wings and stabbed with her hard beak, and it let go to hiss and finally retreat, leaving a trail of blood.

Ally screamed again.

Wrench tried to turn to follow the snake as it slithered away into the jungle and fell over on his side as he shifted back to human.

CHAPTER 32

"Wrench!" Lydia cried, dropping to her knees beside him. Ally fell beside her.

"Uncle Wrench?"

"We've got to get you to the hospital," Lydia cried, cradling his bit hand in her own.

"Can't," Wrench ground out around clenched jaws.

Lydia thought he was protesting the idea of a hospital, then he followed with a gasping, "Can't see…" and started seizing violently.

Lydia held onto his shoulders, trying to keep him from hurting himself.

She was losing him.

All she could do was wrap arms around his trembling muscles and watch his skin go a sickly shade of gray.

Suddenly, the sun above them was blotted out, and she looked up to watch Bastian lower himself into the courtyard like a precise reptilian helicopter, churning leaves as he landed.

Saina hopped off his back, dressed in her lifeguard uniform with a first aid kit in her hand.

"What happened?" the siren demanded, bending over them.

The courtyard still felt very crowded, even after Bastian shifted back to his human form and joined his mate.

"A cobra!" Lydia explained, not willing to let go of Wrench even now. "His hand!"

Saina and Bastian exchanged worried looks as they found the twin puncture marks and the black lines that were already obvious up Wrench's arm.

"I could medivac him to the mainland," Bastian brainstormed to Saina.

"There's not time," Saina replied mournfully.

Wrench groaned. He was drooling uncontrollably.

Ally sobbed.

"What is going on?"

Four heads swiveled to see Scarlet, standing at the entrance to the courtyard. "Wrench!" she said in alarm. "What happened to him?" She didn't comment on Ally's presence.

"A cobra bite," Bastian said mournfully, indicating the swollen limb.

Wrench gave a moan and arched in Lydia's arms. She clung to him, weeping. "Hold on, Wrench," she begged. "You can't leave me."

"Can you help him?" Scarlet asked Saina unexpectedly. Why would she ask Saina?

"Me?" Saina squeaked.

"You were able to sing the goldshot out of Bastian, can you do the same with a neurotoxin?"

Saina blinked at her. "That was different. Bastian was my mate and my magic doesn't seem to work on other people's mates... I don't know if I can do it with Wrench." She swallowed. "But I'll try."

Lydia had no idea what they were talking about. Singing? Goldshot? *Magic?* Wrench was writhing in her arms; it took all of her strength to keep him from hitting wildly out and she was barely following the conversation.

"You can't leave me," Lydia repeated, mouth close to his ear. "You can't go before I tell you how much I love you."

He was growling incoherently—it might have been her name or Ally's that he was trying to say, foaming at the mouth.

Bastian was holding down his thrashing legs, Scarlet was kneeling beside Lydia to help hold down Wrench's arms, and then Saina was singing, softly at first, then with rising intensity.

Lydia felt like she was at the edges of a rushing river, the sound of the siren's voice tugging at her, trying to pull the very essence of her soul from her body.

CHAPTER 33

*W*rench was adrift in an ocean of the worst parts of himself.

Perhaps this death was for the best, he thought suddenly. If he was gone, the people he loved would be safe at last. He would never have to relive the terrible things he had done, never wonder who had unwillingly suffered from the work that he had taken.

He just hadn't expected death to hurt this much.

Every nerve ending was on fire, as if he'd been dipped in acid. It felt like his skeleton was being bent into impossible shapes by his spasming muscles. His panther screamed ceaselessly in his head, a harmony to the creak of his bones giving out.

You can't leave me, Lydia whispered in his ear, and he could feel her arms around him.

They hurt.

Everything hurt.

She'd be better off without him.

You can't leave me, Lydia repeated fiercely.

It would be the best thing I've ever done, Wrench thought, and he let go, ready for the oblivion at the end of the pain.

Only to be yanked back by a thread of music.

The unexpected song, he realized after a moment of agony, had a very specific pull. It wasn't aimed at him, exactly, but at the thread of poison that had wrapped into every fiber of his being.

It was unwinding, untying, unraveling him to get at the toxin.

It drew the cobra's venom from his blood, sucking it from his seized muscles.

It felt like having his skin ripped off from the inside, like every vein in his body was being sandblasted from within.

It was almost worse than the initial poison had been.

Finally, it was done, he was free, and he lay a long moment trying to make sense out of the fact that he was still alive.

"Is he dead?" someone asked. Travis. That was Travis' voice.

Shouldn't I be? Wrench wondered wearily.

"I think he'll be fine." That was Saina's voice, sounding unusually hoarse. "I probably got the toxins from his blood in time."

"His pulse is steady," Bastian agreed.

"Well done." Scarlet's voice.

Shit.

CHAPTER 34

*L*ydia wept in frank relief, cradling Wrench's head in her lap. "Thank you," she told Saina, when she could breathe again. "Thank you so much."

The mermaid was looking fairly gobsmacked herself. "I never knew that siren powers could be used like this," she confessed. "I'm so happy I could help."

"You're amazing," Bastian murmured.

"Is Uncle Wrench going to be okay?" Ally asked, her voice subdued.

She was rather suddenly the center of all the attention in the courtyard as nobody wanted to look at Scarlet.

"Your uncle is going to be fine," the resort owner said mildly. "But I'm left with some questions."

"She needed a safe place," Travis said too swiftly.

"She's been no bother," Bastian added. "None of the guests have seen her."

Wrench mumbled something unintelligible and sat up weakly, leaning heavily on Lydia.

"Wrench didn't want the cartel to know about her," Lydia added quickly. "Her mother is in protective custody until the sting."

They all braced for the worst.

Scarlet took a step forward, and extended her hand to Ally. "I'm Scarlet," she said mildly.

"I'm Ally," the girl replied gravely, shaking the hand gingerly.

"I'm pleased to meet you." Scarlet's voice was utterly neutral. "It was very brave of you to try to fight the snake."

Ally was still clutching the fork, and she gave a lopsided smile. "Snakes can't hurt me," she said proudly. "Papa is a GOOSE shifter, and I will be, too."

The statement met a puzzled silence.

"A goose?" Lydia pressed. She wasn't sure how being a goose shifter would protect the girl.

"A MAN goose," Ally added.

At Lydia's side, Wrench began to wheeze.

For a moment, she was worried he was going to seize again, then she realized he was chuckling. His mirth gained strength until he was laughing helplessly and everyone was staring at them.

"Mongoose," Wrench finally gasped. "She's a mongoose shifter. They're immune to snake venom."

"That's what I said," Ally said in exasperation. "A MANGOOSE."

Lydia giggled almost hysterically. Bastian and Saina burst into laughter, leaning into each other. Travis chortled, holding his sides. Even Scarlet was snickering, a hand over her mouth.

"What?" Ally demanded.

That only made everyone laugh harder, until their eyes were streaming with tears and Travis fell onto the grass because he couldn't stand up anymore.

CHAPTER 35

*W*rench hated being babied much less than he suspected he would. Ally clearly took a lot of enjoyment in playing nurse, and he couldn't complain about getting more time to spend with her as he recuperated in Lydia's room.

But it was only a day before he felt well enough to resent his inactivity and started *thinking* again.

He didn't want to talk about it too much with Ally around, but Laura and Tex took the girl down to the beach on his second day of enforced rest.

"There's still an assassin here," he growled at Lydia. "One that knows about you and Ally now."

"We'll find him," Lydia assured him. "Everyone—especially Scarlet—is on full alert, and we'll make a game plan to flush him out when you're back to full strength."

"You don't deserve this risk. It's my fault this danger is here."

"You don't deserve it, either," Lydia reminded him.

"What if I do?" Wrench demanded. "What if it's all this I don't deserve?" His gesture included Lydia, and Lydia's cozy room, a room that felt more like a home than anywhere he'd ever lived, and the view out the open window. It encompassed the whole island, with all the strange people who had accepted him as one of their own.

He didn't have to look at her to know that Lydia was gazing at him with that look she got—that look that said she wanted to touch him and was careful not to. She'd been thoughtful about how much she casually touched him, and Wrench had caught her reaching for him and pulling back at the last moment several times.

"Do you really think that?" she asked gently. "That you don't deserve happiness? That there's not good in you?"

"If there was good in me, I wouldn't be so good at hurting people," Wrench growled.

"We reflect the kind of people we're around," she reminded him softly. "And if you've never been anything but hurt, that's all you're *going* to be good at."

Wrench started to interrupt her—but to his surprise, she walked past him then, and gestured to him to follow her out into the courtyard. "Come."

A blanket was spread out on the grass, and at first Wrench thought that she had very specific plans in mind. He had no objection to this idea—Ally's arrival and his snakebite had put the kind of crimp on those activities that anyone would expected and he craved having her in his arms again.

But Lydia patted the blanket and not only made no move to remove her own clothing, but put on a pair of flexible leather gloves from her apron pocket. There was a little pile of odd tools to one side and Wrench suddenly wondered if she had a kinky side he hadn't known about.

"Take off your clothes and shift," she commanded him.

He froze in confusion, his ardor dampened.

"Don't look so frightened," she scolded him. "I know you don't like to be touched, but I want to show you how it can be."

No one had ever accused Wrench of looking frightened in his life. When Lydia patted the blanket again, imperiously, he slowly obeyed.

In panther form, he crouched slowly down before her on the blanket, tense and anxious, tail lashing.

Then she slowly began to brush him, a coarse, short-bristled brush in her strong capable fingers.

His panther gave a long sigh of release and slowly relaxed under her ministrations.

She brushed his back with long, hard strokes, and moved down the sides of his neck. Without really intending to, he lifted his head to let her get the front and let out a long purr of contentment. She used her fingers to massage along his jaw and up around his ears. He head-butted her gently, and rolled to one side to let her brush his belly and smooth the fur down over his legs, massaging and brushing as she went.

He purred until he drooled, letting her groom him from nose to the tip of his flexible tail, and caught himself rolling to catch her in gentle claws when she paused.

This ain't exactly dignified, his human reminded him, but his panther was too delighted by the attention to pay him any heed.

She kneaded muscles that Wrench hadn't even known were tense, even relaxing the pads of his big feet. She sat between his front feet and did things to each side of his jaw and down his thick neck that nearly crossed his eyes with pleasure, leaning in with talented fingers to find every knotted muscle and hidden pain.

At last, he lay in her lap, gleaming with some sort of minty oil that she'd rubbed into his fur, and purred in a half-stupor of joy.

"I can do this to your human form, too," she told him in amusement. "If you let me."

Wrench shifted, head still in her lap.

"Right now I'd let you do anything to me," he confessed, feeling languid and relaxed.

Lydia bent over to kiss his forehead. "Anything...?" she said suggestively.

Wrench grinned back. They had some time before Ally would be back.

CHAPTER 36

"*H*ere's the list of people that have arrived since Wrench started working here, that are still here at the resort. Unless our attempted assassin arrived here off the books, this is who we have to start from."

Scarlet adjusted the projector, bringing her tidy handwriting into focus on the screen. The projector must have been a product of the time the resort was first built in the 80s. Lydia was sitting next to Wrench in the darkened room. Only the most trusted of the staff was there—and their mates. As she'd assured Wrench, Scarlet was not taking the attempt on Wrench's life lightly.

The list was frustratingly long; it was the busiest time of the vacation season and people had been steadily moving in and out. Some of the staff had turned over as well, as the isolation of Shifting Sands proved too much for some people to handle long term.

"I do not have record of any snake shifters at all, but people have lied on their applications before. We can eliminate anyone we've witnessed shifting into other forms." She crossed out several of the names herself.

Bastian volunteered, "Julie? That's the one with glasses who hasn't put down a book for more than five minutes in a row? I saw her shift into a deer of some sort on the beach."

Scarlet put a line through her name.

"Those two guys were in the bar when the attack happened," Tex said helpfully. "Couldn't have been them."

Other names were eliminated, but the list was still painfully long.

Graham frowned at the list. "Lars? That the Swedish hockey player?" he asked gruffly.

"Expert!" several of the staff chorused mockingly.

"He's not a bear like he says."

"Oh?" Wrench was all attention. "He could be the type. How do you know that?"

"Ate half the shrubbery around his cottage two nights ago," Graham growled.

"Oh, snap," Breck said. "He's lucky he's still alive."

"We do try to avoid sending our visitors home in boxes," Scarlet reminded them firmly.

"No one wants that review on Yelp," Bastian joked.

"'Excellent food. Great view. Insane landscaper attacked guests with machete,'" Travis mimicked.

Graham looked more amused than offended.

Scarlet cleared her throat. "At any rate, snakes don't eat shrubbery, so we can also eliminate him." She put a neat line through his name.

From the remaining names, they discussed the most likely candidates—the humorless cigarette-smoking man from Lydia's flight, a bruiser with a Russian accent who professed to be a saber-toothed cat, and a black-haired woman who was built slightly but had a quick slyness that everyone agreed was a little suspicious and snake-like.

"A mink would be," Scarlet said, consulting her notes, but she left the star by the woman's name.

"Keep your eyes on these characters in particular," Scarlet told them as the meeting broke up. "Stay in touch with each other, and be smart. Let's go get some work done."

As Wrench went to leave with Lydia beside him, Scarlet paused with them for a moment.

"I will understand if you don't wish to leave your mate's side until this is resolved," she said in a tone that could have been tolerant or just disgusted. "But I do have a request for Lydia alone. Gizelle has been in her gazelle form since the earthquake, and I was hoping that I could have your help trying to get through to her. Jenny's had no luck."

"Of course," Lydia said immediately.

Gizelle had always been shy and skittish. When the Shifting Sands staff had rescued her from a madman's shifter collection, she had refused to shift to human form for months. She still tended to revert to her gazelle shape whenever she was startled or frightened, which was often. With no memories of anyone or anywhere before her captivity, no one was sure how old she was, or where she'd come from before her imprisonment. She was innocent and childlike at times, but her seriousness and the white that streaked her hair sometimes made her seem ancient.

"I'll move the meditation class to the lawn outside the event hall," Lydia suggested. "Gizelle would sometimes join us, and I can stay after class and see if she'll approach me."

Scarlet nodded briskly and left them.

"You know I'm comin' with you," Wrench growled from her side.

"If you do, I expect you to meditate quietly with the rest of us," Lydia teased.

Wrench looked stoic. "Fine."

Lydia almost took his hand, then reconsidered, walking beside him as they went back up to her room to check on Ally. She was startled and delighted when Wrench took her hand of his own volition.

She twined her fingers into his and felt a moment of deep contentment and peace.

CHAPTER 37

$\mathcal{W}$rench tried to decide if meditation class was better or worse than salsa dancing.

One the one hand, he didn't have to watch his feet for fear of crushing one Lydia's unfortunate toes.

On the other, it was every bit as boring and infuriating as he'd feared.

He opened an eye a crack, surveying the others in the group.

"A deep breath in, all the way to the bottom of your lungs. Feel your ribcage stretch. Let your shoulders relax as you breath out again."

The old woman with the unfortunate luggage had her legs twisted into a remarkably flexible pose, back ramrod straight as she followed along with the guided breathing that Lydia was calling out in her calmest voice. She'd been the most surprised of the group to see Wrench join the meditation, and Wrench couldn't decide if she was most put off by the scars and tattoos, the fact that a lowly member of the staff was joining the class, or that he was a man. Whatever the reason, his presence was obviously highly displeasing to her behind a mask of false friendliness.

"Focus on filling your lungs, breathe in."

Beyond the old woman was the cold blonde, looking colder than ever. Her heels and expensive purse were beside her on the grass.

"Breathe all the way out and empty your mind."

The dark-haired supposedly-mink shifter was next in the circle, her long hair pulled back in a sinuous ponytail. Wrench was glad he had joined the class; it would have been laughably easy for one of them to catch Lydia off guard as she sat with her eyes closed.

"As thoughts intrude, let them pass without challenge."

The small group was completed by the bookworm in glasses. It was odd to see her without a book, her eyes closed behind her thick glasses.

"Concentrate on your breathing, evenly out, evenly in."

Beyond them, at the far edge of the lawn, a dainty gazelle was grazing studiously, her big ears flicking back and forth.

"Feel your chest and stomach rise gently as you breathe."

Wrench realized that one of the old woman's eyes was cracked open and she was surreptitiously watching him. He was glad that he'd chosen to wear his mirrored sunglasses, masking his own covert observations. Old habits were sometimes the best. There was danger everywhere.

"Inhale, exhale." Lydia's voice was slow and hypnotic. "You are in a *safe*, restful place."

Just as Wrench was wondering if she didn't sound just the tiniest bit pointed, he heard her in his head, *I always know where you are.*

Wrench bit back a disruptive cough and murmured a gruff, unintelligible apology as he cleared his throat.

One of the girls giggled slightly and the old woman gave a slight disapproving noise.

"Inhale, exhale," Lydia continued serenely. "Thoughts come and pass through and we return to our breathing."

After a few more moments of slow, rhythmic words, Lydia said, "Now let's enjoy ten minutes of silent meditation. Continue to concentrate on your breathing, inhale and count one, exhale and count, one."

Wrench watched her press a button on her phone through one cracked eyelid and then she was quiet.

He was more distracted by the sound of everyone else's breath than his own. The blonde breathed like a metronome. The maybe-mink shifter had a distinct hiss to her breath that made Wrench's shoulder blades tighten. The book-reader almost hummed.

The drone of insects and the distant surf rose up over those close noises, and Wrench could hear the erratic munching of the gazelle across the lawn.

Ten minutes was an eternity, an endless chasm of space and not-quite-silence that Wrench wasn't sure he was going to make it through without fidgeting, and then abruptly Lydia's phone was giving a low chime to end the session. He wasn't even sure what he'd been thinking about, at the end of it.

"Let your body come awake again slowly, and continue to inhale and exhale rhythmically." Lydia's voice was gentle and quiet. "Wiggle your fingers and toes, then your arms and legs. Inhale, exhale. Roll your shoulders back, think about your posture and let your head fall forward and then roll up slowly as you inhale, and exhale."

Wrench followed along, feeling foolish and awkward as blood returned to starved places.

"Take this peace with you on your day," Lydia said in ending. "*Namaste.*"

"*Namaste,*" the others chorused back.

Not expecting the reply, Wrench mumbled his own echo too late, as quietly as possible, but it was masked in the chatter and noise of the women rising to their feet and gathering their things.

Wrench remained seated with Lydia as the others left.

"You did well," Lydia said with a smile.

"Easier than dancing," Wrench said gruffly. The session had not dulled his senses, and he was keenly aware that the gazelle was grazing in their direction, though she was pointedly not quite facing them.

"You're picking that up fine, too," Lydia assured him. "You won't embarrass yourself at the dance tomorrow."

Wrench groaned. "Can't you say I'm still a danger to bystanders and tell Scarlet I shouldn't be allowed to come? I'm still… ah, weak? Ow, my snakebite."

Lydia's laughter was soft and gentle. "Be grateful she won't make you trot once around with all the female guests without partners."

"Doesn't someone else need to stay behind with Ally?" Wrench said desperately.

"Graham is going to stay with her; he's never at the dances and even Scarlet believes he could protect her. She is immune, besides."

Wrench shrugged, sensing the trap closing.

He was saved having to answer by the cautious approach of Gizelle, who, to the astonishment of both of them, went straight up to Wrench and pressed a velvety nose against his shoulder.

"Won't you join us?" Lydia asked softly.

The gazelle flicked expressive ears at her, then sighed, stepped back, and shifted into a skinny, wild-haired girl. She raised dark eyes, not to Lydia, but to Wrench, and he realized that she was not a girl at all, despite her slight form. "You brought a child here," she said achingly.

Wrench exchanged a look with Lydia.

"Yeah," he said reluctantly when Lydia nodded. "My niece. Thought she'd be safer here."

"You were *wrong!*" Gizelle said sharply, drawing away. Wrench balled helpless fists at his side. Any calm he was supposed to have gotten from his meditation was long gone.

Lydia held a sarong out to her and Gizelle stared at it a moment before accepting it and folding it around her naked form. "Honey, do you know who the cobra is?"

Gizelle looked at her blankly.

"The danger," Lydia pressed gently.

"The danger is waking," Gizelle said softly. "It shouldn't wake. It should sleep, and it wakes and it tickles and whispers and the island will break and fall into the ocean and the world will burn." Her voice rose as she continued, until she was crying hysterically and falling into Wrench's arms.

He patted her awkwardly, meeting Lydia's eyes over the crown of Gizelle's white-streaked head.

Lydia was swift to reassure her. "You mean the earthquake? Oh, it's okay, Gizelle. It just happens sometimes. It's over now, it can't hurt you. It's just the ground shaking a little."

Gizelle cried harder, clinging to Wrench.

"I been through lots of them," Wrench added in a manner he hoped was comforting. "They'll wake you up, but mostly they just get your blood going and nothing's hurt."

Gizelle sobbed on him for an awful moment that seemed longer than the endless ten minutes of silent meditation, then abruptly relaxed in Wrench's arms. Then she was pushing back onto her heels. "I smell chocolate," she said eagerly.

"I think Chef is making cake," Lydia said coaxingly.

Gizelle seemed completely unaware of the tears that were still on her cheeks as she bounced to her feet. "Maybe he'll let me lick the batter," she said enthusiastically, then she was scampering off, bare feet silent over the grass.

"That girl ain't right in the head," Wrench said, baffled.

Lydia laughed weakly. "No, not entirely."

Wrench brushed himself off and stood. "Can't figure why she had to weep all over me," he said, frowning down at the tears on his shirt.

Lydia smiled. "I figure you must remind her of Neal. He bonded with her a bit before leaving with his mate a few months back. You have sort of the same look to you."

"Must be," Wrench said briefly.

He hoped he wasn't going soft.

Then he wondered how bad that would actually be.

CHAPTER 38

"*Y*ou did great," Lydia promised, laughing. "My toes are all still attached."

Wrench managed to look some strange mix of pleased and offended behind his gruff facade, and Lydia loved the feeling of his hand at her waist. It was strong and sexy, and she wanted to drag him straight back out on the dance floor, even if he didn't once use anything except the very basic forward and back. He had a sure sense of rhythm, and if he wasn't creative on the dance floor, he was at least steady. Lydia had danced with far worse partners.

"Look out," she teased him. "Scarlet's watching. If you do too well, next time she'll badger you to go dance with all the shy ladies sighing in the wings. These dances always draw more women than men."

Adding weight to her threat, Travis and Tex were trotting dutifully around the room with eager partners while Jenny and Laura laughed together behind the bar. Breck was dancing seductively with a blushing middle-aged woman and Bastian was doing something elegant with the mink shifter while Saina seethed from the side of the room. Even Chef had been dragged from the kitchen and was dressed up and dancing elegantly with Dot, the old woman with short white hair. Magnolia blew him a kiss from the chairs at the edge of the room.

Scarlet was acting as DJ; the loss of their boat gave them no way to get the usual band from the mainland for the event. Lydia felt like it wasn't quite the same as live instruments, but having Wrench at her side more than made up for it.

As Lydia glanced over at her, Scarlet raised her eyebrow and tilted her head towards the few single men standing awkwardly to the side of the dance floor.

"Ah," Lydia said. "I'm not going to be so lucky. But this is a lovely opportunity to get some more information."

Wrench's hand at her waist tightened possessively and Lydia let him draw her in closer. With heels, she didn't have to stand up far to kiss him lightly on the cheek. He growled so quietly that she could only feel it through their body contact, not hear it.

"You could go dance with Ms. Mink," she suggested playfully. "Dancing is a great chance to ask questions."

"I ain't the guy to ask questions," Wrench suggested dryly. "I'm the guy breaking fingers while the other guy asks questions."

Lydia squinted up at him. There was a slight quirk at the corner of his mouth. "Was that supposed to be a joke?" she realized in astonishment.

"Supposed to be, yeah."

Lydia giggled helplessly and squeezed him.

Then he let her go, and Lydia had to fight back her instinct to throw herself back into his arms.

Duty called.

As she clicked across the dance floor in her shoes, she looked critically at her choices. The Swedish hockey player, Lars, looked like he might be lighter on his feet, but he was also gazing across the dance floor longingly at the bookish woman in glasses who was dancing with Tex. He didn't even glance at Lydia as she sashayed towards them.

The Russian bruiser had an unexpectedly innocent look as

Lydia drew closer, gazing wistfully out at the dancers and tapping his fingers against his sleeve. At any other time, this would have made Lydia choose him, but she wasn't here just for dancing. She made the third figure of the group her target, extending an imperious hand to the grim-faced smoker from her flight. She thought his name from Scarlet's list had been Tim.

He looked at her outstretched hand for a long moment before reluctantly accepting it.

Lydia didn't care for the smell of cigarette smoke, and was relieved to find that he was more soap-and-sandalwood scented. He stepped out after her onto the floor with more grace than Lydia had braced for and his hand at her waist—while not Wrench's—was neither desperate nor tentative.

"How do you like Shifting Sands?" Lydia asked, after they had negotiated the lead and settled into a comfortable pattern.

"It's… a nice place," the young man said uncomfortably.

"Enjoying the food?" Lydia pried. Normally, she wouldn't push a conversation if someone preferred only to dance quietly, as this one certainly did. But she was on a mission, and grimly determined to find out who had bitten her mate and might be a threat to his niece.

"Er… it's good," maybe-Tim agreed plaintively.

"What brought you here?" Lydia asked cheerfully, with her best empty-headed smile.

"It's… personal," he said, biting off the end of his words.

Lydia let him turn her, aware of Wrench's gaze attempting to burn holes through her partner.

"Like a contracted sort of personal?" she risked saying, hoping to surprise him into reacting.

But that only puzzled him. "Look," he said crossly. "I'm not sure what you're looking for. I'm only here because my sister didn't want to come alone."

It was Lydia's turn to be surprised. "Your sister?"

She caught his automatic glance towards the librarian dancing with Tex. She was laughing at something he was saying.

"My sister," maybe-Tim repeated.

Lydia sighed. While it was possible one sibling was a deer and the other a cobra, it seemed ridiculously unlikely that the pair were assassins.

Unfortunately, she had piqued the young man's interest. "What do you mean contracted? Like… an assassin?"

Lydia hastened to hush him, and the young man stumbled over his feet as he immediately looked towards his sister. "Are we in danger?" he asked in an anxious whisper.

"You should be fine," Lydia was swift to say, taking the lead automatically as his steps faltered. "It's a personal matter, I promise."

"Who is he after? Has he already made an attempt on someone? Is it a guest?"

Lydia sighed. "Listen, Tim… is it Tim?"

"Tom," he corrected.

"Tom." Lydia said firmly. "I promise that neither you nor your sister are any danger. It's highly unlikely that anything will happen here at a public event like this, and like I said, it's a personal thing. I'm sorry I alarmed you, I was only trying to eliminate suspects and I'm not very good at this." She gave him a winning smile.

Tom was already squinting around at the other guests suspiciously. "What about that brute you were dancing with before? He's got kind of that look, doesn't he?"

Lydia turned them so she could smile across the dance floor at Wrench's glare. "He does, doesn't he?" She said fondly. "It's a useful look, for certain lines of work."

Tom gave her a deeply skeptical look. "Okay then, how about that Russian guy who looks like he did time in Siberia? I saw him shift into something goddamn prehistoric, with fangs like scimitars."

Lydia tipped her head. "That was useful! But I'm afraid we're specifically looking for a snake shifter. He's already made one attempt."

Tom shuddered.

"Who else have you seen shifting?" Lydia hastened to ask. "Anyone you've seen would be helpful!"

"There's that really, really big woman with auburn hair who shifted into a polar bear at the pool," Tom offered. "And, let's see…"

CHAPTER 39

*W*rench glared across the dance floor as Lydia continued dancing a second song with the young man she'd selected.

He used all of the steps Lydia had taught him, not just the one easy set, and even with a handful of other dancers between them, Wrench could tell he was doing a good job of it. They even turned sometimes, where Wrench had stuck to the one safe move, counting under his breath the entire time.

They appeared to be deep in conversation, and Wrench had to ball his fists at his side to keep from stomping across the floor and shoving the man away from his mate.

"Isn't she gorgeous?" Bastian said from his side.

"Yeah," Wrench said before he realized the other man was talking about Saina, who was dancing with the Swedish not-a-bear. There was no graceful way to correct the statement, so he didn't bother.

He made himself stop staring at Lydia like a lovestruck puppy and sweep a glance around the room. Scarlet met his eyes briefly from behind the DJ's table, clearly doing the same. Her expression was serene and unruffled but her eyes were sharp, even from here. She may not expect trouble at a public event, but she was clearly alert for it.

But nothing happened.

Lydia and Saina came back from their dances with more names to cross off of Scarlet's list, but they felt no closer to a culprit by the time the night had grown old than when they had started.

Most of the guests trickled away as the night grew deeper. The white-haired woman, looking two sheets to the wind, nursed a last glass of wine at the little bar, and the last dancers drifted away as the staff began folding up chairs and collecting forgotten glasses.

"We usually split what's left of open bubbly bottles after these things," Lydia said, bringing Wrench a glass. "No use letting them go to waste."

Wrench eyed the fizzy drink skeptical but tossed it down as Lydia sipped hers. It tasted better than he expected, but it tickled distractingly, all the way down. He preferred the burn of whiskey.

The flower in Lydia's fancy updo had started to slip, and Wrench put his glass down so he could tuck it back in. Her hair smelled delicious, and Wrench had to concentrate very hard not to betray his sudden rising need for her. He lingered over tucking a lock of her dark hair back over her ear and loved the way her breath hitched when he brushed her neck.

Just has he was wondering if cottage two was still available for their use, a movement beyond Lydia caught his attention.

The white-haired woman was pushing a bottle away from her on the bar. Her motions were slow, which may have been a product of her inebriation, but it caught Wrench's attention as simply slow, not drunk-slow. Careful-slow. Trying-not-to-get-atten-tion-slow.

"You got the list?" he asked suddenly, his hand on Lydia's shoulder.

"Laura has it behind the bar," Lydia said, glancing in that direction.

Wrench resisted the instinct to tell her not to look. "You remember what that woman's animal shape is?"

Lydia smirked. "Weasel. Ermine, I think? I remember thinking it suited her personality, she was so nosy."

Wrench frowned. "Told me she was a fox." He thought back to the conversation and remembered with a sour stomach what else they had talked about. "I told her I had a sister... and a niece." That had been just a day before Renna ended up in protective custody.

Lydia's smile froze. "She doesn't look like an assassin!"

"She's messing with the bottles at the bar," Wrench told her quietly. "Bottles that you and me and Laura and Jenny mighta been drinking out of later tonight."

Lydia's eyes widened, and she stared at the glass she had been about to drink from in horror.

"What do we do?" she asked quietly.

Wrench's panther had several ideas that centered around the theme of tearing out the woman's throat before she could shift, but the idea of Lydia watching that held him back.

He did a quick assessment of the room. Saina and Bastian had already left—while Wrench couldn't see the dragon being of much use against a snake, Saina's singing gift might have proven useful. Especially if someone got bit. Given the way they had danced the last dance together, he suspected he knew where they'd disappeared to. Or at least what they were doing.

Scarlet was turning off the sound system, bending behind the console to unplug the cords.

Tex was carrying a tray of empty glasses to the bar, where Laura was wiping down the counter and Travis was repairing a chair. They were both chatting cheerfully with the white-haired woman, who was continuing her convincing charade of tipsy harmlessness.

And Jenny was pouring a round of drinks from a bottle that the old woman had been sitting right next to.

Wrench would have given anything for a firearm at that moment and he cast around for something— anything—that he could throw.

As he was considering the aerodynamics of one of the decorative vases, Lydia suddenly sashayed away from him to the bar, her laugh unnaturally bright in the emptying room. "Wait, Jenny, we'll do a toast!"

"Shit," Wrench said under his breath, and he scrambled to follow.

The little woman turned at their approach, and Wrench saw the brief, entirely sober flicker of rage in her face that confirmed every suspicion he had.

Travis was repairing the chair upside down and Wrench bowled it over as he made a straight path to the woman.

"What the hell?" Travis demanded.

Laura and Jenny echoed him in shock as Lydia made it to the bar and swept all of the drinks off in a pool of shattered glass and foaming champagne. The white-haired woman sprang out of her seat spryly, but was trapped by Wrench against the bar with one hand to her throat.

"It's poisoned!" Lydia declared.

Tex sniffed at the bottle. "Sugar, honey, iced tea!" he said in alarm. "This does stink. It's different than rattler venom, but it sure isn't right. Did you drink any?" He looked anxiously to his mate first.

Laura shook her head, eyes big. "This is getting to be a habit," she said weakly. "Jenny?"

Her twin shook her head as well.

His panther panted to be released, to exact painful revenge with teeth and claws, but Wrench only closed his fist around the woman's leathery throat and held on, just tight enough that she was gasping and clawing at him.

"Can't... do... this...!" she choked. "Wasn't... me...!" Wrench tightened his fingers just a little.

"Shift and prove it," Lydia said firmly. "If you are who you say you are, you shouldn't be afraid to shift."

The woman's beady eyes glared back at her, lips turning slightly blue as she snarled wordlessly. Her fingernails dug into Wrench's arms and she kicked at him desperately.

"Wrench." Scarlet's voice was as calm and cool as ever. "If you would kindly give her a little air." She didn't ask him to release her.

Wrench obligingly released the pressure, still holding her out at arm's length.

The woman gasped and spat towards Lydia, who managed to do some sort of dance flutter with her hands and catch the spittle on a napkin she snatched from the bar. She handed the napkin to Tex, who raised an eyebrow and nodded.

"That's the stuff," he confirmed, not even needing to hold it close to his nose.

"Did Blacksmith send you?" Laura demanded.

"You think you can run from him?" The woman didn't even try to deny it.

Wrench tightened his fingers reflexively as Tex stepped forward with a black expression and she gagged until he made his hand relax again.

"Listen good," he told her. "I ain't coming back to that work, and I ain't gonna let him scare me off of doing the right thing. But don't think for a second that I ain't gonna protect what's mine."

She hissed at him, but Wrench could see that she was less defiant than she had been.

"I've got duct tape," Travis offered.

"She could shift out of it," Lydia cautioned, as he started to bind the woman's wrists.

"She can come spend the night with me in my office while we wait for the Civil Guard," Scarlet said mildly. "She attacked a member of *my* staff at *my* resort, and I've got a message for her to take back to Blacksmith."

Wrench gave her a sideways look, wondering if she intended violence.

Dot, taking advantage of Wrench's slight distraction, suddenly slipped from his fingers as she shifted, and struck out towards Lydia's unprotected neck with needle-sharp fangs bared.

Wrench roared and grabbed for the writhing snake, but he wasn't as fast as Scarlet, who caught the snake by the throat with one hand and held her as she snapped her jaws, inches from Lydia's skin.

"I don't care which form you're in for our little talk," Scarlet said coldly, as if holding the giant, thrashing snake with one slim hand was no effort. "If you wouldn't mind cleaning up the hall," she said generally to the staff, and then she was dragging the enormous reptile out behind her. Her heels clicked along the floor as she told it, "Naturally, there will be no refund issued for the remaining days of your stay."

In the silence that followed the sound of the door closing behind her, Wrench gathered Lydia into his arms.

CHAPTER 40

*L*ydia was trembling in shock and relief, and when Wrench kissed the vulnerable skin on her neck that had nearly been bitten, she gave a little moan and sagged into his embrace.

"That was beautiful, what you said about doing the right thing," Breck told him as he started sweeping up the broken glass.

"I been meditatin'," Wrench growled with a straight face.

Lydia snorted and then started laughing hysterically, finally able to pull herself away from Wrench's big, safe arms with tears of laughter streaming down her face.

The twins caught the contagion of humor and laughed until they had to hold their sides and their mates.

Even Wrench was smiling, when Lydia had wiped her eyes and could see him again. "It *was* beautiful," she said quietly near his ear as the others bent back to their cleaning.

"I guess you can say beautiful things when you got beautiful things in your life," Wrench said, looking slightly abashed behind his usual scowl.

"You are *my* beautiful thing," Lydia told him, and was delighted to watch him blush faintly behind his tan.

"I ain't beautiful," he protested.

"You are in that suit," Lydia purred suggestively. "If I didn't want you out of it so badly, I'd never let you take it off."

Wrench cleared his throat.

"You were wonderful tonight," Lydia told him. "You figured everything out before Dot could hurt anyone else."

Wrench shrugged. "Didn't take much thinkin' fortunately."

Lydia stood up as tall as she could so she could put her hands on the sides of his face and put her forehead to his. "Wrench, you are so much smarter and better than you have ever given yourself credit for. I love you, you beautiful, sexy, brilliant man. You are everything I ever wanted, and I—"

The phone in Wrench's pocket chose that moment to ring, loud in the echoing room.

He swore like a sailor, and dove a hand in after it as Lydia stepped back with a sigh. A glance at the screen sent conflict across his features.

"Renna," he said apologetically, and he thumbed it on and turned away as Lydia waved at him to.

Lydia couldn't hear the other end of the conversation, only the slight murmur of a voice, but Wrench's shoulders tightened and then slumped. He turned to her and for a moment Lydia feared the worst.

Then he mouthed, "It's done," and made a conversational noise into the phone.

They talked for several moments while Lydia kept herself busy folding up the decorations and unplugging the lights. A few moments later, Jenny's phone across the room rang.

When he finally hung up, Wrench swept Lydia up into a desperate, crushing embrace. "It's done. They did the sting. They got the bastard, and all the top cronies, and the guy that Renna thought was a mole in the witness protection program. The whole rotten lot of them are behind bars, all their assets frozen. Renna and Ally can go home."

Across the hall, Jenny was sharing the same news, and there were cheers of relief and triumph from the rest of the staff.

"We gotta tell Ally," Wrench said.

"She's probably already asleep," Lydia reminded him. It was well past midnight.

"Yeah," Wrench agreed, finally releasing her. "It'll wait til tomorrow."

"You know what won't wait until tomorrow?" Lydia said suggestively.

Wrench looked hopeful but didn't venture a guess.

"Travis said you'd be replacing the glass at cottage two tomorrow and getting it ready for guests," Lydia told him, tracing a finger along the inside of the collar of his shirt. "That means it's still empty, but not for long…"

Wrench grinned, and before Lydia could stop him, had swept her up into his big arms.

"Eek!" Lydia squeaked happily as he carried her out into the warm, starlit night.

EPILOGUE

A FEW WEEKS LATER

"*U*ncle WRENCH! LOOK what SCARLET got me!"

Ally was standing by the ridiculously over-sized fake tree that took up a corner of the event hall. It had taken Wrench nearly an hour to assemble the thing with Travis, and even longer to decorate it with the white and gold decorations. The Christmas Eve formal had ended without incidents worse than a drunkenly dropped glass and the smallest of fires in a corner where a candle had gotten tipped over.

Ally, drunk with the privilege of a party staying up late with grownups, and giddy with the rush of new presents, was dressed in a red velvet dress trimmed with embroidered holly leaves and glittery poinsettias. She was holding a plush golden teddy bear dressed in a tutu.

"Ally, honey, you don't need to shout," her mother reminded her.

"I just feel SO LOUD with happiness," Ally protested, whispering as loudly as she'd spoken earlier. The ground around her was littered with shredded Christmas paper and open boxes. She was wearing one of the bows on her curly head.

Wrench felt fingers slip into his as he watched her caper around, dancing with her new bear to give Scarlet a thank-you hug.

"You're going to miss them," Lydia said near his ear as Scarlet knelt to embrace his niece, her red hair as brilliant as Ally's dress and accented with a crown of glossy holly.

"It was great of Scarlet to put them up for a few weeks," Wrench said sincerely. "Renna needed a nice vacation."

"Scarlet never fails to surprise me," Lydia agreed. "It was really sweet of her."

"Dance with me?" Wrench invited.

Lydia's eyes sparkled with amusement. "I thought I'd already gotten my Christmas present," she said in delight, putting a hand to the earrings Wrench had ordered for her. They were small silver infinity symbols with black enamel wings.

She put the hand into Wrench's, and he pulled her into the closed position and stepped out.

Wrench concentrated on counting, sticking to the simple, basic back and forth until it started to feel somewhat comfortable. Lydia gazed up at him, contentment and joy in her beautiful face. Dancing close, she was the most gorgeous, sexy thing he'd ever had the pleasure of holding in his arms.

Then he remembered his plan and stepped forward when he should have gone back, colliding knees with Lydia.

"Dammit," he growled, and instead of trying to pick the step back up, he stopped.

"You were doing great," Lydia laughed kindly, trying to gently pull him back into the dance.

He resisted her, but kept her hands in his. "Lydia," he said seriously.

She stopped tugging on him and stilled her feet. "What is it?"

"I'm probably not going to do this one right either," he warned her. "But I gotta try."

She furrowed her brow at him. "Do what?"

Wrench swallowed and slowly lowered to one knee. "Lydia, will you marry me?" He'd tried writing a speech, had scoured the internet for the best poetry, and even asked Breck for advice. (Breck's advice had largely been to *not* get married, never to find a mate, and had involved the word *doom* prominently.) But in the end, he'd decided to stick with the one line, not sure he'd be able to memorize the fancy stuff or deliver it right.

"I'd really like it," he added impulsively, remembering how she'd said she didn't want to be an obligation.

She stared at him, eyes wide and full of happy, unshed tears, and nodded without speaking.

"Shit," Wrench said, letting go of her hands and digging into his pocket. "The ring. I got a ring this time."

The velvety black box was tiny in his big hands, but the simple gold ring on Lydia's finger, when she didn't protest, was an exact fit.

She fell forward, wrapping arms around his neck and he lifted her as he stood. "That was perfect," she said, voice full of emotion. "Yes, yes I'll marry you."

Wrench didn't realize he was holding his breath until he released it, holding Lydia tight to him as he set her back down on her feet.

Applause made him aware that they were the focus of most of the room. Renna gave him a thumbs up from where she sat with Ally falling asleep on her shoulder. Breck dramatically shook his head but was grinning like a sap. Tex whispered something to Laura that made her turn and kiss him. Even Scarlet was smiling.

Travis caught his eye and pointed at something above their heads.

Wrench glanced up. They were standing under mistletoe.

It was as good an excuse as any.

He pulled Lydia into his arms and kissed her soundly.

Her mouth opened under his, eager and hungry. Her body pressed against him, and her bare back felt like silk under his rough thumbs.

Her hands in his short hair felt like fire, and her fingernails scratched lightly down his jaw as she continued to kiss him, desperate and possessive.

When someone shouted, "Get a room!" Wrench could not have agreed more.

He released Lydia's mouth and took her by the hand. "Best advice I've gotten yet," he said wryly.

She smiled at him, hair tousled and lipstick smudged. "Let's take it," she agreed.

They left in a chorus of Christmas wishes and congratulations, but only made it as far as the gazebo in the garden, where darkness gave them privacy they desired.

Lydia unbuttoned Wrench's shirt only slightly more carefully than she had the first time, he shrugged out of the jacket and pulled the shirt over his head when the last few buttons wouldn't cooperate with her trembling fingers. Wrench unzipped her dress and let his hands travel down her sides and up around from behind to cup the breasts overflowing her lacy bra as he kissed the back of her neck.

She moaned in growing need as he pulled her close against him, pressing his own expression of need against her. She turned in his arms and finished shimmying out of her dress while she unbuttoned his pants and worked at releasing him.

There was a brief moment when they were both done removing the last parts of their clothing where they stood and simply looked at each other. Lydia was pale in the faint light, a healthy goddess with blessings at every curve and promises at each tantalizing hidden place.

Then Wrench could not keep from touching her, and she met him halfway, arms rising to stroke his shoulders as he lifted her against the center post and claimed her with his entry. She was wet and ready and as eager as her mouth had been, lifting her legs to wrap around him and take him deeper with each thrust, until they were both in a frenzy of pleasure and desire and couldn't tell where one ended and the other began.

And it was all beautiful and *good*.

A CHRISTMOOSE STORY

I wrote this as a treat for my readers and put it on my site for a short time over Christmas in 2018. It occurs during the events of Tropical Panther's Penance, but stands completely alone.

She was only a few rows ahead of Lars on the small plane, but she may as well have been a hundred miles away.

Lars tried desperately not to stare at the edge of her face, just visible behind waves of mousy brown hair as she bent her head over the book she was holding. The oblique angle and her thick glasses made it impossible to tell what color her eyes were.

If only she would look up, glance back. If he could just catch her attention for a moment, maybe he could make sense of the way the sight of her made something deep inside him ache and awaken. Deep within him, his animal rumbled anxiously.

Whatever it was, it something that was affecting his moose as much as it was the rest of him.

The plane was crowded with people; every seat in the charter was filled. Most of them were chattering cheerfully, gazing out the windows where turquoise sea wrinkled away from the emerald jungle below. They were varied in nationality, but clearly all of them were well-to-do.

Lars glanced at the woman sitting next to him using a tablet. She gave the impression of stupendous wealth, from her perfect, frosty blonde hair to her glittering jewelry and designer clothing. Her tablet had a gold and leather case.

The young woman he was trying not to watch was a stark contrast, and Lars wondered if that was why she had caught his attention, because she was as poor as he was.

But he wasn't poor anymore, he reminded himself. His tablet was as high-end as the one in the hand of the woman next to him, and his clothing was as well made as hers.

But the woman he was watching had simple clothing, and her luggage was a small, battered, secondhand carry-on. Lars hadn't seen her with a phone or any technology, just…books.

Since he had first caught sight of her in the San Jose airport, she had done nothing but read. Book after book, as far as Lars could tell. Judging by the way she carried her bag, it was more books than clothing.

The scowling young man traveling with her had not offered to carry it, despite having an even smaller, more worn bag for himself.

Lars frowned at the man, trying to determine what kind of relationship they might have. They were basically ignoring each other; the man hadn't even taken a seat next to her.

Lars wouldn't have been sure they were traveling together, but there was something about their shared shabbiness, and the close-but-not-too-close way they were with each other that clinched his suspicion.

He was staring at her again, Lars realized, at the tantalizing line of her cheek, and the way her fingers flipped the pages of her book.

The plane gave a little hiccup of turbulence and he watched, hopeful, to see if she would look around. She glanced up only briefly, and then returned to the words on the page.

Even when they had landed, on a postage stamp of an island that didn't even look large enough to put a plane down on, she didn't glance back, only packed her latest book into her bag and slipped into the crush of people exiting the plane.

One of the last to leave the plane, Lars looked at once for her, and was glad to see that she hadn't boarded the courtesy van to the resort yet.

"One last seat!" the driver called.

An old lady pushed forward and Lars let her go, eyes only for the brunette.

She was already taking a seat in the tiny covered shelter that appeared to be all that counted for an airport, pulling out a book. Her companion was glowering generally at everyone — *he* certainly wasn't shy about meeting Lars's eyes. He went to one end of the shelter, lit a cigarette, and silently dared anyone to complain.

Lars's seatmate gave an exasperated sigh and minced in ridiculous high heels to sit beside the real object of Lars's attention.

That left a seat free for Lars, and he darted forward with athletic reflexes to claim the place.

Up close, the young woman smelled like soap and, not surprising, books. Her brown hair, not dark, not exactly light, was soft-looking and inviting.

Sitting next to her was electric — exciting and tantalizing. But she still would not look up at him, utterly engrossed in her open book.

"A half an hour!" the blonde beyond her groused. "That's ridiculous. There's nothing here to do." She waved her phone around in the air. "I can't even get a phone signal!"

Lars checked his own phone and confirmed. "Nor can I."

The blonde gave him a look over her sunglasses. "Swedish?" she asked without seeming particularly interested.

"Soon to be American," Lars said firmly, realizing that he had answered her in the wrong language the first time. "I have..." his English failed him. "I am hockey player," he tried to explain. He was keenly aware of the young woman between them, and wondered if she was hearing him at all. It made him irrationally nervous to think that she might be, and it occurred to him that it sounded like he was a hockey player for fun.

Professional, he wanted to add, but he could not remember the English word for it. The Russian word, and the German, but English was suddenly a cipher. "I play it for team," he tried to explain. "*Expert.*"

The blonde failed to look at all impressed.

The brunette turned another page in her book.

~

*J*ulie stared at her book, and occasionally remembered to turn a page, even though she couldn't make sense of the words on them.

The blond man with the delicious accent was sitting right next to her, so close that she could feel the heat of him, even with the sultry, humid warmth of the jungle all around.

He smelled like new clothing, and below that, a heady mix of sweat and musk.

In her head, her caribou was all attention, absolutely riveted on the man sitting next to them.

He's a hockey *player*, Julie tried to tell her dismissively, but her caribou found the promise of athleticism exciting. *He's not our type*, Julie insisted, continuing to pretend she wasn't a basket case of irrational nerves.

She also didn't want to admit that it was far more likely that she wasn't his type.

She wanted to look up at him, desperately wanted to, but she didn't want to watch his gaze slide right over her. Already, he was talking over her head to the very well-to-do blonde on her other side. Clearly, he was interested in *her*, not Julie.

And who could blame him? Shifters were supposed to be fit and perfect, and here she was, with her poor eyesight and her extra curves and her mousy in-between hair. In the tropical humidity, it was nothing less than frizzy. She wondered enviously how much product the blonde had used to keep her locks so tamed and lovely.

Probably none, Julie realized sourly. She was probably naturally that perfect.

She remembered to turn another page.

The hockey player, who had finally introduced himself to no one in particular as Lars, was continuing to babble in his broken English, and Julie didn't want to admit that she was hanging on every word.

Lars seemed like the most beautiful name she had ever heard.

When the resort van returned, rattling down the winding road to the tiny airstrip, Julie sighed in regret.

This was probably as close as she was going to get to an actual conversation with Lars. She tucked her book into her luggage and lifted her head to meet Tom's eyes.

He took a long drag of his cigarette and held her gaze a thoughtful moment before dropping his butt to stub it out beneath his heel.

~

The jolting ride to the resort was more of the same kind of torture that the plane ride had been. Lars could see the back of the young woman's head and little else, as she bent over a book that he couldn't imagine she was able to focus on between the jaw-rattling potholes.

She was out of the van first, and Lars fidgeted to have to wait until the few people in front of him slowly — soooo slowly — unloaded from the vehicle.

The entrance to the resort should have been enchanting, but the object of all of his attention was already disappearing into the shadowed courtyard beyond, and Lars scrambled to follow.

He was right about her traveling with the surly smoking man — they were standing together at the check-in desk, and he had to remind himself not to crowd too close behind them to be obvious about eavesdropping.

"Welcome to Shifting Sands." The woman behind the desk had improbable red hair, neatly pulled back in a fancy updo. "Do you have your confirmation number?"

Cigarette man looked expectantly at the bookworm, who dug

into her luggage for a worn notebook. "Yes, sorry, here you go."

The woman smiled. It was a cool, practiced smile. Lars recognized it as the one his press agent had been training him to adopt. "No problem. Ah! Julie and Tom Johnson. Congratulations on winning the sweepstake!"

Julie. Her name was Julie.

It was lyrical and utterly perfect for her. He turned it over in his mouth, mouthing it without sound as the woman checking them in began going over maps and procedures.

Lars frowned at the back of Tom's head. Where did he fit in this picture? He had the same last name. Was he a husband? An estranged husband, he thought, from the chilly distance between them. Maybe this trip was a last attempt at rekindling their romance.

The idea made him want to check the man into the desk.

He was alarmed at his own vehemence and he looked with longing at the tiny bit of Julie's face that he could see. What had she done to him? Who was she? Why was he so drawn to her?

Then they were walking away with their luggage and their maps, and Lars stared at them for some time before he realized that the red-haired woman was waiting for him to step forward.

"Your confirmation number?" she asked firmly. Lars recognized that she had already asked that, while he was staring after Julie.

He rattled it off for her, then heard himself speaking Swedish and started to repeat it in English.

The woman waved him off halfway through. "I've got it, thank you," she said in badly accented Swedish.

Lars wasn't quite able to keep from wincing, though he knew that his own English had been twice as terrible today.

"I apologize," she said ruefully. "I only had a book to learn from, I hadn't heard the language spoken."

"No, I apologize," Lars said swiftly. "It was a good try and I appreciate the effort."

He could remember 'appreciate,' but 'professional' still eluded him.

"You failed to fill out the field for the type of shifter you are," the woman said politely, and waited.

Lars froze. *Älg*, he wanted to say, but no, it was elk in English. And an American elk was something altogether different than the European elk. What did they call it? A *moose*.

Then he thought about Julie, and was suddenly frozen with indecision. Girls didn't like prey animals. They wanted predators. Big, fierce predators.

"*Björn*," he said impulsively. "Bear. I'm a bear."

His moose gave a derisive snort, and would have facepalmed if it had possessed the correct appendages.

~

*M*aybe it was the heat. Maybe it was the rich food. Maybe it was the droning insects at night.

Julie couldn't sleep.

She couldn't even read.

She turned off the light after an hour or more of reading the same chapter. It was light fantasy fiction. It should be easy to shut off her brain and escape to the book world, but every time she turned a page, she imagined his voice. It was so rich and wonderful to listen to, even though he appeared to be a self-centered braggart who always seemed to be explaining to someone else that he was an *expert* hockey player.

Not just a hockey player. An *expert* hockey player.

The way he trailed off sometimes, Julie wondered if he wasn't a little slow-headed.

And she *still* couldn't get his voice out of her head, or stop thinking about him.

Every so often, she caught a glimpse of him, of his broad shoulders or his shock of blond hair, and she had to flee, or pretend to find something engrossing in a book, because otherwise, she knew she was going to embarrass herself staring.

After a few moments tossing in the dark, listening to Tom's even breathing from across the room, Julie got out of her bed and crept out of the hotel room in her pajamas.

The resort at night was enchanting. There were Christmas lights up all around, even though Christmas was still several weeks off.

Julie frowned to see them. She would be gone the week before Christmas, back to her ordinary life, her grinding, soul-killing retail job. This was just a temporary escape, a once in a lifetime lucky win. It was lovely living like the other half, but she knew her own dull life was waiting for her return.

There was a book exchange shelf in the back of the bar; maybe a new book would soothe her restless mind.

Like so many public rooms in the resort, there was no distinction from inside space and outside space at the bar deck; the weather here was so beautiful and mild that a mere roof served as plenty of protection.

Julie was looking up at the stars as she walked, listening to the white-noise of the water features, trying to memorize all of it. This would be a beautiful memory to cherish someday in the future.

Then she realized that there was already somebody sitting in front of the book exchange shelf. She frowned, not eager to share the quiet joy of picking out a new book with a stranger, and then caught her breath as she realized that it was *him*.

One bank of the bar lights was switched on, a row of spotlights that did little to illuminate the space. But it lit up Lars's blond head, and the broad expanse of his shoulders.

Inside, her caribou gave a caper of excitement and urged her to approach.

Fear rooted Julie to the spot.

Before she could decide between obeying her animal's fascination with the stranger or her own urge to flee before he noticed her, Lars looked up, directly at her.

❧

*I*t wasn't something he heard—the noise of the waterfalls into the pool below drowned out all the quiet sounds of the night—but something caught Lars's attention and he felt compelled to look around.

She was standing in the shadows just beyond the puddle of lights from the empty bar, but Lars would know her curvy figure anywhere, in any light at all. The moonlight behind her turned her silhouette to silver.

Julie.

He scrambled to his feet and stood there uncertainly for a long moment as they stared across the space between them.

He wasn't sure who started moving first, but they met at a half-lit table halfway between, gazing hungrily at each other. Lars's heart hammered in his chest, and he tried to make sense of what his moose was insisting.

If he'd been drawn to Julie before, it was nothing compared to what he felt now. He *belonged* to her, he was utterly, *wholly* hers. There wasn't a language in the world that could encompass how complete she made him feel, at least no language for tongues.

Then she nervously licked her lips, and Lars thought maybe it *was* a language for tongues.

Her gaze flickered down. "Are you reading that?" she asked breathlessly, and Lars looked helplessly down at the book in his hands.

War and Peace.

"I have already," he said, not sure why he wasn't kissing her. "But the Russian version."

She raised an eyebrow at him. "You read Russian?"

"*Da,*" Lars said. "And German. And a little French. In case I got drafted to a Canadian team."

She blinked in surprise.

"Julie…" Lars didn't know where to go from there.

"You…know my name?" She said it full of wonder. "I never thought you noticed me."

How could I not? Lars should have said. *I never noticed anyone except you.* Or maybe, *You are the only thing in my world now.*

Instead, not wanting to seem like a stalker, he desperately said, "Your name is on your *pyjamas.*"

Julie looked down at herself in sudden consternation, the blush that rose in her cheeks obvious even in the dim light.

"Oh, I...of course. I didn't think anyone would be up. It wasn't...I should have changed...I was just coming to find a book."

Lars wanted to gather her into his arms and kiss away her confusion; it took all of his willpower not to.

"You like to read," he observed.

"Yeah," she said shyly, pushing her glasses up on her face. "Tom keeps teasing me about coming to an exotic tropical island to do the same thing I'd do at home."

"But it's a nicer place to do it, yes?"

Julie gave a low, musical laugh. It was a sound that Lars wanted to coax from her again. "Much nicer," she agreed.

"Where are you from?" Lars asked. He wanted to know everything about her.

"Montana," Julie said. "You?"

"Sweden—er, New York now," he said swiftly. "I am American soon." It didn't feel quite true yet. Should he explain that he had been drafted for professional hockey? He wanted desperately to impress her. But he still hadn't remembered the word for professional, and kept forgetting to look it up on his phone when the rocky resort connection was working.

"I've always wanted to go to Sweden," Julie said wistfully. "It sounds beautiful."

You're beautiful, Lars wanted to say.

She was, with her not-blonde, not-brown hair soft around her face. Her eyes were huge and blue behind her glasses, and her pajamas did nothing to hide the entrancing curves of her figure. She was smiling, slowly and shyly, as they talked. He wanted to kiss her, so badly. His moose was encouraging him to do more.

Ours, he insisted. *Our mate.*

"Your animal..." Julie started to say cautiously.

"A bear," Lars remembered. He'd told the resort that he was a bear. He wanted to tell Julie the truth, but the words were out of his mouth before he could catch them. And once said, he couldn't take it back. Besides, a bear was impressive.

And he desperately wanted to impress her.

"A bear," she said with wide eyes. "Wow. Grizzly? Black?"

Lars had only the faintest idea what the species of bears were called, but grizzly certainly sounded like the sort of tough he was going for. "Grizzly," he said, hoping it sounded appropriately manly.

"And you?" he asked swiftly. "Your animal?"

"Caribou," she said.

It took Lars a moment to resolve the sounds into a word. "Caribou." He should pretend he knew what that was.

"It's basically an undomesticated reindeer," Julie supplied, to his relief.

"*Ren*," Lars agreed. "They are the Christmas deer in America."

To his complete delight, she laughed again. "Yeah! Every year I pull the sleigh at the local children's center on Christmas eve."

"Julie!"

They both looked around in surprise.

Tom was bearing down on them. "Is this jerk bothering you?"

The smile on Julie's face froze. "No," she said faintly.

"Come on, leave my sister alone," Tom said, as if she hadn't said anything. "Don't think I haven't noticed you creeping on her this whole week."

Relief flooded through Lars. *Sister*. They were siblings. Wait… creeping? Lars tried to figure out the translation for that, and could only guess from his tone that Tom thought Lars was being impolite. Guilt replaced the relief. Had he been unwittingly rude?

"Let's go, Julie," Tom said firmly. "You don't need to worry about this prick."

Julie looked between them in consternation, her discomfort at being caught between them clear in the roll of her shoulders and the shy duck of her head. After a moment, she turned away and Tom shot Lars a triumphant look over his shoulder.

"Wait!" Lars cried.

They paused, turning back. Tom's eyes burned with anger. Julie trembled. Did Lars only imagine that she looked as hungry as he felt?

"A book," he said desperately, holding his out impulsively. "Didn't you come looking for a book?"

As if drawn back on a cord, Julie returned to take the book from him. "Thank you," she said weakly. "I…"

"She's not interested in conceited hockey stars who can only talk about themselves," Tom interjected, muscling up beside her. "Learn to take a hint. She can do a lot better than you."

Lars was overwhelmed by his urge to hit him in the face, but wrestled back his moose's instinct. Giving her brother a black eye would probably not endear him to the woman who had upended his world.

"Tom," Julie hissed, turning away. "Let's just *go*."

Lars knew that his best bet was also to leave, before he was tempted to trample Tom into a pulp.

And wasn't Tom right? Julie probably did deserve better than him. She deserved someone smooth and sophisticated. He was only here because he was lucky, and luck was just a thing, not a quality.

His mind was in such a turmoil that the first thing he did when he returned to his cottage was shift into his moose form and browse all the nearby bushes down to ankle-high.

~

"*H*ow could you be so horrible to him?" Julie demanded, once they were out of earshot.

"How could you not have noticed him?" Tom retorted. "He's been absolutely leering at you since we got here. He's clearly some entitled rich sex maniac, and I thought you were too smart to fall for that kind of charm."

Julie tried to tamp down the thrill of excitement at the idea. Lars had been watching *her*? She'd been so busy trying not to stare at him! Her caribou wanted to turn on her heel and chase after, but long experience told her that she would not get rid of Tom so easily.

"Tom," she tried to explain. "There's…something…here. With us. Lars…Lars is my…"

Mate, her caribou supplied with a caper. *Our mate.*

"Your what?"

"My *mate*," Julie breathed, wrapping her arms around herself.

The pajamas that had been so warm earlier felt insufficient against the cool night.

"Your…what?" Tom stopped and Julie walked several steps without him before she realized.

"My mate," she repeated, smiling despite herself.

"He's a moron," Tom said incredulously.

"He's not," Julie defended him instantly. "He knows four languages, Tom. English isn't even his second language."

"He's a hockey player, Julie. An *expert* hockey player." He mocked the accent perfectly. "You deserve better than some rock-headed, over-paid athlete. Worse, he's a *bear*. Predator and prey, they don't mix." Tom patted his pockets and came up with a cigarette, which he lit.

"That's disgusting," Julie said. "You know I hate it."

"I hate *you* thinking you couldn't do better than that vain, shallow jerk," Tom retorted.

"He's not shallow," Julie protested. "And you don't have to protect me."

She couldn't have said why she was so sure…something about the way he looked at her. He spoke a little slowly, like someone struggling through layers of language might…or someone who was as dizzy with unexpected desire as she was.

She wanted to kiss him, to peel him out of his loud, too-new clothing and see what the muscles he wasn't shy about sharing on the beach and pool deck felt like under her fingers. But to her surprise, more than that, she wanted to find out why he read Russian, and what Sweden was like and even how long he'd been playing hockey.

They were at the door of the hotel and Tom paused to take another long drag of his cigarette before stubbing it out and throwing the butt into the trash can. "How could you know that *he's* your mate? I mean, I get that he's good-looking, but…"

"I don't *know*," Julie said, over her caribou's protests. "It's confusing. Overwhelming. But I've never felt like this. My caribou is so sure. And…" she wasn't going to talk about the rest of what she felt with her *brother*. "I just think so," she finished lamely.

Tom looked at her, and not even the darkness could hide his guilt or his anger. "You've thought someone was right for you before," he reminded her, like a knife in the side. "You even said *he* might be your mate."

Julie had no answer for that, unable to articulate how different this was.

Tom shook his head as he opened the hotel door. "Come on, let's just go to bed. I have no desire to sleep through one of the resort's amazing breakfasts."

Julie followed him without comment, turning the book in her hands as she went.

She slept with it under her pillow that night, and dreamed of what she imagined Russia looked like.

~

*T*om lay awake, listening to Julie's steady breath, until dawn started to color the sky. Leaving her to her sleep, he dressed silently and crept out of their little hotel room and down the hall.

He didn't believe in mates, not really. It seemed like a fairy tale, something for gullible shifters or a story for children because it was too hard to explain desire. But Julie's face haunted him; it was the first time she had looked truly happy in longer than he could remember. Whether Lars was her mate or not, Tom was going to find out more about him before he had a chance to hurt his sister.

It was impossible not to know where Lars was staying; his cottage was the first one off the main path, and his porch was not as well screened in greenery as most of the others. He seemed to enjoy sitting out, sunning himself vainly, and had already started developing a deep, glowing tan.

Tom looked down at his own arms. He'd been cautious about sunning, given his starting pallor, but was developing stubborn color. In the early light, it looked pretty pathetic.

He froze at an unexpected sound from behind the hedge. It was a familiar sound, but not one he expected here. It was…munching.

Tom peered around the gate that led to Lars door and confirmed his suspicion. A *moose* was standing in the tiny yard in front of Lars's cottage, chewing viciously at the foliage, its gawky, giant shape utterly unmistakable even without the distinctive antlers.

As Tom watched, aghast, the huge moose shifted back into the hockey player, and bent put on the robe that had been lying on the grass as Tom ducked back out of sight.

Tom retreated quietly, trying to make sense of this.

Lars was a bear...supposedly.

And if he wasn't a bear, what *else* might he be lying about?

He wanted his sister to be happy; she deserved every joy in the world, and he'd be cursed if he was going to let some conceited, untrustworthy foreign *jerk* break her heart. He'd already let her get hurt once, there was no way he was going to do it again.

❧

*L*ars was tired of pretending.

He was tired of pretending that he was comfortable with his money and his new clothes. He was tired of pretending he was a predator. He was tired of pretending not to stare at Julie.

He was just going to find her, and tell her all the things he was feeling, however awkwardly it came out. He was going to confess that he was a charlatan who didn't belong in a resort like this.

Would she forgive him? Or would she find that his deception was too much to accept? Was he too much of a...what had Tom called him? A creeper? The dictionary had helpfully supplied that a creeper was someone sneaky and deceptive. It had also confirmed that 'expert' *was* the English word for 'professional,' but it still didn't sound right to his ears.

But the next morning, Tom intercepted him at the restaurant.

"She's not interested," he said, like a brutal check against the boards.

"Not...interested?" Lars could only repeat dumbly.

"She knows you're a *moose*," Tom snarled. "Did you think she could possibly want to see you after finding that out?'"

Lars could think of nothing. He didn't think of himself as a dummy, but he knew that he sometimes took longer to find the right words than it ought to, which led to him repeating himself, and over-compensating by talking too *much*. And if she knew he was a moose…

"I won't bother her," he told Tom mournfully. "If that's what she wants."

"That's what she wants," Tom said firmly.

Appetite gone, Lars picked at his breakfast half-heartedly and returned to his cottage to find a strongly-worded letter on his door regarding the state of the foliage that he'd eaten the night before.

~

*J*ulie had gotten adept at watching Lars while she pretended to read. She sat with her book where they might see each other and hoped with an excited flutter in her chest that this time he would come and talk to her, prepared to put the book down at the slightest invitation.

But he didn't come over, not even to make loud conversation with someone nearby, as he'd been in the habit of doing.

Now, every time he caught sight of her, he reversed direction so quickly, Julie would have guessed he was on skates.

Was he disappointed that they were mates? Had he found out that she and Tom were dirt poor and only at the resort by grace of winning a sweepstakes? She ached at the idea that he might not *want* her.

She tried a meditation class to clear her mind, failing miserably at it. She took salsa lessons with a beautiful Hispanic woman with a rich accent that she could only compare to Lars's European lilt. She even tried a fancy drink with an umbrella at the bar.

"Are you going to be at the dance tonight?"

Julie looked up in surprise. She had been gazing out over the pool and put her book down absentmindedly. The bartender had apparently taken that as an invitation for conversation.

"Oh, I don't know," she said miserably. It sounded like another chance for Lars to avoid her.

"You should come," the bartender coaxed in his thick Southern accent.

Julie had once liked Southern accents, but there was only one accent she wanted to hear now. "I don't really have anything to wear," she fibbed. She had brought a black dress she'd never had the courage to wear.

"Don't be too put off by the word formal in the description," the bartender said kindly. "We get all kinds of dress styles at these things. It's understood that everyone is living out of suitcases. You should come!"

Julie looked up at him, out of excuses. "I guess," she agreed reluctantly.

~

*L*ars eyed himself in the mirror. The suit was the best that money could buy, perfectly tailored to his broad shoulders. The gold watch was a gift from a technology company courting him to do a commercial. The haircut was hours old from the well-appointed resort spa and perfectly styled with product that even *smelled* expensive. He should feel confident and ready for everything.

Mostly he just felt like a fraud.

Every time they put him on television, he wanted to blurt out that there had been a terrible mistake. He wasn't the hero that they made him out to be. He wasn't the rising star, the next Gretzky. He was just a lost kid who had never felt comfortable in any country, good at fighting and fast on skates.

Now he was expected to wear expensive suits, and vacation at exclusive resorts.

He didn't recognize the young man in the mirror.

That man looked like a bear.

There wasn't a bear inside of him, just a gangly-legged moose that he was wrestling back with sheer force of will.

Julie had liked the bear. There had been awe in her eyes at the idea of it.

Was it only finding the truth that had driven her away? Or was it his awful habit of saying exactly the wrong thing and never finding the right word? She was obviously very smart and well-educated. Probably she saw through every part of his facade from the very beginning. Her brother had been right, she hadn't wanted anything to do with him, clearly preferring the company of her books to any more of his.

He really was a creeper: inadvertently rude, too pushy. Her message of disinterest was unmistakable and he had been inexcusably forward anyway.

Had her eyes, when they met, been as hungry as his, or was he just trying to project his own bone-deep need for her onto someone who wanted no part of him?

Lars shook himself. He couldn't keep dreaming about those blue eyes. He was going to go to the dance and lose himself in glittery social swirl like his agent kept pressuring him to do.

Julie wasn't likely to be there, he thought, with mixed feelings.

It was less complicated when she wasn't nearby, but it somehow eased his heart when she was. He was always aware of her sitting in the dining room by herself, her books her only companions. Even if he wasn't going to pursue her against her wishes, it was comforting to know she was nearby.

~

*J*ulie had regrets.

Sometimes it felt like a lifetime of them, so heavy it bowed her head. And more than anything, she regretted letting her heart run away with her. Tom was probably right, she was probably seeing what she wanted to be there, just like she always did.

Her caribou snorted and pawed in protest, but Julie couldn't trust her any more than she could trust herself.

She also regretted the black dress.

It was a dress for someone who wanted to show off curves, tight through the body and low-cut, with a flirty skirt that ended above the knees.

Julie didn't want to show off her knees, let alone her curves, and here she was, like an exhibition of both.

"If you don't go, you'll always regret it," Tom told her, sensing her indecision. "You have always wanted to go to a ball, and you were so excited about it when you told me about the sweepstakes."

"I was a kid, Tom," Julie reminded him. "A little girl who read too many fairy tales. I'm too old for that nonsense now."

Tom was quiet a moment. "I…miss that kid."

Julie looked at her reflection pensively. "Me, too." Her blue eyes looked unfamiliar with the contacts she was wearing. Reading was always a challenge with them, so she rarely bothered.

"Julie…"

"It wasn't your fault," she reminded him.

His silence was rebuttal enough.

Julie knew better than to argue on the topic, and pulled her hair back from her face. Maybe a braid?

"You should go to the spa, have them do your hair up in some fancy do," Tom suggested.

"Oh, I couldn't…"

"We got a bunch of passes, and it's not like I'm going to go get a manicure," Tom said dryly.

Julie gave a hiccup of a laugh. "But darling, your nails!" she mocked.

Tom smiled briefly, then frowned again. "About that hockey player…" He sounded guilty.

"He wasn't interested," Julie said too quickly, knowing the source of his guilt. "I was probably…imagining things. You…were right."

Her caribou stomped in protest, but she ignored it.

"But you really did like him?" Tom asked reluctantly.

"I have terrible taste in men," Julie reminded him. "I'm glad it didn't go further." The heat in her body just at the thought of Lars turned her words to a flat lie.

"Hang on," Tom said unexpectedly. He got up from the bed

where he was lounging and pulled his duffel bag out from underneath it. He dug into it, and came up with a little box. "I brought your Christmas present," he said unexpectedly. "I know it's early, and I didn't wrap it yet, but...I thought you might want to wear it tonight."

Julie knew what it would be before she opened it, heart in her throat. "You...got it back?"

"The pawn shop held it for me until I could pay it off."

Julie opened the box with trembling hands. "Mom's pearls." It was a necklace of shimmering black pearls, three tapered strands nestled in the red velvet box.

"You couldn't go to the ball without it," Tom told her, frowning to mask his emotions.

Julie threw her arms around his neck. "You're the best brother," she said sincerely.

She knew by the knots in his shoulders that he didn't believe her, but he put his arms around her anyway. "Wear them to the ball, princess," he told her.

"You're coming with me," Julie said, leaving no room for refusal. "I won't go unless you do."

"Dammit," Tom said, but it was warmly.

~

*L*ars wondered why he bothered coming to the dance, hating the music, hating the food. He should just go back to his cottage, or go hit the gym and see if he could work off some of his frustration with the free weights. Maybe he should risk the wrath of the gardener again and go browse in his animal form somewhere no one could see him and realize that he wasn't any of the things he claimed to be.

Then Julie arrived, and it seemed like there was no other place to possibly be.

She paused in the doorway at the other end of the hall. There was a modest crowd of people at the formal dance—not enough that the hall felt crowded, but just enough that he had to move to get a good view of her, and he wondered helplessly as he did so if that made him the creeper her brother had accused him of being.

She was wearing what he recognized was a "little black dress," a garment that managed to mix sexy and sweet in perfect harmony, showing off tantalizing cleavage and shapely legs. There were three strands of dark pearls glimmering at her neck, and her hair was up in a swirl, with little ringlets at her neck. There was something unfamiliar about her, and it took Lars a moment to recognize that she wasn't wearing glasses.

She was, however, carrying a book, and something lifted in Lars's heart when he recognized that it was the thick paperback that he'd given her several nights before.

Then he caught sight of her brother skulking behind her, and he remembered Tom's emphatic declaration that Julie wanted nothing to do with him and realized he was *still* staring.

While he was casting around the room for anything else to look at, the cowboy bartender, Tex, kissed the woman serving drinks and went to intercept the siblings.

As Lars jealously watched, Tex tipped his hat to both of them, then spoke a moment to Tom, who looked surprised and rather pleased as he shrugged. Julie handed her book to Tom, then Tex was giving his hand to Julie and leading her out onto the dance floor.

Lars had to wrestle down his instinct to fly out onto the floor after them and pull her away for himself. Tex's hand was at her waist like he owned her, and he was saying something that made her blush shyly and laugh as he led her into the steps of a dance.

He looked back to find that Tom was scowling at him across the floor, and he scowled automatically back as he thought back through Tex asking Julie to dance. First, he had asked Tom for permission.

Had Lars bypassed some simple courtesy?

Sudden resolve set his feet into motion, and he closed the distance to Tom in a few determined strides.

Tom bristled at Lars's approach, and greeted him with a glare that did nothing to help Lars.

"I am not good with your language," Lars said, point-blank. "I am not good at knowing what to say, or what to do, and I probably have been *creeping*, but I had no meaning to, and I need you to tell me how to make it right because I am for her in a way I have never imagined and I cannot be happy without her."

Tom stared at him, his glare lost to astonishment, and said nothing.

After a moment of silence, Lars fidgeted. "I know I have not been entirely honest," he said desperately. "But I *will* be, I promise."

Tom's eyes narrowed with new suspicion. "What else haven't you been honest about?" he demanded. "Are you even a hockey player?"

"Yes," Lars assured him. "Everyone says I am very good. I just signed a big contract, but I am very afraid that I will not be good enough to deserve it." If he was going to come clean, he was going to come clean about everything, and he was going to do it with his head high. This man was Julie's brother, and if he wanted to win Julie, he was going to get through him first.

"I need a cigarette," Tom said earnestly.

"I don't have one," Lars said regretfully. It would have been a good gesture to politely offer Tom something he desired, he thought.

Tom put the book that he'd been holding into one of the folding chairs along the wall. "Look," he said, drawing Lars a little further away from the nearest people. "My sister says you're mates."

Mates. Hearing it out loud made the word settle into sense. Lars's moose sighed at the rightness of it.

"Yes," Lars said earnestly. "*Yes.*"

"Listen," Tom said, equally serious. "My sister had a boyfriend. He said he loved her, convinced her she was the only one in the world for him. She even thought they might be mates. And he took her to the cleaners. He skipped out of the state with her car, everything she had of value, and left her with tens of thousands in credit card debt. She got kicked out of her apartment and lost her scholarship trying to pay off his debt with a second job."

Lars clenched his hands into fists. "He hurt her," he snarled. "He broke her trust."

"It was my fault," Tom said grimly. "She wasn't that interested in him at first, but I wanted her…I wanted her to be happy. I convinced her to date him, to go out and live a little."

Lars wrestled back his desire to dismantle something with his bare hands. "He hurt her," he repeated. The words he wanted to say didn't translate directly.

Tom continued, scowling. "When you started watching her, I could only think that I needed to protect her. I'm the only family she has. And I wasn't going to let you take advantage of her because she looked like an easy target."

"Easy target?"

"Damn," Tom said in exasperation. "She's as naive as you are, man."

Naive was the same in almost all languages. "I would never hurt her," Lars said fiercely.

"I get that *now*," Tom said, looking conflicted. "But I…I told you she didn't want you."

Lars felt his heart plummet in his chest at the reminder.

"We're being honest now," Tom said. "And I wasn't being honest earlier."

Lars felt his eyebrows knit in confusion. "You aren't a caribou?" he guessed, feeling dense.

"About Julie," Tom elaborated with exasperation. "She likes you. She likes you a lot. I only told you she didn't so that you'd leave her alone. I didn't tell her you were a moose."

A bubble of hope expanded inside of Lars. "She likes me?" he said hopefully. Without meaning to, he turned to search her out among the dancers. She was laughing at something the bartender was saying to her, stumbling a little as he turned her through the steps.

"Man, you *are* hopeless," Tom said in exaggerated disgust. "Go get her. And if you break her heart…" He left the threat hanging.

Lars had to stare a moment longer, not quite able to accept his luck, drinking in the sight of Julie's perfect legs under the swishy black dress, and the bounce of her glossy brown hair. Then he was closing the distance between them.

~

*J*ulie had heard other guests speculate that Scarlet chose her male staff for their good looks; though none of them seemed anything less than competent, they were without exception stunningly handsome and well-built. She recognized the lifeguard among the guests at the dance, and a waiter from the restaurant who had flirted outrageously with her. They were dutifully circulating among the guests, inviting anyone looking bored to dance.

She privately thought it was a good move; it was flattering to have Tex draw her out onto the dance floor, even though she knew it was doubtlessly something he had been paid to do.

He was a perfect gentleman, his touch absolutely professional, his conversation kind. He was a good dancer, too, compensating for the fact that Julie had only learned most of the steps the previous day.

"You're enjoying your stay, I hope?" he asked, when the music slowed enough to allow conversation.

"I have," Julie said automatically, but she knew she said it sadly.

"You're not thinking about a certain Swedish hockey player, now, are you?" Tex teased her unexpectedly.

Julie met his gaze in appalled surprise. Had everyone seen what a goose she'd made of herself over him?

"Aw, honey, don't look like that," Tex said coaxingly. "I know he's a little rough around the edges, but it's clear he's over the moon for you."

Julie shook her head. "No. It's not like that. He's not interested in me." Even the mention of him left her feeling tingling and too aware of her body. Memories of how deliberately he'd been avoiding her the past few days crowded into her head and she miserably stumbled over her steps before Tex could guide her back to the right footwork.

"Hmm," Tex said dubiously. "I'm going to have to disagree with that, sugar." He turned her deftly, and swirled her unexpectedly away from him—directly into the path of Lars, who was bearing down on them with a look of determination.

Her skirt was still swishing into place above her knees as Lars gently took the hand that Tex had released and put his other at her waist.

Her body on fire, Julie let him draw her close, gazing up at him in longing she didn't know how to mask or stop.

He was not as skilled a dancer as Tex, and they collided knees several times when one of them stepped forward instead of back, but Julie didn't care. There was no place in the world she wanted to be more than here, with Lars's hand in hers, with his brown eyes adoring her.

It was every dream ball she had ever imagined, every princess fantasy that had ever crossed her mind. She was the heroine of a book, and here was her happy ending, all six foot something of gorgeous athlete, dancing with *her*, staring down at *her*, holding *her* like she was something precious and fragile.

"Julie," he breathed when the music ended, and she realized that they had stopped dancing several beats before, simply standing, holding each other and looking into each other's eyes like they'd found all the answers to the world there.

She made herself look away at last, as most people changed partners with the new song starting up.

"Julie," he repeated. "Will you come walk with me? I have... confessions to make to you."

Confessions of love? Julie's heart was too full and confused to do more than nod.

She reminded herself that she was not in a novel, and she should be practical, but when Lars led her out the side door into the moonlit garden, she did not feel the slightest bit practical.

When Lars brushed the side of her face with one hand, she leaned forward and he caught her mouth in a kiss so sweet and lingering that Julie thought she might overflow from it.

"You're crying," he said in concern, drawing back and wiping her tears away with careful thumbs.

"I'm happy," she promised. "I just...I thought you didn't want me."

He gave a little growl, gathering her close in his arms, and he kissed her again, less gently, this time. His hard body against her made it clear that whatever else he felt, he wanted her as badly as she wanted him.

"I will stop," he gasped. "I will stop if you ask." His hands were caressing every place her skin was bare, and he was kissing her neck with the same hunger that was burning through Julie's veins.

"Don't you *dare* stop," Julie told him, sliding her hands up under his jacket. "No stopping. *Nyet.*"

They made it a few more steps, deeper into the scented green depths of the garden. Then he was lowering her into one of the flower beds. She tried to remember how to get out her dress, then gave up and hitched the skirt up as he was shrugging out of his jacket and fumbling with his pants.

Then, finally, tremblingly, he was pulling her damp panties down below her knees and Julie had only a moment to appreciate the fine length of him before he was straddling her, and driving into her. She arched up to meet him, crying out in a feral, desperate need as a crest of pleasure broke over her.

His weight on her, his strong arms around her, his ragged breath in her ear, the way he filled her, satisfying her need even as he raised more within her—Julie struggled to find words for what she was experiencing, and eventually stopped trying to think about it and let it wash over her, in wave after wave of bliss.

They rolled together in the flowerbed, and Julie heard fabric rip. Was it Lars's pants, which she didn't remember him fully removing? Or her dress, which at that moment she would cheerfully have torn from her body in order to have more of him against her skin?

She didn't care, and neither did he, clutching her hips as she rode him, turning her over in the fragrant, bruised foliage.

At last, they lay together, spent and panting, and Julie felt like every romance book she'd ever read had fallen sadly short of the mark.

~

*L*ars could have lain in the flowerbed forever, holding Julie's delicious curves in his arms in the tropical night air.

But after not nearly long enough, she gave a great sigh. "I can't believe we're leaving in only a few more days," she said sadly.

A few more days. Lars felt his heart drop at the idea of her leaving. "You couldn't...stay longer?"

Julie gave a hiccup of a laugh. "We couldn't possibly afford it," she said frankly.

Lars chewed on his bottom lip, trying to decide a safe way through the conversation tangle before him. It would have been impossible even in his first language, and having it in his third was a challenge he wasn't sure he was equal to. He wanted to invite her to come and have Christmas with him in New York and never to leave.

While he was still trying to figure out what he wanted to say, let alone how to, Julie continued, "Anyway, it's been really nice at the resort, but...I feel like I don't belong here." She sat up, trying to make sense of how her dress had been bunched up.

"Me, too," Lars could say sincerely as he tried to sort out his own garments. His pants were twisted around both ankles, and he had no idea where his jacket had ended up.

"You?" Julie scoffed. "You're just the sort of famous rich person that a resort like this is for."

Lars sat up, and looked at her in consternation. "I have been pretending as hard as I can. But I...haven't been this for very long," he said honestly. "My parents were poor Russian immigrants to Sweden. I never really had anything until I got signed to the team just a few months ago. Suddenly, I have more money than I've ever realized even existed, I'm getting a green card and working towards American citizenship, and they're putting my photograph on subway walls."

Julie giggled. "Really? Subway walls?"

"Twice life sized," Lars admitted. "I rode the entire city route three times in an order because it was so...ah..."

"Surreal?" Julie supplied, while he was still trying to remember the word.

"Exactly." Lars took her hand. "I am only here because there are some contract problems with other players, and when I asked what to do with my money, this is what they said I might do."

Julie was silent a thoughtful moment. "What would you be doing for Christmas, otherwise?"

Lars looked away. "My parents, they have died," he said, as lightly as he could manage. "Or I would go back to Sweden and have a traditional Russian Christmas, with the most amazing food… oh, the food. I would be hard pressed to say it is better than here, but ah…the *pirogi* and *karachi*…"

Julie was smiling wistfully at him; he could just make out the curve of her mouth in the darkness. "My parents used to do big holiday meals. Turkey and stuffing and mashed potatoes and seven kinds of olives. I remember putting them on my fingers."

"They don't, anymore?"

Julie's smile grew sad. "They died when I was little. Tom had just turned eighteen and we didn't have any other family, so he got custody."

"That must have been hard," Lars said gently.

"It was. He worked so hard, gave up so much. And…he tried to protect me."

Lars gave up his attempt to button his shirt in favor of catching Julie's hands in his own. "Tom told me," he confessed. "About your…boyfriend."

"It wasn't Tom's fault," Julie said immediately.

"It wasn't yours, either," Lars said, equally swiftly.

She blinked at him, eyes bright in the moonlight.

"I should have…"

"It wasn't your fault," Lars repeated.

Julie gave a great sigh and bowed her head, and Lars imagined he could see a great weight resting on her shoulders. "I feel…like I should have known better. Like I should be able to tell when someone is being honest."

Guilt pierced Lars.

"Julie," he said in agony.

She looked up at her, her eyes trusting.

"I haven't been honest," Lars confessed.

Her hands in his froze. "What do you mean?" she asked faintly.

"I'm...I'm not a bear."

She was silent.

This was it. He had broken her trust. Once bitten, twice shy, as the song went. Whatever hopes he had for taking her back to America with him died now.

"What are you?" she asked, her voice utterly neutral.

Lars sighed. "A *moose*."

She said nothing.

The silence ate at Lars's confidence. "I'm sorry I didn't say so at once," he said. "I wanted to impress you, and I thought a bear was...impressive."

Her head was bowed, and her shoulders were shaking. Was she crying? Lars wished he could go back to past-him and punch him in the teeth; the idea of hurting Julie caused such a wretched mix of regret and horror.

The she raised her head, and Lars could see the trails of tears down her cheeks. "I'm a terrible person," he said in agony. "I'm sorry for lying. I didn't mean to hurt you."

Before he could continue, Julie began to laugh out loud. "A moose," she choked. "You're a moose!"

Lars blinked. "Yes," he said. "I should have told you."

She punched him in the shoulder, but it was gentle. "Yes, you should have."

"Please forgive me," Lars said desperately. "Tell me you will forgive me and come live in New York with me and be mine forever and please don't let me spend Christmas without you."

Her laughter faded to something like wonder. "You mean that? You really mean that?"

"It is my first American Christmas," Lars said, hoping it sounded convincing. "Your brother could come. I have an empty house and an oven that isn't in Centigrade. I have no idea how to make a turkey."

"The first thing you do is lie about being a bear," Julie suggested archly.

Lars stared at her in confusion a moment as she dissolved into laughter at her own statement. "Because I am a turkey?" he guessed, trying to figure out the joke.

"Oh Lars," she said, leaning forward to kiss him on the forehead. "You need me."

Lars caught her in his arms. "That," he agreed, "is the truth."

When he finished kissing her, they rose from the flowerbed at last, and he found his jacket lying in the middle of the gravel path.

"Oh dear," he said, surveying the garden. "I fear I am going to get another nasty note from the gardener."

~

Epilogue

As Julie clopped from the ice, tossing her head and making the bells on her harness ring merrily, the gathered children behind her clapped and hollered happily. The music rose as the next part of the entertainment continued on the open-air rink behind her.

Lars met her with a bundle of her clothes. Out of sight behind the bleachers, she shifted, slipped out of the belled harness, and dressed quickly, shivering.

"Your brother seems really grumpy about this," he observed.

"He's cranky because he doesn't have antlers at this time of year, so he doesn't feel like he can really be part of the festivities." Julie pulled the sweater down over her head, and when she struggled out of the neck hole, Lars was waiting there for a kiss.

"It was so sweet of you to give up your last few days at the resort to come here," she said, when he had finally released her lips and pulled a knit hat down over her chilled ears. "The community center kids were really excited to meet a real famous hockey player."

Together, they pulled the tiny sleigh to where Tom waited with the trailer in the parking lot.

"I'd rather have Christmas here, with you," Lars said sincerely. "And Montana is beautiful and reminds me of home. Of Sweden. Which isn't really home now."

"New York will feel like home before you know it," Julie told him reassuringly, slipping one mittened hand into his.

"Anywhere that you are will feel like home," Lars said solemnly, and they stopped to exchange another lingering kiss.

The kiss was interrupted by a loud honk as Tom reached into the open truck window and leaned on the horn.

"Let's go, lovebirds," he scolded. "The community center gets charged double if the sleigh isn't back by eight for the next event."

Julie giggled into Lars's scarf. "Let's go. He's also grouchy because his Christmas present to me this year was to quit smoking."

Lars nodded approvingly. "That's a fine gift," he said. "I hope you find mine half as good."

Julie gave a little caper better suited for her caribou form. "I'm so excited," she said. "I get to give you yours tonight after we drop the sleigh off."

"I will love it," Lars promised, as they hauled the sleigh up onto the trailer.

~

*T*he hall of the tiny apartment that Julie shared with her brother was piled high with shipping boxes already marked with Lars's New York address. Nearly all of them had the word BOOKS scribbled on one end. They would be leaving the following week, and Lars could not wait to make his sterile apartment across the country into a home with the woman who had taken his hand and was dragging him into the kitchen.

"Cover your eyes," she commanded, as they rounded the corner.

Lars stumbled over the edge a box and recovered by 'accidentally' catching Julie in an embrace.

"Whoops," she said without remorse.

Lars's nose had him guessing what his gift was before Julie pulled his hands away from his eyes.

"I found a Russian grocery in the next town over," she said, hopping in place. "I wasn't sure what was traditional for Christmas, so I got a little of everything. I even got the ingredients for piroshki, though I'm not confident I can make them; there are about a hundred recipes on the Internet. And I made Olivier salad. I couldn't believe how much mayonnaise it called for. There's this can of herring stuff I can't read, and something called meat jelly, and Tom made deviled eggs, but they're probably Americanized."

Lars stilled her mouth with a kiss. "It's perfect," he said.

Tom cleared his throat behind them. "I didn't get you anything except the deviled eggs," he said with a shrug. "I figured you were getting my sister, and that ought to last me a few holidays."

Julie laughed and pulled off her coat. "Where do you want to start?" she asked eagerly. "I'm starved!"

"I want to start with your present," Lars said. "There are two parts!"

He rummaged into his bag and withdrew two wrapped packages. One was thin and light, the other thick and heavy. Julie mimed staggering when he put it in her arms. "Which do I open first?" she asked eagerly. Lars put the lighter one on top.

Julie put them both on the last clear place on the counter and tore the wrapping off the tablet, already in a sturdy case and loaded with books. Lars hadn't been able to discern a pattern from her reading habits, so it had mysteries, thrillers, romances, children's books, some non-fiction about Egypt mythology and a wide selection of classics.

"Oh," she said in awe, as Lars showed her how to navigate the screens and adjust the font. "So many books and it's so tiny and light. I've always wondered how it would be to read on one of these. I worried I might miss the feeling of a real book in my hands." She looked up at Lars in alarm as she seemed to realize how that might sound. "I mean, I'm sure I'll love it," she said swiftly.

"That's why I got the next one," Lars said with a grin.

Julie laughed as she tore open the paper. "You got me War and Peace," she exclaimed. "In *Russian!*"

"First edition," Lars said. "I couldn't find a signed version."

"It's perfect," Julie said, putting it down and falling into his arms. "I love it. I'll learn Russian immediately. *Da! Nyet!*"

"I got you something, too," Lars said, looking at Tom over Julie's hat.

Tom looked uncomfortable. "I hope it's on par with deviled eggs," he said awkwardly. "Because seriously, I didn't get you anything else."

Lars fished into his pocket around Julie's arms. "I didn't wrap them," he said apologetically.

But Tom seemed to think this leveled the playing field as he opened the envelope. "Airline vouchers?"

"I want you to come visit us in New York. They're good for a year."

"Thanks," Tom said gruffly. "That will be great."

Julie, still wrapped around him, gave a sigh of contentment. "This is the greatest Christmas I've ever had," she said happily. "You picked these gifts like a pro."

"Like a pro?" Lars had to ask.

"A professional," Julie clarified.

A *professional*. There was the word he had been looking for so long. He had to laugh out loud at himself and bent to kiss Julie as Tom gave a groan of disgust.

"Merry Christmas, everyone," Tom said, turning to plug in the twinkle lights on the little tree.

"Merry Christmoose," Julie laughed near Lars's ear. "Let's eat!"

One hilarious extra...when I was writing this, I didn't know how to write the å character on my keyboard, and I wrote moose as alg instead of älg. Which happens to be algae in Swedish, not moose! Fortunately, I had a Swedish friend read it before posting it on the webpage. I will always picture Lars thinking to himself, "I'm an algae..."

DANCE LESSON

Tropical Dragon Diver was the first of three books in the Shifting Sands Resort series that really leaned hard into fairy tales. This book was obviously the story of The Little Mermaid…with a few very noticeable tweaks. I drew less on Disney and more on much older stories of sirens and their lures. Tropical Panther's Penance was a riff on Beauty and the Beast, and Tropical Christmas Stag would be influenced by Rapunzel, with many liberties.

"Won't you join us?" Lydia invited.

Saina froze in the doorway to the grand event hall. She wasn't lurking, she told herself. Sirens didn't *lurk.*

"I don't want to interrupt," she started to say smoothly, automatically putting a little power into the words. *Don't notice me, I'm not important, not a threat…*

None of her students gave her a second glance, but Lydia's serene face curved into a smile. "You aren't interrupting. You're welcome to join our class. I'd *like* it."

Saina could have kicked herself for forgetting; Lydia had a mate, which muted the effects of her unconscious song. Besides, she didn't actually *want* to use magic on someone who might be...

The idea drew Saina up in surprise.

...who might be a friend.

Lydia was wearing soft leggings and a tank top, sitting on the cool floor of the elegant, echoing room as she led her small class through warm-up stretches. "There are mats in the corner," she said pointedly, and Saina went to get one as obediently as if Lydia had used magic on *her*.

It was a curious fusion class, and Saina forgot to feel self-conscious as Lydia took them through a series of yoga moves, then paired them off to start on very basic salsa steps.

"You've taken dance classes before," Lydia observed, coming to correct Saina's hand on her partner, a tall sepia-skinned woman who still appeared to be ignoring Saina under the influence of her earlier words. "Such grace! Oh, Lana, that's lovely form, perfect."

Saina found herself feeling flustered by the compliment and reminded herself that Lydia was being kind to all of her students; Lydia probably wasn't *really* impressed.

It had been so long since she'd wanted to impress someone that she almost didn't recognize the feeling.

After the class, the other students went chattering off and Saina lingered behind to help put the mats back in the storage closet.

"Thank you," Lydia said. "What kind of dance have you studied before?"

"Middle Eastern style belly dance," Saina said, feeling absurdly shy. "And Hawaiian hula."

"It shows," Lydia said. "You probably didn't need a class this basic."

"I've never done salsa before," Saina said. It sounded colder than she intended, though maybe that was only by comparison to Lydia.

"Have you ever thought about teaching?"

"Salsa?" Saina realized as soon as the word was out of her mouth that it was ridiculous and not nearly as funny as it had been in her head.

Lydia, however, laughed warmly. "I didn't mean salsa. But I have always wanted to learn to hula! Would you teach me?"

"I'm not really qualified…" Saina said hesitantly. "But I could show you some of the moves."

"I'd like that," Lydia said, another of her generous smiles curving her lips.

For almost an hour, they went back and forth sharing moves. Saina showed her the tricks to a shimmy and a kaholo, Lydia showed her some of the fancier salsa footwork. Saina caught herself wanting to sing, stripping all of the magic out of her voice at the last moment, and Lydia laughed with her like they were old friends.

After an awkward parting, where Saina thought that Lydia might hug her and knew she was too uninviting because the idea surprised her so much, she wandered back to The Den. She nodded at Graham in the common room, and walked up the several flights to Bastian's room.

She had a key of her own, now, so she opened the door and went in, trailing her fingers along his unusual hoard.

Mermaids didn't collect things like dragons did, and Saina had never put much importance to owning things. Treasure was only useful for trading to ensure a certain quality of life. Things were expendable…like people, only to be used for advantage and advancement.

But as Saina wandered the room, touching the shining pieces of sea glass and making the seashells chime together, she marveled at the perfect harmony of her mate's hoard. Every item was dear, and she couldn't untangle her attachment from the dragon she loved and the things that he cared about.

She ran her fingers over a gleaming shell at the head of their bed. It was worthless, on any market. Perhaps she could get a few dollars selling it to a tourist. But she didn't want to sell it, she didn't care for what it could bring her. She unexpectedly *treasured* it, just as it was. She cherished her memories of dancing with Lydia, she cared what Lydia thought and how she felt.

Is that what a friend *was?*

500 SHIFTING SANDS RESORT OMNIBUS

Bastian came in to find her laying on her back on the wide bed, toying with the shell.

"How was your lesson with Lydia?" he asked. Gossip spread faster at the resort than even siren song could.

Saina sat up and smiled. "I learned a lot," she confessed.

THE BETTING POOL

I had originally intended to include a scene in the last book where the staff was going over the revelation of what Scarlet was and comparing it to the bets that they had on it. But the pacing of the book totally gallops off after that reveal, and there was no place to squeeze such a conversation in. I had already asked my readers who would have which bets, so it made sense to spin it off as its own story. I always love to hear what people guessed that Scarlet was before they got to the final book! Email me at zoechant@zoechant.com and tell me what you thought she was!

"You want in?" Breck called. "We're updating the pool now!"

Wrench froze at the door to The Den.

"In what?" he growled. The only pool that came to mind was the big salt water swimming pool in the center of the resort, and if Breck was inviting him to that... He wasn't sure what to even think about the offer.

"The betting pool!" Breck explained. He was standing at the kitchen bar, a wooden crate open in front of him. Graham was sitting across from him with an open beer that was perspiring in the humid heat and Travis had some tools and parts spread across the bar as he scowled at some inner workings. "We all have guesses about what Scarlet is. Winner gets the pot."

A betting pool. Wrench relaxed. That made sense. "What's the buy-in?"

"Whatever you've got. Some of us have IOUs for chores or favors in there, there's some cash, Lydia's down for a two-hour massage. Bastian's got a gold choker in here." Breck fished it out and held it up to his throat. "I've got plans for that one!"

"What guesses are taken?" Wrench moved into the kitchen and went for the fridge.

Breck reviewed the page and cleared his throat. "Bastian's got selkie, Laura's got phoenix, Saina has kelpie. Tex has...what is this, *sea* dragon? Graham says harpy." Graham smirked and raised his beer bottle; clearly his choice amused him on several levels. "Chef says an oracle. I've got Gizelle down for angel."

"You can't accept a bet with Gizelle," Travis protested. "She can't possibly understand what the pool entails. That's taking advantage of the poor sweet thing!"

"She wanted to!" Breck protested. "You try saying no to her. This is her buy-in." He held up a brittle-dried flower from the box. "I'm down for big cat—"

"Which is shamelessly cheating," Travis observed. "There are like fifty kinds of big cat!"

"Only five!"

"How do you get five?" Travis wanted to know.

"Tiger, lion, leopard, snow leopard, jaguar," Breck said, looking smug.

"And lynx," Travis insisted.

"Not big enough."

"Speak for yourself," Jenny said, coming into the kitchen behind Wrench. He'd found something left over from the restaurant that looked too fancy to eat, but he had no intention of being picky.

Travis grinned at his mate and bent over his broken parts again.

"You want in?" Breck offered her.

"Scarlet's legally my client," Jenny said quellingly. "I'm sure it's a conflict of interest."

"Has she told you what she is?" Breck wanted to know.

"No," Jenny said firmly. "And I wouldn't tell you if she had."

"What about you, Travis?"

Travis put aside his work and considered thoughtfully. "We don't call it by name," he said. "I'll put in twenty bucks but I don't have it on me."

"Can you write it?" Breck looked wild with curiosity, but his face fell when he took the log back from Travis. "You can't say bear?!"

Travis shrugged. "Old habits die hard. You say its name, you invite it to disrupt your hunt. Scarlet's something with *that* kind of power, you know?"

"You've said bear before," Graham said suspiciously.

"There's bear," Travis agreed. "And then there's…"

"Okay, okay, the-bear-we-can't-say-out-loud for Travis," Breck said agreeably.

Jenny had found herself a snack from the fridge as well and went around the bar to take a seat next to Travis. "I wonder if she's…fae."

"You don't honestly believe in fairies, do you?" Breck said skeptically.

"Not fairies like Tinkerbelle," Jenny said. "More like Shakespeare's fairy queen, or stories of the courts on the other side of the veil."

"Is that a bet?" Breck suggested.

"No!" Jenny insisted. "You are not going get me into your very *questionable* betting pool."

"What about you, Wrench?"

Wrench, mouth full of something he could neither identify nor wanted to in case it was something he might enjoy less for knowing, chewed thoughtfully. Scarlet was certainly powerful. And she was uncanny in her ability to sniff out trouble. Something big, something confident…

"Rhinoceros," he said, once he'd swallowed.

The others all stared at him.

"Rhinoceros?" Breck confirmed. "You sure?"

Wrench cleared his throat. "Well, I read once that a hippopotamus was the most dangerous animal on land. But Scarlet don't like water the way they do. And, well, I wouldn't want to face down a rhino, they move faster that you'd think. And I wouldn't want to face her down either."

They all stared at him and Wrench took a sullen bite of his food. He should've kept his mouth shut.

"That tracks," Travis said with grudging respect. "Wish I'd thought of it."

"She doesn't like water?" Breck said, looking puzzled.

"Well, you never see her on the beach," Jenny observed. "Or that close to the pool, though she doesn't seem to mind rain. Maybe it's just salt water she doesn't like."

Graham just grunted, drinking his beer.

Breck shrugged and started writing on the log, stopping several times to erase. "You could've picked something easier to spell," he complained. "What's your buy-in?"

Wrench grinned. "I'll let you survive that two hour massage with Lydia." He was glad when everyone laughed, because he hadn't meant it all that seriously. "Lemme think about it."

After he'd finished his food, studiously ignoring the chewy thing in the sauce that looked suspiciously like a tentacle, he said, "I ain't got a lot, but there's not a lot here to spend on, either." He put in a twenty.

Breck marked him down, and Wrench dubiously signed the page.

He was undoubtedly gonna get fleeced, but twenty wasn't much to lose, at the end of the day, and he liked that he'd been invited to participate. This whole island was half-mad, and it felt okay to be included in that.

He was *in*.

A NOTE FROM ZOE CHANT

Shifting Sands Resort was honestly like a writing boot camp for me. I learned so much about plotting and characters and the entire craft of writing as I typed my way through these stories in my head. I am very grateful for all of my beta readers and editors; I learned so much from you!

I would love to know what you thought—you can leave a review at Amazon or Goodreads (I read every one, and they help other readers find me, too!) or email me at zoechantebooks@gmail.com. I really enjoy hearing from my readers and I especially love finding out what your guesses for what Scarlet's true nature were before you got to the big reveal!

If you'd like to be emailed when I release my next book, please visit my webpage and sign up to be added to my mailing list at zoechant.com, where you can find a list of all my books. You can also follow me on Facebook or join my VIP Readers Group on Facebook!

SHIFTING SANDS RESORT
COMPLETE TIMELINE

*Shifting Sands Resort shares a world with Fire and Rescue Shifters, and Shifter Kingdom. This is a complete timeline of all three series, with short stories in their appropriate order. This is not at **all** the order I would recommend reading them the first time, as many of the short stories spoil the subsequent books!*

Steps (Tropical Tails)
Roots (Tropical Tails)
Run (Tropical Tails)
Treasure Sense (Tropical Tails)
A Recipe for Happiness (Tropical Holiday Tails)
Firefighter Dragon
Firefighter Pegasus
Royal Guard Lion
Royal Guard Tiger
Firefighter Griffin
Tropical Tiger Spy
Other Duties as Assigned (Tropical Tails)
Locked (Shifting Sands Omnibus Vol 1)
Tropical Wounded Wolf

Unlocked (Shifting Sands Omnibus Vol 1)
Firefighter Sea Dragon
The Master Shark's Mate
Tropical Bartender Bear
Tropical Lynx's Lover
The Storm (Tropical Tails)
Tropical Dragon Diver
Tropical Panther's Penance
A ChristMOOSE Story (Tropical Holiday Tails)
Dance Lesson (Tropical Tails)
The Betting Pool (Tropical Tails)
Firefighter Unicorn
Tropical Christmas Stag
Scarlet and the Christmas Kittens (Tropical Holiday Tails)
(the epilogue of Tropical Christmas Stag)
Lift (Shifting Sands Omnibus Vol 3)
Firefighter Phoenix
Tropical Leopard's Longing
Her Hellhound Bodyguard (Tropical Tails)
(the epilogue of Tropical Leopard's Longing)
Pregnancy Knows (Shifting Sands Omnibus Vol 3)
Tropical Lion's Legacy
Fake Fur (Tropical Tails)
Reunion (Tropical Tails)
Pickled Magnolias (Tropical Tails)
(the epilogue of Tropical Lion's Legacy)
Tropical Dragon's Destiny
A Will and a Wedding (Tropical Tails)
A Hoard of the Their Own (Tropical Tails)
Of Course (Tropical Tails)
Perfect Match (Tropical Tails)
All in the Timing (Tropical Holiday Tails)
(the epilogue of Tropical Dragon's Destiny)
Unreliable Senses (Tropical Tails)
Shifting Sands Academy...forthcoming?

OTHER GEMS FROM ZOE CHANT

The Royal Dragons of Alaska (writing as Elva Birch): A fascinating alternate world where Alaska is ruled by secret dragon shifters. Adventure, romance, and humor! Reluctant royalty, relentless enemies...dogs, camping, and magic! Start with The Dragon Prince of Alaska!

~

Fae Shifter Knights (writing as Zoe Chant): A four-book fantasy portal romp, with cute pets and swoon-worthy knights stuck in a world of wonders like refrigerators and ham sandwiches. Start with Dragon of Glass!

~

A Day Care for Shifters (writing as Elva Birch): A hot new full-length series about adorable shifter kids and their struggling single parents in a town full of mystery and surprise. Start the series with Wolf's Instinct, when Addison comes to Nickel City to take a job at a very special day care and finds a family to belong to.

~

Green Valley Shifters (writing as Zoe Chant): A sweet, small town series with single dads, secret shifters, sweet kids, and spinsters. Standalone books where you can revisit your favorite characters. Start with Dancing Barefoot!

~

Suddenly Shifters (writing as Elva Birch): A hilarious series of novellas, serials, and shorts set in the small town of Anders Canyon, where something (in the water?) is making ordinary citizens turn into shifters. Start with Something in the Water!

~

Lawn Ornament Shifters: The series that was only supposed to be a joke, this is a collection of short, ridiculous romances featuring unusual shifters, myths, and magic. Cross-your-legs funny and full of heart! Start with The Flamingo's Fated Mate!

~

Birch Hearts (writing as Elva Birch): An enchanting series of short stories and novellas. Unconstrained by theme or setting, each short read has romance, magic, and heart. And always, the impossible and irresistible. Start with Prompted 2 for fourteen pieces of sizzling flash fiction.

~

Not sure where to start? Take the quiz at elvabirch.com to find your perfect book!